DESCENDANT OF VALLA

VALLA SERIES - BOOK TWO

ANNA REZES

ALSO BY ANNA REZES

Valla Series:

Unraveling Emily ~ book one

Descendant of Valla ~ book two

Guardian of Latovia ~ book three

Broken Alliance ~ book four

ISBN: 978-1-950657-03-2 (paperback)

ISBN: 978-1-950657-04-9 (hardcover)

Library of Congress Control Number: 2019907455

Cover design by German Creative

First Edition: June 2019

Words Imagined

Hilliard, OH

www.annarezes.com

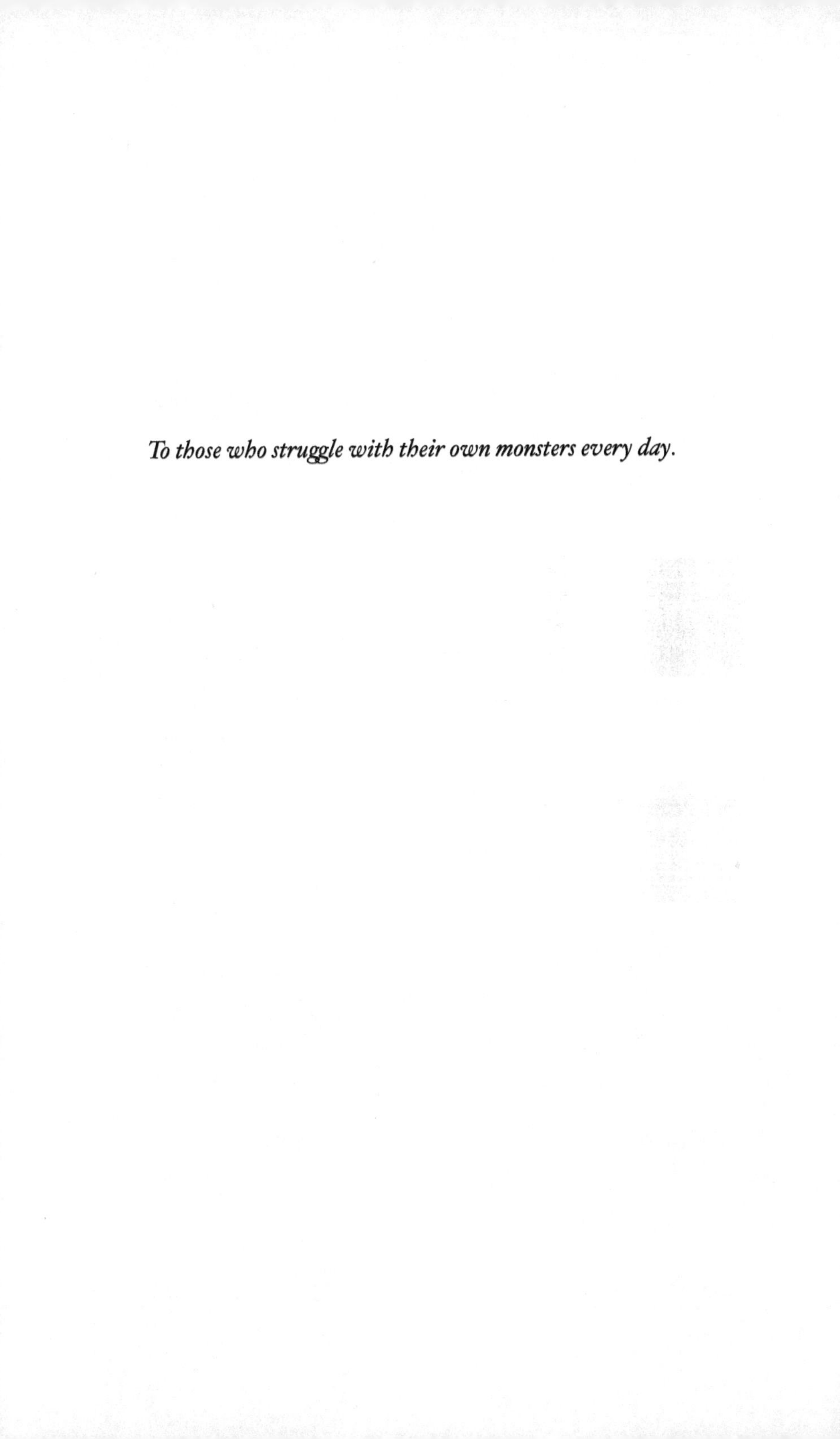

To those who struggle with their own monsters every day.

EMILY -

AS CHILDREN, we learn about monsters. We learn about big hairy beasts or scary shadows that live under our beds. Our loved ones try to convince us there is nothing to fear and eventually we stop checking our closets for the boogeyman.

As adults, we learn the truth about monsters. Not only are they real, but they walk among us in disguise. Some show themselves in significant ways like mass shootings, bombings, beheading the innocent, or crashing planes into buildings filled with people. But there are all manners of evil—thieves, rapists, and killers—lurking just out of sight. We are right to be cautious. We may even take precautions knowing our neighbors, our friends, our families could be hiding demons within. But how do you protect yourself and your loved ones when the monster lives inside of you? And what do you do when the monster takes control?

I thought I was safe. I felt safe, which is precisely what Adelaide wanted me to feel. I knew Valla blood was feared, but I thought I could control it and keep it from turning me into the monster the Olvasho had predicted, but I never anticipated Adelaide.

At first, I prayed for someone to rescue me, but now I wish for death. I didn't know the meaning of pain until evil lived inside my body and ate up all that I once was. Now I am nothing but a shadow—a ghost trapped inside my body.

CHAPTER ONE ~

LATHE PACES outside of his mother's living quarters in the Fort Wayne Mansion. The spacious basement corridor is cluttered with pricy paintings in gilded frames that hang high above rich cherry wainscoting. Crystal wall sconces struggle to brighten the space, while vintage Persian rugs add chaos to the eclectic Victorian style.

Lathe scratches the side of his face where his scars bother him the most. He pulls his hand away, irritated that he feels so out of control. After his mother's initial warning the day before, the Olvasho council started getting all kinds of calls about a disturbance in the Columbus compound. It was where Sky, the leader of the Olvasho, had been staying, and now he appeared to be missing in action, leaving behind a battle-torn building and several dead Olvasho.

Olvasho are capable of a lot, with powers of healing, mental manipulation, and mind-reading. They are also incredibly skilled at hiding in plain sight. They prefer going unnoticed by the general public because no one will stop them if no one knows what they can do. Olvasho don't leave messes to clean up, especially not like the disaster left in Columbus.

The council is still piecing together the facts, and though

Lathe isn't part of the council, he is staying close by, listening to the chatter, and everyone either fears or respects him too much to say anything. He's tempted to go upstairs to see if the council has discovered any new information, but he doesn't want to seem anxious.

He turns to continue pacing but stops short. Down the hall, a young woman appears. Her image flickers, fading in and out. She looks over her shoulder and Lathe catches a glimpse of her emerald eyes as the wind blows her blond hair from her face.

He takes a step forward to get a better look, but in a flash, the image disappears. He snaps to the left, searching, spinning, wondering if it will return. When it doesn't, he goes down the hall to his mother's apartment door. It has been a long time since she has shown images to Lathe. She doesn't mean to be inarticulate, but after years of Sky's abuse and experimentations, she can only describe her visions using riddles.

He works the intricate lock that keeps his mother contained, and her door swings open. As he steps in, the lights flicker then remain steady, something they rarely do.

This room is a stark contrast to the rest of the mansion. It has a clinical feel with sterile white walls and a tile floor. Overhead, fluorescent lights shine down, shielded by shatterproof glass. A small kitchen table sits in a non-functioning kitchenette, while across the room a sleek sofa is sandwiched between rounded side tables. Off the living area, there is a bedroom and a simple bathroom. The furniture in this space is minimalist in style, bolted to the floor in an effort to prevent the woman from unintentionally harming herself.

Closing the door behind him, Lathe turns to find his mother coming out of her bedroom. Her arctic blue eyes appear hopeful.

"My son," she says, coming to him.

"Mother?"

She wraps him in a hug and Lathe takes advantage of the rare moment. He rests his head on top of her light frizzy hair. He hugs her often, but usually to restrain or comfort her. This embrace is a welcome change. Lathe is six-foot-three inches of lean muscle, and though she feels petite and fragile in his strong arms, he knows better than to underestimate her strength. She is one of the few whose gifts manifest physically, and when they do, she is a force to be reckoned with.

"You saw her?" she asks into his shoulder.

"I saw the image. The girl with green eyes."

"She was your half-sister," she says with sadness.

The day before Lathe learned about his half-sister through his mother's manic rant, and now she's making it sound as if something had happened to the sister he has never met.

He pulls back so he can see her face. "What happened?"

"She is so much more now. We must stop them." With a gasp, her eyes become wide with grief, and her fingers dig into Lathe, hopelessly trying to anchor herself to reality. He holds on tight, desperate to keep her with him, but no matter how firm his embrace, he cannot hold the intangible. Her eyes lose their focus, and he watches helplessly as her mind falls into disarray. She pulls away from him and grips the sides of her head. The lights flicker as she bends forward shaking her head as if to clear it.

"Mother, what do you see?" His voice remains calm, though his insides are quaking.

She bends over further, still gripping her head as she shouts, "None of us are safe!"

The temperature in the room plummets as the air begins circulating in gusts that threaten to knock Lathe off his feet. His mother doesn't seem to notice the current even as her curly unkempt hair lifts from her shoulders. Her eyes turn milky just before the lights go out completely, leaving them in darkness.

The room seems to shrink around him as her voice reverberates around the room, hurting his ears. "One evil spirit died, and another is reborn."

"Mother . . ." he says tentatively but is cut off as a gust of wind shoves him into a wall.

"Get out!" she screams in a voice that no longer resembles his mother's but sounds very much like the crazed woman Sky had turned her into.

He stumbles through the dark room, struggling to get the lock to disengage as the violent currents blow around the pitch-black room. When the lock registers, the door flies inward, pulled by the airstream. Stumbling, he rushes to gain his footing.

Using his full strength, he struggles to wrench the door closed as torrents of wind flow past him, out into the corridor.

Without warning, the direction of the current shifts and the door slams shut, dumping him out in the hall.

He sits up, leaning his back to the door as he catches his breath. He looks down the long corridor, noting all the damage caused in those brief seconds it took for the door to close. Shattered glass and broken frames litter the entire hall, reminding Lathe of how badly this could have gone. He knows he needs to be more careful. He can't let his hope of her improvement get in the way of his judgment.

He reaches up to pull his hood back over his head, scratching at that damn spot that always drives him crazy. Lifting himself from the floor, he rushes down the corridor and up two flights of stairs to find out what the council has discovered about Sky's disappearance.

AFTER A SLEEPLESS NIGHT, Morgan gets up to check on her best friend, Emily, who, as of an hour ago, was sleeping soundly. She heard movement upstairs a while ago but wanted to give Emily and Ben some alone time before interrupting them.

She pauses at the top of the stairs, her brows pinching together over soft blue eyes. Emily, along with Morgan's cousin, Patrick, disappeared a few weeks ago after Emily's adoptive father was kidnapped by Sky, the biological father she hadn't known she had. Then early yesterday, Patrick showed up at

Morgan's family home with Emily bleeding and half-dead, bringing to light the secrets Morgan's father and cousin had been hiding. And Emily's boyfriend, Ben, was around to witness the whole thing.

Outside of the guest room, Morgan rolls her neck and brushes a hand through her straight brown hair before twisting it up into a ponytail. Her muscles tense under her workout gear, her body longing to go to the gym to work off some of this worry. Morgan can dominate almost any sport with competitive ease, but outside of athletics, she is a level head with a huge heart. Her friends rely on her, and she usually knows exactly what to do to make things better, but right now, she's at a loss, and it's making her jumpy. She takes a deep breath, trying to force the anxiety out of her limbs before stepping into the guest room.

Morgan is happy to find an empty bed. Emily must be feeling better if she's up and around. Then she sees Ben crouched in the middle of the room with his arms extended toward an open window as if his body froze mid-lunge. He is in peak physical condition, but his muscles are trembling from the awkward stance. Sweat is dripping from his dark hair, sliding down his bronze skin, but he maintains his position.

Morgan frowns. "Ben, what are you doing?"

At the sound of her voice, Ben's quivering legs give out. His hands take the brunt of his fall, and he immediately pushes himself up and rushes to the open window. He sticks his head out, searching.

In a panic, he pushes back into the room, and his eyes do a frantic sweep before they land on Morgan. Instead of an explanation, he brushes past her and careens unsteadily through the doorway. Morgan follows, hopping down the stairs two at a time to keep up with him. Ben is off the front porch by the time Morgan makes it outside.

They find Patrick standing in the driveway, looking satisfied next to his car. The August morning sun reflects off of the expensive BMW he just beat to hell with a baseball bat. Morgan tried to stop him when he first started battering the vehicle, but eventually, she gave up, realizing the car is a reminder of Sky and all the ways he controlled Patrick.

Patrick is usually impeccably put together, but right now his clothes hang off his lean height, looking rumpled and unclean. His short blond hair is disheveled, and his sapphire eyes are red-rimmed. Morgan isn't sure when he last slept.

Ben's heavy footfalls steal Patrick's attention from the car. As he turns to face Ben, the baseball bat slips through Patrick's fingers, clattering to the ground. Morgan watches the panic spread from one to the other like an airborne virus. Ben bends with his hands resting on his knees in an attempt to catch his breath before he gasps, "Emily—"

Patrick takes an urgent step toward Ben, demanding, "How long?"

Patrick doesn't wait for a verbal response, and Morgan assumes he's pulling the information from Ben's thoughts. Patrick marches past them and into the house, letting the front door slam shut behind him.

Ben stumbles before he collapses in the lush grass. Morgan rushes to him, "Ben, are you okay?"

Ben rolls to his back and stares up at the sky, saying, "Emily jumped out the window and ran away, Morgan. It was so fast. She was there and then she was gone." He closes his sad brown eyes. "I couldn't stop her. I tried, but she froze me in that position. I crouched there for almost an hour. I . . . I couldn't move at all."

Yelling from inside has Morgan looking toward the house. A loud crash echoes from the open windows. "I . . . I think I need to get in there."

"Go. I'll be fine."

By the time Morgan makes it into the house, she finds her father, Tom, in a silent stare down with Patrick. Both men have blond hair and blue eyes, giving away their Olvasho heritage.

While Morgan has her father's blue eyes, she didn't inherit his gifts because only women pass down their magic.

The tension in the room is suffocating as the two men glare at one another. Patrick breaks the silence, taking a step toward the door. "I have to go after her!"

Tom moves into his path. "Patrick, you'll get yourself killed! And then she'll come here and kill the rest of us!"

"Why would Emily hurt us?" Morgan asks, walking further into the room, unsure how much of the conversation she's missing from their telepathic dialogue.

Ignoring his daughter, Tom focuses on Patrick. "There is only one reason she'd run away. If you go and track her down, her last gift to us would be for nothing."

"You don't know that!" Patrick shouts, coming eye to eye with Tom.

"Give me another reason," Tom challenges.

Patrick glares at him. "She took Maggie. She loves that dog. Why else would she take her?"

"Don't be ignorant, Patrick. Maggie is a weapon!"

"Dad!" Morgan scolds.

"Look what she did to Ben! You said she turned him into a statue while she fled. You knew this could happen! You knew, and you still threw her at Sky, didn't you?" Tom tosses his hands in the air. "Go ahead and have your tantrum, but because of you forcing her hand, her Valla blood has taken over. The Emily we knew and loved is gone."

"I won't accept that!" Patrick shouts.

"I don't care if you accept it, but for once, listen to me!" He grabs Patrick by the shoulders, looks him directly in his eyes and warns, "You pursue her and we're all dead or worse."

"You don't know that."

"I know better than to risk it," Tom says.

Patrick's lips curl. "You don't even care about her." Shoving Tom away, he walks to the front door.

Tom follows, shouting, "I just saved her life! She's like a

daughter to me, but I will honor her last coherent thought, which was to run away in order to protect us from what she might do."

Patrick turns on him. "Emily wouldn't hurt any of us!"

"You're right, Emily wouldn't, but we both know the person who jumped out that window wasn't Emily."

Patrick opens the door. "No, but we can bring Emily back."

Even across the room, Morgan feels the power Patrick is using to get her dad to back off. The energy freezes Morgan and Tom while Patrick escapes the house, leaving the door to slam behind him. The temporary hold fades away after a few seconds, and Tom stomps after him.

Sensing the escalation, Morgan runs to the door. She finds Patrick standing on the edge of the porch with his head hung low. He beat his car to a pulp just moments ago, leaving him no means of escape. Hoping to prevent a fight, Morgan moves to stand between Patrick and her dad. She isn't stronger than either of them, but she is a weakness for both.

"You're acting like your mother, Patrick!" Tom says from behind Morgan. "Impulsive and ambitious, but never thinking about the consequences."

Morgan gasps.

Patrick shifts angry eyes to Tom, his voice lethal, "How dare you talk about my mother."

"She was my sister first, and I never stopped loving her, but I couldn't let her bad judgment hurt the rest of my family."

Patrick straightens. "Her bad judgment saved Emily's life!"

Tom closes his eyes, takes a breath, then continues, "I never said she didn't do good things, but look what happened to your family—to her family. Your father was murdered, you were brainwashed, and she ended up dead."

Patrick's fists tighten, but Morgan is in the way.

Tom continues, "She's gone, but you should learn from her mistakes."

Patrick turns away and bolts down the steps.

"I'll restrain you if I have to!" Tom threatens.

"Like you could," Patrick says, walking away even as Tom tries to hold him back.

Only then does Morgan remember Ben. She looks to the spot in the yard where she left him sprawled out on his back. Now, he's sitting up, watching intently as Patrick hurries into Morgan's car, grabs her keys from her visor, and takes off.

BURK SECURITY IS Emily's father's company, and in his absence, Chris became the interim head of operations. In his early thirties with auburn hair, a medium build, and a forgettably average face, Chris has been Mark's right-hand man for years. Though he doesn't know about the Olvasho, Mark has trusted him to help with sensitive issues, and so far, Chris hasn't asked too many questions.

Patrick barges into the conference room where Chris is holding a business meeting. The door bangs against the wall and Chris stands from the table as ten faces turn to Patrick in surprise.

"Patrick, wha . . ." Chris begins, but Patrick demands, "Everyone out! Now!"

The room clears out as Patrick uses his extra persuasions over everyone except Chris. He stands, glaring at Patrick from his spot at the head of the table while Patrick shuts the doors, closing them in the conference room together.

"You can't just barge in here like this!" Chris huffs. "We were having a meeting to delegate Mark's responsibilities while he's recovering."

"That can wait. It all can wait. Emily disappeared this morning. I need you to run a search on her. Use your face recognition software or something. We have to find her."

Chris's annoyance shows in his expression, as he calmly

states, "If she shows up on one of our cameras, then I'll let you know."

Patrick is insistent, "No, I need you to tap into a bigger network."

Chris rubs the back of his neck. "I don't know who you think we are. If Mark has that kind of access, he never shared it with me."

Patrick sighs, angry that Emily's father hasn't awakened from his coma. Patrick had kept him alive long enough to get him out of the compound, but now there was nothing else he could do to save him. He blows out a breath. "Mark can't share anything with anyone until he wakes up."

"How long has she been gone?" Chris questions. "You were here last night to pick up her dog, so it can't be that long. Are you sure she's not coming back?"

Patrick glares at him. "You should know better than to question me by now."

"Fine, sorry. I just thought maybe . . ." Chris stops himself. "You know, forget it. How long has Emily been missing?"

"Two hours. You had people looking for Mark immediately. I need you to have them look for Emily."

"Two hours? Patrick, I have a company to run. I can't keep bleeding resources," Chris says. "It's not that I don't want to help. I just have no one to spare. We're already swamped trying to play catch up. Payroll is messed up, everything is behind, and I can't have my guys chase after someone who has been missing for two hours."

"I'll pay you. Whatever you charge, I'll double it. We have to find her!"

"You don't have that kind of money, Patrick," Chris says.

"I have millions in my bank account, and my mentor left me with access to hundreds of millions. I will buy this company if I have to and then you would have to report to me. I thought we understood each other. I thought there was a mutual respect."

"Mutual respect?" Chris barks. "You put yourself and your

needs above everyone else! You burst into my meeting without the slightest notion of respect, Patrick, so do not lecture me or threaten this company! The only reason I haven't had you escorted out of this building is because of my admiration for Mark."

Patrick takes a breath and blows it out, trying to tamp down his anger. He turns to pace away, scrubbing his face with his palms. He spins back to Chris and after a long sigh, says, "I apologize. It's been an exhausting forty-eight hours, and it's possible I'm having trouble seeing outside of my own personal matters. I will be more courteous from here on out. With that said, I ask you to please spare any resources you can." He pulls out his checkbook. "I will pay whatever you need and help the company get back on solid footing, but right now, I need your help with Emily."

SITTING IN HER EMPTY KITCHEN, Morgan rests her elbows against the counter and inhales a deep breath. She drops her head on her folded arms in defeat. She was only beginning to make peace with all the things she has seen and heard in the last thirty-six hours, but that was before Emily made such an abrupt and desperate departure.

"You okay?" Ben asks, sitting down on the stool next to her.

Morgan lifts her head and the words that have been spinning through her mind for the last hour spill out of her, "Why would she leave? Do you think it's an Olvasho thing or maybe a Valla thing? They said she's the last living Valla blood. Do you think she was afraid of the Olvasho finding her? They said Olvasho have a history of killing off the most powerful bloodline."

Ben frowns and shakes his head. "I wish I had the answers, but I'm just as lost as you."

Morgan stands to pace back and forth. "I feel like I need to do something, but I don't know how to help."

"I'm still trying to wrap my head around all this. Em's always been a mystery but . . ." He shakes his head, and his words fade without resolution.

"Ben, she'll come back to us. I mean she has to know we wouldn't let anything happen to her." His eyes close and Morgan places a comforting hand on his back.

"Her eyes . . ." he mumbles with his head down. Lifting his chin, he says, "Morgan, I think your dad might be right. Whoever that was up there, it wasn't Emily. She went to sleep as my Emily, but when she woke, she didn't know who I was. Her eyes were cold, and she felt like a stranger. What if your dad is right? What if she isn't Emily anymore?"

"She's still Emily."

"But what if she isn't?"

"You think what my dad said is true? You think her Valla blood took over?"

Ben shakes his head and shrugs. "I don't even know what that means. I don't know what to think."

Morgan thinks about it for a moment before asking, "You couldn't move at all?"

"It's more like I forgot there was another option. She stole every thought out of my head, making me helpless." He lowers his voice. "What if she's dangerous, Morgan? I love her. I always will, but what if this change is permanent?"

"We got her back the last time," Morgan says, "We can get her back again. Whatever this is, Emily will fight it. She'll come back to us. She's always been stronger than people give her credit for." Morgan goes to the window, hoping to see Patrick return with her car.

Ben comes up beside her, and as if reading her thoughts, he says, "It's probably best he and your dad aren't in the same house right now."

"You're right, but I was hoping for some answers."

"I don't think they have any more answers than we do, Morgan." He wraps a reassuring arm around her shoulder.

Morgan is wistful. "I have always felt lucky, like I won the family lotto. My family was a blessing. We talked openly. I thought we didn't keep secrets. I had no idea my dad was hiding something so unbelievable. Now my mom hasn't left her room since Emily showed up covered in blood, my dad is acting like a raving lunatic, and Patrick just stole my car."

Ben pulls her into a hug. "If you need to go somewhere, I'll take you."

Morgan remains by Ben's side the rest of the day, and Ben seems as comforted by her presence as she is by his. Their mutual fear and confusion brings them closer. But at the end of the day, Ben goes home, and life goes on.

CHAPTER TWO

One Month Later ~

Morgan's feet graze lazy circles on the surface of the lake. Birds sing a joyful song in the afternoon sun while fish swim carefree laps in the shallow clear waters. Summer lingers in the warm September air while leaves begin changing color. Beside Morgan, a thick textbook lies open, but forgotten, against the wide wooden planks of the dock. A soft breeze snags at the book and flips a page, catching Morgan's attention. She came out here to study, thinking it would be peaceful, but the commotion in her head followed her, destroying the tranquil surroundings.

Morgan knows firsthand that everything can change in a heartbeat. In high school, she had a full-ride athletic scholarship coming her way until she tore her ACL. One time hyper-extending her knee ruined her chance at her dream school. Not being one to wallow, she pushed herself harder, studying between doctor appointments and physical therapy.

In the end, she received an academic scholarship to her second-choice school, which took her to Florida. Life was perfect until two drunk college students came into her dorm room and assaulted her. In return for their crime, they got a slap on the wrist, which to Morgan was like a slap in the face.

She moved home, opting to stay with her parents for comfort and safety. She enrolled in a nursing program at a nearby university and found a job as a nurse's aide at the local hospital. She took summer classes, staying in to study while her friends went out. She wouldn't let anything else get in her way. She was unstoppable until a month ago when Emily almost died, and everything she thought she knew about life became something else entirely. She isn't sure she knows how to move forward anymore.

"Morgan, you okay?" Nellie asks, disrupting Morgan's private moment.

Morgan lifts her feet out of the water and stands from her perch on the side of her family's private dock. "Yeah, I'm good."

Nellie's eyes meet Morgan's. "You're a terrible liar. You know you can talk to me about anything, right? That's what sisters are for."

Morgan wishes she was not so transparent. She begged her mom and dad not to drag Nellie into the family secret, and here she is making her sister worry and ask questions. "I'm having guy problems. I'll be fine. Besides, I really need to focus on studying tonight."

Nellie pulls Morgan into a hug. "Let me know if you need me."

"I will," Morgan concedes, letting her sister pull from their embrace.

Once Nellie is gone, the smile melts from Morgan's lips and she bends to pick up her weighty tome of short stories. She steps into the rowboat attached to the dock and frees the tether. Pushing away from the shore, she lets the boat drift across the lake behind her childhood home. She opens her book and attempts to read the same short story she's been working on. It's become the longest short story of her life because she can't focus.

Ever since Emily disappeared, Morgan has had difficulty concentrating. She's never been a good liar, yet she's forced to lie about what happened to her friend. Patrick is the one who came up with the idea, and Ben, Morgan, and Tom agreed that lying was their only option. So the story goes; a guilt-ridden Emily ran off after the car accident she caused put her father in a coma.

But that wasn't the only thing that had Morgan stressed. The escalating tension between her father and Patrick has put Morgan right in the middle. If her father is gasoline, then Patrick is an open flame. To avoid the inevitable explosion, Patrick moved out two weeks ago, and Morgan followed, staying at Patrick's apartment more than she stays at home. But today she needed a break from Patrick's obsessive searching for Emily. She wanted a day to feel normal but is realizing that may never be possible.

The rowboat drifts across the quiet lake until it floats too close to the bank and gets stuck. Morgan makes no move to remedy the situation, but the movement is enough to pull her from her thoughts. She sits in the shallow bank and focuses on the book in her lap.

"You stuck?"

Morgan jumps at the sound of Ben's voice. She swivels to find him standing on the low bank. His nearly black hair is cropped short and his bronze tan has started to fade. Soft brown eyes shrouded in long lashes look down on her. His broad shoulders slouch, and he tucks his hands into the pockets of his jeans, looking uncomfortable.

"No, I'm not stuck," she says. "What are you doing here?"

"I came to see you." He takes a step forward. "Do you mind if I join you?"

In response, she picks up an oar and moves the boat along the shore so he can step inside. Morgan gives up her spot, shifting to the bench facing him. Ben takes her abandoned seat and pushes away from the shore, leading them out into deeper water. Morgan doubts he has much time to work out these days, but teaching Taekwondo has kept him in shape. His long-powered strokes take them out to the center of the lake in no time. Ben lifts the oars out of the water, allowing the gentle current to take over.

As he looks over the lake, Morgan observes him, wondering if he's getting enough sleep. She's been worried about him, but he has kept his distance since the day Emily left.

Ben's gaze shifts to Morgan and they stare at one another for a moment before Ben comments, "You look tired."

Morgan snorts. "Awe thanks, but I'm not the one killing myself by working two jobs. You don't look any better than I do. How is it living with Alec and his mom, anyway?"

Ben shrugs. "About how you'd expect. I'm not there very often, but you're welcome to come over any time."

"I don't have a whole lot of free time," she says, which is true, but it isn't the reason she has stayed away. She's avoiding Alec because somewhere along the way she developed a significant crush on him that would only lead to heartbreak. "So, how are you, really?"

Ben shrugs. "I feel like I'm losing my mind."

Taking a deep breath, she says, "I know. Me too. Are you sleeping okay?"

"No, you?"

"I have medication that's supposed to help me sleep. I haven't been taking it because it gives me weird dreams. I think I'd rather not sleep."

"I get it," he laughs before his expression goes distant. "Has your dad come around?"

"No. He keeps talking about Emily like she's a monster."

Ben scowls. "I should be out there looking for her, but I don't even know where to begin."

"None of us do. It doesn't mean we've given up. Patrick is still following up on every lead."

"Patrick," he scoffs, dragging his hands over his face. "It shouldn't be up to Patrick."

"Patrick is the best candidate we have," Morgan says, looking across the lake to avoid his glare. "Ben, I know you're conflicted when it comes to Patrick."

"Conflicted? That's a nice word for it. Morgan, how are you not conflicted when it comes to Patrick?"

"Because he's trying his best. I can feel it. I mean, really try for a second to put yourself in his shoes. What would you have done?"

"We've been through this before. He's manipulating you. I don't have the same exhausting compassion you have for him. I would have protected Emily from Sky. That's what I would've done!"

Morgan rolls her eyes, unwilling to go through this argument again. "Patrick is a jerk. I'm not arguing that. At least he's trying to make up for it. As much as you hate him, he cares about Emily, and hopefully with his expertise, he can find her. He's our best bet."

Ben starts rowing again as if using his muscles will subdue his anger. His mouth opens to say something, but then it closes with a huff. He drops the oars and rubs his hands over his face. "Damn it, Morgan. I need to do something!"

"I feel the same way, but Patrick is working with Burk Security, and I don't see anything we can do that they aren't already doing."

Ben pulls his face out of his hands. "You and I know her better than anyone. We know how her mind works. We should be the ones following up on leads."

Morgan places her palm on his knee. "We'll get her back, Ben."

He lets out a breath. "That's not enough. If this . . . thing has control of her, then what's gonna happen to her? What is she going to be like when we finally get her back? If we get her back? We need to find her now, while she's still in there. While she can still be saved."

Morgan sees his torment. Not only is his girlfriend missing, but he was kicked out of his home, cut off from his sister, and left feeling undeniably lost.

Tears well in Morgan's eyes and she starts to pull away, but Ben captures her hand in his, saying, "Don't cry because of me."

"Someone should cry for you."

Ben shakes his head and looks at his shoes. "Badass Fletcher with her huge-ass heart. I'm sorry," he whispers, looking back up. "I haven't been there for you."

"Ben, what are you talking about? The floor fell out from under you, and you're apologizing to me. You don't owe me anything, especially not an apology."

Silence falls between them and Ben looks out over the water, appearing thoughtful. The quiet breeze blows Morgan's stray hairs into her face. She brushes them aside, working up the courage to say more, but as she opens her mouth, Ben curses under his breath. "I need to get back to work. I have another class at two."

And just like that, Morgan watches his barriers go back up. He's done talking. Morgan slides back in her seat, asking, "What age are you teaching?"

"My two o'clock class is my three to five-year-olds. The more advanced classes are in the evening." He moves the boat toward the dock.

"What class is your favorite?"

"The advanced classes are cool. I get to spar instead of just demonstrating the moves, but the little kids are funny as hell. Mean too." He laughs. "If it wasn't for the parents' constant hovering, I think the little ones would be my favorite. They're fearless."

"Maybe I'll take a class sometime. Fighting isn't really my thing, but maybe it'd be good to know some self-defense moves."

Ben scowls. "Do you not feel safe?"

She lifts her shoulders. "I just think it might come in handy someday."

With suspicion, he says, "You'd tell me if something happened, right?"

"Don't you think self-defense is something everyone should know?"

"Sure, I'd be happy to teach you some moves."

They make their way to the dock and disembark. While Morgan secures the boat, Ben hesitates to leave. He tucks his hands in his pockets while he rocks slightly from heel to toe, looking anywhere but at Morgan.

Morgan says, "Just spit it out. Whatever it is, you know you can talk to me."

He sighs. "My parents are already keeping my sister from me. Morgan, I can't lose Emily too."

Morgan stares at him for a moment thinking about all the times she's felt the same way. She can't even focus on her school-work. "Okay, let me find out what I can and then we'll go after her, ourselves."

"Patrick will try to stop us."

"It's not up to him," she says.

"But he'll know what we're planning."

"He picks up on my thoughts sometimes, but he's promised not to pry into my mind. I'll let you know when I hear something useful."

"Thanks, Morgan."

CHAPTER THREE ~

PATRICK SPREADS the map across his new coffee table and decides that won't do. He picks it up and tacks it to the wall where he has all the other important information. He steps back and cringes. Great, he's been in his new place for just under two weeks, and it's already looking like a serial killer's hideout. He can't remember why he thought it was a good idea to pin the eight by ten picture of Emily to the wall. It's not like he is going to forget what she looks like. If anything, the photo makes her look more like a victim. Patrick moves to take it down, but stops, feeling like it will mean part of him is giving up on her and that, he can't stand for.

In all this time, they only once caught Emily on camera. She was in Texas, but she was long gone by the time they arrived, disappearing again, without a trace. Chris still has people looking into it, but Patrick is losing confidence in them, just as he is losing faith that Mark is going to wake up. He and his uncle may not agree on a lot of things, but they have been taking turns attempting to heal Mark. So far, they have been unable to bring him out of his coma, but at least they have kept him alive.

Patrick refuses to give up on Emily. He doesn't just miss her —he feels entirely lost without her. He stares at her picture on his wall of nonsense, remembering the first time he laid eyes on her.

The sun was shining, a slight breeze blowing, and it was about seventy-five degrees. Ultimately, Patrick thought it was pretty nice out considering he was stuck in Ohio. He craved the beach. He missed the sun reflecting off the water as he rode the waves, just him, his surfboard, and the ocean. He missed the solitude. As long as he continued to keep Sky happy, he could maintain his illusion of freedom. Sky expected excellence from him, and if Patrick didn't perform, he would never see the beach again. His life might be a far cry from perfect, but it was more comfortable to do what Sky demanded, even if it meant he'd had to sell his soul many times over.

He didn't have time to think of the beach; he had a job to do—someone to find—and he was on the clock. Patrick was the best guy they had, and he was up for a challenge, but this was a waste of his time. Sky sent him here without a solid lead, without a lead at all in Patrick's opinion. A female Olvasho around the age of eighteen was not enough to go on, but clearly, Sky was becoming desperate.

Patrick was becoming desperate, too. He wanted to get the hell out of Ohio, especially before winter rolled around. He would lose his mind if he was still here when it started snowing. He was unable to convince Sky that this was a lost cause, so here he was, searching everywhere, even campuses mid-summer. He wasn't having any luck here at the community college. Maybe he'd try his luck at the university down the street. He jingled the keys inside his pocket eager to leave.

Seeing so few students on campus, he wandered toward the parking lot. He stood against a stone wall calculating his odds. Really, he just wanted to drive his baby around a little more. The new top of the line beamer was a gift to help soften him up for this damn assignment. He guessed it helped a little. Not only was it fast, but it drove beautifully. He jingled the keys in his pocket again, weighing his options.

Forget it. He was done for today. He pulled away from the wall and took a few steps to leave when he spotted a young woman a few steps ahead. Her big gray eyes were pointed at the giant clock that covered one side of the large brick building. He watched her sigh and her shoulders slumped. "Crap! I was in such a hurry to leave the bridal store; I didn't realize I'd be an hour early." Her thoughts came to Patrick, burrowing themselves inside his mind without any effort of his own. It was bizarre.

He stared at her as she continued to walk forward, oblivious to his attention. She looked pitifully sad, and he wondered how she hadn't noticed him. He was used to being seen.

He dropped the keys in his pocket and turned to follow the light-haired young woman who was invading his thoughts. He kept his distance, thinking she may turn and acknowledge his presence, but she was too enthralled in her own deliberations.

He knew he was wasting his time watching her. She was not the one Sky was looking for; she couldn't be. Sure, she was a female around the age of eighteen, but her eyes were gray, and she could barely be considered blond. It didn't fit. Sure, she'd spoken into his mind, but perhaps her mind was a little quirky that way. He'd come across other unusual things. He encountered a man a few years back who couldn't be mentally manipulated. It was an anomaly in his genes that made him immune to Olvasho abilities. It was extremely rare, but it happened every once in a while. So, she wasn't the one Sky was searching for, but Patrick couldn't help his curiosity. Nobody said he couldn't have a little fun on the job.

She turned a corner, readjusting her book bag on her shoulders. She fussed briefly with her long hair, freeing a few strands from under the shoulder straps as she continued her lazy pace across campus. Patrick soon realized she had led him in a circle, and he thought perhaps she had discovered he was following her.

He gave her a little more space and eventually she sat down on a bench, setting her bag next to her. She was digging in her backpack and didn't notice a dark-haired, muscular guy approach. Patrick wondered how anyone could be that oblivious to their surroundings.

She looked up, startled. Patrick moved a step closer, feeling protective even though the thought was irrational.

She pulled her face together as she spoke. "Oh! H . . . hey, Ben. I didn't know you were taking summer classes."

Her voice radiated through Patrick's mind. Her words were amplified for him, despite the distance. "Why is he talking to me?" He heard her *think, causing him to suck in a breath, beyond amazed. It was not new for him to hear someone's thoughts, but to hear them so crystal clear like she was gifting her thoughts to him personally from such a distance was something that had never happened to him before. Something about this girl was very unique, indeed.*

"Oh," she said in a beautifully shy voice, feeling self-conscious. "So, what do you think?"

Patrick continued to stare at her with fascination. He not only heard her words and thoughts, but he felt her every emotion. He could see her face now that she was looking at this young man in front of her. Her skin was deliciously pale. Her thin frame appeared delicate next to the broad shoulders of her visitor.

"About what?" she mumbled. Patrick was curious as to what her friend said to make her feel so uncomfortable. He sensed her racking her brain for something to say, and she was about to mention a wedding when her friend cut her off. Patrick wondered if she was getting married. Surely, she wasn't. She looked far too young. He inspected her hand, relieved when he didn't spot an engagement ring.

"I'm sorry," she whispered, and Patrick felt himself get angry over her apology. Why would she apologize to him? But he realized her friend was looking just as confused by her apology.

She stood dramatically to walk away, but she lost her grace as she fumbled with her bag, clumsily flubbing up her escape attempt. The friend caught her hand, staring at her with a look that brought it all together. He was in love with her, and she had no idea.

Patrick was an idiot for listening. Something was peculiar about this girl, but she was clearly not who Patrick was looking for, and evidently, she was just as complicated as most girls her age. Bored, he started to walk away, annoyed when he continued to hear her thoughts even after trying to block her out.

Her mind spoke to him, and he realized he was walking further into the courtyard instead of toward his ride. Patrick looked to another student sitting beneath a tree and went over to him, attempting to refocus his attention so he could get this girl out of his head.

"You guys are like brothers to me," he hears, but it is not the guy he

was hovering over; it was that girl. "Well, maybe that's a stretch," her thoughts spoke even louder in his ear.

"How irritating," Patrick said aloud. The student under the tree looked up, startled by his sudden closeness. While Patrick glared down at him, the student quickly gathered his books and scurried off. Patrick found satisfaction in the way the stranger feared him. He leaned against the tree trying to calm himself. It had been so long since he'd lost control and now this ordinary little twit was in his head.

He felt her eyes fall on him. Despite his irritation, a pleasant heat filled Patrick, and a smile took his face as she inspected him. He ran a hand through his hair, determined not to let this unimportant female get the best of him. He was pleased to know she thought he was attractive. She was envious of his tan. He felt her gaze shift away, and he took the opportunity to look at her. Her gaze flicked back to him as if his eyes had called to her. Their eyes met briefly before she quickly lowered her gaze.

Patrick continued to watch her interact with her friend, feeling bitterness when he made her laugh, but soon pity replaced the bitter feelings as Patrick noticed the look on the guy's face. It was clear she meant the world to him, but she was instinctively closed off from her feelings. This guy so obviously wanted more from her, but she denied him; yet, Patrick couldn't seem to get her to stop handing intimate parts of herself to him. It overwhelmed him with feelings he thought long dead. She was stirring emotions deep within him. He both hated it and longed for more.

The girl watched her friend leave, holding on to her denial. She turned back to her bag and resumed digging, ending her search with a granola bar in hand. Crumbs spilled out in her lap and down her shirt as she ate her messy snack. Patrick was amazed by her complete lack of grace. Once she finished, she stood, leaning forward to brush the crumbs away. He couldn't remember the last time he'd been so intrigued and entertained by someone. His body was shaking with laughter at this awkward young woman.

He felt the moment her eyes landed on him. Her gaze was hot, a sensual caress. Patrick returned her emphatic stare, only to get a short look of horror before she turned her entire body away from him. "How embarrassing! He's been watching me!" He heard her thoughts. She threw everything in her bag, and Patrick felt a sudden panic. He couldn't let her escape. He started toward her.

She began to walk away, but glanced back, searching for him. Patrick smiled, watching as her body hesitated, then stopped. He felt her wrestling to free herself from his pull. He felt her fight her attraction to him, but they were magnets drawn to one another by a force they couldn't overcome. She thought he was beautiful, but she thought it strange that he was dressed so formally. He hadn't needed to wear a suit today. It was just a habit; something Sky ingrained in him. Always be the best-dressed person in a room. He continued walking to her, feeling a giddiness inside of himself. He'd never been more intrigued by someone in his life.

Overwhelming fear consumed his thoughts. He wasn't sure if they were his own or hers. He suspected it was both, but he couldn't keep himself away from her, walking straight toward the danger unraveling him. Her fears echoed in his mind. "Look away, Emily! Look away! If this is how you feel from far away, imagine how he'll affect you up close. You can't talk to him!"

Patrick fumbles with that thought. She didn't want to know him. But how could that be? She was angry with him. Patrick felt a sting he hadn't experienced in nearly six years. She'd already concluded that he wasn't worth knowing and suddenly he felt unsure of himself. He was an inconvenience she had no interest in entertaining. She didn't want him, and he felt shattering devastation at her perception of him.

She pulled out her phone to answer a pretend call, and unsure what to do with her rejection, Patrick shifted his direction at the last second. She looked up through her lashes and he thought for a second, she might have changed her mind, but she wore her determination like armor, closing him out, severing her emotions from his thoughts as if severing a lifeline.

Patrick looked forward, placing a hand in his pocket and palming his keys, desperate to escape the emotions she had unsettled in him. He was close enough now that he could smell her sweet scent, so close that he could have reached out and touched her soft skin, or brushed the hair from her face, or snapped that delicate neck to put an end to these emotions she'd stirred in him. He continued forward one step at a time.

"What a bizarre boy, why is he behaving so strangely?" Her thoughts

reached out to him once more, falling like a noose around his neck, strangling him. He had to detangle himself. He had to make it stop, but he couldn't. She made him powerless to do anything but listen. "Why am I reacting so irrationally?" She questioned herself as Patrick rounded the corner of the path, needing to escape to his car.

The sound of a key in the apartment door causes Patrick's mind to scatter. He spins to face the door just as Morgan pushes it open.

Her gym bag is slung over her shoulder and her hair is still wet from her shower. "Hey, Patrick," she says as she swings around to face him. Her gaze cuts right past him and her blue eyes go wide. Her smile melts into a grimace. "Doing some decorating, I see. Looks like all you need is a string to connect all the clues and a tinfoil hat to keep the aliens out of your head."

Patrick responds by spinning back around to look at his project. He scratches his forehead, saying, "They're clues to finding Emily."

She scrunches her nose. "I think you might be using the word *clue* a bit haphazardly."

He knows she's right. He has next to nothing. The wall is just a cluster of random ideas he has come up with on the nights he can't sleep.

Morgan moves forward, taking it in. "The map is new. Did you find something?"

"I thought it might speak to me."

"And?"

"It's just a piece of paper, Morgan. I'm losing my mind."

Morgan laughs. "You might be able to think more clearly if you could sleep. Have you tried those sleeping pills?"

"The same ones you refuse to take."

"I'm not refusing," she says stubbornly.

Patrick changes the subject. "Tomorrow I'm driving out to Maplesburg."

Trying to hide her surprise, she asks, "What's in Maplesburg?" Even though she knows exactly what is in Maplesburg, his childhood home filled with a lifetime of old memories. He avoids talking about it and has never shown interest in going before. "Did you find something?"

"My parents hid some artifacts. They're probably pointless, and Sky's men already combed through it years ago, but maybe they missed something. My parents had some pretty ingenious hiding places."

"Can I come with you?"

"I can do it on my own," he says, hating the idea of going at all. It was the last place he was truly happy and he's afraid of the emotions it might bring up. Going alone feels too difficult, but pride keeps him from asking for favors.

"I think I should go with you," Morgan insists.

Patrick jumps at the opportunity, but still finds a way to keep her at arm's length. "Okay, but you're staying in the car."

CHAPTER FOUR ~

MAPLESBURG IS NOT SO MUCH a burg as it is a dozen houses clustered together in the middle of cornfields and wilderness. There are no stores or gas stations within ten miles. It's a two-hour drive from Patrick's apartment in the city, and as promised, Morgan stays in the car while Patrick wanders into what is left of his childhood home.

The sidewalk leading up to the house is cracked and hidden under waist-high grass and tree-sized weeds. Carnivorous vines devour the outside of the house leaving only portions of the faded blue siding to peek through. Windows are cracked and broken. The tiny paths through the thick weeds prove four-legged critters have made Patrick's old home their own.

"It shouldn't be taking him so long," Morgan mumbles after a half an hour of sitting alone in the car. She gets out to stretch and glances at the sun beginning its downward descent. "Ah, screw it. He can be mad if he wants." She quickly tromps through the tall grass, only slowing once she gets close to the house.

Cautiously, Morgan enters through the front door. The horrid smell of animal excrement is overpowering. She pulls her shirt over her nose as she walks across the room.

"Patrick," she calls, but there is no answer.

She makes her way around a torn couch, taking in the rickety furniture and the cheap plastic frames hanging on the wall. There are toys scattered on the floor, left out as if awaiting someone's return. A small television lays broken on the floor in the corner next to a collapsed table.

It's hard for Morgan to imagine Patrick being poor, but he was raised without wealth by parents who loved him and gave up everything to do what they believed was right. And now Patrick has returned to this place—despite the painful memories—so he can continue his parent's fight, even if it means sacrificing himself in the process. He feels bound to Emily in a way Morgan is afraid to question.

The light coming through the window is fading, and she doesn't want either of them to be here when the current residents—whether raccoons or possums or something more wicked —awaken.

"Patrick," she calls again, moving through a doorway into a kitchen.

The smell worsens and the setting sun struggles to shine through the filthy windows. She notices an open door and peers down into a musty basement staircase filled with cobwebs. A small glow comes from the bottom. She hesitates. Would he really go down there?

She turns away and moves to check the door across the room. She hears a faint sound and freezes. Holding her breath, Morgan stands at attention like a meerkat on high alert. She waits for the noise to come again and sure enough, the tapping of claws across a wooden surface nearby sends her feet flying into motion. She rushes through the kitchen toward the basement. Moving down onto the narrow top step, she prays that small glow is coming from Patrick. She pulls her phone from her pocket and opens the flashlight app horrified to see the number of spiderwebs lining the rickety staircase. But spiders are the least of her worries as the nocturnal critters in the kitchen come hunting.

"Patrick? Are you down there?" she calls, inching her way down the steps.

In response, Morgan hears a thud. She hurries down the last few steps, searching the dark space as she goes. Light comes from an open door down the way. She runs the length and turns into a room, discovering a flashlight lying abandoned in the doorway. She sweeps her phone through the room and finds Patrick lying on the floor shaking violently.

"Oh my God, Patrick!" Morgan rushes to him, collapsing next to his vibrating body. She drops her phone to the floor and cradles his head in her lap to keep it from banging on the hard floor. She tries to think logically. But she can't think.

His eyes roll to the back of his head.

"Patrick, I don't know what to do. I don't know what to do!"

Her mind reverts back to her CPR training from the hospital and she examines his body, spotting a chain dangling from his fisted hand. She pulls the chain and a sapphire gem slips out of his tight grip.

The shaking stops immediately. His tense body relaxes, and his head flops to the side in her lap.

"Patrick?" She drops the delicate chain to the floor and lays her fingers on his neck, right over his hammering pulse. His breathing is erratic. "Patrick, it's me, Morgan. Can you hear me?" She waits for a response. And she waits. And she waits.

When she realizes his breathing and pulse are the best response she's going to get; she opens his hand to inspect the blistering burn across the center of his palm. Then she looks to the necklace on the floor. The nickel-sized gem appears to be darkening in color, its sapphire color turning onyx. Morgan picks up the dainty chain and brings it closer for inspection. Her fingers graze the gem, tingling at the touch. A wave of dizziness has her swaying to the side.

"Don't touch it," Patrick rasps.

She drops the necklace and tears of relief flow from her eyes. "Patrick, are you okay?"

He reaches up and wipes a tear from her cheek. "Now I am." He begins to get up, but Morgan pushes his shoulders down.

"Don't you dare! You scared me. I need you to lie here for a minute, so I know you're okay."

With a nod, he lays his head back down on her lap.

"God, Patrick, what happened?"

"I'm fine, Morgan. I promise." He tips his head toward the jewel lying on the floor. "I came here looking for that necklace.

"Looks like you found it," she says with a wry smile. "And it looks like it was killing you."

"I'm guessing that's why my parents kept it locked up and hidden down here. It was supposed to neutralize the gifts of an Olvasho. I think I activated it wrong."

"How did you activate it?"

"With a drop of blood," he says.

"And what were you supposed to do?"

"I don't know. I must have read it wrong." He sits up and faces Morgan. "I thought I told you to stay in the car."

"Yeah, thank God I never listen to you." She looks back to the necklace. "Are you going to take it with you?"

"Yeah. I suppose I'll try again later."

"Just promise you'll do it when I'm around."

Patrick stands up, offering a hand to help Morgan to her feet. "I'll be more prepared next time. Come on. Help me with this stuff. I'm sure the raccoons are already awake upstairs, and there are bats down here."

THEY GATHER the items Patrick found into two boxes. Several books take up one box while the other is filled with an assortment of things, including the dangerous necklace which Patrick places in a velvet pouch for protection. He doesn't quite know how the accessory works yet, but he felt the powerful magic it contains.

Morgan insists on driving. Patrick wants to argue, but he thinks better of it. Spending the last hour in his childhood home brought up memories he's unsure how to handle, and that damn necklace took too much out of him. He slumps into the passenger seat and within minutes the exhaustion takes its toll on him and he falls asleep.

Long ago Patrick taught himself not to dream, but today he broke all kinds of rules. His dream begins with the sound of waves crashing against a shoreline. As it unfolds, Patrick finds himself standing on a beach watching the midnight waves roll over the ocean. The sky is dark with the new moon and the stars hang like dazzling lights high above.

The waves splash onto the beach, spraying Patrick with a fine mist, vying for his attention. In his three-piece suit, the heat of the night feels stifling, and beads of sweat gather at the nape of his neck and slide down his back. He removes his jacket and lets it fall to the sand as he walks forward unbuttoning his vest and discarding that, too. The ocean breathes, whispering his name on its breath while an enticingly cool mist continues to coax him forward.

He slides one shoe off, then the other. His body tingles as he moves closer to the brine. The breeze beckons him, and the waves turn gentle, lapping seductively, luring him into the calm waters. When his feet sink beneath the surface, the current picks back up guiding him deeper, drawing him into its depths.

The water is up to his waist now, making his pants heavy while his shirt clings to his wet body, but it's not enough. It won't be enough until he's completely submerged. He goes under, tasting the salty ocean on his tongue. It's a tease, making him desperate for more. He dives deeper into the inky cold depths until his lungs sting in the best way. The burning makes him feel alive. He knows he's drowning, but he plunges further into the bottomless chasm, captivated by the dark waters surrounding him. All the answers are here, hidden in the deep abyss. He just needs to go deeper.

Desperate for air, his lungs betray him, and he gasps for air.

He wakes with a choking sound.

His sudden coughing fit draws Morgan's attention from the road. "Are you okay?"

Dusk has turned to night outside the car windows, and Patrick is grateful there are no streetlights to illuminate the interior of the car. It's dark enough that she doesn't notice the sweat trickling from his forehead. Patrick wipes it away when her eyes go back to the road. He clears his throat, trying to steady his voice before speaking. "Not entirely back to myself is all."

"I know today took its toll on you. We'll be home in twenty minutes."

Patrick licks his parched lips and tastes the salt from the ocean, the dream sticking to him like a hangover after a night of drinking. He wonders what the hell caused him to have such a surreal dream. It was vivid and terrifying, yet deep down, there is an overwhelming compulsion to visit the dream once more. He feels all the answers he's been searching for are there, hidden in the depths of the ocean.

CHAPTER FIVE ~

A FEW WEEKS later ~

"PATRICK, do you know what you're looking for in all those?" Morgan asks, eyeing the stack of ancient looking books sitting on his coffee table. The hard bindings are barely holding together, and the yellowing pages are brittle.

"I'll know it when I see it," he says, carefully flipping through pages.

"Can't I help?"

"Don't you have your own homework? I thought nursing school was supposed to be difficult."

"I'm good at multitasking," Morgan notes, taking a seat on Patrick's couch. His apartment has an open modern feel and is scarcely furnished. Morgan is convinced most of the furniture is too stiff to be comfortable, but she's slowly breaking it in. She's taken over his spare bedroom and the place is starting to feel like home. She's especially grateful he took down the serial killer wall he had going on in the living room.

"This isn't something you can help with," Patrick says, turning another page.

His obsession with finding Emily is making him more irritable as the days pass, and Morgan feels an overwhelming urge to help in some way. "Isn't there anything else I can—"

"No, Morgan."

After a while of silence, Patrick closes the tome in his hands, places it on the floor, and moves to the next book. As he scrolls the table of contents, Morgan says, "Ben has tried repeatedly to contact his sister. Patrick, do you think she will call him? I mean, why hasn't she called yet?"

"Maybe you were wrong," he says without looking up. "Maybe she won't call."

"I just wanted so much to be right," Morgan says, grabbing a book from the coffee table, determined to help anyway.

Patrick glances up from his book. "I know you feel bad, but life doesn't always give you what you want."

Morgan avoids his eyes, looking for a title in the faded binding while she works up the courage to ask him for help.

"You're killing me, Morgan. Just ask."

"I know you have a full plate looking for Emily. I still wish you would let us help you with whatever you're planning."

"Morgan, there is nothing you or Ben can help me with. And I don't have time, nor do I want to interfere with someone else's family affair. My only concern is getting Emily home."

"I want her home too, but can't you spare an hour—"

"Stop wasting my time with Ben's problems."

"That sounds exactly like something Ben would expect you to say. Don't you want to prove him wrong?"

"I'm manipulative and heartless and only look out for myself. Perhaps Ben is correct in his assumptions. I certainly haven't denied his allegations. I have nothing to prove to him, nor do I care what he thinks of me. Why are you trying so hard to prove him wrong?"

"Because I know you. I know you're not heartless, Patrick. Molly is the only family he has left. He's tried nearly everything to reach out to her, but his parents are keeping her from him. What if it were you?"

"I would count my blessings that my family wasn't dead."

Morgan sets the book down on the coffee table. "I'm your family, and I'm not dead."

"You know what I mean."

"Patrick," she says in a small voice. "I'm worried about you."

He looks up from his book. "I'm painfully aware. It's annoying, and I don't recall anyone electing you my keeper. You're free to go any time."

"I'm not going to abandon you."

"Technically, I never invited you, nor did I intend for you to stay."

"You never had to ask and if you think you're getting rid of me that easily, you can forget it."

He looks back down at his book, as he says, "Your parents miss you."

"Oh, really? I saw my parents this afternoon. When was the last time you spoke to them?"

"I've come between you."

"Emily came between us. And stop changing the subject!"

"Morgan, enough!" he scolds with a stern look. "I am not your patient. Stop trying to fix me! I can't think with you nagging me. Honestly, I could get more done without your constant pestering!"

Morgan stands from the couch, crushed by his words. "I'll get my stuff and be on my way."

"Morgan, I'm not kicking you out. I know you're more comfortable here than you are at home right now."

She turns to face him. "I'm glad I'm so transparent, Patrick. It must be nice to know what people are thinking."

"I've obviously upset you."

She clenches her jaw, feeling the heat crawl up her neck. She walks back toward him. "Patrick, you upset me all of the time with your words and little jabs. I usually brush it off because I know you don't mean it, but I wasn't aware that my caring about you was considered nagging."

"Morgan, you want me to be someone I'm never going to be."

She rubs her jaw, refusing to raise her voice. In a controlled voice, she says, "Maybe, you're right. Or maybe your biggest fault is feeling the need to manipulate everyone into thinking you're a heartless bastard." Morgan starts down the hall to the guest bedroom.

"I am a heartless bastard!" he calls after her.

She turns around and stares at him. Does he really believe that? She opens her mouth to argue but thinks better of it. Shaking her head, she turns back around and goes to pack her things.

As she's shoving things into her bags and fighting back angry tears, a knock sounds at the front door of the apartment. After a moment she hears talking from the living room. She never considered Patrick might have other friends. She's never seen him with anyone else or heard him talk about anyone. Curious, she goes to the bedroom door to eavesdrop.

"Well?" Ashley asks, standing in the doorway of Patrick's apartment. Her ultra-blond hair hangs in loose messy curls, and she's wearing skintight jeans that show off her tall slender frame. In an attempt to get Patrick's attention, she's wearing a plunging V-neck, showing off her best assets, but he's immune to her blatant flirting.

She looks past him into the mostly bare apartment waiting for him to answer.

With an impatient sigh, Patrick says, "They're just things. Decorations don't matter. I'm only here until I move to the next place."

"That doesn't make any sense," Ashley says, moving further into his space. "It's your home, Patrick. How can you relax when everything looks so . . ." She looks around the open space. "Empty?"

Ashley and Emily used to work together at the pet supply store, and after Emily went missing, Ashley stuck around, bonding with Morgan even though the two were about as opposite as two people can be. Right now, Patrick is annoyed that it wasn't Ashley who went missing instead of Emily.

Patrick sighs and moves directly in front of her to grab her attention. "I appreciate your concern, but I like my space the way it is."

"Of course, you do," Ashley says, her eyes clinging to his body.

Patrick knows she's wondering what he looks like naked, but he isn't in the mood to be fawned over. Everyone always wants something they're too afraid to ask for. Even his cousin was afraid to ask him for a favor, but then again, didn't he give her every right to be intimidated. Even as he stands here with a salacious Ashley, Morgan is packing up to leave him.

"Ashley, doll, as flattering as this is, did you have a purpose for being here or are you only here to criticize my apartment?"

"Are you always so blunt?" she questions, raking him with hungry eyes as she fiddles with a strand of her platinum hair.

"Yes," he says, smiling an irritated smile. Ashley stops breathing, taken by him. He used to love getting that reaction, but now it feels worthless.

Feeling impatient, Patrick takes a peek at her thoughts to remind her of her purpose for being here. "Ashley, the party?"

"Oh, how did you know? Did Morgan already invite you? She said she wasn't going to. She said I'd have to invite you myself."

"Ashley, I'm not coming to your party."

"Why not?" she pouts.

"Because I don't want to."

A look of shock crosses her face before she shrugs it off, saying, "Blunt. I guess that's your way, though. I can respect that."

He frowns. "You shouldn't."

"I still want you to come, but I can't make you, so I'll just see you another time." She turns to walk out the open door.

Patrick starts to close it when Ashley spins around to stop him. "Are you in love with her?" she asks, unashamed. "Emily, I mean. Are you in love with Emily?"

Patrick isn't one to be taken off guard, but people don't usually say what they're thinking, especially if it's going to make the person they're speaking to uncomfortable. Ashley manages to both make him uncomfortable and take him off guard at the same time.

After a moment of thought, he answers, "Emily is important to me."

Hand on her hip, she frowns. "That's not what I asked."

"That's my answer," he says, closing the door, but Ashley stops him again, pushing it open further.

"You're hot, like, way hot, which I'm sure isn't lost on you. I mean just standing here talking with you is kind of hard because most of what I wanna do is like, totally inappropriate."

"What's your point?"

"You're alone. Morgan says you don't have a girlfriend and haven't since she's known you. I know you like girls because I've seen it. I show up like this," she gestures to herself, "and throw myself at you and nothing. You didn't even look at my cleavage. Even gay guys acknowledge my cleavage. So, I'm trying to figure out why someone like you is alone. Is it because of Emily?"

"Goodnight, Ashley." Patrick attempts to close the door, but her palm slaps against it.

"Morgan is worried about you. She's going through a rough time. I thought coming here and throwing myself at you might give you a way to blow off some steam. I get that's not what you need right now and you blowing off my party and asking me to leave is fine, but don't ignore Morgan. Her best friend just ran off and she's worried to death over her. You can be a dick to me all you want, but be gentle with her. She's fragile right now."

"Ashley," he says in his sensual voice. She stares up at him and her dark eyes go nearly black with lust. "You are a tenacious, beautiful young woman, but I'm no more interested in your opinion than I am in your body. I'm going to close the door now."

Her mouth opens into a little O just before Patrick closes the door between them. As Patrick takes a deep breath to pull himself together, he hears Ashley laughing outside.

"You're a freak, Patrick!" Ashley shouts, before clicking away on her heels.

Memories bombard his body like a ship taking on water.

"Freak!"

He was twelve-years-old again, walking down the sidewalk away from the group of pubescent boys.

"That's right. Go run to Mommy!" a boy shouted.

"Leave him alone, John!" a girl yelled.

"Shut up, Lexi!"

"No," Lexi shouted back. "What did he do to you?"

Patrick knew. Lexi had a crush on him and because she was talking to him, John wasn't happy. Neither was Patrick. Not that Lexi was unpleasant, but Patrick knew she was too nice to him. He mostly ignored her, but it only encouraged her to try harder.

"Come on freak!" John yelled, "You gonna face me or what?"

He was thinking about the "or what" when . . . Thwack. The first rock hit him in the back of the head.

He couldn't wait to get his gifts. Then he could diffuse situations before they began. He would be left alone. Lexi wouldn't have even known he'd existed and then there would be no conflict. He could pass through school like a shadow. He was counting down the days.

"Patrick," Morgan's voice brings him back to the present.

Damn it. He's leaning with his palms against the door, his head hanging, looking like he'd been kicked in the gut. He straightens, trying to pull himself together, but he struggles to put the past behind him and move on. The seal he placed on his past is loosening. Sometimes—like now—the memories would sneak up on him out of nowhere.

"Patrick, don't pretend you're fine." Morgan's forehead crinkles with concern. "Please just act like you're feeling for once."

He peers at her, losing the lie on his lips. Flashes from his life are coming and going in the painful rhythm of his heartbeat. One second he's here with Morgan, the next he's plagued by years of torture. *A teenage girl appeared on her knees before Patrick, her angry face fading in and out of view while Patrick struggles to block the words she was shouting at him.* Morgan is speaking to him, *but he was watching the girl. Sky stood next to him, encouraging him to finish what he started. This wasn't like his mother. Patrick had his wits about him as Katie knelt before him. Her angry words echoed through the room. "He'll kill you for this!" Patrick hoped like hell those words were true, as he stepped forward. The girl whimpered, fear showing through her bravado.*

"Patrick!"

Squeezing his eyes shut, Patrick focuses on the present while his breath comes in sporadic gasps.

Morgan's voice is frantic as she shouts, "Patrick, let me go!"

Opening his eyes, he realizes Morgan is across the room, unable to move because he paralyzed her with his thoughts. He releases her as the room begins to spin and he reaches to the wall for support but misses and falls to his knees.

Morgan rushes forward sliding down to her knees. Patrick attempts to hold her off by throwing out a hand, but he's lost control. He tries like hell to stay in the present, but Katie keeps flashing in and out of view. *The look of hate and fear in her eyes broke him, but he didn't let it show. He had a job to do. Duty always came first.* Pure agony pours out of him in the shape of a roar, but the terrible noise, however awful it sounds does nothing to relieve the pain he still feels in his cold, black heart.

Morgan's arms wrap around him. Her touch feels like a lifeline. Her thoughts pour into him, becoming his own and he gets lost in her worry, her concern for him. Him, a selfish, murderous bastard, who has lived a life looking out for only himself. Yet, through Morgan's connection, he sees himself the way she sees him, and she thinks he's worth caring for. She loves him regardless of his faults and sees him as redeemed, even when he holds no hope of redemption.

Patrick lifts his arms to wrap around Morgan, holding her to him, finding solace in her reassuring touch. "Morgan, you don't know what I've done," he confesses, fighting his emotions.

She holds him tight, saying, "I don't care. You aren't that person anymore."

Burying his face into her shoulder to hide his distress, he chokes, "That doesn't erase who I was."

"You're right, but no one said redemption was easy."

For the first time in years, he breaks down sobbing, as Morgan holds him in her arms. She loves him despite him feeling completely unworthy, despite his past sins. He doesn't know how long they stay kneeling on the floor in a tight embrace, but it's long enough for Morgan's and his knees to ache, though she would never complain.

Eventually, Patrick pulls away, watching her wipe the tears from her face. If he didn't know it before, he knows it now—Morgan has a beautiful soul.

"Morgan, none of us deserve you. You're too good for this world and crying doesn't make you weak," Patrick whispers to her. "It shows how deeply you feel. You suffer for us, while we pretend to be strong. Your beautiful heart bleeds into each of us through your endless compassion. We don't deserve your love or your loyalty."

Morgan takes a shuddering breath and begins crying in earnest. "I told you, you're not heartless."

CHAPTER SIX

EVERYONE LEFT the office hours ago, except for Patrick and Chris who sit in anticipatory silence. Chris's team found another lead, a rumor really, but it gives them both hope.

"I'll pack up the van and drive out there," Patrick says, standing.

"Vince is already looking into it," Chris says. "Wait until he gives us more intel. He should be in contact within the hour. By the way, thank you for helping on the Maple Avenue case. I don't know how you fixed it so quickly."

"I told you, I've got skills," Patrick says, wanting to get back to the topic that actually matters. "It's already nine o'clock and Vince reported the first tip four hours ago. We should call him and check to see what he's found."

Chris shakes his head and the phone rings. He raises an eyebrow, "Well, here we go. It's Vince."

Patrick grabs the phone and answers, demanding, "What'd you find?"

The feminine voice sends chills through his body. "Patrick, you must stop." Emily's voice comes through the speaker, yet it sounds entirely different. "I am starting to think perhaps you are a man obsessed. Save yourself the trouble and don't bother coming after me. I will be long gone by the time you arrive. And just like Texas, I won't leave a trace for you to follow. If you keep sending people after me, I might even be forced to use more aggressive techniques." The line goes dead.

Patrick curses as he throws the phone across the room.

Chris's eyes widen and he asks, "What the hell was that?"

"That was her!"

The phone rings from the floor, the screen cracked. "You're buying me a new phone," Chris says, picking up his broken phone. He answers and listens for a moment while Patrick paces, dragging his hands through his hair.

Chris says, "Hold on Vince, I'm gonna put you on speaker. I need you to repeat that."

Switching to speakerphone, Vince's voice comes through the phone. "It's a bust. There is nothing here. If she was here, she isn't now."

With his hands on his hips, Patrick closes his eyes and shakes his head while Chris wraps up the call.

Once Chris is off the phone, Patrick says, "Pull your men back."

"What?"

"This isn't working. She's just manipulating them. Who knows how many times they've come in contact with her." Before Chris has a chance to ask what he's talking about, Patrick says, "It's one of those things I can't divulge."

"You're serious?" Chris asks.

"Yes. Pull your men out. I'll handle it on my own," Patrick says before walking out.

MORGAN WIPES the sweat out of her eyes and hits the next ball. She came to the batting cages straight from the gym. She was hoping to vent some of her frustration after finding out Ben got a letter from his parent's attorney threatening a restraining order if he tried to contact his sister again.

She doesn't understand how a family could be so cold. On top of that, Morgan's grades are slipping, evidence she's been too distracted to focus. She's even considering dropping classes.

There has been no progress in finding Emily, and Patrick told Burk Security to stop their efforts. Patrick is going to try to do it all on his own. It pisses Morgan off that he won't let her get involved. It's just as Ben said; Morgan feels she needs to do something.

Morgan swings the bat and sends another ball flying into the net. She finishes out her round and steps out of the cage.

On her drive to the apartment, she is salivating over a shower, comfy clothes, and comfort food. When she walks in the door, Patrick doesn't even look up from his laptop long enough to say *hi*. Usually, she would say *hi* anyway, but not today. She walks through the living room and back to the bathroom where she takes a long soothing shower. When she emerges in her pajamas, she heads to the kitchen for some ice cream.

"Emily left a trail," Patrick says from his spot on the couch.

She stops in her tracks to stare at Patrick.

He's still not looking at her as he continues, "She's been wiping memories as she goes, but I started looking for the bizarre, and after sifting through the complete rubbish, I found some interesting information." He looks up and she moves toward him. "Look here." He turns his laptop to face her.

A cherry red Ferrari takes up the center of an article on the computer screen. Morgan moves in closer and reads the title aloud, "Teen gifted Ferrari for serving her community." She leans forward to read the rest of the article, but Patrick pulls the laptop back around in his lap, so she takes the seat next to him on the sofa.

He begins clicking away on the keyboard while explaining, "This particular teen was doing community service at the psychiatric hospital where Emily visited her mother. But that's not all." He tilts the screen toward Morgan with a photo of the facility. "That same day, three patients were released. I visited earlier today and with some persuasion, I found the doctors were confused, patient charts were missing, and the cameras from that day went down from a storm. But here's the thing." He clicks over to the next window showing a sunny forecast. "Not a cloud in the sky that day." He points at the screen as he exclaims, "This has to be Emily!"

"But why?"

"I'm unsure why, but I tracked the Ferrari back to Mr. Everett Cetrone."

"Ben's dad?"

"The one and only. According to paperwork, it was a charitable donation to a local organization, except the organization doesn't exist."

"When did this happen?"

"August 6th, the day she disappeared, and on the 7th the Ferrari was given to the teen where Emily released three patients and left with the facility's van. A van that nobody seems to remember. Three days later the same van is seen in Oklahoma where it was towed for blocking a private drive."

"What's in Oklahoma?"

"Nothing anymore. I tracked her to Michigan next and although she's made trips here and there, I think she might have a place she keeps going back to in Michigan."

"Patrick that's amazing! You found her!"

"I think I may have to go and see. It could be a dead end. She could've gone anywhere."

Morgan sags into the sofa and says, "It's still progress."

"It's more than we've had. Nonetheless, it could be a dead end, just something to throw us off her trail."

Patrick rests his head back on the sofa and sighs as his eyes fall shut.

"How long has it been since you've slept, Patrick?"

Bloodshot eyes burst open. "I haven't had time to sleep. This is more important," he says, pointing to the computer.

"Let me help you look into this," Morgan says.

"Sure, grab your computer."

She sits there for a moment, shocked that he's taking her up on her offer to help. She springs from the sofa to retrieve her computer from her room.

When she comes back into the room, she asks, "You really talked to her, to Emily?

"Yes."

"What did she sound like?"

He hesitates. "She sounded like a different person."

"And you really told Chris to call off his men?"

"Emily has been manipulating them this whole time. Who knows how quickly we could have found her if she wasn't twisting everyone's thoughts around?"

"I still can't believe she spoke to you. We will get her back, Patrick."

CHAPTER SEVEN

THE FOLLOWING week ~

SIX A.M. COMES TOO QUICKLY for Morgan. She knew she shouldn't have stayed up so late doing research the night before.

Yesterday, Morgan and Patrick tracked Emily to a condo in one of the tallest buildings in Grand Rapids, Michigan. When Patrick refused to let her go with him, Morgan went to the gym to vent her frustrations, and what she came up with, was a plan to get around Patrick.

She leaves her hair down, letting the straight brown locks fall to the small of her back. Summer is over and soon her freckles will disappear along with her tan, but for today she rubs a smooth layer of foundation over her nose and cheeks to hide the freckles that plague her through the sunny months.

While Patrick is still sleeping, she goes outside to wait. Ben pulls up in his Corvette. She throws her overnight bag in the trunk before opening the passenger door. "Good morning," she says, falling into the seat next to him.

"Hey," he greets as she shuts the door. The car moves

forward, and he glances at the cup in her hand. "What are you drinking, and why is it green?"

"I always have green smoothies for breakfast," she replies, clicking her seatbelt in place. "It's healthy." She takes a sip through the straw.

He pulls out of the driveway and glances at her. "It's gross, isn't it?"

She holds it up for him. "Here, try it."

He pushes it away. "I'm not drinking that!"

"Coward," Morgan coughs.

"Fine." He grabs the cup and takes a sip. Thrusting it back at her, he makes swallowing look painful.

Morgan laughs. "Delicious?"

"That's disgusting! Why would you drink that?"

"I told you. It's healthy."

He opens his glove compartment and grabs a pack of gum. "There are better ways to be healthy." He pops a piece of gum in his mouth and leans to the side pulling his wallet from his back pocket. He hands it to Morgan.

"What's this for?" she questions, tucking her drink between her legs.

"The fifty bucks you tried to give me the other day. Slick putting it in my car, but I don't need it. I'm not a charity case, Morgan."

She thought she had gotten away with sneaking him money, but she does as he says, and takes the money back. Her eyes go to his driver's license and she laughs. "No way, Ben! You look like a pedophile in this picture!"

"You've never seen that before?"

"No, I would've remembered. When did you have a mustache?"

"It was a dare." He rolls his eyes. "Alec has a way of talking me into stupid things."

"Does he ever!" she laughs. "It's just his way with people, isn't it!"

"What's going on between you two, anyway?"

She gives an incredulous laugh. "Nothing!"

"Bullshit! You've had an open invitation and you haven't been over in the last month."

"I'm busy."

"That never stopped you before. And it's not like you're avoiding me, so what happened between you and Alec?"

"Benjamin Isaac Cetrone, are you being nosy?"

"I wanna know if I need to kick his ass."

She smirks. "I could kick Alec's ass all on my own, thank you."

"Morgan, I'm serious."

She sobers. "Nothing happened, okay. Alec is Alec and will always be Alec. He just gets under my skin sometimes."

"Did he try to sleep with you?"

"No, Ben. He didn't try to sleep with me any more than he's always tried to sleep with me. It's just flirting. In his own way, he knows I'm off limits. Let's just drop it, okay?" She fiddles with his wallet, feeling flustered. Morgan finally asks the question she's been dying to know. "Why did your parents kick you out?"

"Lots of reasons. Emily was the nail in my coffin though."

"But she was gone before they kicked you out."

His jaw is hard and his eyes straight ahead. "My parents and I aren't much for talking. It doesn't matter. They don't matter. I just need to get Emily back and make sure my sister is okay."

"I'm sorry, Ben. I wish there was a way I could help more."

"You are helping. You're helping me get Emily back."

"Patrick's gonna be pissed we went without him."

"That's his own fault for not letting us help sooner."

"How long of a drive is it?"

"Five hours."

THE ANSWERS ARE HERE. Patrick can feel them lurking beneath

him. He swims deeper until the ocean absorbs his body and constricts the air from his lungs. The pressure this deep underwater is painful and the dim light from above is all but extinguished, eaten up by the depths. The temperatures plummet the further he goes, but he has to keep going. As if conditions aren't severe enough—his temptress—the ocean, throws him into a whirlwind of underwater currents. His body is tossed around like a child's toy. He fights to stay in control, but quickly loses his battle when he invites the salty water into his lungs.

He wakes with a gasp; thankful Morgan isn't around this time.

THEY ARRIVE in Grand Rapids at noon. Despite the overcast, dreary weather, downtown is alive with activity. Long-standing Gothic buildings line the narrow streets. Many of the historic structures have been remodeled, blending the old with the new by adding clean lines and contemporary architecture to the original Gothic design. People stroll down the sidewalks, taking the time to say *hi* to one another as they go about their daily routine. Morgan feels the artistic vibe of the city and almost expects to find an easel painting standing on the old brick sidewalk. A yawn breaks her concentration, and she looks back to the road ahead, eyeing the soaring tower as it comes into view.

Ben and Morgan pull up to the tallest building downtown, and Morgan wonders if they should continue. The two exchange a glance before Ben gets out of the car. Morgan shoves her reservations down and follows. She pulls a picture of Emily up on her phone as they head into the lobby.

A woman in uniform stands by the reception desk, and as they head towards her, she asks, "Can I help you?"

Morgan's heartbeat kicks up a notch as she steps forward, holding out her phone. "Have you seen this woman?"

The clerk's eyebrows pinch before she smiles. "Of course."

"Is she in apartment 1200?" Ben asks, coming up behind Morgan.

"No," the woman says. "She stays in the penthouse when she visits."

"Do you know if she's there now?" Morgan asks.

The woman steps back, resting against the counter. "She went to a business meeting and then I believe she's headed out of town."

"Do you know where the meeting is?" Ben asks, "She's a good friend of ours and we wanted to say *hi* while we're in town."

The woman looks back and forth between them. Patrick could pull this information from her much faster. Morgan notices the woman's hands are shaking and when she speaks again, there is an edge to her voice.

"You guys don't seem like the type of people she surrounds herself with." She looks between them again with pursed lips. "Look, I don't know what you guys are trying to do, but—"

"We're trying to stop her," Morgan interrupts.

Ben gives her a sharp look, but Morgan ignores him. "The truth is we used to be friends with her before . . . well, before. But now we just want to stop her from doing the things she's doing."

The woman completely lets down her façade, wilting into the counter until it's practically holding her up. Her voice shakes and tears come to her eyes. "Mr. Powell lived in the penthouse for years. He built this building, and there is no way he would just give it to her. Not ever. Everyone acts differently around her like they're brainwashed or something. I watch the cameras, so I know when she's coming and going, but I've never interacted with her."

Morgan reaches out, taking the woman's hand. "Do you know where she is?"

She reaches behind her to grab a business card from the

counter. "Here." She hands it to Morgan. "That's where you can find her, but are you sure you want to?"

"We'll be okay," Ben says.

"I hope so. I hope you know what you're doing."

"Thank you for your help," Morgan says before she and Ben leave.

There is a heavy silence on their walk to the car. Ben types the address into his phone while Morgan contemplates what they will do when they get there.

When Ben starts driving, Morgan asks, "Should we call Patrick?"

Ben glances at her. "Not until we know we have her."

"But what if we need his help?"

"The second we call him; he'll tell us to go home."

Morgan doesn't argue. She knows he's right, but as they pull up to the office building, she takes out her phone to send Patrick a quick text. Then she thinks better of it, deleting the message and putting her phone back in her pocket.

The building's lobby overflows with elegance from the shining stone floor to the elevated ceiling dripping with gleaming lights. The office they are looking for is on the ninth floor, so they head for the bank of elevators. Morgan's hand goes to her pocket, debating again whether to contact Patrick, but ultimately, she leaves her phone where it is and boards the elevator.

Soft music fills the compartment on their ride up, and Morgan bites her lip as she watches the numbers ascend. Tension builds the higher they climb.

Beside her, Ben appears stoic, but his body is stiff, his muscles contracting.

"What if she doesn't recognize us?" Morgan asks, wiping her sweaty hands on her jeans.

"She will."

"How can you be so sure?"

"I'm not sure. I'm desperate. I saw how scared that woman

was back there. I've gotta believe Emily's still in there some-where and that she's not all monster."

"I really hope you're right," Morgan says as the elevator doors open.

CHAPTER EIGHT ~

THE CONFERENCE ROOM has floor to ceiling windows that over-look the city. The other three walls are made of clear soundproof glass allowing Ben and Morgan to watch the meeting in progress. Eight people gather around the oblong table in the center of the room. Seven of those individuals are wearing suits in varying shades of gray to match their salt-and-pepper hair.

The eighth, a young blond woman, is wearing a formfitting white dress. Perfect loose curls lay against the smooth skin of her exposed back, the only area that her white dress doesn't cover. The high neckline and long sleeves almost cover enough skin to make up for the drastic mid-thigh hem. Red polished fingernails tap against the conference table as she uncrosses her pale silky legs. She pushes back to stand on her red spiked heels. She leans forward to plant a palm against the table, having terse words with the man opposite her.

He looks angry, but as she speaks, his face loses its emotion, until his blank expression turns into a smile and he stands from his seat to walk around the table and shake hands with the bombshell at least half his age.

Morgan feels frozen in her spot watching her friend, only this isn't Emily. Her dad and Patrick warned her. Even Ben warned her, but Morgan had to see with her own eyes. The woman before her carries herself differently. Her hair is lighter. Her already slim body is thinner than before.

Morgan turns to Ben, but his eyes are stuck on the woman in the conference room. The woman who is and isn't Emily.

"Ben, what do we do?"

Ben takes a step forward. "We confront her."

As if she can sense his movement; Emily turns around, looking directly at them, her shining emerald eyes startling against her fair complexion. She raises an eyebrow and her painted crimson lips curl into a lazy grin. The softness her teenage face once possessed is entirely gone.

She turns back to the men, addressing them before walking to the door. As the glass door opens, Morgan and Ben take a step forward.

Emily lifts her arms out to the side, greeting, "It's so nice of you to visit, old friends!" The voice is the same, but the tone is different. The words are wrong. Everything is wrong. The hairs rise on the back of Morgan's neck, warning her, screaming at her that this was a mistake. She reaches for her phone.

"No, no," Emily says, waving a finger at Morgan.

Morgan feels her mind bending to Emily's will. She feels herself put her phone back in her pocket, but it isn't her decision. Emily is implanting her own thoughts and even though Morgan knows it's wrong, she can't fight it. It's confusing, almost disorienting to feel someone else's thoughts.

"Let's go get some fresh air," Emily says, before turning to lead the way.

Morgan can't tell if she's following because she wants to or because Emily is making her. She tips her head to look at Ben, and his eyes reflect her worry confirming Morgan's suspicions. The way Emily took control of them seemed alarmingly effortless.

Morgan gets so lost in finding out which thoughts are hers and which aren't that she doesn't comprehend climbing stairs until she reaches the top and a door opens, sending a cool breeze to blow through her hair.

She snaps to as she steps out onto the rooftop. The cool wind feels frigid up here. Morgan saw only twelve buttons on the elevator, so she's guessing they are roughly thirteen flights up. She folds her arms and fights a shiver.

Emily stops and turns to face them, saying, "You both must really be desperate. Desperate and stupid. Emily ran away so I wouldn't hurt you."

Morgan tries to wrap her mind around that sentence.

"You thought her seeing you would give her a change of heart? Ha. It's not her you should worry about." She moves to Ben, appraising him. "She doesn't control this body anymore."

Her hand strokes his chest. "I can see what she likes about you, Benjamin. She still wants you, but you'll never be enough. I should kill you right here. Get rid of the temptation."

Emily moves out of his way and he begins walking forward, toward the edge of the rooftop.

Morgan tries to move, to grab Ben's arm, but she forgets how to use her limbs, so she shouts, "Stop. Ben, Stop!"

"He can't help it," Emily says, her cold green eyes flipping to Morgan, "Just like you can't."

Morgan's eyes go wide before her limbs remember their function and her feet carry her forward. She watches helplessly as Ben climbs up on the ledge. That's when her tears begin. She's right behind him, climbing up only a few feet away and through her tears she sees Ben gritting his teeth against Emily's compulsion, but it's no use.

The door to the stairwell bangs open, but Morgan can't see anything except for the hundred-foot drop in front of her.

PATRICK STEPS out onto the rooftop in his three-piece suit and smooths his hair, horrified by the scene in front of him. Morgan stands on the very edge of the building with her back to him. A few feet away, Ben is in the same position. Emily stands safely in the center of the rooftop between Patrick and the edge of the building.

Patrick's body responds to Emily, hope blossoming at the sight of her. She is as beautiful as ever in her short white dress.

"Patrick," Emily purrs, sashaying towards him. "How nice of you to join us."

Suddenly Morgan and Ben turn around to face Patrick.

"Let them go," he demands, stepping forward.

In return, Morgan and Ben both take a step back, closer to the ledge.

"Now, love, I don't appreciate people telling me what to do."

"Emily," he says in the calmest voice he can muster. "Will you please let them go?" He takes a slow step forward with his palms reaching out in surrender. But as he takes a step, so do Ben and Morgan who are teetering at the edge of the rooftop.

Patrick stops.

Emily purses her lips, her eyes narrowing. "That's disappointing. Patrick, you've changed."

"So have you," he says.

"When you were with Sky, you wouldn't have hesitated to let them die as long as you reached your goal. And now you're going to let me escape because of them." She waves a hand toward Ben and Morgan.

Patrick looks to Morgan whose balance wobbles and her tears fall harder.

Emily grins. "Hmm, what about just one of them then?"

Ben lifts his leg, teetering on one foot.

Patrick reaches out with his mind until he clutches Ben, forcing him back onto both feet. Morgan squeals and Patrick mentally grabs her, too.

While Patrick focuses on keeping them alive, Emily strolls up and places a kiss on his cheek. "Until next time, Patrick."

Morgan and Ben are still standing on the ledge. Emily hasn't broken her connection, and it takes all of Patrick's concentration just to keep them from moving. The stairwell door bangs shut behind Emily, and beads of sweat trickle down Patrick's forehead.

His body shakes with the effort and after several moments, Emily severs her connection. Patrick collapses, falling to his knees. He bends forward, his palms against the cement. His shoulders rise and fall with each breath. His head is screaming from the pressure and he wipes the drops of blood from his ear. He lifts his head, glaring at Ben and Morgan as they get down from the ledge, and cling to one another with trembling arms.

Patrick tries to speak, but he can't catch his breath. He lowers his face as he attempts to regain his voice.

Ben and Morgan move closer. While Ben hangs back, Morgan bends down to help Patrick, but he pushes her away, breathlessly scolding, "Don't touch me!"

Morgan backs away, standing by Ben.

Between his panting for air, Patrick says, "What . . . the fuck . . . are you guys . . . doing here?"

Morgan says, "We were trying to help."

"Help?" Patrick wheezes and quickly spirals into a coughing fit. Morgan rushes to him, but he holds out his arm to fend her off.

Once his coughing ceases, Morgan voices her concern, "Patrick, there is blood coming from your ears."

He wipes it away with a shrug, grits his teeth, and pushes himself to a standing position. "Do you feel like you just helped out?" he rasps. "Or do you feel like you got in my way and almost died?"

"We didn't think she would hurt us," Morgan reasons. "She didn't hurt Ben before."

Patrick's eyes flick to Morgan, his lips curling in disdain, "She isn't Emily anymore!"

Morgan lets out a breath, and cries, "I know that now." She

moves into his space and wraps her arms around him in a hug, whispering, "Thank you, Patrick."

Patrick steps out of her embrace. Looking down at her, he says, "Go home."

"Pat—"

"Go home, Morgan."

"I'm sorry," she whispers, and Ben grabs her arm, guiding her toward the stairs.

"Ben?" Patrick calls.

Ben pauses, looking over his shoulder.

Patrick continues, "If you ever put Morgan in danger like that again, I will throw you off a building myself."

"Noted," he grumbles and continues into the stairwell.

As soon as the door closes behind them, Patrick collapses.

CHAPTER NINE

One month later ~

"Wow, he's really good!" Ashley chimes from across the small table. The trendy coffee shop is getting crowded as the patrons who came in for a quick cup of joe decide to stay to listen to the live music. The old building has high ceilings, creaky wooden floors, and large windows that overlook the busy street. Fall is mid-swing, bringing chilly weather that does nothing to deter the foot traffic through this part of town, and the coffee shop's rich aroma and eclectic flare seems to draw people in. The cafe is organized chaos with mismatched chairs tucked under an assortment of wooden tables while the walls proudly display local artwork.

It's big for a coffee shop, but the ambiance makes Morgan feel right at home. As the smell of expresso wafts through the air, she takes a sip of her drink and stares at the guitarist up on the small platform in the corner.

"Yeah, who knew," Morgan says, turning to Gavin. "You're his best friend. Did you know he could play?"

"I had no idea," Gavin says, looking just as surprised as Morgan feels.

"You're kidding. None of you have ever heard him before?" Jeremy asks while running his fingers through Ashley's hair, the platinum strands looking stark against his dark skin.

They shake their heads, all eyes glued to Ben playing his guitar.

"When he invited us to his new job, I assumed he'd be making our lattes," Morgan says, setting down her drink.

"I almost didn't come home this weekend," Gavin adds, rechecking his phone. "Where the hell is Alec? I swear, the asshole is gonna be late to his own funeral."

Morgan laughs, "No, he'll be on time for that because he won't be responsible for getting himself there."

"Hey guys," Alec says, coming from behind Jeremy.

"'Bout time," Gavin says, while Ashley moves her purse from the seat they were saving for him. None of them were expecting him to bring a girl with him, but there she is, pretty, petite, dark hair, pouty lips. It all amounted to one thing—another notch in Alec's notorious bedpost.

Alec takes a seat, inviting her to sit on his lap. Morgan rolls her eyes, grabs her drink, and focuses on Ben who didn't sing, but he didn't need to. The guitar sang for him.

Alec motions to the girl in his lap, "This is Sadie."

They all give half-hearted hellos before all eyes fall back on Ben.

"Where's Ben . . . holy shit!" Alec exclaims when he finds him on stage. "When did that talented fucker learn to play the guitar?"

"He's pretty good," says Sadie.

Morgan holds tight to her drink, fighting the urge to throw it in the chick's face. Ben is better than pretty good.

After a moment, Alec turns to Morgan who is unfortunate enough to be sitting right next to him and Sadie. "How you been, Fletch? I haven't seen you for a while."

"Busy with work and school."

"Yeah, how's your job going? I heard you give sponge baths now. Please tell me you have some Victoria Secret type hotties you get to scrub down."

Morgan frowns, wondering how she let this happen. She knew better than to fall for this idiot, but it happened anyway. She fiddles with her cup feeling out of control. "You have no idea what I do. I get people ready for surgery. It's definitely not sexy."

"Come on, just let me pretend."

"You can pretend all you want, but it's important to me that you know I spend my day with old pendulous breasts and sagging scrotums," Morgan says. "There is nothing sexy about it."

"You're such a prude." He laughs. "You probably have a thing for sagging scrotums. You'll make some eighty-year-old very happy one day."

Giving him an exhausted look, Morgan sets her cup down and changes the subject. "How is it possible you didn't know Ben plays? He's been living with you for months. Didn't you see his guitar?"

"Nope."

Sadie, still perched on his lap, chimes in, "I've probably been occupying too much of your time, baby." She turns in his lap to kiss him, which quickly turns into more. Their tongues meet and their hands stray as they trade saliva.

Ashley mumbles something about low standards, while Jeremy pretends to cough in an attempt to cover up her words, but his cough turns into laughter halfway through, and Gavin nearly spits out his drink. By the time Sadie moans, Morgan has had enough.

"Seriously, Alec!" Morgan's chair screeches as she shoves away from the table to walk toward the bathroom. Ashley's chair scoots back too, and she catches up to Morgan in the ladies' room. Morgan leans against the sink with her head lowered.

"You okay?" Ashley asks.

"I'm fine," Morgan huffs. "I just can't stand him sometimes."

"You can drop the act with me. I know you're in love with him."

Her head shoots up. "I am not! He's immature and misogynistic."

"Misogynistic? That means weird sex stuff, right?"

"No, it means he hates women," Morgan explains.

"I don't think that's his problem!" Ashley argues. "He likes them a little too much."

"Does he, though?" Morgan questions. "I don't think he cares about them at all. God, I'm such an idiot."

"It's okay. Just take a breath."

"I just walked away like a child throwing a temper tantrum. I don't want to be like this, Ashley. It just makes me so mad because the Alec out there," She points toward the door, "that isn't the real Alec. And if it is, I hate who he's become. But I have to find a way to at least pretend he doesn't affect me." She sighs, "I should probably go apologize."

"Umm, no, you just need to stop," Ashley says, grabbing Morgan's wrist. "You have no reason to apologize. He's the slut putting on a show. Now here, wear this." She pulls lipstick from her purse and hands it to Morgan.

"Why?"

"Because you have beautiful full lips and it will draw his attention there. He'll be kicking himself for bringing that girl with him."

"Ashley, I don't—"

"Trust me!" Ashley insists.

When they leave the bathroom, Ben is putting his guitar away. Ashley goes back to the table while Morgan approaches Ben, asking, "Ben, how many more secrets do you have stashed up your sleeve?"

He stands from his crouch to give her a hug. "Thanks for coming out." He pulls back to look at her. "Are you wearing lipstick?"

"Yeah, Ashley made me. Sometimes it's just easier to do what she says than to fight her. But seriously dude, what's with the secrecy? None of us knew you could play."

"Music has always been private to me. I used to play for Molly, and I played for Emily a few times. I heard they were looking for some live music here and I figured, why not make a few extra bucks."

"So how did it feel to play in front of so many people?"

Ben smiles. "It felt good. Better than I thought it would. Guess it helps that you guys didn't boo me off stage."

Morgan shrugs. "I paid everyone off before you started."

Ben laughs as he picks up his guitar case. "Well keep paying them, cause they asked me to play again next Friday and if all goes well, it might become a regular gig."

"Ben, that's great!"

"Yeah, and it's not far from the apartment I found."

"You found a place! Why didn't you tell me?"

"It's not a big deal. The place is tiny, but at least it'll be mine."

She hits him in the arm. "It is a big deal! When are you moving?"

"This weekend. It'll only take one trip to get my stuff out of Alec's, and I had to order furniture so that's being delivered."

"Ben that's huge!"

He shrugs. "How are things going with Patrick?"

"He's not so bad. Still a little bitter about us being the reason Emily got away, but he's mostly forgiven me." She winces. "You, on the other hand, should probably steer clear of the apartment."

"I'm not looking to make friends with Patrick. I don't care if he hates me. I'm just as pissed we lost her."

Morgan sighs and they head back to their friend's table. On the way, several people stop Ben to tell him how great he sounded. One person asks the questions Morgan is wondering so she finds out that Ben learned to play the guitar with the help of YouTube, and he's been playing since fourth grade.

Before they reach their friend's table, Morgan says, "So how's everything else going? How's the maintenance job?"

He shrugs, "It's all right. I don't like working nights, but it frees up my schedule so I can teach lessons throughout the day. It all works."

"I hope you're getting enough sleep."

He turns to face her when they reach the table. Giving her a look, he says, "Morgan, you don't need to mother me. I'm fine."

"Okay," she says, showing her palms in surrender.

Looking at the table, Morgan is relieved to find Sadie in her own seat. The group pulled over two extra chairs for Morgan and Ben. Unfortunately, they kept Morgan's seat right next to Alec's. While everyone bombards Ben with questions and praise, Morgan sits down and pretends like Alec isn't there.

Alec leans into her, bumping her with his shoulder, as he softly says, "Sorry I made you so uncomfortable. I'm not trying to push you away. I miss you, Fletch. Life is more fun when you're here to put me in my place."

Morgan looks up and his eyes go straight to her lips. "Alec, you don't need me to put you in your place."

"Yes, I do," he says. "I'll always need you."

"Doesn't Sadie keep you in line?"

He looks away from her lips and shakes his head. "None of them do."

"Then you should learn to do it on your own."

His hazel eyes meet hers. "You're still mad at me?"

"I've known you for a long time, Alec. You're better than whatever this is you're pretending to be."

"Is that why you've been avoiding me? Because you're disappointed."

"No. I told you. I'm busy."

"You make time for Ben."

"Ben needs me."

"You don't think I need you."

"You have Sadie."

He rolls his eyes. "Exactly. I have Sadie. Shouldn't that tell you how much I need you? And Ben doesn't need you. Emily left him. He's just gotta move on."

"And that's why he needs me, 'cause his other friends give him crappy advice."

"Don't blame me, I come from a broken home," Alec postulates. "What kind of advice should I be giving him? Sulk and wait around for Emily. I know you're her friend, but doesn't it piss you off that she just up and left? Especially with her dad still in a coma and Ben's parents disowning him. I thought she gave a shit, but maybe we didn't really know her."

"I don't think we know the whole story. But telling Ben to go out and find someone else isn't going to take away what he's feeling."

"It might take it away for a little while. And it definitely will help him feel less alone."

"Is that what you're doing?" she says pointedly. "With Reece, with Sadie, with . . . what was her name, Beth? Do they help you feel less alone?"

"Are you jealous, Fletch?"

"I just hope you're getting tested regularly."

Alec bursts into laughter, breaking their private conversation. Everyone at the table looks at them. Morgan notices Sadie's glare, but Alec is oblivious. He wraps an arm around Morgan and pulls her into his side kissing her temple.

"Fletcher, I've missed you. Stop avoiding me and I'll promise not to be such an ass."

"You mean there's an on/off switch?" Gavin asks. "What the hell man? I never got that offer."

"It's reserved for special occasions."

"And what's the special occasion?" Ashley asks.

Alec responds, "I've missed the shit out of you guys, and

Benny Boy is gonna be a superstar, taking his friends along for the ride. Right, Benny Boy?"

"I'll punch you in the face if you call me Benny Boy again."

"Come on, bro. You're talented as fuu—"

Morgan clears her throat, noting the family at the next table.

Alec stutters, "Talented as sunshine and rainbows."

"Words of encouragement spoken by a true gentleman," Ashley comments.

"You guys love me!"

"Yeah, we do," Sadie says, placing a hand on Alec's thigh. Morgan rolls her eyes and looks away as her hand makes its way up, up, up. That movement tears Alec's attention away from Morgan, and after Sadie leans into Alec's ear to whisper something, it's suddenly time for them to go.

"We'll see you guys later," Alec says, as they make a beeline for the door.

Ben says, "So much for him missing us."

Ashley suggests, "Maybe we should neuter him."

"Did you hear that?" Gavin says, with his hand to his ear. "Her panties just dropped."

"You're assuming she had any on," Jeremy adds.

Ashley elbows him and he gives her an innocent look, saying, "What?"

"On that note," Morgan says, sliding out of her seat. "I'm going to take off. I have some studying to do. Ben, you were great! I'll be here every Friday for the foreseeable future so long as I'm not working."

Ben stands at the same time she does. "I'll walk you out. This isn't the best neighborhood."

"I'll be fine. I have my pepper spray."

"You know how likely you are to end up spraying yourself instead of your attacker and you know how close you have to be? I'll walk you out."

"Before you go all Sensei on me, look." She points to the

front window. "You can see my car from here. So why don't you just watch to make sure no one kidnaps me."

"Fine."

"Thanks, Ben, you're like the protective big brother I never had."

"And you're a lot like the pain in the ass sister who won't talk to me." Ben wraps her in a hug.

When Morgan pulls away, she turns to the table. "Gavin, I'm glad you came home this weekend. I'll see you guys later."

"Don't forget about my party next week," says Ashley. "You promised you'd come."

Morgan rolls her eyes, knowing she never made that promise. "I said I *might* be there."

Morgan makes her way to her car with the feeling she's being watched. She looks over her shoulder as she unlocks her door and sees Ben watching through the window. Maybe his talk got her feeling paranoid, but the little hairs on the back of her neck are standing on end.

She hurries into her car, locking the doors behind her. She waves to Ben before pulling out onto the street. Headlights come up behind her and she winces at the halogen lights reflecting in her mirrors. She speeds up, but those lights stay on her, causing her heart to race. She turns left, then right, then another left while those halogens continue to glare in her mirrors. She merges onto the freeway and the vehicle behind her flies past.

Realizing she was overreacting, Morgan lets out a long breath, but as soon as she relaxes, that niggling feeling returns. She takes inventory of the cars around her as she continues driving. After exiting the freeway, and making a few unnecessary turns, the same blue car remains on her trail.

She runs a yellow light, but the blue car flies through it too. As her breaths come quickly, she calls Patrick in panic.

His lungs are burning. He's out of breath.

Freezing waters are pulling Patrick underwater. Darkness wraps its arms around him, welcoming him home as he sinks further into the abyss. The ocean was once his temptress, luring him into her depths with whispers of promises. Now she is a bully, teasing and taunting Patrick with answers she won't allow him to reach.

His eyes close against the turbulent currents tossing his body. He's pulled deeper into the darkness. Something unseen slithers along his skin, proving there is more to fear in the dark than just the icy water. A creature brushes against him and Patrick gasps.

He wakes coughing. He leans over the trashcan next to him, unsure if he's going to vomit this time. The dream keeps visiting him, becoming more frequent with each night that passes. Almost every night for the last three weeks he's had the same dream. It makes for restless nights, which is why he dozed off on his couch this evening. The dreams change a little each time, but they always end when Patrick's lungs fill with water. He usually wakes gasping and spitting up water that was never really there in the first place.

He dry-heaves into the trash until he's certain nothing more is coming, then he pulls himself up, wiping his mouth on the back of his sleeve. He stands to get a glass of water when his phone starts ringing. He answers on the second ring.

"Morgan—"

"I'm being followed!" she shouts through the speaker.

Alarms go off in his mind, but he keeps his voice steady. "Where are you?"

"At the apartment. I'm just turning into the parking lot."

"I'll be right there," he says, pocketing his phone and running out of his apartment door.

Mentally he reaches for her and finds her close enough for him to pick up on her thoughts, which is a relief because he can protect her. He spots Morgan weaving her way through the maze of parked cars. The car following is pursuing her closely.

Patrick reaches for the mind driving the other car and is met by a wall, confirming his suspicion that they're dealing with an Olvasho. Patrick tamps down the barriers to his own thoughts and forces all of the tension out of his posture.

Morgan drives straight up to Patrick and pulls her car into the yellow "no parking" zone right outside the building. Patrick keeps his pace casual, appearing as if he doesn't have a care in the world. He leans his body against Morgan's car door just as she reaches for the handle, forcing her to stay put.

The blue car passes at a crawl and Patrick makes eye contact with its driver. Patrick would recognize the scarred face anywhere, but as if to make a point, the driver smiles and looks to Morgan. The threat is unmistakable, reminding Patrick that even though he is free of Sky, he is not invincible.

Once the car is gone, Patrick opens the door for a shaken Morgan.

"Patrick, did you see who it was? Why were they following me?"

"Go on up and get inside. I'll park your car and be right in."

"Patrick . . ." she hesitates.

"Go!"

She hurries into the apartment while Patrick parks her car. When he enters, she's on the edge of the couch anxiously awaiting him. "Who was that?" she asks, standing up.

"His name is Lathe. You have no reason to worry. Lathe barks, but he doesn't bite. He's an Olvasho sent to check on me since I've declined to check in after Sky's death. He must have seen us together at some point. By following you, he was demonstrating how easy it would be to exploit my weakness. It was a fear tactic to get my attention; however, in making his point, he's also made me angry. I am not a good enemy to have, Morgan."

"I have every reason to worry, and what do you mean you haven't checked in? Who were you supposed to check in with?"

"The Olvasho council."

"You guys have a council?"

"The leadership is broken. What was once built to protect and hide the Olvasho has become a place for the corrupt to gain power and leadership over the weak."

"How many Olvasho are there?"

"Hundreds, maybe thousands. It's hard to tell. There are fewer than there used to be, and many have gone into hiding. Some neglect their abilities, which causes a problem down the road when their grandchildren suddenly have these gifts with no guidance or understanding."

"I had no idea there were so many."

"Morgan, they won't touch you. They're afraid of me. So, when I tell you I'll keep you safe, I mean it."

WHEN LATHE'S mother told him he had a half-sister who killed their father—the father Lathe wanted dead all his life—he expected his half-sister to be a cold-blooded assassin. However, everything in Lathe's research proves contrary to his initial belief.

Emily grew up in a boring town in Ohio, went to public school, had friends and a family. She lived a life so far removed from the life Lathe was dealt. Because he didn't have the luxury of a childhood, a family, or anyone to support him unconditionally, it's hard not to envy her soft life. Lathe grew up knowing how much was expected of him, and if he wasn't strong enough to handle it on his own, people would die. How is it that his untrained half-sister breezed in and killed the man he was unable to kill? He suspects it's only because of her Valla blood that she survived. He should probably be thanking her instead of choking on bitter indignation, but there is too much he can't quite swallow.

For one, Lathe knows Patrick is involved, and wherever Patrick is, death is sure to follow. He figured Patrick had a hand in Sky's death, but there are so many mysteries from that night.

He thought about approaching Patrick, but he can't do that alone, and he isn't ready to let people know he found the identity of the Valla blood involved.

He's been hoping Emily is the only remaining member left of the Valla bloodline, but it's a guessing game at this point. He thought the bloodline was gone entirely until the night Sky died. He wasn't close enough to feel it personally, but there were too many witnesses claiming to have felt the pull in their blood.

Before all of this, he thought the power of the Valla bloodline had been grossly exaggerated over the years—a ghost story of sorts—but after listening to statement after statement, he could no longer deny the possibility that the Valla bloodline not only remained, but far exceeded any Olvasho abilities he had encountered, aside from his mother. He should have notified the council as soon as he found her identity, but his mother's words always came back to him, "Your father's blood runs through her veins. She is your sister, but her demon blood reigns. She will fight it, but she cannot win. Valla will rise again!"

It made sense that she was Sky's daughter. Sky had a plan for all his children. Most likely, he was keeping her hidden; otherwise, there would have been a manhunt underway. Lathe speculates over the many mysteries, but he doesn't really know. He needs answers, which is why he's here. He kept his trip a secret, afraid the others would make a mess out of things. And deep down, he feels the need to protect Emily. She's family, after all.

Lathe drives back to the coffee shop, parking around the corner. He pulls his hood up over his head and exits the car. The moon hides behind heavy clouds, and Lathe finds the shadow of a full tree to hide beneath while he watches the coffee shop from across the street. Looking in through the window, he observes the remaining patrons. He did as much research as he could before approaching Emily's friends. He recognizes the muscular guy with dark hair and guitar to be Ben, Emily's boyfriend. Ashley is the girl with platinum hair. She used to work with Emily, and the other guy, Gavin, graduated with Emily. He's unsure who the dark-skinned man next to Ashley is. He'll have to do more research.

Ashley and the unknown man leave first, and a few minutes later, Ben and Gavin get up to leave. As they are walking out of the coffee shop, Ben receives a call.

He places the phone to his ear, saying, "Yeah?"

He scans the parking lot as he listens to the person on the other end of the line. "No," he says, casually observing the area. "Okay." His eyes go right over Lathe without pause. "I don't see them, Morgan. I'll look around and let you know if I do."

Ben eyes the pavement around him as he tucks his phone away.

"What'd she want?" Gavin asks.

"She lost a glove. I guess it fell out of her pocket. She was asking if it was here."

"Why'd she have gloves. It's not that cold."

"You know Morgan. She's always prepared for everything."

Lathe smirks, wondering at Ben's quick lie. He has no doubt Morgan called to warn Ben about the scarred man following her. Now Lathe knows that the two of them know things the others don't. Ben and Morgan are keeping secrets, but what is their connection to Patrick?

Ben and Gavin look around for a make-believe glove before giving a bro hug and going their separate ways.

Lathe follows the Corvette, careful to make sure Ben doesn't notice him.

"I DID my research on you. What happened to the big fancy house and Ivy League school?" Lathe asks from across the console of the car.

Ben is seated in the passenger seat. He was fairly compliant getting into the car, or at least he didn't show any outward signs of distress, but Lathe feels his resistance. Ben is trying to fight the mental hold Lathe has on him, but it's not enough to keep him from spilling his guts.

"My father kicked me out the day Emily left. He thought I was dependent on him and that I couldn't survive without his money. He thought he knew how to control me. Screw him and his money. I don't care about either."

"Who do you care most about?" Lathe questions, sure he knows the answer.

"Molly."

"Your sister," Lathe says, hiding his surprise. "What about your girlfriend?"

"I love them both."

Love? Lathe wasn't expecting that. Obsession, infatuation, he can understand, but love? He can tell just by talking to Ben that his feelings for her are real. Emily never coerced Ben and Lathe is relieved by that much. "Tell me how Emily killed Sky."

Ben shakes his head, but not in refusal, more like he's still questioning everything he's seen and heard. Even now as Lathe pulls memories out of him, Ben is skeptical, but eventually, he answers, "Sky was feeding off the souls of," he gives Lathe a dirty look, "other people like you. Emily set them free, and without the souls, Sky died."

"Are you sure she set them free?"

"How can I be sure of any of this? I believed her when she told me. It's why she almost died."

"Why didn't she die?"

"I don't know. Maybe her Valla blood protected her."

Lathe rolls that around in his mind before asking, "You love her, but aren't you afraid of her?"

"I'm not afraid of Emily, the real Emily, but I'm afraid of what she might do."

"Do you think she plans to return?"

"No, but if she does, I'd be worried if I were you," Ben says with rebellion in his voice, trying like hell to pull away from Lathe's mental hold.

"Emily had to know we'd come looking for answers. She left you unprotected. You've gotta be asking yourself why she would abandon you?"

Ben manages a glare toward Lathe, growling, "You don't know the first thing about her."

"Are you sure your loyalty isn't misplaced? Olvasho are manipulators. The better liar you are, the further up the food chain you crawl. Sky was at the top until Emily took him out. By all rights, that would leave Emily right at the very top of the hierarchy."

Ben is silently fuming, resisting the urge to say any more.

Lathe smiles despite himself. He actually kind of likes this guy. "Let's talk about Patrick."

This time Ben answers without restraint. "He's manipulative and arrogant, like you. I don't trust Patrick, but Emily does. She doesn't care that he led her directly to Sky. He's the reason she almost died, and now . . ." His eyes go wide, and he clamps his mouth shut.

"Now, what?"

Ben takes a deep breath, fighting it, but eventually, the words come out anyway, "It isn't her. Her eyes are cold. She's different."

"Valla," Lathe supplied.

"I don't know, but it never would've happened if Patrick hadn't shown up."

"Patrick is a predator. He'll attack when you aren't looking, and toy with you like a fucking cat until you're begging for death. My girlfriend was one of many who didn't survive Patrick. She got in the way on his climb into Sky's pocket."

Lathe fights the anger seething through his veins. He has to keep his head on straight. Too many people are counting on him, and no one knows where he is. If anything happens to him, his mother will die and who knows how many she'll take to the grave with her. He's the only one that can care for her. Sky might be gone, but they are all victims left to suffer from years of his cruelty.

Lathe turns to Ben and says, "Morgan went running to Patrick tonight. Why would she do that? What's the nature of their relationship?"

"They're roommates. They only met this summer, but they became close. Morgan is too compassionate for her own good."

Lathe thinks about that, remembering how Patrick had protected Morgan earlier. That is wildly out of character for Patrick, especially because Ben says they are only roommates, not lovers, but something doesn't quite add up. "Are they sleeping together?"

"No."

"Interesting. Why not?"

"He's in love with Emily."

"But you're her boyfriend?"

Ben shrugs.

"Why would Patrick protect Morgan?"

Ben rolls his eyes. "She seems to think he cares about her."

"Benjamin, you know far too much about us. I suspect Morgan knows just as much, if not more. If it weren't so dangerous, I would wipe out all of your memories of us, but I can't do that without putting you at risk for brain damage. I can't believe Patrick was so sloppy. Now, forget we had this talk. If anyone asks, you went for a walk to clear your head. Now, get out of the car."

Ben steps out of the car and their entire interaction is erased from his mind.

CHAPTER TEN ~

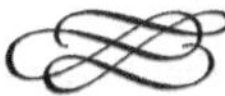

THE FOLLOWING week ~

MORGAN SHOWS up an hour early for work at the hospital. She takes the elevator up to the fourth floor. Stepping off, she passes the nurses station. She's never worked on this floor, but she visits Mark so often the nurses greet her by name. Just as Morgan is about to enter room 407, the nurse steps out and closes the door behind her.

"I'm glad you're here," she says quietly, ushering Morgan away from the room.

"Has there been a change?" Morgan asks, feeling hopeful.

The nurse lets out an empathetic sigh. "Unfortunately, there has been no change in his mental state, though his other wounds have healed, and the swelling is gone. The latest brain scans are just as confusing as the first. That's not why I pulled you out here. Samantha is in there. She's not in a good place."

"What happened?"

"Her bridal shower is next week. She extended an invitation to me but warned me she might postpone the wedding until he wakes up." She pauses. "Morgan, the chances are . . ." She stops herself from expelling more bad news.

Morgan nods her understanding. The evidence says it's much more likely for Mark to pass away than for him to wake up. Even the optimist in Morgan acknowledges his one in a million chances. Neither Morgan's dad nor Patrick have been able to reach Mark's psyche, though they keep trying.

"Thank you. I'm glad you're taking such good care of them."

"I'm doing what I can, but it breaks my heart. Samantha is a sweet girl. Have you heard anything about her sister?"

Morgan shakes her head, whispering, "No."

"Even if she returns, I don't know how Samantha will feel. It's sad to see these families fall apart. I see it all the time. It just makes me wonder if every family is one tragedy away from unraveling."

They stand in silence for a moment. Morgan holds back her tears, wishing she knew how to fix it. Eventually, she says, "I'm going to go visit with her for a while. Thank you for the heads up."

"Good luck, sweetheart," she says before walking away.

Morgan opens the door slowly, easing her way into Samantha's heartbreak. Samantha's long mahogany hair is swept to the side, dangling over one of her delicate shoulders in thick waves as she leans over her father in the hospital bed. Samantha looks up, her face reflecting her recent weight loss, evidence she's been absorbing stress instead of food these days. Her brown doe eyes spot Morgan, and she smiles, her dimpled cheeks looking hollow.

"Morgan, I'm so glad you came by. He's doing better today. Look at his face. He almost looks like he's smiling, and the cuts are healing so nicely. I've been putting coconut oil on the scars. I read an article that says coconut oil helps with scarring. I want him looking his best when he walks me down the aisle." Samantha flips her hair over her shoulder and walks to the end of the bed. She pushes his blanket to the side, exposing his thin legs. "The doctors don't sound very optimistic, but I know my daddy, and he's going to wake up. I might have to postpone the wedding a little, but he's going to walk me down the aisle." She bends his knee slowly before straightening it out and then repeats the process as she continues explaining, "They said he would probably need some physical therapy since he's been lying here for so long. I've been helping him keep active, so his muscles don't waste aw-ay." She hiccups the last word before bursting into sobs. She doubles over, laying her head on top of Mark's leg.

Morgan goes to her, resting a comforting hand on her shoulder. "Samantha, it's okay. Here, sit down." Morgan guides her to the chair next to his bed. "I'll do his exercises this time while you tell me what's going on with you."

Samantha collapses in the chair, falling into herself. She wipes the tears away, explaining, "I have a bridal shower next week and I don't even know if I'm getting married. I don't know what to do with this. My dad is in a coma and Emily . . . I'm so worried about Emily. How am I supposed to get married without my family? Dan's mom doesn't want to postpone. And we don't know if Dad is going to wake up. And my sister — I get so mad at her. How could she do this to me? Then I start to wonder if maybe she's dead and that's why she hasn't come back."

Morgan says, "Emily is not dead."

"I'm so angry with her, but I still miss her so much," Samantha whispers, wiping tears. "And everyone keeps going on like nothing's wrong, but I can't. How am I supposed to live my life like this? This is supposed to be the most exciting time in my life, but I've lost my family. I don't know if I'm ever going to get them back and it feels like it's killing me."

"They aren't gone, Samantha. Emily will come back, and your dad will wake up," Morgan reassures, making empty promises she knows she shouldn't make.

"You must know something I don't then because my dad's not improving. The nurses said he hasn't made any signs of progress in weeks and the cops don't care about Emily. The trail ran cold two-seconds after she disappeared and no one's even looking for her. I don't know what to do." Samantha wipes at the mascara under her eyes.

"We all want to find her. We're looking, well, Patrick is looking," Morgan divulges.

"Really? Because I've already hired a private investigator, but he didn't get very far," she says; then with new hope, she asks, "Has Patrick made any progress?"

"Umm, nothing concrete."

"I want to talk to him," Samantha insists.

"Yeah, okay." She pulls out her phone. "Just give me a minute," she says, before walking out into the hall.

Surprisingly, Patrick doesn't seem upset. Lately, everything was upsetting him, so Morgan is relieved to find him docile. She hangs up and walks back into the room.

"He agreed to drop by before the bridal shower next week."

"Perfect. Thank you, Morgan. Thank you."

CHAPTER ELEVEN ~

MORGAN HAS HOMEWORK TO DO, but she's already dodged too many of Ashley's parties, and she knows she won't be able to escape them all. Besides she's overdue for a fun night. Most of her friends are away at school, and she is still dodging Alec; which means her social group consists of Ashley, who wants to party all the time, Ben, who doesn't have time for her, and Patrick, who is scaring her more each day. She is spending most of her time alone in the safety of her cocoon, but she misses the old Morgan, the social butterfly, the outgoing athlete, the fearless, driven woman she no longer seems to know.

When her shift ends just after eleven, she changes out of her scrubs and into her costume for the party. Slipping into black leggings, a red football jersey with tube socks and sneakers, she waits until she is in her car to smear black lines under her eyes. The drive to Ashley's is quick, but finding a parking spot near her campus apartment is next to impossible. It's midnight by the time she secures a spot three blocks over. The late hour does nothing to slow activity. She finds herself walking among rowdy party-hopping college students.

The old Morgan would love this, but that Morgan didn't appear to be showing up tonight. She feels worse with every step she takes. The dark streets put her on edge, and when a guy jogs past her to catch up with his friends, she freezes with fear. Her memory from the terrible night in Florida—the night that nearly destroyed her faith in humanity—haunts her. She tucks her hand into the pocket of her coat, holding tight to the protection of her pepper spray.

Eventually, the number of street lights begin to increase. By the time Morgan reaches the duplex Ashley shares with her two roommates, Morgan is more at ease. She steps onto the porch, moving aside as a group of girls in devil horns and tiny red dresses come giggling out the front door. They stumble past her, laughing their way down the steps.

She grabs the door the girls left standing open, wondering again, how she let Ashley talk her into coming to this thing.

She enters, traveling through the living room and moves toward the back of the house. She takes a detour through the dining room to avoid the couple making out in the hall. In place of a dining table, Morgan finds a group surrounding a ping pong table. She continues into the kitchen at the back of the duplex where everyone is chanting, "Tink, Tink, Tink, Tink!"

In the middle of the commotion, Morgan finds Ashley in her short, shimmery green Tinker Bell costume chugging beer through the hose of a beer bong. Morgan sits down on an abandoned stool and watches as Ashley gracefully drains the last of the beverage without dribbling or gagging. Once finished, Ashley throws her arms in the air and everyone cheers. As the next person steps up to take her place, Ashley spots Morgan and squeals, rushing to her. "You came! I can't believe you actually came!"

"I told you I'd come."

"Yeah, but you never come. I'm so happy you're here. And you dressed up. Look how sexy you are!" Ashley chimes. "Let me get you a drink."

Morgan looks down at her costume, wondering which part of it is sexy. She hasn't even taken off her coat. Maybe Ashley is already drunk. "Ashley, I can't risk getting caught drinking under-age. I could lose my job."

Ashley tilts her head. "How old are you?"

"Twenty."

"My mom's a lawyer. I'll make sure she takes care of you if anything happens, but nothing is going to happen!"

"No, Ashley. I told you I'd come hang out, but drinking isn't my thing."

"Fine, fine," she concedes. "I'll get you a non-alcoholic beverage."

"Thanks," Morgan says, but Ashley is already walking away.

"Hey, babe." Morgan flinches at the masculine voice against her ear, flashing back to that night again. She reaches for the pepper spray at the same time she spins around to find Ben standing by her stool. She leaves the spray in her pocket as her insides settle and she reaches forward to hug him. "Oh, thank God you came."

"How did Ashley talk you into coming to this?" he asks.

"She made me feel lame."

"And you fell for it?"

Morgan confesses, "Not only fell for it. Look what I'm wearing." She slips off her coat and drapes it over her arm.

He steps back to appraise her. "I like it. Too bad you aren't the actual quarterback. If you were, then maybe we wouldn't suck this year."

"Ben, you have way too much faith in my athletic talent and Ashley is going to kill you for not wearing a costume."

"I can take her. I was already running late. I had to stop by Alec's to pick up a couple of things I left there. It was supposed to be quick, but I got sucked into talking to his girlfriend. I didn't have time to deal with a costume."

"Why'd he even bother to have you talk to her? By the time you learn her name, she'll be old news to him."

"Not Sadie, I think he's serious about her. They've already been dating for a couple of months."

Morgan gasps. "Sadie from the coffee shop?"

He nods his disapproval, then shrugs and says, "It's the longest relationship he's ever had. But they seem . . . happy."

Unable to hold her tongue, Morgan spits, "He's an idiot!"

Emily said Alec would break her heart, so she stayed away from him. Nothing about him is good for her. In fact, he has very few good qualities to speak of. So, why can't she stop thinking about him? Why does the thought of him in a relationship make her so incredibly angry? She knows Alec is a dog, a dirty, untrustworthy mutt of a dog, yet she continues to think of him as the Alec she grew up with. She misses that Alec.

"Anyway, I didn't mean to leave you stranded with Ashley," Ben says, drawing her out of her thoughts.

"And what's that supposed to mean?" Ashley says, handing a can of soda to Morgan and keeping the bottle of vodka for herself. She looks Ben up and down. "You're not wearing a costume," she says with outrage. Grabbing his hand, she drags him out of the kitchen. Morgan follows as Ashley pulls him up the stairs and into her bedroom.

Ashley points to a pile of clothing on her bed, "Choose wisely."

"You can't be serious," Ben says, eyeing the costume pieces scattered across the bed.

"It's a costume party, Ben. You put on a costume, or you leave."

He steps back, crossing his arms on his chest. "There are other people here without costumes."

"I didn't invite them. I invited you."

"This is stupid," Ben says, sifting through the assortment.

Morgan sits at Ashley's desk, draping her coat over the back of the chair while Ashley sets the bottle of vodka down so she can readjust the top of her strapless Tinker Bell dress. She checks herself out in her full-length mirror, fluffing her hair and reapplying lipstick.

Ben picks up an eye patch and a pirate hat. "By the way, next

Saturday we're having a little get together at Alec's to celebrate his birthday. There won't be costumes or fifty obnoxious coeds, but it should be fun if you guys want to come." He looks directly at Morgan and continues, "I think you should come even though you're not a huge fan of Alec right now."

Ashley is still leaning into the mirror when she laughs and says, "Only because she hates herself for being desperately in love with him."

Ben laughs while Morgan gasps, betrayed by the truth. "No, I'm not!"

"Give it a rest, Morgan. We're your friends," Ashley cajoles, turning to face her. "You can stop pretending."

Realizing this may not be a joke, Ben looks to Morgan, studying her reaction. "Morgan?"

Her eyes are on the floor, but they dart up when she realizes how guilty she must look. She doesn't want to admit it to Ben, but her face gives her away like it always does.

Ben whispers, "Morgan, no. You . . . you know that can't happen. He's—"

"Relax, Ben. I don't want to have feelings for him," she admits, standing from her seat.

Ashley chimes in with her infinite wisdom. "The heart wants, what the heart wants."

Ben shakes his head. "You're way too good for him."

Too good, that's what she tells herself every day, but hearing it from Ben makes her stick up for Alec. "He's your best friend."

"I know."

"He took you in when you had nowhere to go."

"I know."

"He'd do anything for you, and you think I'm too good for him?"

"Yeah, and Alec would agree with me. Morgan, I'd give my left nut for the guy. You're right, he's my best friend, but so are you. You know what he's like, Morgan. Alec is . . . he's not . . ."

Ben fumbles with his words before stating, "I will never let anything happen between the two of you."

"It's not up to you," Ashley argues with her hands on her hips.

Ben becomes angry. "Morgan and Alec. Never! I'd never let that happen."

"Let it happen?" Morgan snaps, standing up. "I'm not looking for it to *happen*, Ben. I know Alec is a dog. He sees what he wants, he takes what he wants, and he leaves what he's had. Or he did! Apparently, that's not him anymore. Now he's ready to settle down with Slutty Sadie." She shoves her unopened drink into Ben's chest. "But even if . . . No, even when he dumps her, it doesn't mean I'll be throwing myself at him. I have standards, Ben, but Ashley is right. It's not up to you."

She grabs the bottle of vodka from the desk. "I'm not fragile," she says, before storming out of the room, leaving them speechless.

"What the hell just happened?" Ben says, dumbfounded.

"Why are boys so stupid?" Ashley responds.

"How is this my fault?"

"Imagine for a moment that you start having all of these feelings for one of your best friends. Now say that friend didn't show you the same interest. You want to remain friends, but the whole time you have these like feelings that just keep growing. Sound familiar?"

"It's not the same as Emily and me."

"I'm not saying it is, but imagine Morgan reacting to you and Emily like you just did about her and Alec."

He rubs the tips of his fingers over his lips, thinking. "It's not the same, Ashley."

With sympathy, she says, "Is it because you have feelings for Morgan?"

His eyes flick from the door to Ashley. "What?"

"You love her," Ashley observes. "It must be really confusing for you."

MORGAN WANDERS DOWN the hall taking a swig of the clear liquid. It burns as it hits her throat, and she wishes she had held on to her soda. Instead, she takes another gulp from the bottle, hoping it will cure her. She's been trying so hard for so long, but she can't hold it all together anymore. She feels like a screw-up.

She makes it to the kitchen before Ben and Ashley catch up to her. They try to reach for the bottle, so she hurries to take a few more swigs which turn into big gulps. Lowering the bottle, she winces at the terrible taste. While Ashley rips the bottle from her grip, Ben hands her the open can of soda. She takes it, all too happy to get the vodka taste out of her mouth.

Ashley asks, "What happened to—can't get caught drinking underage—and—isn't my thing?"

"I changed my mind," Morgan says, feeling the warmth settling in her belly.

"Morgan, I know you're not fragile," Ben says.

"Of course she's not fragile. She's a BAMF!" Ashley announces, eyeing her half-empty bottle of vodka. "Did you drink all of this?"

"Yeah, it's not very much," Morgan replies, "I don't feel any different."

"Not yet, you don't," Ben says, taking the can from her hand. "Have you eaten anything tonight?"

"I ate around six."

He grabs a bag of chips from the counter and demands that she, "Eat."

"Ben, I'm not a child. You don't need to take care of me," Morgan argues, still angry at him from a moment ago. "Just because Emily left doesn't mean you get to coddle me!"

Ben becomes terrifyingly still, and Morgan hates herself for hurting him.

"Ben, I'm sorry. I didn't mean that . . ." she pleads, but he doesn't stay to listen to her apology. He turns around and walks away without another word.

Ashley's eyes are enormous, staring in shock.

Morgan covers her face and mumbles, "I'm such a bitch. I don't know why I said that. I should leave. Coming here was a bad idea." She turns to leave.

"Oh no, you're not!" Ashley grabs her arm. "In about five minutes you're going to be sit-down-on-the-floor-because-the-world-is-spinning drunk!"

"No, I'm not. I didn't drink that much."

"You definitely drank more than that much! It's 80 proof."

"I don't know what that means," Morgan replies, feeling a warmth spread through her limbs and her body feels like it's floating—like gravity forgot its job. Lighter, she decides she feels lighter. Morgan smiles happily, her eyes losing a bit of focus.

"Crap! I need Ben. Stay here." Ashley runs after Ben.

Morgan turns to the sexy angel next to her and explains, "I'm an adult. I am not drunk. And I don't have to listen to anything Ashley says." The angel laughs, as Morgan wanders into the dining room.

She finds a few people playing ping pong and leans against the wall to observe the game. Deciding the two playing are not a good match, she asks, "Can I play?"

The girl on one end immediately offers her paddle, looking relieved. "Be my guest," she says, letting the ball bounce past her. Morgan takes the paddle and steps forward. Her opponent across the table is a smiling Spartan from the movie *300*. Morgan notices he has a cute smile and shredded abs and the perfect chest for a Spartan. Clearly, he wore this costume to flaunt his muscles.

The Spartan asks, "Do you know the rules?"

Morgan nods.

"Are you any good?"

"I've never played, but how hard can it be?" she responds.

He serves the ball and Morgan hits it, but it goes off to the left.

He smirks. "Guess that answers that," he says, before retrieving the ball.

He hits another ball toward Morgan, and she knocks it back to him this time. The ball goes back and forth a few times before Morgan knocks it past him. He's not smirking anymore.

He skeptically remarks, "Never played before?"

"Promise," Morgan says, feeling a lot more like she's floating. "Cross my heart." With her finger, she makes an exaggerated crisscross over her chest.

"You're lying," he accuses.

"No, she's just a natural," Ben says, coming from behind Morgan.

The sight of him makes Morgan jump up and down like a lunatic. "Ben! You came back!" She runs to him and throws herself at him in a full body hug. Ben catches her, wrapping his arms around her.

"Oh, wow," Ashley says, following Ben. "Starting to kick in, huh?"

Morgan backs out of the hug and shakes her head in disagreement even though she knows she feels different. "Ashley, I feel just fine. In fact, I'm about to beat this foxy spartan in my first ever ping pong match." She makes sure to enunciate every word to emphasize how clear-headed she's pretending to be.

"Foxy Spartan?" her opponent questions with a sexy grin. "Hate to break it to you, but I never lose."

"We'll see about that."

The match continues and Morgan stays pretty focused on the game. Soon a crowd begins gathering around them. It becomes increasingly difficult to follow the ball, and Morgan realizes it's going to be impossible to convince her friends that she isn't drunk when she keeps swinging her paddle too late.

"How many points does this game have?" she asks.

The Spartan laughs. "I thought you knew the rules."

"I know them enough to beat you." She leans against the table for a minute to balance herself. "What's the score?"

"Nine to nine," Ben answers.

"It's eleven," Ashley says, holding up her phone. "I just looked it up. Table tennis official rules go to eleven."

"Ooo, I didn't know we were in such an official game," Morgan sings, this time looking like a lunatic, but she's helpless to stop it. Before her mind completely clouds over, she hits the ball across the table, and it goes right past the guy.

"Hey, cheater! I wasn't looking!"

"Well, you better pay attention, cause you're about to lose!" Morgan leans on the table and fans herself with the paddle.

He asks. "What's your name?"

"Morgan."

"Morgan, how drunk are you?"

No use in denying it anymore, she holds up her thumb and index finger arranging them until they showed him an incy-wincy bit.

"You're lucky," Ben says to the guy. "She would've wiped the floor with you by now if she weren't trashed."

"Benjamin Isaac Cetrone! I am not trashed!" She stands with her hands on her hips only to realize the ball is coming for her. The ball hits her in the chest as her paddle rests at her hip.

She looks to her opponent. "Well played."

He smiles, "I'm Josh."

"Well played, Josh."

"I should be thanking your boyfriend for distracting you." He nods toward Ben.

"Ben is not my boyfriend," Morgan laughs.

Ashley chimes, "She's single."

Josh does a quick sweep of Morgan and asks, "How are you single?"

Ben groans inwardly, holding himself back, while Ashley gives him a knowing look.

"Don't try to butter me up with your words and lick-able abs," Morgan responds, "I'm not stupid. This is game point."

His eyes are glued to hers, and a smirk plays on his lips. "So it is."

She serves the ball to him. He swings, missing the ball and the winning point goes to Morgan. She throws her arms up to celebrate her triumph, but through her haze, she notices Josh looks far too happy for a loser. Her arms fall as she accuses, "You let me win!"

"Of course not!" he says, walking around the table to meet her.

"I demand a rematch and this time try not to let me win. Or are you afraid I'll beat you for real."

He laughs under his breath. "I didn't let you win."

"I don't believe you," Morgan says, looking at Ben to back her up, but he just shrugs.

Josh leans in and places a kiss on Morgan's cheek, saying, "The game wasn't what I was aiming to win."

Morgan's cheeks flush from the alcohol, or maybe it was his nice words or the way his abs feel against her greedy fingers. The alcohol offers her the feeling of invincibility, so she leans into the shirtless Spartan, already forgetting his name.

CHAPTER TWELVE

MORGAN WAKES with her head resting on her arms currently draped around the white porcelain throne. She doesn't remember giving the toilet a hug, or even whose toilet she's hugging. As she unwraps herself, nausea spikes and vomit burns up her throat, so she leans over the open seat. Once finished, she flushes the toilet and folds her body into itself on the floor. She has no idea where she is or how she got here.

A hand pulls the hair out of her face and, she groans against the soft touch.

"Here, try to drink this." Ben sets a bottle of water next to her.

Morgan looks up. "Ben." She smiles a pathetic smile. "What did I do to myself? My whole body hurts."

"Do you think you're done puking for a while?"

"I don't know."

"Drink the water. You've gotta rehydrate."

Morgan pushes herself up off the floor. "Where's my phone? I have to call Patrick and—"

"He called last night. He knows you're safe."

"I need to take a shower and get home."

"You've been up most of the night. You need to sleep. Here's a t-shirt for you if you want to change, but the best thing you can do is sleep. One day of sleep isn't going to kill you."

"I need to brush my teeth." While coming to an ungraceful stand, she groans, "Ugh, I think I'm dying."

Ben pulls open a drawer and sets an unused toothbrush on the sink. "You need to eat something. Do you want me to get you a cheeseburger? Ashley said cheeseburgers are good for hangovers."

Morgan glares at him. "If you mention a cheeseburger one more time, I'm gonna barf."

"I'll make you some toast. See if that helps."

He leaves the bathroom and Morgan looks in the mirror to find her black face paint smeared all over cheeks and forehead. She washes her face and brushes her teeth before Ben steps back in with a plate of toast.

"Ben, I really don't want that."

"Eat it anyway," he says, picking up a slice and putting it up to her mouth, forcing her to take a bite. "You kinda owe me."

She glares at him and takes a bite. She makes a face and chokes down a few more bites.

Satisfied, Ben sets the plate down, saying, "I'll stop force feeding you and give you some privacy."

She wants to be angry with him, but she did this to herself, and he's been nothing but helpful. "Thanks, Ben, for everything," she says, as she closes the door behind him.

Her head throbs as she changes out of her leggings and Jersey. Ben's t-shirt comes down over her hips, so she leaves her dirty clothes in the bathroom.

Ben has a studio apartment, so as soon as she walks out of the bathroom, she sees him lying on his back in bed with his arm draped over his eyes, snoring softly. The apartment is pretty empty since he only just moved in and it's void of furniture except for a queen bed, a dresser, and a recliner in the corner.

Stepping forward, she realizes Ben left a glass of water and

Tylenol on the dresser for her. She takes the pills before lifting the blankets and sliding in. Ben startles awake at the movement.

"Sorry," Morgan whispers.

"I didn't mean to fall asleep so fast. How are you feeling?"

"Terrible. I'm sorry I ruined your night."

"I'm glad I was there. How much do you remember?"

"I was awful to you, Ben, and you still took care of me."

"Don't worry about it."

She grabs his hand. "Thank you, Ben. I don't know what I'd do without you."

He squeezes her hand and speaks softly, "Go to sleep."

Morgan dozes off holding his hand. Ben watches her sleep for a while, contemplating the truth of her words from the night before. He doesn't think she remembers what she said to him in the car on the way to his apartment. But watching her sleep like this, he understands everything she'd said. It freaks him out a little, but not enough to pull away from her.

"I'm in love with him, Ben, and . . . and you know the thing is . . ." Morgan drifted off into thought, looking out the window. Without warning, she spun back toward him. "I made out with that guy tonight. It felt good to be wanted, but I'm glad you stopped us because I didn't care about him. Alec is a moron, but I love it, I mean him. I love him. He makes me laugh and . . . And I should be in love with you, Ben. We would be perfect together and don't say you've never thought of it before. Think about it, we're friends, we're outgoing—or at least we used to be, we're attracted to each other . . . well, maybe, are you attracted to me?"

He looked at her and then back to the road.

After a moment of silence, she continued, "You'd be lucky to have a girl like me, you know if Emily and Alec weren't in our lives. Emily is my friend even if she tried to kill us. I would never ever get in the way of you two. I told her about Florida. I wasn't going to tell anyone, but I told her, and maybe I'll tell you."

"Morgan, you don't need to tell me."

"I want you to know," she said solemnly. "They tried to rape me, Ben. I fought so hard, and they still overpowered me. I wasn't strong enough."

She seemed to sober at the thought. "It's a secret though. You won't tell anyone, right? No one knows except my mom and my dad and Emily and . . . Patrick probably knows cause he sneaks into my head. It's weird cause I like living with him, but I don't like that he knows way too many personal details. That's really why I came home. Not cause of Patrick. Cause of those assholes in Florida. I lied when you asked me if I felt safe. I'm always scared, but I feel better living with Patrick, and I feel safe when I'm with you. Did you ever like me? It doesn't matter because you love Emily and I'm in love with an idiot."

Ben kept his eyes on the road, wishing she would stop confessing all these things to him. When he looked back over at her, she was looking down at her phone. She must have taken it back when he wasn't paying attention.

"What are you doing? Give me the phone." He held his hand out for it.

She leaned away from him, putting the phone up to her ear. He reached for it, but she tilted her body toward the door. The phone was ringing, and he had a sick feeling about who she was calling.

"Morgan, give me the phone!" he demanded.

"Fletch?" Alec's voice comes through the phone.

"Morgan, give me the Goddamn phone." Ben pulled the car to the side of the road as Morgan said, "You're an idiot, Alec!"

"Shit," Ben muttered, shifting into park as soon as the car came to a stop.

"You're an idiot, but I can't stop thinking about you," she said before Ben ripped the phone from her.

"Hey!" she shouted, trying to take it back from him.

Ben put the phone to his ear and said, "She's drunk. She doesn't know what she's saying."

"Ben?" Alec mumbled.

"Benjamin Isaac, give me my phone! If I want to tell him how I feel, then I'm going to tell him!"

Alec questioned, "What the hell?"

"She's drunk and upset. I'll talk to you later, man," Ben hung up and looked at Morgan who was suddenly very quiet. Shit, she was crying.

Her feet were tucked up on the seat, and then just as quickly, she was wrenching open the car door and leaning out to throw up.

Ben reached over to hold back her hair. After a moment she leaned back in her seat.

Ben said, "We're only five minutes away from my apartment. Do you think you can make it?"

She nodded, closing the door. Her tears had streaked the black marks painted on her cheeks and she stayed silent for the rest of the ride.

Once they made it to his apartment, she rushed to the bathroom. Once again, he held her hair out of her face while she vomited. When she finished, he brought her a bottle of water. As he handed it to her, his phone chimed in his pocket, and he pulled it out to see a text from Alec.

Ben cursed, pulling out Morgan's phone to find she'd been texting Alec confessions throughout the night. He didn't know how the hell he missed it.

"Morgan, I'll be right back," he said, and she groaned, resting her head on the toilet seat. Ben walked into the other room, dialing Alec.

"What the hell?" Alec said as his greeting.

"I need you to ignore it, man. I need you to forget she sent those, okay? Delete them and pretend it never happened."

"She thinks she's fucking in love with me?"

"Tonight, she's said all kinds of crap she doesn't mean. I'm serious, man. I'm going to delete these messages and so are you. This never happened."

"What did happen tonight?"

"We went to Ashley's party. Things got out of hand," Ben said before he was interrupted by the sound of retching coming from the bathroom. "I gotta go, she's throwing up again,"

"Shit, okay, later."

They hung up and Ben went back into the bathroom to soothe Morgan as she emptied the contents of her stomach. Eventually, he tried to get her to move to the bed, but she refused to leave the bathroom, so he brought her a pillow and blanket, continuing to comfort her into the early morning.

CHAPTER THIRTEEN

THE FOLLOWING NIGHT . . .

ICY WATERS and burning lungs have become familiar to Patrick. He can't help but hold his breath, even knowing it could be over with his next inhale. But Patrick holds his breath, allowing the dark waters to carry him deeper, guiding him closer to the creature in his dreams. He's hoping for answers, but he has to find the beast first. Then the dreams may stop, and he might finally be able to get some sleep.

He feels movement next to him, so Patrick opens his eyes underwater to view the predator waiting to consume him. Something brushes against him and then disappears. He is left alone in the dark waters watching for the monster to reappear. He catches darting movements in the sea before the creature's glowing eyes are just before him. He expected them to look cruel or perhaps be predatory red, but none of his planning prepared Patrick for her breathtaking luminescent-blue eyes with an endless depth. Devastated by the matching crystals staring right through him, Patrick gasps. With his inhale, the sea comes burning into his lungs.

Patrick jerks up on the couch, gasping for breath. He coughs violently, eventually throwing up into the trashcan Morgan provides. Setting the trashcan aside, he puts his head between his legs, struggling to take in enough air. The dreams have become routine, although, Morgan doesn't usually witness the full extent of his suffering. He hopes he didn't say anything aloud while he was dreaming. He didn't mean to fall asleep in the living room again.

He cradles his head in his hands, hoping to stop the living room from spinning. He's all too aware of Morgan's worried eyes diagnosing him. She learned to stop asking about his dreams, but they've been escalating.

"Patrick, it's getting worse," Morgan whispers, placing a reassuring hand on his back. "I'm worried about you. Isn't there something I can do?"

Patrick peers up at her and the room tilts with the movement. Everything is spinning, so he squeezes his eyes shut, and the dream comes flooding back to him. Those crystal eyes. It felt too real to be a dream, but he doesn't have visions, and he would know if someone was tampering with his head.

"Is it the same dream every time?" Morgan asks, pulling him back to reality.

"More or less," he answers, relieved the room has finally become stationary.

"What happens in your dream?"

"Talking about it won't change anything."

"It might help me if I knew what was going on before you actually suffocate one of these days."

"My dreams aren't going to kill me."

"Are you sure? You wouldn't budge when I tried to wake you."

That takes him by surprise. "You tried to wake me?"

"Yeah. If you held your breath any longer, I was going to do CPR."

"I'm drowning," he says in a rush. "In my dream, I'm drowning."

"But you always wake up before you drown?"

"It ends when I inhale the water."

"Can you breathe it in right away? Wouldn't that keep it from getting worse?"

"I'm not really in control," he says.

"There has to be some way to make them stop. Could there be something helpful in one of these books?" Morgan points to the table where he keeps the collection they brought back from Maplesburg.

"I haven't found anything to help with the dreams, but the red book on top helped me discover that the combined blood of Isa, Leona, and Valla activates the necklace."

"Patrick, what if the necklace is what caused the dreams. They started after our trip to Maplesburg. What if it's some kind of curse or something?"

"That's not how the necklace works. We aren't witches, Morgan. We don't go around cursing things."

"From what you described, that necklace is full of magic you don't really understand," she argues, picking up the red book. "I'm going to start reading to see what I can find out." She opens the book, scrolling through the first page before setting it back on the table. "Okay, you go through that one. It's in that crazy writing." She opens another book, satisfied that it's written in a language she understands.

Patrick stands from the sofa. "I saw Samantha today," he says out of the blue. "Apparently, you gave her my number. She called earlier asking if I found anything. She was about to cancel her bridal shower and postpone the wedding. I met with her and convinced her to continue with her wedding plans. I wiped her memory of our encounter and I plan to check on her at the bridal shower to make sure the wedding is on track. Now, we just need to get Emily there in time."

"Do you have any new leads?"

"No, but I will. First, I need to brush my teeth to get rid of this taste."

CHAPTER FOURTEEN ~

October 31st ~

Patrick throws the book across the room. He is done with this. He keeps running into dead ends, and he doesn't know where else to look. He's exhausting all of his resources. He found Emily once. He thought he would be able to find her again, but with each dead end, he feels her slipping further and further away. He should never have forced her into her fight with Sky. He should've done what Ben said and protected her from the beginning. Or better yet, he should've walked away and stayed away from her that first day on campus.

He remembered walking away from Emily, who was mysteriously getting in his head. He was running away to avoid the ugly feelings she had awakened inside of him. His feet hit the pavement one after the other, but he was barely aware of his actions. His mind was reeling, consumed with the frustrating aberration. She hadn't wanted him.

The BMW locks disengaged as Patrick approached his brand-new car. He opened the door to get in when a feminine voice stopped him.

"Hey," she called, followed by her friend's giggles.

Patrick stood straight and gazed at the three attractive women standing next to his car. He'd let them sneak up on him, something he learned long ago not to do. It was obvious they weren't a threat, but he'd let his guard down.

"So, is this your car?" One of the girls asked him.

He was usually smooth, but they'd approached at a bad time. "You mean the one I'm getting into?" he questioned, irritated by their obvious flirting. "Well, I should hope so."

"Maybe you could give us a ride," another girl said. All three were looking at him in anticipation.

They were cute. Maybe he hadn't lost it. Maybe the girl from earlier was broken or something. She'd been oblivious to things that were sitting right there in front of her. Clearly, it was her issue, not his.

"So . . ." one of the girls said, moving closer. "What'll it be?" She stroked Patrick's arm and cocked her head.

He looked over the three attractive women hitting on him and then looked back toward campus. "Sorry babe, I'll have to take a rain check. I have a class to attend."

They sighed and complained, disappointment making them whiny, but Patrick wasn't interested. He shut his car door and took long strides back to the giant stone building. Her presence was like a beacon calling to him.

He took a seat in the back of the classroom, and his eyes were drawn to her right away. She had a notebook on her desk as an ancient looking man hobbled on a cane towards the podium. Patrick felt her fondness of the decrepit old man even as he questioned the odds of the professor surviving the day, let alone the semester. As the class went on, Patrick found his strange obsession hunched over listening carefully with her chin perched atop her fist. She was genuinely engrossed in the man's stories. Maybe the professor was interesting. Patrick wouldn't know. He was having a difficult time listening because he was too focused on the young woman with gray eyes and dark blond hair. Emily.

While the rest of the class fell asleep or typed word for word notes, Emily, continued to jot down notes here and there. Mostly she was listening, completely uninterested that Patrick existed, and this deeply disturbed him. He had to make her notice him.

The professor dismissed the class a couple of minutes after four o'clock. He watched her look at the time, then grab her notebook and bag as she stood with urgency. She rushed up the aisle of the lecture hall while loading the things in her bag. Patrick moved out of his seat right before she came up the last few steps. She was barely paying attention, but she stopped herself just shy of crashing into him.

"Oh my God! It's him! Why does he smell so good? Why does he have to look so great?" Her thoughts came screaming into Patrick's psyche.

He turned around to face her and couldn't help his delighted laugh, relishing in her attraction to him. "You're terribly clumsy, aren't you?" Patrick said in a sensual tone. "It's rather endearing to find such a beautiful woman whose movements completely contradict the elegance a body like yours suggests." It was a jab, but he couldn't help himself.

She was gawking up at him. "What the hell?" Her thoughts were angry. She tried to step around him, but Patrick moved into her path, while she intentionally avoided eye contact. "Allow me," he said, pushing the door open. He stood in the doorway, wanting her to brush up against him.

She squeezed by him, narrowly avoiding contact as she sped out the door without a word. "Until we meet again," he said just loud enough for her to hear.

She took off in a fast walk and he caught himself smiling again. It was strange the effect she seemed to have on him.

He waited outside the building of her next class and listened to her indistinct thoughts. He found comfort in the fact that she was thinking of him, even if her thoughts weren't all positive. She thought Patrick was in her humanities class, which reminded him that he needed to register or at least get the books if he was going to pretend. A small part of her was excited to see him again even though the rest of her was angry for thinking of him at all. Patrick relished in the fact that he excited her.

When she came out of the building, Patrick followed her out to the parking lot, feeling like a stalker. Trailing people was part of his job. He didn't know why this would feel any different. He followed a few cars behind her for about twenty minutes, surprised to find she lived only a little ways away from where he was staying. He wondered if she knew his cousin, Morgan. They would be about the same age.

He parked down the street from her house and smiled again when he realized she was still thinking about him. She stepped out of her car, slamming the door. "Stupid Boy!" He heard her thoughts loud and clear. Once she was inside, he pulled his car up a little closer to inspect the out-of-date house and quickly realized that it might not look like much, but the security on the house was no joke. Surveillance cameras were well hidden around the exterior, but it was part of Patrick's job to notice that kind of thing. He counted five cameras and suspected there were more. He thought his car was still out of range but made a mental note to touch up his background in case anyone ran a check on him. Patrick backed up and turned the car around, going back the way he came, hoping to avoid any cameras he might have missed.

The drive to his uncle's house was just a few minutes outside of town. He cruised at a comfortable eighty miles an hour on the country roads but remembered to slow down properly this time, so he didn't hit the gravel driveway and send rocks flying. He pulled down the long drive, noting the absence of other cars, grateful he'd have the house to himself for a little while so he could do his research in peace.

He was used to being left alone in the most luxurious of accommodations, but he felt that living with his only living relatives could be useful to help him learn the area. His family didn't know what he had been sent here to do or who he was working with, but it was in their best interest not to know. They were nice people, which only gave him more reason not to hang around. His uncle knew Patrick could blow his cover, but he also knew they were the only family Patrick had left since his father disappeared when he was six and his mother died when he was fifteen.

Patrick parked next to the house, grabbed his briefcase, and took the sidewalk around to the front door. He still couldn't believe they didn't lock their house.

He was staying in the bedroom next to his cousin, Morgan. He thought he'd be able to get close to her and pump her for information but found that part of his plan wasn't working out. She kept an active social life like a typical nineteen-year-old, but Patrick found it annoying how mature and lovable she was. It also didn't help that some days when she was home, she would lock herself in her room and cry. She was an emotional basket case after being assaulted in her dorm this past spring. At least she tried to hide her misery. He gave her props for that.

Entering his temporary room, he locked the door behind him. He sat on the bed, punching in the code on the locked briefcase and then another password on the encrypted computer inside. Once he was granted access, he typed in the address he just left.

After a brief search, he learned that Mark Burk, a forty-two-year-old man who purchased the home with cash thirteen years ago, had two living daughters and was twice widowed. His first wife, whom he was only married to for six months died of a drug overdose. His second wife, married fifteen years, died six years ago. After a brief investigation, her death was ruled a suicide. Patrick explored further and found that wife number two, Selma Burk, had schizophrenia and was institutionalized for the last three years of her life.

Patrick looked up the daughters. Samantha Lee Burk, twenty-two, had just graduated with her bachelor's degree in Education. He found a recent engagement photo along with information about her sorority, her transcripts, old parking tickets, all her social media, and memorial photos from Selma's funeral. Patrick scrolled back to the top, typed in Emily Burk, and hit enter.

She was a seventeen-year-old high school graduate from the same school Morgan had attended. Patrick smiled, happy with the new information, but soon became frustrated when he couldn't find anything recent on social media. She had apparently deleted all of her accounts. In her senior yearbook, her name appeared twice. Once in the required mugshot and in the second, she was standing with three guys. Patrick recognized the guy from earlier as Benjamin Cetrone. The other two boys were listed as Alec Garner and Gavin Clark.

Patrick went back to social media to find Emily mentioned in several posts. None of them were kind. He discovered Leah Young was behind most of them and found it interesting that her brother Daniel Young was about to marry Emily's sister.

Patrick scrolled through Emily's bank statements and found she worked at a pet supply store. She'd had a variety of odd jobs over the years and Patrick wondered if the family was poor. The house looked like a dump, but with all the security surrounding the house, he knew there was something worth protecting. He began to hack into Mark's financials, but an alert came up. What was this guy hiding?

Now Patrick understands what Mark was trying so diligently to protect, and he had obliterated the security Mark worked so hard to put in place. He shouldn't have manipulated Morgan into introducing him to Emily. He shouldn't have set foot in Emily's classroom. Emily would have stayed safe if he hadn't ruined her chances of a free life.

Patrick goes back to the bottle of bourbon and decides to drink from the bottle instead of filling up another glass. He heads back to the couch where he continues to beat himself up over his mistakes as the sun sinks in the sky.

MORGAN ENTERS the dark apartment and flicks on the lights, startled to find Patrick sitting on the couch with a bottle of bourbon in his grip. Morgan moves forward with caution. "Patrick, what are you doing?"

He doesn't look up as he answers, "I fucked it all up."

Morgan takes a deep breath as she sets her things down. "Patrick, this wasn't your fault. Even Emily said that much."

"Morgan, you lie because you love me, but please stop. I know I fucked it all up and now I can't find her. I'm the reason for all of it."

"You were doing what you needed to do in order to survive."

"I wanted Sky to be proud of me. I mean, how messed up is that? I hated him, but I also needed his approval. I wanted to please him and stay on his good side, Morgan. In his own twisted way, I thought he loved me, and I didn't want to be expendable, so I tried to impress him."

"He twisted your thoughts. He brainwashed you, Patrick."

"Then why do I miss him?"

Morgan's eyes go wide at his admission, and she's glad he's not looking at her. She has no idea how to respond.

"He was all I had, Morgan, and his praise felt good. I was his favorite. It made me feel important, but he also killed my family and tortured me. How sick is it that I loved and hated him at the same time?" He takes another swig from the bottle.

"It sounds like Stockholm's syndrome," she says, taking the bottle from him.

He sways on the couch, completely drunk. He looks to Morgan with sad eyes and confesses, "I killed people for that monster. I can't take that back, but I thought I didn't have a choice. I did. I should'a died instead'a killing them."

"Why don't we get you to bed?" She sets the bottle on the table and offers him a hand.

He looks up at her with glazed over eyes, gaping. "You're an angel." He looks away and shoos her. "Go away! I can't die yet," he slurs, "not till I get her back."

"Patrick, I'm not the Angel of Death. Come on," she coaxes, "I'm even going to lie right next to you to make sure you don't die in your sleep."

Patrick nods, accepting the hand she offers.

CHAPTER FIFTEEN ~

November ~

MORGAN IS RUNNING LATE. She covered when two of her coworkers called off. It didn't help that they had particularly difficult patients, and she was covering the entire floor. Her eight-hour shift quickly turned into ten, but she left with enough time to shower and change before going out. She promised Ben she would come tonight.

She pulls into the parking lot and has to circle twice before finding an open spot. She hurries out of her car and right into a puddle. She shakes the water off, but it's already soaked through her shoe. With a groan, she continues her way into the coffee shop. The place is packed tonight. Ben is playing an upbeat song, and she's surprised to find Alec sitting next to him using his hands to beat on a djembe drum. The whole place is held captive, transfixed by the melody. People in the audience are moving with the music.

Morgan's stare lands on Alec. His face tilts to the floor, eyes closed as the beat flows from him like it takes no effort at all. This is the Alec she loves. The carefree Alec who—despite the crowd of onlookers—looks comfortable in his own skin, who isn't making crude jokes, but is filling the room with his incredible energy.

His eyelids open and his hazel eyes land on her. He smiles big, showing off his swoon-worthy dimples. He looks delighted to see her and that feeling tingles through Morgan's whole body. She smiles back, matching his excitement.

"Excuse me," someone says from behind Morgan, breaking her trance.

She moves forward, realizing she's blocking the entrance. She pushes through a small crowd of girls who are practically drooling over the guys on stage. She goes to the counter to order her drink and leans against a back wall out of the way.

When they finish their song, Alec stands to bow. His charisma has everyone eating out of his hands. He steps off stage, and Ben continues into another song as Alec makes his way to Morgan.

"Hey, Fletch," he greets, scooping her into a hug that lifts her off her feet. She throws her arms around him for support.

By the time he sets her back down, she's breathless.

"How the hell are you?" he asks, stepping back.

"Good. I'm good." Her wet shoes and bad day are long forgotten.

"How's that dickweed cousin of yours?"

"Patrick? He's—"

"Right over there." Alec gestures to the other side of the coffee shop.

Her eyes follow, and sure enough, Patrick is leaning against a wall looking like he'd rather be anywhere else. Morgan scrunches her brow, staring at him. Patrick doesn't look her way, although she's sure he knows they're talking about him. Morgan wonders why he didn't tell her he was coming tonight.

She looks at Alec, saying, "I've been bragging about Ben. He probably wanted to see for himself."

The barista calls her name and Morgan takes a few steps to

grab her drink from the counter. When she turns back around, she almost runs into Alec. "Whoa, you're right there."

"Here I am," he says, grinning.

"I didn't know you'd be playing tonight."

He doesn't respond, but his eyes are glued to her like she's the only person in the room.

"Why are you looking at me like that?" she asks, feeling the heat creep into her face.

"How am I looking at you?"

"I don't know. Just—"

"Come sit with me," he says, wrapping his arm around her shoulder. He pushes her forward, guiding her to a two-person table in the corner with a reserved sign sitting on the top.

Morgan asks, "The band gets a table?"

"Ben gets a table, but seeing how we're the only ones here who know Ben, I guess we have dibs," he says, as they sit across from one another. Alec leans forward. "You and Patrick are pretty close. Do you want to invite him over?"

Morgan laughs. "He would already be over here if he wanted to be."

"Have you guys always been close?"

"No. Our parents had a falling out years ago, so we only met this summer when he came to stay with my family."

"But you're close now, right?"

"Yeah, I guess so."

"Why is he here tonight if it's not to hang out with you? It can't be to see Ben. From what I've heard, they hate each other."

"Why are you so worried about them?" Morgan questions.

"I guess I'm still trying to put it all together to figure out what happened over the summer."

Morgan sits back. It takes her a minute to compose herself. "What do you mean, what happened?"

"To Emily and her dad, to Ben, but mostly what happened to you? I want you to tell me what really happened this summer," Alec says, resting his elbows on the table.

Morgan is drowning in secrets and the fabricated story is her only life preserver. She knows she's a lousy liar, but she's rehearsed this lie so many times that it has become second nature; yet, at this moment she wants to tell the truth. "I eh' . . ."

"Come on Fletch, it's me."

Suddenly, the lie is right there on her lips, spilling out, "On their way home from Colorado, Emily and her dad were in a car accident. Emily walked away without a scratch, but her dad was severely injured and fell into a coma. They don't know if he'll ever wake up. Emily couldn't deal with the guilt, so she took off."

Alec's eyes flit to the table, appearing disappointed as he leans back in his seat with a sigh.

"What?" Morgan questions.

He shakes his head. "I don't know why you guys are lying to me. Why would Emily take off?"

"She couldn't handle it."

"Bullshit."

"Excuse me?"

"Bull. Shit," he enunciates. "Emily took so much crap through high school. You guys were close. You know what she went through, and you think she'd just up and leave because of one accident. I don't buy that for one fucking second."

"Maybe it was all too much," Morgan suggests.

"Then explain what happened to you?"

"To me?"

He tilts his head. "Stop acting stupid, Fletcher. We both know you aren't."

"I really don't know what you're talking about."

"Who is this?" Looking at her sideways, he gestures toward her. "I miss confident Morgan. Who the fuck is this imposter that took her place? I don't know her."

"Alec . . ."

"Who did this to you? I'll kick their ass!"

Unsure what to say, she avoids looking at him and gazes toward the stage where Ben is playing a soothing song.

Alec follows her gaze and curses, snapping Morgan's attention back to him. "You got a thing for Ben," he accuses.

"What?" A smile lights her face as she laughs.

"You looked at him," he says in defense.

"Yeah, cause he's on stage. I love Ben, but I don't have a thing for him. God, Alec, you're a moron."

"Now that's closer to the Morgan I know. Look, I even got you to laugh. I miss your laugh."

That wipes the smile from her face. She sits back, unsure of when she leaned toward him.

"And there it goes," he says with a frown. "You're a social butterfly, Fletch. You always have been. According to social media, your life was booming this summer with girl's nights and hanging with old teammates. Then August hit and you disappeared. You told me what happened to Emily, but what happened to you?"

"Are you stalking my social media?"

"Hell yeah, I am! Twitter, Instagram, Snapchat, Facebook. I've got 'em all covered."

"I've been busy with school. I don't have time for—"

"Try again, 'cause you know I'm not buying that shit." He leans forward on his elbows. "You forget that I've known you for sixteen years."

Morgan thinks for a moment, wondering how she can explain without telling him too much. With a sigh, she begins, "When I tore my ACL three years ago, my teammates ditched me. I'm not complaining. I understand, but Emily stuck by me when I was lame and couldn't do anything but sit around. It wasn't out of pity. It was because she valued our friendship. She's always been different and most people at school hated her for what they couldn't understand. She pretended it didn't bother her, but I know it did.

"She kept people from getting close, but I was one of the lucky few she let in. And I know she would do anything for me. She's one of the strongest people I know, Alec, but one day she realized she couldn't handle it anymore. One of the people she loves most might never wake up, and so she ran before she could lose anyone else. I want to be there for her, but I can't. And you're right, this isn't Emily. She wouldn't abandon Samantha when she's supposed to get married next month. She wouldn't leave when her dad is in a hospital bed dying. She wouldn't leave Ben hours after telling him what he really means to her. Emily—the strongest person I know—wouldn't do those things, but guess what? She did, and if she's gone, then something must really be wrong, but I'm helpless to do anything. I'm at a loss and I guess this whole thing changed my priorities."

Alec leans in, his hazel eyes on her as he reaches across the table and grabs her hand. "So, what are your priorities now?"

Her heart is hammering as his hand rests on top of hers. He has beautiful masculine hands. She didn't know hands could be so tempting. His thumb moves back and forth in a soothing motion and for a moment she forgets he asked a question.

Breathless, she finally says, "Getting through one day at a time."

"You're something special, Fletcher."

"You're not so bad yourself."

"I have to ask you something?" he says, leaning closer.

Her heart gallops in her chest at the prospect of what might come next, but Morgan pulls away, dragging herself out of her daze before they destroy their friendship with words and actions they can't take back. "No Alec, I will not have sex with you in the bathroom."

With a quick smile, he says, "Damn, you thwarted my plans, again."

"You've had your turn for questions. It's my turn."

"Ask away," he says with confidence, leaning back in his seat.

She betrays herself by asking, "Why do you care?"

His face shows disbelief, followed by anger. "I'm not always a dick, Fletch."

"I didn't say you were. I'm not used to the twenty questions from you, is all."

He scowls. "I usually don't have to push so damn hard to get you to open up to me, but I always care about you," he says, sounding cross. "Do you really think I haven't noticed you avoiding me? I've known you since preschool, Fletch."

Despite his harsh question, she smiles, remembering preschool Alec. "You're the one who gave me my nickname." Her smile grows and she can't keep herself from laughing.

Alec fights a smile. "Oh great, now you're making fun of me."

"I never made fun of you!" she corrects.

"No, but you were bossy. You made me your project, trying to play teacher all the time."

"Kids are mean. I was trying to help you," she says in her defense.

"You'll be happy to know I've been able to pronounce my R's for quite some time now, Mowgan."

She laughs aloud.

He throws his hands up. "See, you were making fun of me!"

"Do you remember the time in kindergarten with Ryan Bollard?"

"Are you kidding me? How could I forget! You were so pissed. I've never seen you so angry. You jumped out of your seat, marched right up to him in your stupid plaid jumper and stomped on his damn foot as hard as you could. I was humiliated. I didn't need a girl fighting my battles."

"I think I did a fine job sticking up for you. I broke two of his toes and he went crying to the teacher."

"I remember that, too," he says through a laugh. "You were sitting in your chair looking all innocent as he pointed you out to the teacher. She was so confused. You're lucky no one else saw you."

"He was a bully. And he was making fun of you. He got what he deserved, and no other kindergarteners messed with you after that."

He howls with laughter. "That's because he told everyone I did it! Once he realized the teacher didn't believe it was you, he started pointing at me. You're the reason I got my bad boy reputation."

She laughs louder, tears coming to her eyes. Then she shakes her head. "I'm so sorry," she says between laughs. "I know it's not funny. I got you in so much trouble."

He smiles, but all of a sudden seems to snap out of the hilarity. His dimples disappear as his face turns thoughtful. His look sobers Morgan, and she listens as he says, "You're the reason I started standing up for myself. You were my hero. You've always been my hero. You're too smart, too kind, too talented, too much of a badass. You'll always be better than everyone around you and you've never even considered it. You're gonna do amazing things, Fletch. You'll leave us all in the dust."

"I'm not better than you," she says, staring into his hazel eyes. After a moment, she adds, "Or anyone."

He looks at her with his eyebrows cocked. "Why did you come back from Florida?"

She gives a sad smile. "Doesn't seem right, does it? Years of careful planning and working my butt off and I end up back where I started."

"You can plan the shit out of your life, Morgan. The thing most people don't get is life doesn't give a shit about your plan."

"Life had its own plan for me," she returns. "I know this is where I'm supposed to be. At least for now."

"I'm not complaining. I'm glad you came back. But I am curious what brought you back."

She admits, "I didn't feel safe there."

"Do you feel safe here?"

"You mean, like right now?" she says with humor, giving him a once over. "Or in general?"

"You really don't remember, do you?" he says with dejected amusement.

"Remember what?"

"Nothing," he replies, seeming to snap out of his funk. "I gotta get back up there. He only has a couple songs left." He stands up and stoops to kiss the top of her head. "God, I've missed you. It's been really good spending time with you again."

"Ditto," she says, unable to look him in the eye.

He stands there for a moment, almost like he has more to say, but when she finally looks up, he smiles, showing off those sexy dimples and then walks away. Ben is in the middle of a song when Alec picks up the drum and jumps right in, bringing the beat out of the melody. Morgan sits there, transfixed. She knows Alec loves attention, yet he gave up most of his spotlight to be with her this evening. She also notices something else. He hadn't mentioned Sadie. Not even once.

After a while, Patrick takes the seat across from Morgan. He doesn't say anything. He sits there and pretends to listen to the music, but she doubts he's really there for the band. She figures he'll tell her what he's up to in his own time, so she doesn't question his motives and they sit together in companionable silence.

When the guys finish their set, Morgan waits for them to pack up their things. She watches from the table as they talk to their admirers.

"They sounded good tonight," Patrick comments from across the table.

Morgan continues to watch the emptying stage. "I'm surprised you came."

"I didn't come for them."

"I figured as much." She turns toward him, asking, "So why are you here?"

"Lathe is in town."

Chills spread over her skin and she shivers. "Patrick, why didn't you tell me?"

He shrugs. "I just did."

She makes a sound of disapproval and complains, "Have you seen him? What does he want?"

Patrick stands from the table, ignoring Morgan's questions

and says, "Ben, you sounded excellent tonight. You have quite a talent."

Ben approaches their table eyeing Patrick cautiously before turning his head to Morgan. Morgan pushes her chair from the table, the legs scraping against the floor. She stands and steps into Ben, wrapping him in a hug.

He's stiff as he wraps his arms around her. His eyes move to Patrick and Morgan steps away. Ben asks, "Why are you here tonight, Patrick?"

"Lathe is in town," Morgan answers for him.

Ben's eyes shift to Morgan and back while he addresses them both, saying, "What does that mean for us?"

"Well, we already know he's had his turn with you," Patrick says. "Your mutual hatred for me playing in your favor, I'm sure."

"I already told you, I don't remember talking to anyone."

"Lathe isn't sloppy. He wouldn't leave you with a memory of him."

"So again, what does this mean for us. What does he want?"

"At first, I thought he was taunting me, but now I think it's more likely he's discovered Emily's identity. This could be very bad for us. Lathe is less likely to corner you if you are in a group. I believe he's alone, which is peculiar, but it also means he'll be gone by morning. It's not safe for him to leave his home for too long."

"That doesn't sound good," Morgan says.

Ben asks, "Why does he hate you, Patrick?"

With an intense glare, Patrick says, "I'm sure you can imagine what I might've done to piss him off."

Morgan jumps in, saying, "So, he spoke to Ben when he was here before and he tried to get to me. So, who else would he go after?"

"Samantha, but she's with Dan and his family tonight making her a difficult target. He won't risk the exposure. It would be pointless for him to go after Mark."

"What are you talking about?" Ben questions. "Mark is a sitting duck."

"Lathe wants information, and Mark's psyche has been run through a blender. Lathe won't hurt him, of that I'm certain. He won't hurt anyone except, maybe Morgan."

"What?" she squeals, "Why me?"

Ben answers, "Because you're the only one of us who Patrick actually cares about and he really hates you, Patrick. Again, why is that?"

"Many people hate me. How am I supposed to understand their reasoning? It's unlike Lathe to hurt Morgan. He has a week spot for women, and once he met you, he wouldn't be able to harm you. I just don't want him to know everything you know. Not yet anyway."

Ben grimaces, fighting his temper. "That's cold, Patrick." He pulls Morgan into his side. "Her safety should rank higher than your secrets."

Patrick stands back and looks at the two of them side-by-side. He senses something that wasn't there before. At his assessing look, Ben's memories from the night of Ashley's party flood to the forefront of his brain and Patrick dissects his thoughts.

Morgan asks, "What are you doing?"

Tilting his head to the side, he says, "I could ask you the same."

"Hey, Patrick," Alec says, joining the group.

"Alec." Patrick nods in his direction. "I'll let you guys visit. Morgan, I'll be outside when you're ready." He turns and leaves.

Alec questions, "What was that about?" He eyes Ben's arm around Morgan. "You guys okay?"

Morgan pulls away from Ben. "Yeah, he's . . . I gotta go. I'm sorry guys. You sounded great tonight. You should team up more often."

She hugs Ben and then moves to give Alec a hug. He swoops

her up and when he has his arms around her, he whispers, "You sure you're okay?"

"Yeah, Alec. I'm fine."

He doesn't let go, though. Instead, he says, "Promise?"

"Promise," she replies.

He lets her go but holds out his hand, pinky up. Morgan gives a small grin and wraps her pinky around his.

Seeming satisfied, he says, "See you later Fletch."

"Bye guys."

Once she's out of earshot, Ben questions, "What were you guys talking about earlier?"

"We were just catching up."

Clearly upset, Ben accuses, "You didn't tell her about the night of Ashley's party, did you?"

Alec shakes his head, watching her walk out the door. "She really doesn't remember."

"I told you. She doesn't remember much from that night."

Alec justifies, "She was drunk anyway, so it doesn't matter."

"It does matter. She might've been drunk, but she was serious. I know I told you it didn't mean anything, but I lied. You're the reason she was drinking. She was mad when I told her you and Sadie were getting serious. You need to tell her, Alec."

"I will. I just don't want to fuck this up. I need some time. I mean, it's Morgan."

"I invited her to come by for your birthday tomorrow night. I invited her before I knew about . . . you know. Think you can have your shit together by then?"

"Guess I'll have to."

CHAPTER SIXTEEN ~

Across town, Lathe sits on a barstool, leaning forward to rest his elbows against the bar while he swirls his half-empty glass of whiskey. He keeps his hood up and his head down as he watches her from the corner of his eye, waiting for the right moment. She is tipsy as she sashays up to the dart board to retrieve the darts she and her friend's boyfriend threw. The boyfriend is checking out her ass, while his girlfriend talks distractedly to a group of friends. Lathe can't blame the guy. Those tight jeans do a fine job cupping her ass and showing off her long legs. After retrieving the darts, she reaches up to write on the chalkboard a few feet away. She is keeping track of their scores, while he keeps track of how many times her shirt rides up to show off her belly button ring. After jotting the scores from this round, she turns with a smile and bounces back to her opponent, handing him his darts.

Her peppiness is getting on Lathe's last nerve. She flips a platinum lock of hair over her shoulder and spins to take aim with the dart held delicately between her fingers. She's good. Even he can admit that, but her mannerisms are driving him crazy. Her toothy smile, the way she unconsciously touches her full lips when she's thinking, and the way those sinfully dark eyes taunt him. He straightens in his seat and takes another sip of whiskey. He doesn't even like whiskey, which is why it is taking him so long to down the liquid.

Too focused on her group of friends, she hasn't looked at him once in the past hour and a half of him observing her. He is used to people-watching, but watching Ashley tonight, makes him feel like a creep. His eyes float back to her as she throws her hands above her head to high five her opponent after he hits the bullseye. The guy grins and points towards their drink table. She laughs as she grabs a shot from the table and downs it like a pro.

The girlfriend turns around just in time to watch her boyfriend bite his lip and adjust his pants while watching Ashley's ass.

"Busted," Lathe breathes.

The girlfriend instantly turns angry and begins to cause a scene, hitting her boyfriend with her purse over and over while drunk crying. Ashley slips away, escaping the escalating scene. With an eye-roll, she abandons her group of friends for the bar. She leans in next to Lathe and places an order for a rum and coke.

She points to the stool next to him. "Is someone sitting here?" she asks Lathe. He keeps his face tilted down as he shakes his head no.

"Cool." She hops up on the stool. "Are you here alone?"

He nods a yes.

She leans forward against the bar to look at him. He's thankful she's sitting on his good side, although he's not sure why it matters. "Are you just shy, or are you a creep? I've noticed you watching me."

Lathe blinks, surprised by her words, surprised she noticed him at all. He was a practiced expert when it came to going unnoticed. He wasn't sure when he slipped up. He opens his mouth to answer her when the shouting from the other end of the room gets louder, and glass shatters across the way.

Ashley and Lathe both look to the commotion. Ashley's

friend is throwing a tantrum and is about to get kicked out of the bar. Without looking away from her friend, Ashley shouts to Lathe over the crowd, "That's Bethany! She's my roommate. She breaks up with her boyfriend at least, like, three times a week. They're a freaking tornado, but they always come back to each other. It's disgusting!" Ashley snorts and swings back around on her stool. With a sharp intake, Ashley hisses, "Oh, shit, what happened to your face?" Her hands come up to cover her lips, looking as if she wants to stuff the words back into her mouth.

That's twice she's surprised him in the last two minutes. Lathe is used to people gawking and whispering, but it is rare for someone to verbalize such a harsh response. He leans in, and in a mock whisper, he says, "Usually people don't speak so loudly when pointing out someone's flaws. I didn't come up to you and say, 'Why the hell is your hair so damn blond?'"

"Hey," Ashley grabs at her hair. "I pay a lot to get it this blond! I like my hair."

"I like my face."

"It's a nice face. I never said I didn't like it." Ashley responds, tucking her heels up on the rungs of her bar stool. "It's got character. You know, like, it makes you more distinguished or something."

Lathe lifts a brow and tilts his head to the side. "What's wrong with you?"

"I get called a bitch a lot, but I think I'm just more honest than most people. I can leave you alone if I'm making you uncomfortable, but I'd also like to point out you're the one who's been staring at me all night. What's your name?"

"Lathe."

"Lathe, I'm Ashley." She reaches out to shake his hand.

After they shake, the bartender places her drink on the counter in front of her and walks away. Ashley grabs it and fiddles with the straw. "So, seriously Lathe, how did you get those scars? It had to have been something horrific."

He raises his one good eyebrow and shakes his head. "It really wasn't."

"I don't believe you, but I get that you don't want to spill your guts to a complete stranger. If it helps, you can ask me anything you want."

"You used to work with Emily Burk." It isn't a question. He just wants to see how she'll respond.

"Yeah, how did you know that? Wait, are you for real stalking me?"

Lathe snorts, unable to contain his surprise. "Aren't you the least bit frightened by me?"

Leaning onto the bar, she purses her lips and searches his face. "Should I be, Lathe?" She bites down on her straw and waits for him to answer, her inky eyes lifted to his.

"Why did you come over here if you knew I was watching you?"

"Well, because either you were too shy to say hello and I thought I'd give you a chance, or because you were waiting to kidnap me in the parking lot and you're much less likely to kidnap me if I've seen your face and others can identify us together." Absently, she twists a lock of hair around a long-manicured finger. "How do you know Emily?"

He's stunned by her, by this girl who has been skipping and giggling around tipsy all evening. But as he looks at her up close, her eyes are focused, and her thoughts are clear. He realizes she holds her liquor better than most. She brings the straw to her lips and Lathe's eyes lower to her mouth, a tiny knowing smile curving those luscious lips.

"Lathe," she says, placing her drink back onto the bar with an eyebrow raised in question. "You're staring at me."

That breaks him out of his thoughts, his mind taking an unexpected detour. He clears his throat. "Emily and I seem to know a lot of the same people. We've never actually met, but I'm curious to know what she's like."

Ashley confesses, "You kinda remind me of her for some

reason. Work isn't fun without her. She was always coming to me with her guy problems. She's like, a hottie magnet. Is that why you're asking about her? Because I gotta say, that ship has sailed. I tried to steer her in the right direction. I think she made the right decision in the end, but oh my God, it breaks my heart to see it all fall apart. I feel so bad for Ben, poor guy. Do you know him?"

"Yes, we met recently."

"You probably couldn't even tell that he's totally heartbroken."

"Was she involved with anyone other than Ben?"

She purses her lips, twirling that lock of hair again. It's distracting. Lathe is half tempted to reach out and tug it out of her hand, but he sits back, waiting for her response.

She untangles her fingers from her hair and taps a finger against her lips. "You know, it's hard to say."

"What about Patrick?" he supplies.

"Aren't you the little gossip," she giggles. "I think Patrick is more interested in her than she was in him. She slapped him when he kissed her."

Lathe likes what she's telling him, and he hasn't needed to use any mental persuasion at all. Ashley is an open book.

Ashley continues, "She seems like the only person who could resist him. Well, I guess her and Morgan, but that's only because they're cousins."

"Cousins?" Clever, Ben kept that little tidbit to himself. He told Lathe that Patrick met Morgan this past summer and they became close, but he neglected to say they were related. That meant Patrick had family that no one knew about.

"Yeah, they only met this summer. I guess their parents had a falling out or something."

"Are they related on her mother's side or father's side?"

"I don't know."

"Ashley, you have been very helpful." He throws money on the bar and stands to leave.

She catches his hand. "That's it? I'm helpful, and now you just leave?"

"Yes, that's generally how this works."

She lets go of his hand. "How what works?" She's scowling at him with uncertainty written all over her pouting face.

"Er . . ."

"Oh my God, you just wanted information about Emily, didn't you?"

"Yes."

"You said you haven't met her. Are you in love with her too or something?"

"Or something."

Those inky eyes narrow to slits. "You're being incredibly vague."

With a huff he sits back on his stool, facing her as he peels the hood back from his head. He watches her eyes travel up his scalp where the scarring rendered the left side completely hairless. He shaves the rest of his head to keep a consistent look. He leans in. "Ashley, do I look like the type of person who needs to explain myself?"

She squares her shoulders. "How would I know? You haven't told me a damn thing about yourself. I could list the number of things I know about you on one hand."

"Firstly," she holds up one finger, "you stalk girls in bars even though you look as if you'd rather be anywhere else." She holds up a second finger. "You're super embarrassed about your scars, which only make you look like a badass." A third finger joins the others. "You ordered whiskey even though you think it's disgusting." Four fingers. "You—along with every male I know— are a bit obsessed with Emily." Her thumb pops out and she wags her fingers. "And you're attracted to me, even though you're pretending not to be because it makes you feel . . . ashamed, maybe." She drops her hand. "I can't tell what that look is."

Pegged. She has him pretty well pegged. She wasn't as ditzy

as she let on. "You're not what I expected. I'll give you that." He stands from his stool and begins walking away.

She jumps off her stool and after a few strides, her hand catches his arm. She complains, "That's not fair! You got your answers. Can't you give me mine?"

He spins to face her. "What answers?"

"The least you can do is tell me what happened to you? I bet it hurt like hell."

"You paid for your hair. I paid for my face."

She grants him a laugh. It's a beautiful sound. He breathes it in, wraps it around himself, curls it into a ball and tucks it away for safe keeping.

"How 'bout an honest answer? Unless you're afraid," she taunts.

She's goading him and he knows she's doing it, but he can't stop himself from grabbing her arm and leading her to a booth not far out of their path. It's a bit quieter over here, so he doesn't have to shout to be heard. She sits on the opposite side of the table and pulls her legs up on the bench beneath her, sitting cross-legged like a child. Her eyes come up like twin shadows peering into the light. She looks hopeful and excited to know about him. He tries to convince himself that she's just morbidly curious, but he's holding his breath, unsure why she affects him as much as she does.

He looks her square in the eye and takes sick pleasure in telling her the brutality of his story. "I grew up taking care of my ill mother, but when I turned fifteen, my father was going to take custody of me. He was a terrible man and I didn't want to go. About a month before my birthday, I was at a bonfire. At the end of the night, it was just me standing there watching this fire die when I realized I'd rather burn alive than live with my father. I had been poking at the fire, so the metal rod was already in my hand. Everyone would assume it was an accident, that I tripped and landed on the burning rod."

Ashley accuses, "No you didn't!"

"No, I didn't. My girlfriend was there, and I wouldn't do it in front of her, but it's where I first came up with the idea. It wasn't until the following week when the perfect opportunity presented itself.

"I was a busboy at a local diner, and we were particularly short staffed one morning. My boss got a call from the school saying his daughter was sick and he needed to pick her up. The school was just around the corner, so the trip would only take a few minutes. He asked me to keep an eye on things for him. I horribly abused his trust because the second he was gone, I got to work. I wanted to disfigure myself so my dad wouldn't want me. The pain was excruciating. I passed out as the burning oil ate my skin and woke in a hospital bed. No one ever questioned if it was an accident, because what kind of person would do that to their own face?"

Ashley leans back in her seat. "You are the craziest person I've ever met. How could you do that to yourself?"

"There was no other choice. My mother depended on me. She would die without me, and I knew my father wouldn't want me if I were disfigured. The recovery was more painful than I imagined, but my mother is alive today because I look like this."

Ashley's eyes glisten as they watch him. "I can't tell if that's the sweetest or most horrifying story I've ever heard. Is any of it true?"

"All of it is true."

She leans forward, resting her arms in front of her on the table. "But how did you do it? I mean, like, how did you physically, mentally, emotionally have the courage to inflict that kind of pain on yourself? Weren't you afraid of going blind?"

"I can't say I was thinking very clearly. I only know that I was desperate enough to risk it."

"And your father refused to take you because of this?" She waves at his face.

"He took one look at me and his disgust couldn't have been more obvious."

"So, your goal was to become disfigured?"

He nods.

She shakes her head, saying, "It didn't work."

Lathe laughs until he realizes she's saying exactly what she's thinking.

"You didn't make yourself ugly, Lathe. You made yourself stand out more, but this . . ." She leans forward reaching out to touch his face.

"Don't touch me!" he says, leaning away from her. He flips his hood back over his scalp and rests his head against the back of the booth.

She drops her hand and settles back on her bench, but her eyes are all over him. She uses them to caress his face, inspecting the grooves and ridges in the discolored skin across his cheek and up to his forehead where his hoodie now covers his scalp. Her eyes dip to his scarred lip and then down his jaw and neck. Her eyes drop to his chest and then flick back up to his eyes. "Do you have scars everywhere or just your face?"

He is so thrown off. He doesn't know how to react to her, so he does what he knows. He compels her. She's very compliant with no idea he's compelling her. It's clear she has no knowledge of the Olvasho like the others. She is a friend to his half-sister, a self-proclaimed bitch, a bleach blonde who uses too many *likes* in her sentences, and who makes him uncomfortable with her invasive questions. Once he realizes she's already given him all the information he needs, he wipes the memory of him from her mind, stands from the booth, and leaves.

LATHE LOOKS into Morgan more closely and quickly finds her parent's address. He drives out to the country house, feeling bitterness as he sees the lake out behind the house. These people live such a different life than he does. He parks in the driveway and decides to go up to the front door. Before he reaches the door, he senses another Olvasho. The porch light flicks on, and a middle-aged man steps out the door.

"What's the meaning of this?" Tom asks, closing his arms over his chest as he takes in Lathe's size and scars.

"Thomas, I take it," Lathe says, stepping onto the porch. "My name is Lathen Andrew Vallor. Before you jump to conclusions, I only included my surname so you would know it's pointless to fight me. Sky bred me for strength, but I am nothing like my father. I mean you no harm. I have questions and so long as you answer them, I won't report you to the council."

"You say you're nothing like him, but you're threatening me."

"Threatening to expose you is a bit different than murdering you and stealing the souls of everyone you love. You see the difference?"

"The rumors are true, then. He discarded you because of your scars."

"Yes, but it seems he was determined to find my sister."

Tom pales. "You know about her!"

"I know she's from Valla lineage. I know that your estranged nephew, Patrick—Sky's second in command—discovered her and led her to Sky. I know your daughter, Morgan, is Emily's best friend and now she is living with Patrick. There are a lot of things I know, but I was hoping you could clear a few things up before I take any of this information back to the council."

"You've kept it from them?" Hope blossoms through his expression.

"The council is flawed but necessary. Their reaction to things can be harsh, so I wanted to scope things out first," says Lathe. "After all, she is my half-sister."

"She *was* your half-sister," Tom corrects. "She isn't anymore."

Lathe sighs. "I was afraid of that."

Tom invites, "Come inside and we'll talk."

CHAPTER SEVENTEEN ~

THE NEXT DAY ~

MORGAN PULLS UP in front of Alec's ranch style house and immediately regrets agreeing to come. His home is on the smaller side, but it's only ever been Alec and his mom, and his mom was usually working. Morgan spent a lot of time here over the years, and she never considered the size of the house, but tonight it feels too small, especially if Sadie is going to be here.

Taking a deep breath, she steps out of her car and walks right up to the front door. She rings the doorbell and steps into the house, the same way she's done for years, but everything about tonight feels different. She walks the short hall into the living room where Ben and Gavin look up from their video game, greeting, "Hey, Morgan."

Seeing them calms her nerves a bit. "Gavin, I didn't know you'd be here this weekend."

"Yep. Alec would kick my ass if I didn't come home for his birthday."

"Morgan, is that you?" Alec's mom, Cindy, calls from the kitchen.

Morgan walks around the corner into the kitchen and finds Alec's mom at the island adding the finishing touches to his birthday cake. The wide bottom tier is decorated with fondant icing and appears to be wearing pinstripes in multiple shades from navy to baby blue. The white top tier is thinner but taller. The navy fondant suspenders stand out atop the white buttoned-down dress shirt. A frosted navy bowtie adorns the top and Cindy is pealing navy candy buttons from a sheet of wax paper and placing them delicately in a row under the bowtie.

"Hi, Cindy."

"I thought I heard you in there." Cindy smiles, wiping her hands before greeting Morgan with a hug. "I heard you were back in town. What have you been up to?"

"I'm working at the hospital and taking classes. Homework has been eating up all my spare time lately."

"Well, it's so nice to see you. I'm glad you could make it tonight." Her voice turns to a whisper, "And if I'm being honest, I miss having a girl around here I can talk to. These girls Alec dates, well . . . they aren't you."

"I heard he was getting serious with Sadie," Morgan says, hoping she'll tell her that it isn't true.

Worry wrinkles Cindy's forehead and she sighs before saying, "You know, I feel like I did the best I could with him, Morgan. He just doesn't think with his head a lot of times, and the types of girls he dates, well, I don't think he even likes them. I want the best for him, but no, never mind. I shouldn't be talking to you about this. I'm sorry, Morgan. I'm just blabbing away."

Morgan has a lot of follow up questions she wants to ask, but they are already in dangerous territory, so she says, "So what about you? Have you been seeing anyone?"

Cindy says, "I don't know how people find the time. Between the diner and my cleaning business, I'm too busy. I barely see Alec as it is, and once he starts working for his father, I'm afraid I'll never see him."

Morgan chokes. "He's going to work for his dad?"

Cindy nods. "He didn't tell you? I'm not happy about it, but it will be good experience and it pays well. He'll need more money now that he's moving out."

Morgan blinks. "He's moving out, too?"

Cindy's face shows concern. "Oh, honey, he hasn't told you yet?"

"No." Morgan recalls their conversation from the night before, realizing he hadn't really spoken about himself at all. "I guess, he didn't mention it last night and we've barely seen each other in the last few months."

"He and Sadie are planning on getting an apartment together. They . . ."

The doorbell chimes and Cindy pauses. From the living room, Gavin yells, "Come in!"

Morgan feels like her heart has been ripped out. He is going to move in with Sadie.

When they don't hear the door open, Cindy rolls her eyes, saying, "I guess they aren't going to get it. Could you? I'm almost done here, and Alec should be here any second."

"Of course." Morgan walks back through the living room where Gavin and Ben are immersed in their video game. She feels numb as she heads down the hall and opens the door to find Ashley and Jeremy standing on the stoop.

"Hey," Morgan greets, "I didn't know you guys were coming."

"We're just swinging by. I needed to see you." Ashley explains, "After the party last week, I wasn't sure if you'd be here."

"Why?" Morgan asks, inviting them in.

As they enter, Ashley whispers, "You know, because the texts you sent to Alec."

Morgan tilts her head. "What texts?"

"Oh my God, do you not remember? Why do you think I've been checking up on you all week?"

"Checking up on me? Is that what those texts were about?" Morgan asks, pulling out her phone.

"Duh!"

Morgan scrolls through her texts and sighs, "Ashley, there is nothing here. I wasn't texting him."

They are gathered in the front hall when Ben enters from the living room. "Hey guys, are you staying?"

From the living room, Gavin yells out, "Alec is on his way."

There is a weird tension in the air, and finally, Jeremy breaks away from Ashley and heads toward the living room, saying, "I heard there would be cake."

Ashley and Ben are staring at one another as if trying to communicate telepathically.

"What's going on?" Morgan asks. "Why are you guys acting weird?"

"You deleted them," Ashley accuses Ben.

Ben says, "Ashley, let's talk about this later. Now isn't the time."

"Ben?" Morgan questions. "Was I texting Alec last Saturday?"

Ben rubs his face, his jaw tight with tension. "Morgan . . . it wasn't a big deal. I told Alec to ignore them. You were drunk and I didn't want you to be embarrassed or start acting weird around us."

"Ben?" Her face falls. "What did the texts say?"

He thinks about lying but concedes to tell half-truths instead. "You told him that he's an idiot and that you like him."

"Is that all?"

"Basically."

"I . . . I can't believe you deleted them." But she can. He was trying to protect her because he probably knew Alec and Sadie were moving in together and she had made a complete ass out of herself.

Ben steps forward. "Morgan, I'm sorry." He tries to pull her in for a hug, but she pushes away.

"It's . . . it's okay. I get it. I guess . . . I don't know. I'm gonna go help Cindy with the cake." She walks away, leaving Ben and Ashley standing by the door.

As soon as Morgan reaches the kitchen, Cindy is placing the fondant cake out for display. Morgan knew the woman was talented, but she has outdone herself this time.

"Wow, Cindy, that looks amazing! Alec is gonna love it."

"You know, I think it might be my favorite."

Morgan hears commotion at the front door and then. "Happy Birthday, Alec! Happy birthday, man!" And a repetition of good wishes until Alec and Sadie make their way back to the kitchen.

Alec rounds the corner and looks straight at the cake.

"Happy birthday, baby," Cindy greets, moving forward to hug her son.

Alec's eyes go soft as he wraps his mom in his arms, whispering, "Momma."

Morgan swoons. She loves the way Alec is with his mother. He clearly has a huge soft spot for the woman who gave birth to him. She's been a single mom from the moment she found out she was pregnant, and although Alec knows his father, the man had never been involved. Cindy never even asked for child support, which is why she works two jobs and in her spare time makes cakes for fun and for extra spending money.

Alec pulls away from his mother and his eyes fall on Morgan. "Happy birthday," she says in a small voice. She manages a smile, but embarrassment floods her. She thought that yesterday meant something. He looked at her differently last night, and now she knows why.

Alec pulls Morgan in for a hug while Sadie looks over the cake. "Oh my God, Miss Cole, this is so cute!"

"Thank you, Sadie. You know how Alec loves his suspenders."

Alec laughs, pulling away from Morgan at the same time Sadie says, "It almost looks too good to eat, but you know the baby wants some cake." She places her hands over her belly and Morgan fights a gasp.

"Sadie!" Alec reprimands with a scowl on his face.

"Oops," Sadie says sweetly, looking to Morgan.

Morgan holds herself together, all the pieces clicking in place, the reason Alec is still with Sadie, the reason they are moving out, the reason Alec is selling his soul to go work for the father he hates.

Morgan plasters on a smile, studiously avoiding Alec. Focusing on Sadie, she gathers as much enthusiasm as she can muster, saying, "Wow, that's exciting news!"

Sadie smiles, continuing to cradle her perfectly flat stomach, before giving Morgan a look filled with pity. Using a deceivingly sweet tone, she consoles, "Sorry, I tried to persuade Alec to tell everyone sooner to avoid an awkward situation like last weekend."

If looks could kill, Sadie would be dead several times over from the glare Alec gives her. "Sadie!"

"What?" she says innocently, "I just bet she wishes she would've known before saying all that stuff to you."

Morgan's cheeks are burning now. Sadie is out for blood and Morgan is not that kind of girl, but she knows the type. At this point, anything Morgan says Sadie will twist against her and she is already mortified.

Morgan doesn't respond to Sadie, but instead looks to Cindy, who by her expression knew about the baby, but appears to be putting together the pieces she's missing. Morgan says, "Cindy, it was great catching up with you. I'm going to call you about a cake for my dad."

"Of course, dear," Cindy says, wrapping her in another hug. "You have my number. Call me anytime."

Sadie makes a noise at the back of her throat, and Alec grabs her shoulder, pulling her from the room, and dragging her to his bedroom. As soon as they're gone, Cindy turns to Morgan, saying softly, "I'm so sorry. That girl is a bitch. I've tried to like her. I have, but I don't know what Alec is thinking, and now there's a baby. I think it's my fault. He doesn't want to run out on her like his father ran out on me, but that girl is bad news."

She reaches for Morgan's hand. "I had no idea that you and Alec—"

"It's nothing. Obviously, Sadie views me as a threat, but I . . . Alec and I are friends and I hope they can figure this thing out. I'm sorry, I'm just gonna go."

Cindy sighs, "I wish you didn't have to leave, but I understand. Give me a call about that cake, or anytime, really."

"I will." Morgan pulls away from the counter that's been holding her up and heads back through the living room full of silent friends who just overheard their entire conversation.

Gavin and Jeremy are sitting on the couch playing a two-person video game, acting like nothing is wrong while Ashley stands with her back to Ben's chest. Their hands interlace in front of Ashley like the two of them are posing for a prom photo. Except, their expressions are hostile. Ashley's face is red and unsmiling while Ben looks exasperated. He lets go of Ashley as soon as Morgan enters the room, and she realizes he was restraining her.

"I'm okay," Morgan reassures Ashley, "but I think it's best if I leave."

"I'm gonna kill that bitch," Ashley threatens.

"Maybe you should go, too," Morgan suggests. "We don't want to ruin his birthday."

Ashley shakes her head, fuming, "Sadie's the one who ruined it."

Morgan gives Ashley a hug. "Thanks for having my back."

"We all have your back," she says into her ear. "Alec is the one letting this happen."

Morgan pulls away, very quietly justifying, "She's having his baby."

"So!"

"Ashley, shh," Morgan hushes. "We'll talk later."

"I can blow off Jeremy and we can have a girl's night, or screw that, we can have a girl's night with Jeremy."

"Maybe another time. I'm going to go home and hang out

with Patrick." She turns to the guys on the couch, saying, "Bye, Gavin, bye, Jeremy. I'll see you guys later."

Jeremy waves from the couch while Gavin drops his controller and vaults over the back of the couch to give Morgan a bear hug. "Love you, Fletch. See you next time, hopefully without the drama," he teases.

Morgan gives a self-deprecating laugh while Gavin leaps back over the couch to pick up his discarded controller, complaining, "Dude, you're cheating!"

"I'll walk you out," Ben offers to Morgan.

Ashley is still standing there looking pissed.

"Promise me you won't make this worse," Morgan says to Ashley.

"I make no promises, but I'll try," she agrees.

Morgan gives her a look, saying, "Ashley—"

"Fine," she huffs, "Jeremy, we gotta go."

"Give me a minute," he says, staring at the TV, his fingers moving quickly on the controller.

Ben walks Morgan to the door, whispering, "I'm sorry. I didn't know Sadie knew about the texts."

She turns to him. "Did you know about the baby?"

"I didn't find out until the other day and I wanted to tell you, but I didn't think it was my place. It needed to come from him, and I guess—"

"It doesn't matter, Ben. I'm the one who sent the texts, and even if I knew, I can't say that I wouldn't have sent them anyway. It's my fault. You already went above and beyond by taking care of me that night." With a sigh, she asks, "Did I do anything else that I don't remember?"

Ben looks to the side, before revealing, "You told me the real reason you left Florida."

She sighs, and her eyes fall closed.

He grabs her hand and squeezes, saying, "You also told me that we would make a perfect couple, you know if we weren't in love with other people."

Morgan laughs, "Wow, I really shouldn't drink. I mean, I can't say my logic was necessarily wrong, but I don't feel that way about you, buddy."

"That makes two of us, but I do care about you, Morgan, and if you need anything, I'm here for you." Opening the door, he offers, "Do you want me to take you home?"

"No, you're his best friend. You need to be here for his birthday. Don't worry about me. I'm fine. Love you, Ben," she says, leaning in for a quick hug. He places a kiss into her hair before letting her go.

She leaves the house, but before she reaches her car, she hears, "Morgan! Wait!" She turns to see Alec running after her.

"Alec, I'm fine," she reassures him, placing a hand on his chest, to keep him from coming closer. "I guess I sent you some texts last week, but I don't remember them. I'm sorry. I don't even know exactly what I said. I didn't mean to upset Sadie or be the reason you can't enjoy your birthday."

"Morgan." His eyes burn into hers. "I'm sorry about Sadie."

She doesn't know what he means, sorry she's pregnant? Sorry she's a bitch? Sorry he's with her?

He clarifies, "She says things without thinking sometimes."

Harsh laughter escapes Morgan. "Don't apologize for her, Alec. She knows exactly what she's doing and obviously felt the need to stake her claim. I just wish she wouldn't have made such a spectacle out of me, but I guess I kinda did that to myself."

"You didn't," he argues.

Morgan continues, "I don't know how we spoke for so long yesterday and none of this came up. You're moving. You're going to work for your dad. You're having a baby. I don't even know what's going on in your life anymore. I know I'm your oldest friend, but maybe our friendship has run its course."

His face falls. "Fletch?" he says, stepping forward.

"I shouldn't have been here tonight, Alec." A tear falls and she quickly brushes it away. "I don't belong here anymore." She turns and walks toward her car.

"Morgan, wait."

She pauses with her back to him. He keeps using her real name, and it hurts because she wants it so much. She wants him so much.

"Sadie was there when I got your messages. She read them before I even knew you sent them. I . . . I wouldn't have shared them. It wasn't like that."

Morgan walks around to her driver's side, letting the dark camouflage her tears.

"I don't want to lose you, Fletch. I told her that I wouldn't lose you. You're too important to me."

She looks at him over the top of her car, her lips trembling "Goodnight, Alec. Happy birthday."

She feels like she is saying goodbye for the last time, and the thought makes her tears come more quickly. Alec doesn't say anything as she climbs into her car, but she's never seen him look so sad. She forces her eyes forward as she drives away, but when she looks in her review mirror, he's still standing in his yard watching her drive out of his life.

CHAPTER EIGHTEEN ~

SINCE THE MOMENT Patrick met Emily, she had been unraveling everything, undoing all he had worked so hard for. After they disembarked from their Fourth of July boat ride, he strolled away as if he were still in control of the situation, but it was a lie, like everything he had been told. If Emily would have killed him on the boat—the way he had planned—he would not be torn between his duty to Sky and what he knew in his heart was right about Emily.

"Patrick," Uncle Tom called across the lawn after he'd left Emily on the beach with Morgan.

Patrick looked up, feeling lost and angry at how he had let everything get so out of hand. She was making him question every single thing he was taught, everything he believed in. He was losing control, becoming soft. She was more dangerous than anything he'd ever dealt with, yet he wanted to cradle her in his arms and protect her from anyone who would want to harm a hair on her head. She was making him careless. He tried to gather his calming aura as he walked towards his uncle.

Tom clapped a hand on Patrick's shoulder and took in his faded misty eyes, saying, "She got to you, didn't she?"

"What?" Patrick asked, feeling unusually perplexed.

"Oh, come on, you've gotta realize it by now. She's the last Valla blood. And you aren't going to tell a soul."

Patrick glared at his uncle. "You knew all this time and you didn't report it?"

"What's there to report? She's just a girl," Tom scolded. "Besides, hasn't she proven it to you, yet? Valla doesn't mean demon. They are not interchangeable and the sooner you realize that, the better."

"How dare you!" Patrick breathed, "I've kept you safe all these years. I could've easily reported you for hiding my mother!"

"I was hiding you, too!" his uncle said. "Or have you forgotten that? Your mother helped a Valla, something you could be accused of yourself, Patrick. After meeting Emily, do you really think she is what they say she is?"

"It doesn't matter what I think. She is a Valla!" Patrick said, still feeling weak from his encounter with Emily.

Tom pulled his phone out of his pocket and held it out to Patrick. "Here. Go ahead, call them. Tell them what you've uncovered."

Patrick glanced down at the offered phone. He looked up again. Tom's eyes were staring straight back, calling Patrick's bluff. Shit, his uncle could see right through him. Patrick hadn't gotten his strength back enough to hide his emotions from another of his kind. The only reason Emily hadn't seen it was because she was just as weak.

"Do you want me to dial for you?" Tom continued.

Patrick pushed the phone away and moved past him without a word. He walked around for a while trying to clear his mind. He ended up on the other side of the lake sitting next to the weeping willow where he and Emily had sat not so long ago. While he watched the sunlight sink below the horizon, he made his decision, knowing it would be the dumbest thing he would ever do, but he couldn't turn her in, not yet, not now.

The apartment door opens, snapping Patrick out of his memory. He knows he needs to stop reminiscing, and he blames his lack of focus on his lack of sleep. Morgan walks through to the kitchen counter and drops her keys and purse. Patrick watches the emotions pour out of her in thick waves of indigo, the colors representing disdain and despair as she fights for control over her feelings.

She turns to face Patrick who stands from his spot on the sofa. As soon as they lock eyes, Morgan's face falls and tears rain down. Patrick walks the short distance and pulls her into his shoulder, saying, "I'm sorry, Morgan."

She sniffles and pushes out of his embrace, looking up with accusing eyes. "Patrick, you knew, didn't you?"

He grimaces. "I found out last night when I saw Alec at the coffee shop."

"Why didn't you tell me?"

"It wasn't my place to tell you."

"Since when do you honor that kind of thing?" she asks.

"Since my cousin taught me how to function as a normal human being."

"I'm serious Patrick. Wasn't your place? I get when Ben says that because Alec is his best friend, but you? Why didn't you warn me before I left tonight? I had no idea what I was walking into. You said you would protect me!"

"Yes, from danger. Emotional distress over your love interest hardly qualifies as danger."

She steps back. "Are you really that indifferent?"

"What would you have me do, Morgan? Manipulate him into breaking it off with his baby mama? Would that make you feel better? You knew this would end in disaster. Emily told you Alec would break your heart. And while I can alter his mind and make him lust for you, I can't change his heart."

"I wasn't asking you to change or manipulate anyone, but thank you for explaining how the heart works," she growls. "You could have warned me about the baby. I thought you at least would do that much for me." She takes off her coat, throwing it over a kitchen chair before walking into the living room. She stands with her hands on her hips, too angry to sit. After a moment she jerks toward Patrick, accusing, "Is this because we went to find Emily behind your back? Are you still angry with me?"

Patrick rubs his temples. "No." He picks up his laptop from the coffee table and sits back down on the sofa. "You would be hurting, regardless. This way Alec got to see how he hurt you. Now, if we're done with your blubbering, I'd like to tell you what I found."

"Done?" She throws her arms out. "Oh my God, Patrick, you don't understand how feelings work, do you? I was not only heartbroken but completely humiliated tonight."

"Morgan, I'm sorry, but before you continue blaming me, I need to tell you what I found on Emily."

Morgan wipes her tears away, momentarily distracted. "You found something?"

"I picked up on her trail again." He spins his laptop around to face her.

Morgan leans in, eyeing the security footage that is playing on a loop. Emily is walking into a hotel lobby.

"Where did you get this?"

"I searched her past patterns and found that she was commuting the hour from Grand Rapids to Grand Haven to take the ferry to Chicago. She ghosted in Grand Rapids, but she's still doing something in Chicago."

"When is this footage from?"

"Tuesday?"

"This past Tuesday?" Morgan says with excitement.

"Yes, it's still a few days old but—"

"Patrick," she says, "this is amazing. You found her."

They stare at the screen for a moment with all the thoughts and words floating aimlessly around inside their heads.

Without looking up, Patrick says, "I'm sorry about the baby. And I'm sorry you love someone you can't be with."

"I'm sorry I blamed you." Morgan points to the screen. "This is more important. Finding Emily is more important than my love life."

Patrick gives her a warm smile and says, "Go grab your computer. I have some leads for you to look up."

"Awesome." Morgan runs to her room to grab her laptop.

MORGAN AND PATRICK are mid-search when Patrick's spine goes straight and he looks to the front door, saying, "Ashley's here."

"What?" Morgan looks up from her screen and then grabs her phone from the coffee table. "Oh, crap! She kept texting me earlier, so I put my phone on *Do not disturb*. I have sixteen texts and five calls. Oops." She looks up, her expression dripping with guilt, just as Ashley bangs on the door.

Morgan closes her computer and sets it on the table before jumping up to get the door. As she opens it, she says, "Ashley, I'm sorry. I didn't see—"

Ashley pushes past her. "I don't care, woman! I have to pee!" She rushes down the hall and slams the bathroom door behind her.

"Okay?" Morgan closes the door and leans against it. "So much for her being worried."

Patrick chuckles from his spot on the sofa. "I don't think her need to urinate diminishes her worry for you. It was just a bit more pressing."

Morgan steps away from the door and joins Patrick in the living room again. Ashley comes out after a few minutes and settles down in one of the lounge chairs. She tucks her feet up under her and grabs the throw blanket from behind her to wrap around her shoulders. Once she's settled, she looks to Morgan. "I was worried about you, but you seem much better now than you did earlier. I'm still going to stay with you tonight to keep an eye on you."

Morgan laughs. "Because you're concerned?"

"Yes. Of course. And also, one of my roommates broke up

with her boyfriend last night, and they just got back together, so I cannot go home tonight!" She pouts. "Please don't make me go home tonight."

"Of course, you can stay here. Right, Patrick?" They both look to him expectantly.

Patrick glances up from his computer. "She's not staying in my room."

Ashley focuses on his sapphire eyes. They remind her of something. What it is, she couldn't say. It doesn't matter. At least she doesn't have to go home tonight.

"Whoa, wait!" Patrick's eyes shoot back up. "Ashley, what were you just thinking about?"

She looks confused by his question.

He continues, "Just a second ago when you looked at me, what was going through your head?"

"Umm . . ." She looks to Morgan who appears just as interested in her answer. "Maybe you guys shouldn't live together. You're becoming weird!"

Morgan laughs, but Patrick's eyes are glued to Ashley with such intensity that she shifts uneasily in her seat. "Right now, I'm thinking you remind me of the weird guy I met at the bar last night."

Patrick's body relaxes and he grins. "Please elaborate."

"He was . . ." Ashley pauses, purses her lips and her eyes wander up to the ceiling as she focuses on the previous night. "Maybe I was tipsier than I thought. I can't seem to, like, remember very clearly, but I know I met a guy. He was staring at me and . . . his face. He had an awful scar." Her brows scrunch in concentration. "His name is Lathe. I remember because I thought it was weird."

Morgan jerks her head to Patrick who is wearing a slightly amused grin. "Ashley, did he ask you questions about anyone?"

Her eyes jerk to him. "How did you know?"

Patrick asks, "Who was he asking about?"

She squeezes her eyes closed and rubs her temple, eventually shaking her head in defeat. "I don't know."

"But you remember him?"

"Yeah." She points to her face, saying, "He has a huge scar on one side of his face, extending up into his scalp, and God, his eyes. They're so blue." She points to Patrick. "Even bluer than yours."

He raises a brow, noting that Ashley hasn't come on to him at all in the short time she has been here. Maybe she has a new crush. "Ashley, do you remember what you told him?"

"Why is everybody asking me weird questions? I get the feeling you already know who I'm talking about. I think he said he knew you. Did you put him up to this? Is that why he was acting so strange?"

"I do know him, but I didn't put him up to it," he says, as his fingers start moving on the keyboard and his eyes lower back to the screen, finished with the conversation.

But Ashley isn't finished. "He seemed surprised that Morgan was your cousin."

Patrick's eyes flick up to her, followed more slowly by his chin. In a hurry, he closes the computer, sliding it onto the coffee table as he jumps up from the sofa.

"Morgan, have you talked to your dad today?" he asks while grabbing his keys from the counter. When he hears her resounding, *"No!"* he grabs the doorknob and rushes out of the apartment. The door closes with a bang, and Morgan and Ashley stare at each other.

Ashley curls the blanket tighter around her. "What the hell was that?"

Morgan shrugs, hiding her worry behind a joke. "You're right, living together has made us weird."

MORGAN IS wide awake in bed with her thoughts wandering back to Alec. The look he gave her as she left him standing in his front yard has her crying silent tears. She wipes them away as they fall, but her pillow captures the evidence. She flips it over, thinking she has her tears under control when she hears the apartment door. She carefully slides out of her bed, so she doesn't wake Ashley. She makes her way out to the hall and finds Patrick waiting for her.

"So?" she asks expectantly.

His back is leaning against the wall with his shoulders slumped and his arms folded tightly across his chest, radiating tension. "Your dad is okay. Lathe went to your parent's house last night looking for him. He wanted answers and your dad gave them to him. He said Lathe had most of it figured out and your dad filled in the remaining pieces. The only good news is that Lathe is keeping things to himself for the time being, but we don't know how long that will last. Lathe may have promised he would keep your dad's secret, but the council may find out on their own."

"His secret?"

"Your dad changed his identity twenty-five years ago to get away from the Olvasho so he could lead a normal life without their interference. They think he's dead."

"What!" Morgan tries to process this new information. It's another huge secret her dad kept from her. She thought they were done with secrets. She shakes her head and gets back to the topic at hand. "So, what is Lathe after exactly?"

"Emily," he says simply. He runs a hand through his hair and sighs. "He wants to know what we're dealing with. He wants to know where Emily is, how she managed to kill Sky and free those souls, and he wants to know if Emily will kill us all. I think I'm going to have to talk to him."

"Is that safe?"

He sighs, his eyes falling closed. He turns to head to his room. "It's something I'll think about while I try not to drown in my sleep tonight."

Morgan crosses her arms over her chest. "That's not funny."

He leans his forehead against the wall, keeping his back to her and says, "I'm sorry, Morgan. I'm exhausted. Let's talk tomorrow."

"Sleep safe, Patrick."

He smiles as he steps into his room.

CHAPTER NINETEEN ~

November 4th ~

Despite the absence of an invitation, Ashley insists on going to Samantha's bridal shower. Morgan tries to tell her it's inappropriate, but Ashley claims Samantha won't care as long as she brings a gift. Patrick was already tagging along, so Morgan decides why not add another.

The three of them pile into Morgan's car with Patrick at the wheel. Months ago, Patrick bought a silver utility van to replace the BMW he beat to hell. Morgan thought it an odd choice, questioning his decision in the beginning, but the van was handy moving things into the apartment. The previous night before Ashley showed up, Patrick told Morgan he had a mattress and all sorts of electronics in the back of the van in case he would have to go on a road trip to find Emily.

The three of them pull up to the hotel and Patrick drops the girls at the door before parking the car. The lobby is regal with an elegant sign to point them in the direction of the bridal brunch. Morgan and Ashley enter the dining hall, greeted by rich hardwood floors and a dozen white linen covered tables surrounded by gold Chiavari chairs. Fragrant white roses decorate each table, filling the room with a fresh floral scent. They are nearly the first to arrive, so Samantha spots them right away.

"Oh my God!" Samantha gasps. She rushes over to hug Morgan and then turns to Ashley.

"Hi, I'm Ashley. I hope you don't mind that I'm here. I begged Morgan to bring me. I'm a friend of Emily's, and I was dying to meet you."

"I'm glad you came, Ashley. It's nice to meet you. I haven't met many of Emily's friends."

Morgan says, "My cousin, Patrick, is parking the car. He should be in any minute."

"Thank you for persuading him to come."

"I really didn't have to convince him. He wants to help."

Something distracts Samantha, and she places a hand over her lips. Morgan looks behind her to see Patrick walking into the room.

Ashley whispers, "It should be a sin for him to wear that suit. He's way too distracting."

Samantha makes a noise of agreement while Morgan rolls her eyes. She acknowledges his good looks, but she also knows how much pain he hides beneath his charming smile and handsome body. Most of the time she wants to reach out and take his hand in an attempt to help him carry his burdens.

Samantha smiles radiantly at Patrick and blurts, "You're a psychic, aren't you?"

Inwardly Patrick cringes, disgusted by the Olvasho who prey on desperate people by posing as psychics. He smiles, offering his hand. "It seems you're the one with the psychic abilities."

"Not really," she says, placing her hand in his. "You remind me of another psychic I knew. I don't really know how to explain."

"I don't like to label myself, but I do seem to have abilities that sometimes come in handy with finding missing people."

"You were friends with Emily?"

"I still consider her my friend. That's why I'm not giving up on her."

Samantha takes a staggering breath before saying, "Thank you." Then she glances at the table next to them. "Come, sit with me; let's talk before people get here."

The four of them sit around a circular table. Samantha turns to Patrick and asks, "Do you think you could help my dad? He's having trouble finding his way back to—"

"Samantha?" Dan approaches.

Samantha spins on her chair to face him. "Oh, Dan, I want you to meet some of Emily's friends. This is Ashley, Morgan, and Patrick. He's helping us find Emily."

Dan's eyes narrow on Patrick. "Is he now?"

"I am," Patrick says, with his alligator smile. "Would you like to join us?"

Samantha is oblivious to the tension. "I need to catch up with Grandma Willow. I'll stop back in a few," he says seamlessly while he glares at Patrick. He kisses Samantha on the cheek before walking away.

"You've got a good one there," Patrick comments to Samantha.

Samantha touches her cheek where he kissed her and seems to swoon, "I know."

Patrick looks to his cousin, then flicks his eyes to Ashley, communicating that he needs Ashley not to witness what's about to happen.

Morgan turns to Ashley and says, "Oh, I forgot the gift from my sister. It's in my trunk. Ashley, will you please get it for me? It's in a little silver box. It's either in the trunk or the back seat."

"No problem, I'm sure I can find it."

Patrick hands over the keys and Ashley walks away. Morgan turns back to the conversation between Samantha and Patrick.

He takes her hand in his, increasing his control with physical touch while maintaining close eye contact. He digs deep into her psyche until he finds a comfortable space to filter her deepest thoughts. Patrick quickly becomes overwhelmed by how much this young woman loves her family. Her pain feels tangible even before he digs into her mind.

"Samantha," he speaks, "you don't need to worry. You know in your heart Emily will come home, and her disappearance has nothing to do with you." He feels his words resonating in her mind. "Your dad would not want you to change the date of the wedding because of him. The guilt is not yours to bear. After today, you will no longer believe in psychics or feel responsible for what is happening to your family. Now, forget we had this conversation and go say *hello* to Grandma Willow."

He stares silently for a moment, taking extra special care of her before pulling away.

She doesn't seem to skip a beat. "Great to meet you, Patrick. Let me know if you find anything." She smiles. "I need to go say *hi* to Grandma Willow."

Soon she's gone and Patrick acknowledges Morgan's scowl. "You're the one who dragged me down here and now you're going to critique my tactics," Patrick complains.

"Have you ever done that to me?" she questions.

"Of course not." He reaches his hand out to graze her cheek. "You're family. You're much easier for me to manipulate."

She hits him with the back of her arm. "Don't you dare!"

"I promise you I have not and will not ever manipulate you with my mind unless you give me a reason."

"That was comforting right up until the end, Patrick."

Ashley drops the keys on the table next to Morgan. "I couldn't find your sister's gift. Maybe you left it at home. It sure as hell isn't in your car and it's freezing out there."

"I'm sorry, Ashley. I must have left it at the apartment. Thank you for looking."

Leah walks up to the table. "Hey, Morgan," she says while staring at Patrick.

"Leah," Morgan replies.

A coy smile plays on Patrick's lips as he looks up at Leah,

unveiling his most seductive grin. "Leah?" he says, coming to a stand.

Leah's eyes are huge as she watches him stand with lust in her eyes.

Patrick reaches out to her, gently pulling her hand into his. He presses a kiss against her knuckles, letting his lips linger, and with a sensual voice, he says, "My name is Patrick, I'm Morgan's cousin and a good friend of Emily's. I've heard so much about you."

Her eyes round when he says the bit about Emily, but then he wraps his arm around her shoulder and says, "I would love to have a private chat." His words soothe her worries, and just like that, he leads her away from the table.

Ashley is gawking. "What the hell was that?"

"Did Emily ever tell you about Leah?" Morgan offers.

"No, is she another girlfriend of Emily's that she didn't mention?"

"The opposite, actually. Leah has always been incredibly cruel to Emily."

"Then why the hell is she here?"

Morgan frowns. "Leah is Dan's sister. She'll be Sam's sister-in-law soon."

Ashley glares after Leah. "So why would Patrick . . . what's he doing?"

"I'm not sure I want to know." Morgan chews on her bottom lip as she watches the two together.

Ashley narrows her eyes at Patrick. "He's in love with her, you know . . . with Emily. He's, like, totally gone over her, isn't he?"

"Yes, I think he is."

"Yeah," Leah answers wistfully.

Patrick lifts a dark curl from Leah's shoulder. "You know Emily Burk?"

She tries to cover her disgust, but there is a glint of hatred in her eye. "Yeah . . . why?"

"I would like to know what she did to you to make you dislike her so much."

She's reluctant to answer and Patrick senses her embarrassment. "It's okay; you can trust me." He pulls her intimately close, giving her the persuasion she needs to tell him what he wants to know.

"She stole my seventh-grade boyfriend. Well, he was going to be my boyfriend, anyway. It was supposed to happen at my birthday party, but then Emily's mom died, and it totally ruined everything. He didn't even come to my party because he was feeling bad for her and she didn't even want him. I don't know why he likes her. I mean, she's not even cute, and she went crazy after her mom died. Her dad had to lock her up in a psych ward for weeks. She came back to school and it's like the whole school could only talk about how strong she was when really, we all knew she was just shy of the loony bin. I mean, are you kidding me! A lot of people have parents die and they don't make a scene."

Patrick gives an exaggerated frown. "You poor thing, you had it so rough."

"I know, right?" She bites her lip as she looks up at him.

"Did she ever say anything to you about any of your hate mail or the rumors you spread?" Patrick inquires, reaching out with his mind to take inventory of the room.

"She didn't have the guts to confront me. She made Ben do it for her. What a joke! She has him wrapped around her finger. It's a turnoff. I don't even like him anymore.

Patrick leans in, whispering, "Thank heavens you got over Ben when you did, you know, before he lost all of his money."

"Oh, I know!" Leah says, eating up every word he feeds her. "Poor Ben. I feel bad for him, really. She messed with his head and then she ran off and basically killed her dad. She's bad news. Samantha is better off without her."

"Is that so? I guess, I only knew Emily for a short time, but she left me with quite a different impression." Patrick slowly guides her toward one of the tables at the front of the room. "I believe this is your table," he says, pulling out a chair for her.

"I don't have to sit down, yet." She looks at him with confusion.

"I think you'd better sit down for this."

She looks confused, but she sits down in the proffered seat. He scoots her forward and leans down to whisper, "Sit tight, I'll be right back."

With a grin, he turns and taps on the shoulder of the woman a couple of steps away. She pivots to face him, and Patrick smiles pleasantly, although, what he wants to do is scrub away the fake tan and layers of makeup that hide such a beautiful face.

"Hello, Mrs. Young." He holds out his hand for her to place her dainty polished fingers in his palm. "My name is Patrick."

"Oh, please. It's Judy."

"Judy, I just had the pleasure of meeting your daughter. You two look so much alike, you could pass as sisters. Your husband is a lucky man."

Judy places a hand against her chest, his words causing her to blush. "Well, that's very kind of you to say."

"Just speaking the truth," Patrick says seamlessly. "Would you please join our table?" He directs her to Leah's table and pulls out a chair for Judy. "If you would have a seat, I believe you two have a few items to discuss."

Leah looks at him in confusion. "Aren't you going to join us?"

"No, this should be between the two of you. Leah, you should tell your mother what you told me about Emily. And please don't stop there. You want to confess everything you've done."

Leah looks betrayed, her mouth gaping while Patrick smiles and encourages, "Go on, you will feel better when it's over."

Leah turns to face her mother and unable to stop herself; she starts at the beginning. "Emily umm . . . stole my seventh-grade boyfriend . . ."

Patrick walks away, heading back to Morgan. As he slides into his seat next to her, he finds that she and Ashley are glaring at him. "Ladies, do we have a problem?"

Ashley leans forward, pointing in the direction of Leah and her mother. "What the hell was that?" Ashley crosses her arms on the table while Morgan takes a sip of her drink.

Patrick smirks. "I thought Leah might feel better with a clear conscience, so I persuaded her to tell her mother about all the ways she's treated Emily over the years."

Morgan chokes on her drink, and Ashley slaps her on the back while Patrick hands her a napkin.

Ashley looks up from Morgan's coughing fit and plants firm eyes on Patrick. "How the hell did you convince her to confess all of that to her mother? You only talked to her for, like five minutes. How can you be sure she's confessing anything?"

Patrick nods in Leah's direction. "Trust me, she's confessing."

Morgan finally stops coughing and takes another sip of her drink while all three of them stare toward Leah's table. Leah is wiping away tears while her mother looks shocked.

Ashley turns to Patrick, accusing, "What? Did you promise to go down on her in the bathroom or something?"

Morgan manages to swallow this time before bursting into laughter.

CHAPTER TWENTY ~

THOSE EYES. Crystalline blue eyes with specks of silver haunt Patrick throughout the day. And at night he hopes to find them staring back at him. He promised Morgan he would run from the ocean threatening to drown him, but he can no longer withstand the temptation. He stays in the sea as long as he can, praying for those crystalline eyes. He needs them, even knowing they could be his death.

The color of midnight surrounds him, and if it weren't for the waves shoving against his body, he would forget he was sinking in the freezing water. He doesn't fight the current from pulling him under. It's taking him to the only place he wants to be and the deeper he goes, the closer he is to those eyes. But with the depth comes the pressure constricting his chest. His lungs burn for oxygen, but he holds his breath and enjoys the stinging pressure as he pushes himself further into the abyss.

Something smooth caresses his skin and he turns to look for his sea enchantress. The mysterious beast is lurking in the waters next to him. Her bewitching eyes seem to glow as she nears him. Her lips don't move as she speaks to him. *"If you don't breathe, you will die."*

In his mind, there is no choice. He would rather die than lose focus on this glorious beast. It's taken so long to get her to reveal herself to him. He needs her.

"Patrick, I'm not going to let you die."

His enchantress swims closer, wrapping her aura around him just as the first compression hits his chest.

"Breathe, Patrick!"

A breath is forced upon him, causing him to gasp. His lungs fill with sea water as he reaches for his enchantress, but her crystal blue eyes are already fading into the dark sea.

"Oh, thank God!" Morgan calls, as Patrick sputters and gasps for air.

Patrick opens his eyes and wonders what happened to gravity as the world does summersaults beneath him. He squeezes his eyes shut, waiting for the room to stop spinning and the floor to stop shaking beneath his shivering body. He manages to catch his breath and opens his eyes to discover he's on his bedroom floor. Morgan is crouched over him; her image becomes solid, even as the room behind her continues to tilt and sway. His throat burns, and his body is wet and dripping on the carpet. Morgan helps him sit up as the room continues to whirl around them.

"Did you give me mouth to mouth?" he wheezes.

"You were turning blue, Patrick. I just saved your life."

Patrick doesn't respond. He keeps his head down and concentrates on breathing.

Morgan continues, "You were holding your breath, weren't you? You know if you inhale the water, you'll wake up, but you don't want to wake up, do you?"

"Are you watching me sleep now?" he sputters.

"Patrick, you made a promise to me!"

"Morgan, I'm in my bed. It's three in the morning. How did you know I wasn't breathing?"

She huffs, "Normally, I might beg you not to get mad at me,

but after this, I'm glad I installed an apnea mat in your mattress."

"You did what?"

"It tells me if you stop breathing for more than twenty-seconds and if I didn't put it there, you'd be dead. Are you trying to kill yourself?" she asks, cutting through the bullshit.

Patrick acknowledges he's let too much of his training slip away. Where he used to be meticulous, he's become negligent. Morgan, the most candid girl he knows, slipped something into his bed without his knowing. He's still pissed. "I can't believe you're asking me that again."

"You might be insulted, but I'm trying to understand."

"No, I don't want to die. It's hard to explain. There's something in my dream, a creature, she's . . . she's magnificent, and she comes closer every time, but I can't quite . . . It's like she is waiting for something. I'm so close to figuring it out."

"Is it death, because you were pretty close to figuring out what that's like."

"Morgan, I'm not some asshole thrill seeker. There's something there. I can't explain it, but this creature has these eyes, and I can feel her getting closer every time. I just have to—"

"Stay away! That's the only way you should end that sentence. You have to stay away from the sea monster trying to lure you in with her temptress eyes."

"It's not like that. It's almost as if I'm looking into the eyes of God."

"Good Lord! Do you even hear yourself? Do you think God would drown you in your sleep?"

"Morgan—"

"Patrick, you scared me tonight! I thought you were going to die!"

"I'm not going to die."

"I might not understand all of your Olvasho abilities, but I know you aren't invincible. Patrick, I need you. You." She presses the palm of her hand against his chest for emphasis. "Promise me you'll stop this."

He looks into those soft eyes of hers. She is the only person left on this earth to have faith in him. She loves him and he promised to protect her. As much as he needs to know what is lurking in his dreams, he needs Morgan more.

"I'll stop, Morgan. I promise."

CHAPTER TWENTY-ONE ~

STILL UNDECIDED IF she wants to go inside, Morgan shivers against the icy November winds. Deciding she has nothing to lose, she ducks inside the café. She moves forward to take a spot in the long line as she looks around for the guy who invited her here.

She doesn't know his name, but she keeps running into him at the campus library. They've been exchanging glances for weeks and today before he left the library, he asked her to meet him here. She gave him a non-committal maybe and he left. She notices the handsome stranger at the far end of the counter, waiting for his meal. She searches the menu scrawled in chalk behind the counters as she unwinds her scarf.

A person behind the counter calls the name *Preston*, and her library friend steps forward to pick up the tray with his food. He turns to find a spot to eat and sees Morgan. He smiles and walks towards her, saying, "You came!"

She isn't entirely sure she made the right choice, but he has a great smile and she grins back at him. "I've never been here before." She looks back at the menu. "What's good here?"

"Everything."

"What did you get?" she asks, peeking at his tray.

"Today, I ordered the quiche. Usually, I order the pulled pork or the veggie wrap. Tough decisions. Whatever you do decide, I hope you'll come sit with me."

"Sure."

After she orders and her food is ready, she finds his table and sits across from him. He has a laptop open next to him, which he closes and pushes aside as soon as she sits.

"You got the veggie wrap. You won't regret it. It's delicious."

"I think I might be more excited about the fries," she admits, picking one up. "So, you're a student?" She pops the fry in her mouth.

"Yeah, I'm a senior. My name is Preston. What about you?"

"Morgan. I'm a sophomore in the nursing program."

"Nursing is a great career choice. Do you know what type of nursing you want to do when you're finished with school?"

"There are a lot of great options. I guess I'll narrow them down as I go. What about you? What are you in school for?"

"Architecture."

"That sounds interesting. What kind of architecture are you planning to do?"

"The kind that pays well."

Morgan laughs, "Well, that's one way to decide."

"You have a great laugh."

"Thank you," she says, sounding unsure. "What I meant to ask is what type of architecture do you prefer?"

He thinks for a moment before answering. "I guess what I would love to do is urban design because it incorporates buildings, landscape, and green design. In all likelihood, I'll end up in commercial architecture because I have more connections in that field, and I know what it pays."

"There are more important things than money. Will you at least try to do what you love?"

"What do you mean?"

"If you love urban design, I think you should at least try to go that route. Granted, I don't know how difficult that might be, but do you really want to look back on your life and regret not following your dream?"

He stares at her long enough for the silence to become awkward.

Morgan bites her lip. "Sorry, I know you didn't ask for my opinion. I bet you're regretting your decision to invite me." She pops another fry into her mouth.

A genuine smile graces his face. "You're such a breath of fresh air, Morgan. You said you're a sophomore, but you seem mature for a sophomore. Let me take you to dinner tomorrow night. I want you to dress up so I can take you to a fancy restaurant and spend an exorbitant amount of money on you."

"I'm flattered, I am, but I don't have time to date right now."

"Listen, if there is anyone who understands being busy, it's me. I'm not asking for a lifelong commitment or even a relationship. I'm asking for one date. One night with delicious food and great company. Come on, let me spoil you."

She thinks about it for a moment, before answering, "Okay. But tomorrow doesn't work, and I work evening shifts at the hospital, so I don't have a free night until next Thursday."

"Busy girl."

She shrugs, "I told you I don't have time to date."

"It's okay. I think I can wait a week to spoil you."

"You should know I'm not a fancy girl."

"I don't believe you."

"I was more into the homecoming game than the dance. Don't get me wrong; dressing up can be fun. I just want you to know what you're up against here."

He laughs. "So, I take it you watch football?"

"I do."

"Pro or college?"

"Both. But I prefer college football. What about you?"

"I'll watch both, but I'm more into Pro. The Cowboys are my team. I was born in Texas. My family moved up here when I was ten."

"Oh, I bet you miss the warm weather."

"On days like today, maybe, but Texas summers are miserable. I still have family out there, so I visit fairly often."

"You don't have the Texas twang," she teases.

In his best southern drawl, he says, "Nah, I don't reckon I do, ma'am."

Morgan laughs aloud. "That's terrible! I guess you just weren't meant to be a Texan."

"You've barely touched your food. I'll stop asking you questions so you can eat."

Time passes quickly, and the next thing she knows hours have passed. Morgan knows it has everything to do with Preston. She gets lost in him, talking and laughing. They exchange phone numbers before leaving, and Morgan is glad she came.

MORGAN DOESN'T USUALLY DRESS up, at least not in dresses; nevertheless, her date with Preston is a dress-worthy occasion. Knowing full well she is out of her league in the dress department; Morgan contacts Ashley for help. As it turns out, Ashley has an endless supply of dresses and invites Morgan over to peruse her wardrobe. Ashley owns party dresses, evening gowns, and preppy dresses for those times she's forced to meet her parents at the country club.

"I can't picture you at a country club," Morgan says, flipping through the dresses.

"Thank you. I pride myself on that."

Morgan gives her a questioning look.

Ashley shrugs. "I haven't had the best luck with my parent's country club. It's basically like a grown-up clubhouse for stuck up people who want to exclude everyone they feel is beneath them. My parents are awesome, Morgan, but I don't like who they become when we're there. Everyone glosses over everything that actually matters."

Ashley lays on her stomach in bed with her head propped in her hands while her feet swing in the air. "So, what's this guy like, anyway?"

"Ashley, I already told you. He's a couple of years older than me, a senior. He's going to school for architecture—"

"Blah, blah, blah. I mean, what does he look like? How does he make you feel?"

Morgan pauses in her pursuit; turning to face Ashley, she leans against the door frame. "He's great. He makes me laugh. He's generous and kind, a gentleman. He has a welcoming smile and green eyes, brown hair that was a mess of short waves when I saw him, but that was only because he had his hair tucked up under a hat most of the morning. He's athletic, but not bulky. He goes to the gym every morning at six a.m., so he's disciplined. He's maintained a four-point—"

"And there you go back into the boring stuff," Ashley says, dropping her face to the bed.

"What are you looking for, Ashley? What do you want me to say?"

She looks back up, asking, "Does he excite you or are you just doing this to get over Alec?"

Morgan turns back to the dresses and begins scooting hangers.

"Either way, it's totally fine with me," Ashley supplies. "I simply want to know what kind of advice to give you. And I want you to be honest with yourself, so you don't end up getting hurt."

Morgan turns back to her. "He does excite me. It's just that he's so different from Alec that it's hard to compare the two. Preston makes a lot more sense than Alec ever did. We have so much in common, and he makes me feel like I'm exciting. I know it looks like he's just a rebound, but that's just bad timing. When I was with him, Alec didn't even cross my mind. I like Preston."

"Okay, so we need to make you look sexy for your romantic

date. Just bring the dresses you want to try over here," she instructs. "I'm still trying to figure out how it's possible you don't own a little black dress. It's every woman's right of passage to own and wear a little black dress at least once."

Morgan shrugs off her comment and lays her selection of dresses on the bed.

"Those are all boring!" Ashley rolls to her back. "Morgan, you are killing me!" she complains, scooting over to sit on the side of the bed. She picks through the dresses and as Morgan slips into one, Ashley groans and moves to her closet.

Morgan realizes this dress is neither flattering nor date material. She takes it off and Ashley hands her another. Morgan slips it over her head and struggles with the multiple beaded straps and quickly realizes this isn't a dress she put in the pile.

"Ashley, what is this?" Morgan complains, pulling at the hem of the skirt which barely covers her thighs. She spins around, catching a glimpse of the back in the mirror, or lack thereof. "I said fancy, not slutty."

Ashley admires Morgan. "If I can ever get you to go out with me, you are definitely wearing that dress!"

Morgan pulls the dress up, getting the beads caught on each other as she lifts it to her shoulders. "Help," she squeals.

Ashley helps Morgan out of the beaded contraption and grabs the next dress which Morgan deems perfect. Short, but not too short, fitted, but not clingy. It is somewhat basic, but the simplicity makes it classy. It is also black.

Ashley stands back and smiles with pride. "I told you. Every woman needs a little black dress."

Morgan says, "I'm beginning to see your point."

THE VERY NEXT DAY, Morgan is standing in front of her own mirror in her borrowed dress and black heals second-guessing her decision. Knowing she's done all she can do; she moves to the kitchen.

She's fiddling with everything, emphatically cleaning and straightening. She scoots the canister of sugar over an inch and slides it back. "Why am I so nervous?"

From the living room, Patrick says, "I think that's normal for a first date. Stop second-guessing yourself. He is a fool if he doesn't see your beauty."

"I shouldn't even be doing this! There are more important things to do. I should be helping you tonight." She slides her fingers through her long silky hair.

"You haven't had a chance to breathe in how long?" he asks, walking over to her. "You deserve this, Morgan. Besides, he's already here."

There is a knock at the door. Morgan blows out a breath and moves to open it but panics at the last second. She presses her back against the door, whispering, "Patrick, will you do your thing? You know, your little mind reading thing to make sure he's not a creep. I just . . . I can't handle . . ."

He stands in front of her, brushing his fingers down her arms. "Of course, Morgan. I will interrogate him if necessary." He winks.

Her shoulders relax as she exhales, "Thank you, Patrick."

Patrick gives an encouraging grin and steps into the kitchen while Morgan opens the door. She smiles up at Preston, who looks handsome with his wavy brown hair tamed and styled. He's holding a bouquet of yellow tulips. Her joy is evident in her expression. "Oh wow, yellow tulips are my favorite!"

"I remember," he says with a grin. "You look beautiful tonight."

"Thank you. You don't look so shabby yourself." Morgan takes the bouquet and steps back so he can come in. "Let me just put these in water and then we can go." Morgan gestures to Patrick as she passes him in the kitchen. "This is my cousin and roommate, Patrick. Patrick, this is Preston."

"It's nice to meet you," Preston says.

"The pleasure is mine," Patrick responds, stepping forward to take Preston's hand in a masculine shake. "Morgan has told me a little bit about you. You sound like a decent man. Any noteworthy skeletons in your closet, Preston?"

"Patrick!" Morgan scolds.

Patrick releases his hand, saying, "I have all the faith in you, Preston. I have no reason to believe you'll disappoint."

With a smile, Preston turns to look fondly at Morgan. "I don't plan on letting her down."

Patrick steps in and takes the flowers from Morgan. "I'll take these. You go enjoy yourselves."

"Thank you, Patrick," Morgan says, before grabbing her purse and coat.

"I HAVE to see you again, Morgan. I know you're busy, so I'll wait if I have to, but when can I see you again?"

"The only night I'm free is . . . well, technically, it's tomorrow, but I promised my friend I'd come see him. He plays the guitar at the coffee shop down on Fifth and Main. You can come with me if you'd like. It's nothing fancy, but he's an excellent musician."

"It's a date," he says, stepping in closer with a serious look on his face. He leans in to press his lips against hers, and her eyes flutter closed as their lips meet.

She pulls back slightly, breaking their kiss. "Can you pick me up by seven tomorrow?"

"How about six and we can grab a quick meal beforehand?"

Her cheeks hurt from all the smiling she's been doing this evening, but she can't help herself. She gives him one last grin, saying, "Perfect."

He dips his head to give her another sweet kiss, and when he pulls away, he says, "Perfect."

She's still smiling, and this time it's accompanied by a delightful shiver. She could get used to this feeling. She ducks her head and reaches for the doorknob. As she backs into her apartment, she sounds slightly breathless. "Thank you for a wonderful night."

"I look forward to seeing you tomorrow."

After one last look, Morgan closes the door between them and leans into it. Tonight was perfect, absolutely perfect. He took her out to a new posh restaurant downtown where the atmosphere was pure elegance, the service was stellar, and the food was to die for. Preston wasn't lying when he said he wanted to spend an exorbitant amount of money on her. She'd never had such an expensive meal. That said, her favorite thing tonight was Preston. She loves the way they spoke so easily, the way his eyes stayed on her the whole evening, the way he treated her like she was the most important thing in the world.

Patrick's voice comes from the living room. "Looks like you had a good time."

She turns slowly, keeping her eyes closed, still picturing the evening in her mind. "It was wonderful," she says on a sigh, opening her eyes. She gasps, stumbling over her words. "How did . . . where did . . ."

Maggie is sitting at Patrick's feet. The scarred Doberman Pinscher looks pleased as Patrick strokes her head.

Patrick explains, "I felt drawn to Emily's house this evening, and look who I found sitting under the yellow tape in the front yard."

"Maggie," Morgan whispers, stepping forward on wobbly legs. "Did . . . did you find anything else?"

"No, and I didn't sense her presence either, but I think she sent Maggie back to us. Why else would she show up now?"

Morgan pales. "Do you think . . ."

"No, I don't think she's dead. If anything, I think this means she's fighting to regain control."

Morgan bends down, reaching a tentative hand out to

Maggie. When the dog nudges against her hand, Morgan moves closer, petting Maggie with both hands, noting, "She's so thin."

"I'm not sure when she last ate a proper meal. I picked up dog food on our way here. She ate so quickly she made herself sick."

"Poor thing. Were you able to get anything from her? Do you think she can lead us to Emily?"

"Her mind works differently than a human's, and right now she's exhausted. I think she's had a very long trip. Maybe after we both rest, I'll be able to discern what I'm sensing from her."

Morgan looks up from Maggie. "What can I do?"

"You can go dream about the spectacular evening you had. Preston is very taken with you. I'm delighted someone besides me finally sees your value."

She blushes.

"I'll make myself scarce should you decide to invite him in after your next date."

Her blush grows. "Patrick!"

"What? Most roommates have signals. I just thought you'd like to know that I can sense when I'm not wanted, and I won't give you a hard time. I'll quietly disappear so you can ravish one another."

She shakes her head, coming to a stand. "I'm going to bed unless there is something more I can do to help with Emily."

"No. Maggie and I are headed to bed as well," he says, standing from the sofa.

CHAPTER TWENTY-TWO ~

As promised, Preston picks Morgan up at six. It's a mild day, warmer than usual for mid-November. Preston drives Morgan into the city and parks a few streets over from the coffee shop.

"Seriously, where are you taking me?" Morgan says while getting out of the car.

He looks like a kid with a secret. "You'll see!" He rounds the car to meet her on the sidewalk. He takes her hand in his and leads her down the street. They pass several restaurants, but he continues walking.

"You're killing me!" she complains, pulling on his hand.

He turns to face her, pulling her body into his. He caresses her cheek and lowers his lips to hers. It starts as a simple kiss but deepens as they lose control. Their tongues mingle, and she clutches the front of his jacket, forgetting they're in public as she releases a moan.

A passerby whistles at their very public display of affection and Morgan laughs into his mouth as they separate. He holds her face in his palms, unready to let go, confessing, "I've wanted to do that since the moment I left last night."

She bites her lip. "I'm glad you did. We should do that again sometime, just maybe somewhere a little more private.

He gives her a chaste kiss and weaves his fingers in hers before they resume their walk. "It's just up here."

He pulls her down a side street filled with food trucks. Her eyes widen in excitement. She looks up at him and he laughs at her expression.

"And here I was worried you were taking me to some fancy restaurant again. Preston, this is amazing!"

"I thought you'd like it; besides, I spent all my money last night."

She gives him a worried look.

"Relax, Morgan. I'm kidding." He nods his head towards the row of trucks. "So, what'll it be, princess?"

"Will you look at me differently if I get a hotdog?"

"Are you kidding me? I come here once a week just to get my gourmet hotdog fix."

They enjoy their wieners at a nearby picnic table, and twenty minutes later they're headed to the coffee shop. They arrive a little early, finding Ben sitting at the reserved table up front. "Oh, Preston, I want you to meet one of my best friends. He's the one performing tonight." She grabs his hand and leads him over to Ben.

Ben stands as they approach, and Morgan lets go of Preston long enough to hug Ben. Once she steps back, she says, "Ben, I'd like you to meet Preston. We met at the campus library."

Ben reaches his hand out to Preston. "Nice to meet you."

Preston looks to Morgan as he says, "Morgan's been raving about your music."

"I guess you'll see if I live up to the hype." Ben notices the looks Preston and Morgan are exchanging and wonders when this became a thing between them. He also hates that she brought him here tonight because Alec is going to be blindsided and most likely throw a tantrum, not that he has any right to complain. Morgan looks happier than he has seen her in a long time. He should be hugging this new guy for putting that smile on Morgan's face, but he also wants to check into the guy properly.

"Hey guys, give me a minute. I'll be right back. I need to make a call. Feel free to take the table." Ben makes his way outside and dials the number he never expected to call. It rings twice.

"Is Morgan all right?"

"Hello to you too, Patrick. Yeah, she's fine. She's with this Preston guy. I take it you've met him?"

"Yes, we've met."

"What's your take on him?"

"He's a wanted fugitive. Killing young brunette women all over the United States."

"You're such a prick, Patrick. Come on, what's your read on him?"

"Are you jealous or concerned? It's hard for me to get a good read on you over the phone."

"I know you give a shit about her. I do, too. You know what happened in Florida. I will rip this guy's throat out if he hurts her. I need to know he's good enough for her and it takes a lot to be good enough for Morgan!"

Patrick sighs. "I'm not sure anyone is good enough for her, but he's a good guy. He treats her like gold. Just watch the way he looks at her and you'll see it. He isn't perfect, but he's quite an improvement over Alec."

"So, how's she gonna be when Alec gets here tonight?"

"I guess you'll find out. I'm otherwise occupied, or I would be there myself, because yes, Ben, as you so eloquently pointed out, I do care about her. Imagine that—there is a heart in this cold Tin Man after all."

"What are you doing that's so important?"

"Finding your girlfriend. I'm making progress. Not sure if Morgan told you, but Maggie showed up last night."

"What?" Ben can't breathe. "What does that mean?"

"That, hopefully, I'll meet up with her soon."

After a moment, Ben says, "You're in love with her, aren't you?"

"Let's not get carried away."

"Patrick?"

"Yes, Ben. I would die for her. I will give her whatever she needs, but in no way am I in competition with you. She has always been very clear about her feelings for you."

"I don't understand your relationship with her, but I know you're important to her. It's been three months, and the last I saw her she tried to kill me. By now she probably has a new handful of suckers falling in love with her."

Neither of them likes the way that statement makes them feel because, in all honesty, they don't know. They know very little about what is happening, and the doubt starts clouding Ben's mind.

Patrick is the first to break the silence. "I think I just realized how hard this must be for you. I love her, but she's never been mine to lose. She admitted her feelings for you just before she disappeared and then you lost her and yet you didn't, but you could at any moment and the not knowing must be torture."

Ben is speechless for a spell before responding, "Don't forget all the other shit going on in my life, Patrick. You left out some stuff. Maybe you could also bring up my parents kicking me out, my sister disowning me, and my shitty studio apartment that I pay for by working three jobs. I mean, if you're gonna pile it on, then go for it."

He looks in the windows of the coffee shop and realizes he's late. "But it'll have to wait. I've got to get to work." He hangs up and walks back inside.

BEN IS in the middle of his set, and the crowd sits captured by his music. Morgan and Preston sip from their drinks while leaning across the table towards one another in an intimate conversation. They don't even notice the approaching bombshell until she invades their table. Ashley grabs an empty chair and pulls it right up to their table for two.

"Hey." She plops down in the seat, eyeing the two of them. Turning to Preston, she says, "I'm Ashley. Are you the architecture major graduating this year?" Ashley looks to Morgan conspiratorially and adds, "Or is this one of the others?"

"No, Ashley, you've got the right one. This is Preston. Frank and Jeff were both busy tonight."

Preston is silent for a second before smiling and saying, "It's funny you mention them because I was just out with a Frank and Jeff last night. I hate to break it to you, but they both have STD's."

Ashley looks at Morgan, saying, "I like him. Can we keep him?"

Morgan laughs and reaches across the table for Preston's hand. "Yeah, I think I'll keep him, at least for a little while."

Ashley pops up, saying, "I've gotta go grab my drink. I'll be right back."

Ashley turns to find Alec glaring at them from the drink counter. When she approaches, she says, "Before you decide to mess this up, we need to chat. You're only mad because it's not you. Morgan actually likes him and she's happy. She deserves this, Alec. So, like, before you decide whether to sit with us or leave, remember you fucking let this happen. There is no one to blame but yourself, so don't make her pay for your mistakes more than she already has." Before Alec can respond, Ashley grabs her drink and is off.

Alec isn't sure whether he wants to stay. It's true, he will be moving in with his pregnant girlfriend in a few weeks, but his friendship with Morgan is too important to lose, so he swallows his pride and decides to join them. He reaches the table just as Morgan's date leans in for a kiss.

"Hey, Fletch. Hey, Ashley," Alec greets.

Ashley spins around on her seat. "If you're staying, we should just move that table over here." She gestures to the next table.

"Eh, yeah, okay, sure," Alec responds.

Once they move the table and get settled, Ashley sits next to Morgan.

Noticing the happy couple is no longer holding hands, Alec says, "I'm Alec," before taking the seat next to the new guy.

"Oh, Alec, Morgan has told me about you. I'm Preston. Hey and congratulations, I heard your girlfriend is expecting."

Alec wants to punch him in the fucking face. He swallows his rage and says, "Yeah, thanks, she's due in May."

"That's huge, man. Really exciting. I graduate in May and I thought that was big, but you're going to be a father. Wow!"

"Yeah, it was a shock, but we're excited."

Ashley asks, "Have you thought of names?"

God, is it too late for him to change his mind. He needs to get the hell out of here. As if sensing his panic, Morgan's foot taps his ankle under the table. He knows it's her because she uses the stupid secret code they invented in first grade. Two taps, a break, and another tap. They used it as a sign of solidarity whenever one of them got in trouble, but Morgan never got in trouble. It was always him, yet she never gave up. The taps said, "We're in this together. You and me."

She was his best friend until he was held back in the second grade and he realized he was too stupid for her. She was always getting A's and smiley faces while he was getting in trouble. He only goofed off because he couldn't understand the words he was supposed to be reading. They didn't find out he was dyslexic until fourth grade and by then, their group of friends had expanded, and they didn't see each other as often.

She taps the code against his ankle one more time and he smiles, his panic subsiding as he focuses on Morgan. God, he's a fucking moron. But Ashley was right. Morgan deserves to be happy.

"We've talked about names," he says, answering Ashley's

question. "We don't have anything picked out. You said you're graduating in May?"

"Yes, but I'm going on for my masters, so I'll still be in school for a little while longer."

Alec doesn't like comparing himself to this guy, but he can't help it. Preston is the kind of guy Morgan deserves, someone smart, who has his life together. Not a guy who lives at home with his mommy. Not a guy who depends on his bastard father for a damn job. And definitely not a guy who runs out on his psycho girlfriend after he knocks her up. God, he really needs to get the fuck out of here.

CHAPTER TWENTY-THREE ~

BEN'S PHONE rings as he loads his guitar into the trunk of his Corvette. He hesitates to answer, wondering why Patrick is calling back so soon.

Eventually, he picks up. "Patrick, I was joking about you rubbing my shitty life in my face."

"I'm not calling about that. You need to come over here tonight. I found her. I found Emily, or at least I'm ninety percent certain it's her."

"Are you serious?" Ben asks, feeling a trickle of excitement mixed with fear.

Patrick continues as if Ben hadn't spoken. "I'm leaving tonight and Morgan is going to want to come with me. I won't allow it. I won't put her at risk. She listens to you and I promised I wouldn't compel her."

"You're leaving tonight?" Ben shuts his trunk and rounds the car.

"Yes. Can you be here in the next half hour?"

"Yeah, I'll be right over," Ben says, trying to hide his anxiety. He hangs up and climbs into his car.

PRESTON WALKS Morgan to her apartment door. With regret, he says, "I really wish I didn't have to cut the evening short, but I have to finish a paper that's due tomorrow morning."

Morgan's eyes go wide. "Why didn't you tell me earlier? We didn't have to stay the whole evening."

"That's exactly why I didn't tell you. I wanted to spend time with you."

"Well, maybe on our next date we can stay in and study, because I want to spend time with you, too, but I've got a lot of homework."

"Are you saying you'll make time for a third date?"

She smiles. "That's exactly what I'm saying, but it's still true that I don't have time for this," she teases.

He leans in. "And neither do I." His lips touch hers once, twice. She wraps her arms around him, drawing him into her. Their mouths open and their tongues mingle. The heat of this kiss is so much hotter than their earlier kiss, and it goes on uninterrupted, giving their hands time to explore.

Morgan realizes they either need to take this inside or say goodnight, but it feels too good, so she doesn't pull away until her lips feel bruised and she's out of breath. They stand with their foreheads pressed together, long enough to reign in their desires and catch their breath. Then Preston steps back. "I hate that I have to leave right now."

"It's probably for the best. My roommate has been in one of his moods all day, and we both have homework to do."

"Goodnight, Morgan." He takes a slow step backward, then another and finally turns to walk away.

"I'll talk to you soon," she calls after him.

Instead of responding, he pulls out his phone and begins typing. She wonders what's so important that it can't wait. Then her phone chimes, and with a big smile, she pulls it out of her coat pocket watching as he stands behind his open car door.

She reads the message from him. **Morgan, I'd really like to keep seeing you. Exclusively.**

She is still smiling as she types back. **Are you asking me to be your girlfriend?**

His response is quick. **Absolutely.**

She looks up to find he's watching her expectantly. She bites her lip and then looks down to text back. **You know I really don't have the time but screw it. Yes, I'll be your girlfriend.**

He strides towards her with a triumphant smile. He doesn't stop. He crashes right into her, one hand going around her waist while he cups her cheek. Their kiss starts back up, white hot, but he pulls back before they get too carried away.

"I'll see you later, babe," he says, as he pulls away.

"Later, boo," she calls in return.

Looking worried, he asks, "Those names aren't gonna stick, are they?"

With a laugh, she shakes her head. "No."

"Good."

With that, he walks to his car while Morgan turns around and walks into the madness that has become her apartment. The living room furniture has all been shoved to one side of the room to make space for the carpet of paper covering the entire floor. Thank God Preston hadn't come in.

Closing the door behind her, Morgan mumbles, "What's going on here?"

Patrick hollers from his room. "I know where she is!"

She takes her eyes from the hundreds of pages strewn across the floor and carefully walks toward the bedroom, unsure she heard him correctly. "What?"

"I found Emily."

She turns into his room and finds Maggie lying on his bed while he's throwing things in a duffle bag. "Really?"

"Ninety percent sure! Make that ninety-five," he says, while carelessly tossing items in his bag.

"Is that what the mess is about in the living room?"

"Yes, I had to lay it all out and follow the trail." He stops packing and walks to the living room to show Morgan.

Patrick walks across the carpet of paper, pointing at a sheet. "You see, here? This was when she stole the Ferrari." He spins and points down at a different sheet. "Then over here she took the van out to Oklahoma where we found out about the Grand Rapids and from there . . ." he points to the picture under her foot. "The incident in Arizona."

She already knows this chain of events. "Patrick, stop! How did you find her?"

He looks up from the papers and says, "Tigers." Then he continues his manic behavior by rushing back to his room.

She follows after him. "What do you mean, tigers?

He lifts his bag and walks into the bathroom. "I mean tigers. Two tigers went missing from the zoo." He grabs a toothbrush and a few other items before brushing past her again.

"Are you leaving right now?"

He spins to her, saying, "I need to leave before she moves on."

Morgan panics, realizing this is happening now. "Let me grab a few things!" She takes off toward her bedroom.

He shakes his head, but she's already gone. He takes the few steps to her room and leans against the doorframe. "Morgan, you aren't going with me."

She turns from throwing clothes in an open backpack and says, "I won't get involved. I just want to be there to help you. I'll stay out of the way."

"No. You aren't coming."

She resumes packing, saying, "The hell I'm not! Patrick, you can't go alone. What if something happens to you? It's too dangerous!"

Taking slow steps into the room, he explains, "Exactly, it's too dangerous for you. I'm not as easy to kill. Besides, if this doesn't work, I'll need you here to warn the others."

She pauses her packing to look at him, letting her bag hang

from one hand while crumpling a shirt in the other. "Warn them of what?"

"You've experienced firsthand what Emily can do. She took control of your every thought. I'm not as easy of a target, but as you've pointed out to me in the past, I'm not invincible. So, after I leave, I need you to warn your dad and help him prepare for the worst just in case things go poorly."

Morgan stares at him with a look of horror. "No," she whispers. "There has to be another way. A plan where no one dies or becomes a zombie."

"I don't foresee it playing out that way, but I'd like to have a contingency plan in any case. And I won't put you in danger."

"What's plan B?" she questions, throwing her half-packed bag on the bed.

"Plan B is doing nothing, and I've already established I won't do that."

"Patrick, do you even have a plan?" She balls up the shirt in her hands.

"I will figure it out as I go. There is no other choice. You still don't understand what she is!"

"I know *who* she is," Morgan defends, throwing the balled-up shirt to the bed.

"We become different people when we don't have control over our thoughts. She almost had you jump off a building!"

"But she didn't do that to you! Emily is still in there! She's gotta be fighting it."

"She is fighting it. She sent Maggie here to get me." At the mention of her name, Maggie rushes into the room and sits at attention beside Patrick.

Morgan rubs her face with both hands in frustration. She takes a few deep breaths attempting to calm herself. More together, she says, "Patrick, I have a plan B, or I guess it's more like an idea, but it's not exactly legal. However, it might come in handy, especially if things start to go bad."

Disliking her secrecy, Patrick impatiently filters her

thoughts. "That is not a bad idea, Morgan. I don't know why I didn't think of that."

"It's because you're too close. You need back up, Patrick! You can't always do everything alone."

He steps forward, gripping her shoulders. "Thanks to you, I am not alone. I might be making this journey by myself, but I will call you every day and keep you up to date on everything I do. I put Emily in grave danger once. I will not make the same mistake with you. Besides, I need you to stay here and take care of Maggie while I'm gone."

"You're not taking her with you?"

"The goal is to go unnoticed. A vicious looking Doberman is sure to draw unwanted attention."

A knock at the front door interrupts their conversation, but neither of them moves to answer it right away. Soon they hear the door open and Ben calls, "What the hell is all this?"

Morgan smirks, saying softly, "This might be worse than the murder wall you had going a while back."

"Oh, I'm aware I come across as a complete lunatic, mad rambling and all."

"How would I have explained all of that to Preston?"

"Well, he probably wouldn't have asked you to become his girlfriend."

She laughs while Ben calls, "Morgan?"

Patrick releases her shoulders, and she walks out to meet Ben.

Patrick finishes packing his things before joining them in the kitchen. He sets his duffle bag on the kitchen table and walks over to Morgan, who is standing with her back to the counter.

"Morgan, before I leave, there is something I need to do, and I need you to trust me on this."

"Imagine that," she says.

Instead of responding to her sarcastic tone, he continues on a serious note, "I need to put a protective barrier around your mind. As soon as I leave, Lathe will most likely visit, if not others. I need to make sure you have something in place where they can't manipulate you or get information out of you unless it comes willingly."

"How are you going to do that?"

"It's simple," he lies. "Come lie on the sofa."

It is not simple. The only reason he hadn't done it before is because of how dangerous it is. He read his mother's journal dozens of times—with lots of concentration and practice in between—until he felt he was getting the hang of it. He is far from mastering it, but their time has run out, and a little protection is better than none.

It takes about thirty minutes to finish putting the barrier in place, and although Morgan feels no pain, it completely drains Patrick.

Ben witnessed it all, feeling a pang of sympathy for Patrick. He can see Patrick is hurting, but he doesn't say a word about it.

CHAPTER TWENTY-FOUR ~

A LITTLE BEFORE two in the morning on November eighteenth, Patrick leaves town. If everything hadn't taken so long the night before, he would be hours closer to Emily, but even he has to admit the extra time taken to procure plan B could very well save his life, along with others.

Now Patrick is driving, staring into the sunset for the last several hours as he follows the sun west. He traveled through a time zone a while back and he knows another is coming up soon.

Sixteen hours in and it's time to stop for gas, again. So far, traffic hasn't been bad, mostly because Patrick has been mentally manipulating drivers out of the way. This little town of Winona, Kansas is still three hours short of Denver.

He knows he won't reach the zoo until after it closes, but he figures the fewer people, the better. After a quick stop, he's back on the road. And before he knows it, he's passing through the second time zone and entering Colorado.

He pulls up to the zoo at seven. The parking lot is basically empty, aside from zoo personnel. It doesn't take much for him to manipulate and charm his way back to the tiger exhibit.

It takes him a few hours of sorting through people's stories and minds to finally get anything of use, but he hits the jackpot when he finds the security office.

Emily hadn't had them delete the footage of her visiting the zoo. The sight of her makes him gulp back the terror aroused just by watching. He recognizes her, but she looks vastly different. Her hair is lighter and longer, and her curvy, petite body is even thinner than before. But the most significant difference is the way she carries herself. She is a lioness on the prowl, a self-possessed threat sauntering through crowds of unsuspecting potential victims.

This isn't the self-aware Emily he knows. This isn't Emily at all. This is her demon-blood at work. This is Valla.

She gives a small wave and winks at the video camera, clearly intending for Patrick to view this footage. She wants him to find her.

Chills run down his spine and apprehension pools heavily in the pit of his stomach. She is setting a trap for him and he knows the only way to get her back is to walk right into it. He knows how dangerous she is, but the longer someone else has control of her body, the harder it will be for him to get her back, and he fears it may already be too late.

He can't focus on that right now. He needs to stay positive so he can find her and take her home.

He takes a digital copy of the recording with him as he leaves the zoo. He also takes the footage from the parking lot, so he can search for the license plate attached to the vehicle Emily was in only two days ago.

Patrick won't let this trail go cold.

It's only nine-thirty, but he feels heaviness weighing him down as he drives away. He hasn't slept in over forty-eight hours and he knows he needs to take a shower and crash, but first, he needs to find out where Emily ran off to after leaving the zoo.

He stops at a gas station where he climbs into the back of the van with his laptop and begins a search of the license plate number. While the plates are running, he lies down on the twin mattress to rest his eyes.

Next thing he knows, the sun is streaming in through the windows, rousing him.

"Damn it."

He pulls himself up and awakens the sleeping computer and there on the screen is the information he was searching for. The clock tells him it's seven a.m. He overslept and he hadn't given Morgan a call as he had promised.

He picks up his phone, dialing Morgan.

"What did you find?" she says in place of *hello*.

"She was at the zoo a couple of days ago. I tracked down the plates of the stolen vehicle she was traveling in and found it parked outside a hotel two states over. I'm headed there to check it out now. How is everything there?"

"It's . . ." she hesitates, "It's okay."

Patrick knows she doesn't like staying with her parents, but it's the safest place for her while he's gone. "As suffocating as it may feel, you are safer there," Patrick reassures.

"Are you on your way to the hotel now?"

"Yes. I've lost too much time already. I'm on the road to Missouri, now. I'll text you when I get there."

"Everyone needs sleep, Patrick, even you. Be safe."

"You do the same, Morgan." He sighs. "Talk to you soon."

PATRICK KEEPS Morgan informed as he follows Emily into Chicago. She's playing a game of cat and mouse with him, providing him glimpses, just enough to give him hope. The day before Thanksgiving, Patrick spots Emily as she's driving down a busy Chicago street.

He hails a cab and follows, but as soon as he gets close, his cab driver swerves into oncoming traffic and plows into a fire hydrant. Patrick hits his head on the divider as water explodes from the busted hydrant.

The cab driver fights his airbag, looking confused. He stares in shock at his crumpled car.

While the driver is still dazed, Patrick jumps out of the cab and runs down the street, trying to catch the license plate number of Emily's car. But she's gone, vanishing into the aftermath of the accident she created. Patrick stops running and once the adrenaline fades, he feels the bruise forming on his forehead where he hit the divider.

Once he's back in his hotel room, he gets a bag of ice for his head and calls Morgan.

"Anything new?" she answers.

He explains what happened, and then asks, "What's happening there?"

"Nothing that exciting or terrifying."

"How are things with Preston?" he asks, trying not to be single-minded.

She sighs. "Preston flew out to Texas to spend a week with his extended family. I don't know if things are going to work. Even when he's here, we're both too busy to spend time together."

A FEW DAYS LATER, Patrick is still in Chicago, but he's getting closer. He can feel it. Emily is toying with him by leaving a trail of clues to keep him interested.

On Wednesday night, the week after Thanksgiving, Patrick calls Morgan. "I found the hotel she staying at here in Chicago. I think this might be it."

Patrick can practically hear Morgan's pacing.

"Patrick, it's the middle of the night. Promise me you'll sleep before catching up to her. You have to be able to focus, otherwise—"

"I will get a full night's sleep. I'm also past due for a good grooming. I promise I won't be reckless, Morgan."

CHAPTER TWENTY-FIVE ~

NOVEMBER 29TH ~

AN ATTRACTIVE BRUNETTE stands at attention behind the mirrored front desk. "Hello, sir. Are you checking in?" she says in a professional tone.

Patrick rests a hip against the desk. He is wearing a fitted navy suit, sans a tie, because it felt too much like a noose around his neck and he wasn't going to make it that easy for her. Crossing his ankles, he takes in the extravagant modern-industrial chandelier. Something is niggling at the back of his mind. There is something about this lobby, something about this hotel that feels familiar. He can't recall being here before, yet he knows that chandelier didn't use to be there, and the entire ceiling used to be covered in intricate gold detail. And the front desk used to be . . . he turns to look at the other side of the lobby . . . over there.

"Excuse me, sir. May I help you?"

Snapping out of his thoughts, he focuses on the woman behind the desk and says, "Apologies. I was distracted by this fascinating lobby." Leaning towards her, he gives a seductive grin, saying, "I see it's not just the lobby overflowing with beauty."

She blushes, giving him a coy grin. "Mr. Glenn, it's a pleasure to meet you. Though I'm disappointed we couldn't have met under different circumstances."

Patrick's heart skips a beat, realizing Emily must be anticipating him. It confirms his suspicions that this has all been an elaborate trap. "I wasn't aware you would be expecting me," he says, keeping his seductive grin in place.

She shakes her head, explaining, "Oh, no Mr. Glenn, it isn't me who is expecting you."

"Please, call me Patrick." He tries to invade her mind but runs into an impenetrable barrier.

"I admit that tickles a bit, but I'm afraid that won't work on me, Patrick." She taps her head and smiles, explaining, "She didn't want you to manipulate me." She approaches him from around the desk. "Now, if you would follow me, I'll show you up."

She leads him to a secluded elevator and taps a key card against an electronic scanner. "This elevator will take us directly to the bar, which is where she prefers to spend most of her time."

Stepping into the elevator, Patrick asks, "How long has she been staying here?"

"Only for the last few months, on and off." The elevator doors close and as the elevator rises, she continues, "It's been wonderful having her here and just wait until you meet Copper and River. She's taken quite a shine to them. They are her favorites, but I'd say you're a close third. I hope for your sake, you all hit it off. They can be pretty intimidating."

"I'm sure we'll hit it off. I've been told I'm a bit of a people person."

Lifting a brow, she says, "That you are, Patrick Glenn. That you are."

The elevator stops and music blares from the other side of

the doors. Patrick feels the beat of the music vibrating through the floor. He comments, "Sounds like some party."

"It's always a party, Mr. Glenn," she says, and with a ding, the doors open. "This is where I leave you. Enjoy the celebration."

Patrick steps off the elevator, but seeing the giant crowd, he turns back and asks, "Any idea where I might find Emily?"

"Who?" she questions, looking confused.

"Emily!" he shouts to be heard.

"Emily?" she asks, as the doors close between them.

Patrick turns back to the party. The same modern industrial theme he saw in the lobby is continued up here. The concrete floors, exposed beamed ceiling, and raw wood and metal materials mix with modern shapes. Stunning light fixtures hang above a mirrored wall stacked with alcohol, making the moderate-sized bar look twice its actual size. Slightly tinted floor to ceiling windows wrap along two sides of the room, letting in warm colors as the sun sets. A strobe light hangs over the designated dance floor. The place is packed with swaying men and women, and no one seems to notice their newest arrival.

As Patrick makes his way to the bar, a huge roar permeates the room. The crowd parts to reveal a giant white tiger with glowing yellow eyes proudly sitting in the corner of the room. The tiger stands from his haunches and prowls forward. There is no reaction from the crowd except for opening the passageway for the tiger. Patrons continue their laughing and dancing, but it's all wrong. There is not an ounce of emotion in the room as if someone has contrived their behavior.

He pulls out the gun he stashed in the back of his pants and points it at the beast prowling in slow motion toward him. Its mouth twitches and a snarl reveals big sharp teeth. It creeps forward, salivating at the idea of tearing flesh from bone. Finger on the trigger, Patrick knows he should shoot, but instead, he takes a step toward the violent creature. He tells his feet to stop, but they move one after the other, carrying him forward until the gun is just a few feet shy of the tiger's head. The giant cat relaxes, sitting down at Patrick's feet.

A voice comes from behind Patrick, stopping him cold. "Such beautiful creatures. It'd be a shame for you to kill one another."

"Emily," Patrick breathes, lowering his gun and giving the tiger his back so he can face the real threat.

She is standing away from the crowd, her black dress and flowing blond hair making her stand out like a fallen angel. The long sleeve plunging mini dress covers just enough skin, leaving very little to the imagination as it clings to her body in the most enticing way. Her long blond waves flow past her breasts. Her naked legs and nude heels give her the illusion of height making her all the more tempting. Even from across the room, her eyes stand out. Startling green orbs stare back at Patrick, and he has to calm his galloping heart and tamp down the desires burning from within. Even after all his time with Sky, he has never had a moment where he felt this exposed. He knows he would grant her any request, no matter the cost.

The volume of the music lowers and again Patrick questions, "Emily?" but even to his own ears, he sounds helpless, all his confidence washed away.

"No, love," she says, consoling him with her words. A second white tiger walks alongside her. "Do you like them? River is my favorite," she says, motioning to the tiger next to her. "Look. His blue eyes remind me of you."

"So, this one must be Copper," he says, referring to the one next to him.

She nods, instructing, "Follow me."

She pivots to glide across the room with confidence and poise.

Someone slips the gun out of Patrick's hand and he doesn't try to fight it. He lets it go and follows Emily, because he will follow her anywhere. The tigers and a few mind slaves follow them into a private room and close the door behind them. The room is cozy, done up in warm colors with a sofa and matching armchairs facing a fireplace with logs burning in the hearth.

Emily turns to Patrick, her hands politely folded behind her as she makes a spectacle out of surveying him. Tilting her head, she concludes, "I see why Emily is so attracted to you, Patrick Glenn. She's in here you know, in this body, in my mind. I have control, but I feel her desire for you. She feels bound to you. I suppose nothing bonds two people together like shared trauma."

Unfolding her hands, she reaches out to slide delicate fingers down his chest. "You want me. I can feel it." Her fingers fold into his lapel and she guides him closer until her chest grazes his. Her hands dip under his jacket and begin slipping buttons from their holes. His hands wrap around her wrists, stopping her attempt at undressing him. She rests her palms against his chest in surrender and he releases her. Before he can move away, she says, "Why are you fighting this?" Her palms glide up his chest. "You want Emily, but you'll never have her because she's in love with someone else." Her hands slide to the nape of his neck, her fingers splaying in his hair. "But I'm not," she purrs against his lips.

Patrick's eyes close as he inhales her scent.

"That's it, Patrick. You know you want this." She pauses, turning to instruct her mind slaves to leave. The room empties except for Copper and River, who lie like sentries in front of the door. Patrick watches the tigers until Emily tilts his jaw to face her.

"You can't manipulate me, Valla," he says in a low voice.

She sneers. "I prefer you not call me by that name, and I don't have to manipulate you, Patrick. I know you want this." She guides his hand to her breast, slowly directing it down her curves to the small of her waist.

Patrick grips her waist pulling her tight against him. In response, she molds her body to his, feeling his level of excitement pressing into her belly.

Fighting and giving in simultaneously, he growls, "I want Emily, not you."

"You can have us both," she breathes.

Lowering his chin, his lips descend, hovering over hers, but not pressing against them. He remembers what her lips feel like against his own. The one kiss he shared with Emily so many months ago had been gentle. It had been a tender reminder that neither of them was alone, but right now, he doesn't want gentle. He is not capable of gentle. Right now, he is desperate and yearning.

His heart races as he pulls her closer, his fingers twisting in the material of her dress, struggling to contain the desires he's been controlling for so long. Too long. He breathes her in, pulling in her scent, touching her skin, feeling her curves until pulling away is not an option. He dips his head, closing the distance, claiming her lips, possessing her the way he's always wanted.

She only encourages him, moaning into his mouth and moving against him in a sensual rhythm. He struggles to realign his wants with his needs and breathes, "Let me see her."

"I am her, Patrick. I possess her mind and body. What else do you need?"

"Just a glimpse of her and I'll stop resisting," he says, panting against her.

"She's deprived herself, never giving into what she wants. She will deny you, but I'll give you all of her, Patrick."

He breaks away from her, pushing her body back with so much force she has to brace herself against the sofa to keep from falling over. He rests his hands on the front of his thighs, fighting to catch his breath.

Tugging her dress back in place, she sits on the arm of the sofa. Crossing her legs, she looks at him with venom in her emerald eyes. "You're still trying to be her white knight, Patrick. It'd be sweet if it weren't so pathetic. She doesn't love you, and she'll never give you what you want . . . but I can."

"You're a liar." He shakes his head, his senses coming back to him.

Her laugh is a foreign sound. It's such a vile contrast to Emily's heartfelt laughter. Patrick holds back his wince, pulling himself back up to his full height.

"Isn't that the pot calling the kettle black?" she says, moving closer to him. "Don't forget who you're talking to, Patrick Glenn. I'm not some young girl. I know you better than you know yourself. You want to be a hero, but you never will be. You're still trying to save Emily, but all you've done is fail her. You led her to a father she wasn't strong enough to face, which only forced her to awaken Valla. Then you failed to notice Valla until I stole possession of Emily's body and mind. Emily's last conscious effort was to run away to protect everyone from us, and instead of respecting her last wish, you come here, making her sacrifice null and void. You fail her over and over again and call it love."

"Excellent job twisting the story," he comments.

"Those are all facts," she states. "You're incapable of love, Patrick. People like you and me, we were not built for love. We were raised to collect power, not morality. Love is a lie, anyway."

Patrick reasons, "Your mother loved you. She gave her life so you could live."

Her laughter is a menacing threat that claws at Patrick's resolve. "Patrick Glenn, I thought you were smarter than this. After everything you've seen, after all the lies you were told, haven't you questioned the origins of your ancestry? The fairytale you were told is a lie. The story you told Emily, a work of fiction. Facts so easily get lost in translation, and everyone wants good to win, but rarely is it that cut and dry. Very few people knew the truth in the first place, but they all died or were too frightened to share their story."

CHAPTER TWENTY-SIX ~

AFTER HEARING the Olvasho origins so many times, it is a tapestry inside Patrick's mind. Like a child's nursery rhyme, he can recite it word for word. But the mere thread of doubt has Patrick tearing at the seams of the once indestructible tapestry.

The woman before him wanders over to the tiger she calls River. She weaves her fingers in the thick mane of white hair, saying, "White tigers are beautiful creatures. River, here, is just over five-hundred pounds and in the wild, he's at the top of the food chain. Well, almost. Humans are their only predators, but humans don't just kill them. They capture these spectacularly rare creatures and turn them into sick, inbred beasts to be kept in cages for enjoyment."

Patrick looks at the tiger. With a sigh, he asks, "Your point?"

"If tigers learned how to outsmart humans, there would be nothing keeping them from earning back their top spot in the food chain. The world would be better for it, and tigers wouldn't torture humans like humans torture them."

"So, you're an animal rights activist?" he asks, full of skepticism.

Her lips curl into an aggravated grin. "It's a metaphor."

"For what?"

"Me. I'm the tiger! And they forced me into a cage for their enjoyment. But I grew stronger until I outgrew them in both intellect and strength. But unlike the tiger, I wanted to make them pay."

"So you tortured and killed hundreds?"

"You don't even know who I am. You know nothing about my story. You call me Valla, but I am Queen Adelaide, Valla's mother. No one cares about my story. No one cares about my pain. I was born in poverty and forced into a brothel as a child. I don't imagine I have to go into detail about the horrors of life as a child raised in a whorehouse." She pauses, waiting for him to react.

He schools his features and casually sits down in an armchair. He leans back, crossing his legs. Once he's settled, he looks up and motions with his hand for her to continue, determined to look bored, although her words are shaking him.

She looks impatient. "Comfortable?"

He shifts in his seat. "Not really. I suppose these chairs were chosen for their aesthetic purpose rather than comfort."

With a sigh, she takes a seat on the sofa to face Patrick and pats the seat next to her. "The sofa is comfy. You're welcome to join me over here."

Patrick's eyes flash as they watch her short skirt inch up her thigh. He catches her knowing smile, as he says, "I believe you were telling me of the horrors of living in a brothel."

With a calculated glare, she continues, "I had a friend around my age. Because of neglect and lack of medical care, she was on her death bed at fourteen. It made me desperate to escape. I wanted to save both of us. So, when I discovered an abandoned dagger, I stole it. No one paid much attention to me. They thought I was too dumb and broken to fight back. They saw me only as a beautiful young toy they could abuse for their pleasure, much like these magnificent tigers.

"No one expected me to fight back, but the anger from the injustice gave me the strength I needed to cut into their flesh.

I relished in their suffering. I found that I quite enjoyed killing.

"With blood soaking my hands, I went back to rescue my friend, but it was too late." She glares at him. "I see the way you're looking at me." Her smoldering look would make a weaker man shrink. "Remind me of how many men and women you destroyed in your time with Sky, and yet, you never confronted the man who held you prisoner."

"We are not the same," he says in defense.

"No, I am much stronger. I conquered the ones who held me captive. All the darkness I stored in my soul, I pulled forth and used as a strength. And when I crossed paths with Pelagia, a powerful healer and wielder of magic, I learned everything I could from her.

"When I moved on, the magic that had been so beautiful in the hands of Pelagia, turned dark. It gave me power, youth, and beauty. I became queen of many realms, and as my husbands expected me to bear children, I refused to introduce more innocent lives to suffer in this wicked world. I took my children's lives before they were born. In return, their lives gave me strength and youth. I moved from one prince to another. I lived many lifetimes, surrounded by the beauty of my making until Reyshen, Pelagia's descendant, caught up to me. She didn't like how I was using the gifts her great-grandmother shared with me, so she suspended my powers. She wanted to lock me up, but I'd rather die than live in a cage. I was pregnant with Valla at the time, and she was failing in my womb, but instead of miscarrying my child, I traded her death for my life."

"What about Leona and Isa?"

A look of disgust crosses her face. "They were never my children. King Edmond saw me through what he thought were miscarriages, thinking I was desperate for little girls. In hopes of appeasing me, he came home one day with two baby girls with blond hair and blue eyes just like him. Though blond hair and blue eyes was my preference in lovers, I had no desire to have children, especially peasant children."

Patrick wants to point out that she, herself, was born a peasant, but he needs to hear the rest of the story.

She continues, "I was stuck in some sort of purgatory for fifteen years until Reyshen died. Then I could sense Valla. We were connected somehow, and our connection grew the more she used her power—my power. Soon after, I realized I could live through her. I possessed her body to kill the king because he deserved to die. He was the one who called on Reyshen. He was the reason I was once again imprisoned.

"Each time I stepped back into Valla's mind, I tried to show her she didn't need to be afraid. She was powerful. No one could stop her, but she fought me. I gave birth to her, and she didn't appreciate what I'd given her. She tried to get rid of me, she even tried to kill herself, but I wouldn't let her die. She simply couldn't see that her power was a gift. Then she fell in love with a man who helped her lock me up inside, taking away my control.

"She gave birth to a daughter. I only wanted women to carry my power, so males were unable to survive in her womb, something I'm glad to see passed on for all generations of Valla's bloodline. After Valla's daughter was born, she contacted her step-sisters. Their joined powers were enough to overpower Valla who held me inside like a prisoner while her sisters killed her, and I died again." She stands up as if the sofa is on fire, her anger flowing like lava from a volcano. She sears Patrick with a look. "Very different from the fairytale you grew up knowing."

"Why are you telling me this?"

She walks around the coffee table and sits on the edge right in front of Patrick. Recrossing her legs, she says, "Because, Patrick, you and I are not so different. Sky kept you locked in a cage for years. He tortured you. I know what that's like. You cling to Emily, just like I clung to my daughter. We protect them, but they don't want us. Emily will break your heart, but I won't.

I will appreciate you and treat you like a partner." She leans forward. "There are some lines this body—or the minds inside this body—won't allow me to cross." She uncrosses her legs and rests her delicate hand on Patrick's thigh. "But with you, she is different. With you, she lets her guard down and I know she would make an exception." She glides her hand up his thigh.

Wrapping his hand around hers, he stops her movement. He stares at their linked hands for a moment, fighting to keep himself in check. Absently, he rubs his thumb across the soft skin of her fingers, but immediately stops when he realizes what he's doing. He looks up to see she had not missed it. The sultry smile curving her lips and her temptress eyes have him leaning forward before he can catch himself.

Seeing his tells, Adelaide moves onto his lap. Surprise momentarily freezes Patrick's movements. He breathes out in a rush when her breath tickles across the sensitive skin below his ear. Her lips press teasing kisses along his neck and his eyes close in an attempt to remember his purpose. She nibbles lightly and he groans, shifting her in his lap. She places his hand on the smooth skin of her inner thigh.

He can't seem to control himself and his fingers dig too firmly into her leg. Just as he forces himself to release his grip, she moans against his neck and pulls back to place her hands against his chest. They stare eye to eye.

"I thought maybe I'd have to persuade you, but since you have entered this room, I haven't had any reason to control your mind or body. There is an undeniably strong connection between us, Patrick."

He rests his forehead against hers. "I'm here for Emily," he grinds out.

"Emily is here. She is safe. I will protect her, and you can help me keep her safe." She wiggles on his lap, rubbing against his sensitive parts. Her skirt rises and his hand moves further up her thigh, his finger brushing the silky material of her panties.

"Stop resisting," she pleads against his lips.

And just like that he caves, pulling her into him, welcoming her tongue in his mouth as his hands explore.

She unbuttons his shirt, pulling it open. Then she pauses, pulling back. Her eyes go straight to his necklace. With a questioning frown, she reaches out for the onyx.

Her fingers tingle as they graze the gem. "How did you get this?"

"Isn't it beautiful? It gives power to the one who wears it. I found it in the old artifacts my parents had stashed away."

Her eyes fall back to the gem. "Do you know where they found this?"

"No, but they traveled all over when I was young."

"It used to be mine. I was wearing it when my daughter so cruelly caged me."

Patrick looks shocked. "I had no idea." He reaches up behind his neck and unclasps the necklace, holding it out to her. "Then it is still yours. Turn around."

She turns and holds her hair to the side, making it easier for him to clasp it together. Patrick lets the gem fall against her chest and she spins back to face him.

"It tingles. I don't remember it doing that before."

He tucks his hand into his pocket, sticking his finger with the pin he has hidden there, as he explains, "That is the magic igniting again. The tingling is only temporary." He reaches out for the onyx. "It looks better on you," he says, letting a drop of his blood touch the surface.

His blood triggers the gem, making it glow bright blue, while her eyes go wide, and she shrieks in agony. She claws at the necklace, trying to remove it. Her fingernails rake across her chest, ripping into flesh but the gem has already begun to burn her skin. Her frantic hands go still as her body goes limp. Patrick lowers her to the floor where she starts seizing, the same way Patrick seized the first time he held the necklace. She's staring up at him, as he holds her head in his lap.

He hates to watch this. He doesn't want Emily to suffer, but he has to wait it out. He needs to make sure Adelaide is gone before he makes the pain go away for Emily.

Hot breath against the side of his face has him turning to see the giant white tiger hovering next to him. River's sky-blue eyes glimmer as his mouth curls into a snarl.

"Damn," Patrick says, ducking to the side. He drops Emily's head onto the floor and rolls away from the imminent danger. The move allows him a brief reprieve, but the growling tigers are coming at him from both sides. "Stop!" he commands, but they aren't listening to him.

CHAPTER TWENTY-SEVEN ~

THE BELL CHIMES on Lathe's phone and he looks down to see there is a disturbance with his mother. He pulls up the feed from her room to find nothing but darkness. Switching to the infrared camera, he sees his mother sitting in the middle of her living room with objects circling her head.

He rushes down the flight of stairs to the basement and enters her darkened chambers. Lathe flips the light switch by the door, but the room remains bathed in darkness.

"Mother, it's me. Please turn on the lights."

"No, no, no, no, no, no, no . . ." his mother repeats, her voice becoming softer and softer until her words fade completely.

Lathe lights up his phone, holding it out, so he's able to see in front of him. He finds her curled on the floor beside the sofa. She whimpers when the light illuminates her features.

"Mother, what do you see?"

"Gore," she whispers, uncurling from the fetal position. Looking at him with cloudy eyes, she says, "Gore . . . And an army of horned beasts and fire. Fire burning everything." Looking startled by her words, she shrieks, "Fire burning everything!" She folds back into a ball covering her head with her arms. "No, no, no, no, no, no, no."

Lathe breathes out a sigh and puts his phone away. He crouches to sit on the floor next to her. His back rests against the side of the sofa, and he places a reassuring hand on her back as he begins to sing softly.

> *"There once was a girl with golden hair,*
> *with eyes so blue and skin so fair.*
> *Blessed with gifts so rare and pure,*
> *nobody knew what she'd endure,*
> *His soul was black with sins so dark;*
> *this covetous man claimed her heart,*
> *He took her wits, destroying her life;*
> *she lived each day with pain and strife,*
> *Until one day when her belly grew,*
> *the babe inside she hardly knew,*
> *His innocent life saved her own,*
> *her reason to live for him alone,*
> *Others seem to think she's blind,*
> *but there are visions in her mind.*
> *I'll always love you, so I'll stay,*
> *protecting you 'til your last day."*

By the time he's finished, she is clinging to him, her head buried against his chest. He holds her, rocking gently as the lights flicker.

"Lathe," she breathes, pulling back. "It's been so much worse ever since . . . ever since he died. Your father, do you think he was protecting me?"

"No, Mother. I don't think Sky was protecting you. I think this is because of what's happening, with Emily, or Valla. You said there was fire?"

"I could stop her," she says, her clear blue eyes becoming round in her face.

"Yes, I know, but it's not safe, Mother."

"I wish I could control it. I wish I could . . ." Her eyes become unfocused, taking her to another place.

"Mother?"

Gasping, she jerks her head to the other side of the room as she watches a scene play out before her.

He tries to bring her back. "Mother?"

She whispers, "Adelaide." Her body trembles.

Chills crawl over his skin, "Who?"

Her unseeing eyes grow wider, and she gasps, "No, Adelaide! You must help her."

"Who is Adelaide? I don't know who that is."

She turns to him. "Go to her!" she shouts as the lights start flashing on and off. "Go! You must save her!"

"Okay," he soothes, getting to his feet. "Okay, Mother, I'm going to her."

She watches him leave, but inside her mind, she shouts for him to stop so she can explain everything. She just sent her son off to die.

She gets to her feet and runs to the door, but it's locked up tight. She turns to push the panic button to call him back, but as she turns, she notices a tiger standing across the room.

Forgetting herself, she moves back into the living room to get a better look at the brave feline. Most animals are too afraid to come near her. Before she reaches the tiger, it fades away.

Her son forgotten, along with her fear, she forces the lights off and goes to sit in the place the tiger was standing.

Hot breath against his skin, the snarling tigers come at Patrick from both sides. "Stop," he commands. But they aren't listening to him. He looks down to the woman lying on the floor, and her lips curl into a snarl just before her eyes roll back in her head.

Copper pounces and Patrick dives to the side, shouting,

"Stop!" He spins around, and both tigers are standing next to him, their snarls gone, their eyes directed at him, awaiting his next command. Patrick looks down to see Emily's eyes are closed and her body is quiet. Adelaide is no longer in control, and now the tigers are listening to him.

"Heel," he commands, and the tigers sit. Patrick kneels next to Emily. He pulls a glove out of his pocket and onto his hand before picking the gem up off of her skin. There is a burn indent from where the gem began melding into her chest. "Come on, Emily," he whispers. "Come on, wake up."

Patrick sits with her for several moments before her eyes open and her face turns sad as she finds Patrick looking down at her.

"Emily?"

She shakes her head. "No, Emily is barely holding on. I'm afraid my mother has broken her will to live."

"Valla?"

She nods, saying, "There can only be one entity in charge of this body at any given time. Much like a modern-day vehicle, there is only one driver's seat. The three of us are stuck in this vessel, none of us able to get rid of the other, but we all have an influence. Adelaide took the driver's seat months ago, before Emily even understood she was sharing her vessel. We haven't been able to regain control, although we have tried."

"But Emily is still in there?"

"She is," she says, her gaze not connecting with his. She takes a deep breath and continues, "Queen Adelaide must be stopped. She fed off the vitality of her unborn children for decades so she could stay young and beautiful forever.

"My father, the king, suspected an evil spirit possessed my mother, so he called upon a shaman, Reyshen, the great-granddaughter of Pelagia, the woman who gave my mother her gifts. Reyshen didn't approve of the ways Adelaide was using her grandmother's gift, so she sought to destroy the evil queen. But when she found out Adelaide was pregnant, she tried to save the baby.

"The only way for my mother to escape was death, so she stole my peaceful afterlife. She gave me all the life she had stored up, leaving me with remarkable capabilities, but she robbed me of parts of my soul. Trying to compensate, my soul latched on to my mother's, and eventually, Adelaide became a part of me. She haunted me, and it only got worse as I grew.

"By age fifteen, Queen Adelaide began possessing my mind and body while I slept. She killed Reyshen and the king. My father was a kind man, and he did not deserve to die. Neither of them did. Reyshen shared her gifts with my step-sisters before she died, but my sisters were still afraid of me. So, I ran away to a place where I wouldn't hurt anyone else.

"But I did. My mother demanded revenge and continued possessing me when I slept. I chained myself in the wilderness, but when I awoke months later, I was surrounded by mind slaves and dead bodies with only a faint recollection to what she had done.

"This went on for years, until I fell in love with a man named Jonathan. Together, we found a way to repress my mother from taking over. Isa, Leona, and I discovered we could charge this gem with magic to suppress Adelaide. It took a drop of blood from the three of us to activate the stone.

"Adelaide was drawn to the necklace but was completely unaware of its power over her.

"I lived happily for the next year. I married Jonathan and had his child, but his love shifted to fear when the necklace started losing its power. He feared for our daughter's safety, so we called on my sisters. He believed they were coming to strengthen the magic in the necklace. It would've taken just a drop of blood from each of us to restrengthen it, but that was not my plan. I called on my sisters to put an end to my suffering. With Adelaide repressed, Isa and Leona euthanized me like the rabid animal I had become. I was diseased by evil, destined to die. I shattered

Jonathan's heart with my betrayal, but I thought it was the only way to protect my daughter.

"What I didn't realize is the magic used to kill me would ricochet and kill my sisters. Without the three of us, no one knew what to believe. Our families turned against one another and Valla blood was deemed evil. Generations have paid dearly for our mistake."

Valla looks heartbroken, but she continues, "My sisters and I didn't know our souls were cursed. I guess I made that discovery first. I thought I was in Hell, eternally damned for the sins of my mother, but the fire licked at my skin like a lover's caress. I was stuck, trapped in this in-between, a purgatory of sorts, where all I could do was wait and observe. I was cursed to watch as generations of my bloodline were persecuted and killed. Emily is my only remaining heir."

Her demeanor shifts, no longer reflecting the past. Valla's nostrils flare and she snaps, "Patrick Glenn, you think you love her, you think she needs you, but you've already betrayed her by coming here. You have broken every promise you have made her, every vow."

"I'm here because she wants me to be. Have you even asked her what she wants?"

Her smile twists as she shakes her head, accusing, "You think you're here to rescue her?" A sorrowful laugh escapes her. "She chose you to come here because she was counting on you doing what no one else could. She wants you to kill her, Patrick." She clears her throat. "After all of the terrible things you have done, she asks you to do the one thing you cannot do."

Dread fills Patrick because he knows her words are true. "Can you save her?"

"I already saved her once," Valla answers. "During her fight with Sky she called on me for help, opening a door she didn't know was there. I've been waiting a long time to be of use, and I've tried to help others in the past, but none survived, until Emily. You and your uncle kept her alive long enough for me to intervene and heal her mortal damage. Our souls merged, and it was beautiful. But as we were recovering, my mother's soul found us—she always finds me—and she took control. Tell me, Patrick Glenn, what are you planning?"

"I need a drop of her blood mixed with mine to activate the stone. If what you're saying is true, then the necklace does work."

"It's only a temporary solution. It won't last."

"We'll take the temporary solution until we find a permanent one. I need to take Emily back to her family. They need her. I need her. The Olvasho need her."

"Adelaide is very strong right now. It may take a while for Emily to regain full control of her body. And then there are the mind slaves to contend with. Some of those people Adelaide has controlled for months. She steals their thoughts and fills their minds with her own ideas, possessing them from afar like puppets. They will need a lot of help finding their way back."

"I'll fix it."

"You are talented in many areas, Patrick, but your lack of self-awareness will be your downfall. You mistake your obsession with Emily for love."

"There is no mistake. Her feelings will never match mine. I accept that, but I will love her regardless of her affections."

"She will not be happy with you for bringing her back," Valla warns. "She is not the Emily you once knew. Adelaide has controlled her every thought, every action for months. She will need help adjusting to her life."

"I know, but she's strong. She can do this."

"She is capable, but she may not be willing."

"Are you going to bring her back to me?" Patrick asks, becoming impatient.

"I will try. Once I activate the necklace, my connection to her will fade, not as much as Adelaide's, but I won't be able to lend her my strength. It will be up to you to help her. My mother must be eliminated. That will probably entail my demise, and I will happily die if it means destroying the evil that has plagued our families for generations. I trust you'll find a way, Patrick." She pricks her finger and touches it to the stone still in Patrick's hand. The second her blood makes contact; the gem glows emerald. She winks and her eyes fall closed with a peaceful smile.

THE SKY GETS dark so early now, and Morgan feels tired after her anatomy class. She has checked her phone at least twenty times to see if she has missed a call from Patrick. Hours have passed since he last checked in, and she is scared for him.

Morgan sends him another text before her long trek across the university campus. Student parking is on the North side and her anatomy class just so happens to be in the most southern building. When she started classes, the walk didn't bother her because the sun was still in the sky and she didn't think the Olvasho were dangerous to her. But with the season change, the sky is dark this time of night and it leaves her feeling even more vulnerable to the Olvasho.

Morgan huddles into her coat and scarf before stepping out into the unpredictable weather. Tonight is not particularly cold, but it is windy. The smell of rain fills the air, indicating a storm is on the way. As she walks, she notices other students are keeping their heads down in an attempt to ward off the gusty winds. Her path is reasonably well lit with the blue emergency lights every so often, but dark shadows from trees and buildings leave Morgan feeling leery. A sudden breeze whips Morgan's hair into her face and she fights to tuck it back into her hood. As soon as she does, her scarf blows in front of her and by the time she gets it under control, she discovers a man walking next to her.

Looking down at her, he says, "Morgan, I think it's time we talk."

The lamplight above shines down on his heavily scarred features, causing Morgan to gasp. "Lathe?" she breathes, taking in the deep grooves of discolored skin that mold his once beautiful face into something out of a nightmare. Whatever happened to him must have been horrific. On instinct, Morgan reaches out to comfort him, but he steps back confused by her movement.

He didn't hide his scars in an effort to become more intimidating, but it has the opposite effect on her. Lathe wonders what is wrong with these women, first Ashley and now Morgan. His eyebrows pinch together as a grim line takes his uneven lips. He grabs her wrist and pulls her out from beneath the pool of light.

Triggered by his touch, the words Patrick implanted in Morgan come pouring out of her. "You forced me into my role with Sky. Had you not destroyed your face," Morgan pauses, realizing the harshness of Patrick's words flowing through her, but she is helpless to stop them. "Had you not destroyed your face," she repeats, wincing, "I would've had a chance at a normal life. Do you think my life has been any easier than yours? I didn't ask for my years with Sky. I didn't want any of it. I didn't choose the things I have done, or the horrors done to me."

Patrick's words continue to pour from her mouth. "You can compel Morgan if you want, but it's unnecessary; she will give you any information you desire. I know you have a need for revenge, but harming Morgan will not take away your pain. Morgan is a beautiful soul. Knowing her has changed me, and for what it's worth, I am sorry about Kay . . . Katie." Tears fall from Morgan's eyes as Patrick's words come to a close.

Lathe stares at her for a moment. With a short laugh, he looks down at her and says, "Patrick thinks too much of me. I am not above revenge." He grabs her wrist again. "Come with me."

CHAPTER TWENTY-EIGHT ~

EMILY ~

I THOUGHT I WAS SAFE. I felt safe, which is precisely what Adelaide wanted me to feel. I knew Valla blood was feared, but I thought I could control it and keep it from turning me into the monster the Olvasho predicted. I never anticipated Adelaide.

Valla was there too, looking out for me like a big sister. With the little control we had, we kept Adelaide from killing people. It took all of our strength, but together, we were able to accomplish at least that much.

In the beginning, I prayed for someone to rescue me, but somewhere along the way, my prayer changed, and I began wishing for death. I didn't know the meaning of pain until evil lived inside my body and ate up all that I once was. Now, I am nothing. I'm a shadow, a ghost. I let the numbness consume me most of the time. But I was alert and aware the second I sensed Patrick, so I watched him through Adelaide's eyes.

I saw the way he looked at her, the way he reacted to her. I saw the moment he gave in and wanted to believe it was me. I wanted to believe it was me too. Then I remembered I sent

Maggie to find him so he would come here and kill me, but I saw no malice in his eyes, and I was afraid for him. Adelaide was a master of manipulation, and Patrick walked so willingly into her trap.

Then I felt her shock and pain the moment he betrayed her. Every second she grew weaker, and Valla and I became stronger until Adelaide lost control over my body. I didn't grab power. I didn't want it. I wanted to die.

So, Valla took control and spoke to Patrick. She explained the truths and I saw his concern. I heard his words, but he has no idea. The Emily he once knew is no longer. He just isn't willing to believe it.

Valla comes back to me, saying, "Emily, either you take over or Adelaide will. I can feel her growing stronger."

She's right. I feel her gaining strength.

"Emily, the necklace will work, but you have to be in control of your body before it's placed against your skin," she explains.

"Thank you, Valla. For all of your help with Sky and all that you've done to help me through."

"I will always help you, Emily, for as long as I am able."

I OPEN my eyes for the first time in months and everything seems brighter through my own eyes. A tiger stands at my side, its snow-white fur radiant against the black stripes. Blue feline eyes stare at me as my mind melds back into one with my body. All of a sudden, pain overtakes me. It's Adelaide. She's fighting to get back into the driver's seat. The pain is so intense that I don't notice Patrick approach until he kneels next to me, placing a hand on my shoulder. With a startled breath, I turn to him, my alarm melting into sorrow, and I plead, "Kill me, Patrick. Kill us! Please. I can't hold her much longer. She grows stronger by the second."

"No, love, you need to fight. You can do this. You hold the power, not her!"

"Patrick, I'm not strong enough," I argue through gritted teeth.

"You have to be," Patrick says, holding the bloody emerald in his gloves hand. "We need you."

I whimper, closing my eyes against the pain. "I don't care, just let us die."

"Please, Emily, I need you."

Hands fisting, head throbbing, I fight the demon in my mind. Tears of agony rain down my face and Patrick leans forward to wrap the emerald necklace around my neck. The gem lands on my chest, sizzling against my skin. Patrick catches me as I fall back. He lays my exhausted body down on the sofa, his fingers combing through my hair. I feel him press a kiss against the side of my head and his serene ocean waves caress the confines of my mind. I welcome them in, taking all the comfort he offers until his healing waters become a soothing balm against my exhausted mind.

CHAPTER TWENTY-NINE ~

EMILY REGAINS CONSCIOUSNESS, aware of her dark thoughts. Fear binds her body, its parasitic tentacles crawl up her spine, making it impossible to move. Her eyes flash open as she attempts to clutch the only remaining thread of reality. Everything has betrayed her, her thoughts, her mind, her body, but her eyes have always given her a glimpse of the truth.

Right now, her eyes tell her she's lying on a mattress in the back of a moving utility van with a white sheet draped over her. She props herself up on an arm and searches the space. The two rear windows reveal a dark sky with a glimpse of the sun above the horizon. She turns to look behind her to see who's driving and finds Patrick at the wheel. He's deep in thought, trying to work out his inner turmoil by grinding his molars back and forth. He doesn't know she's awake, yet.

Pushing the sheets to the side, she notices she's still wearing the white t-shirt and shorts Patrick made her change into at the hotel. She attempts a full body scan but is immediately overwhelmed by the crimson liquid soaking through the white material of her t-shirt. Blood drips through the hands she frantically presses against the wound. The liquid pools around her on the mattress.

She lifts the hem of her shirt to press her hands against the gaping wound in her abdomen, but it only grows.

She's lost too much blood.

She should be dizzy.

The pain should be all-consuming, but all she feels is panic. She must be going into shock. She hyperventilates while she makes another desperate attempt to staunch the bleeding.

"Emily!" Patrick is there, grabbing at her hands. "Emily, calm down."

She shoves him away, trying to save him from whatever is tearing her apart from the inside. He comes right back, trying to grip her hands. She swings her arms and kicks her legs, all the while, trying to maintain the blood loss.

"Emily, it's not real."

She is shrieking and panting for breath. She is dying. Patrick stops advancing to sit on the opposite side of the mattress with his back against the wall, saying soothing words she is unable to comprehend.

"Emily, whatever you're seeing. It's not real."

Her shrieking turns into sobs, and she still can't breathe. She folds herself into a ball, curling up like a fetus in a womb. And like a fetus, she needs her mom. But she's alone with Patrick and she's bleeding to death. She thought death would feel different.

She looks up to Patrick, asking, "Why? Why did you let them do this to me?"

"Emily, whatever it is you're seeing, it isn't real."

His answer confuses her. She looks down at the sheet pressed against her chest and the blood is . . . Gone. She shoves it away and discovers her clothing and body are intact.

She looks down at her open palms and the blood returns, dripping through her fingers, running down her arms, crimson drops are staining the white sheet. She's shaking, and her breath is rapid as she attempts to scrub the blood from her arms.

"It's not real," Patrick repeats, trying to grab ahold of her wrists.

"If it's not real, then what am I seeing?" She blinks and the blood vanishes. Her ears are ringing. Everything is spinning. Patrick's arms are around her, pulling her into his lap and holding her there.

She whimpers into his chest, "I'm losing my mind, Patrick. I can't . . . I can't even trust my eyes. You . . . you should've killed me."

"It will get better," he reassures, pressing his lips to her temple.

"And if you're wrong?"

His head rests on top of hers and the question goes unanswered. She sobs into his chest, pleading, "If it doesn't get better, I need you to do it, Patrick. I need you to end it. I can't go back to that. Some things are worse than death." She looks up into his glistening eyes. "Patrick, I'm begging you. Don't let me go back."

"Emily . . ." Tears slip from his eyes.

"It's mercy, Patrick. It's mercy. Not murder."

MORGAN SITS on the couch in Patrick's apartment. She glances at the computer sitting on the coffee table. She can reach out and grab it, but with Lathe hovering over her there isn't much she can do from there.

Lathe leans against the side of the couch, rubbing at his temples when suddenly he snickers, saying, "You're so obvious with your thoughts."

"I never pretended not to be," Morgan shoots back.

"You put far too much faith in Patrick. Do you know what happened to Katie, or did he just compel those words out of you?"

Morgan shakes her head. In a small voice, she says, "He never told me, but—"

"Patrick is a black widow, Morgan. Do you know what that means?"

Morgan swallows, not wanting to hear it from him. "I'd prefer to hear it from Patrick."

"Patrick is too much of a coward to tell you."

Morgan focuses on her lap where her hands wring together. When she glances up, Lathe is watching her hands. He knows she doesn't deserve this treatment, but Patrick left her here for Lathe to find, trusting Lathe not to destroy her the way Patrick destroyed Katie.

"Katie and I grew up together. She was my girlfriend, the only good thing in my miserable life and Patrick used her as a plaything before murdering her in cold blood."

Morgan tries not to react, but traitorous tears fall from her eyes.

Lathe leans in, close enough for his breath to tickle her ear. "And he abandons you, knowing I would come for you, knowing I want revenge for Katie. He left you at my mercy. Me, Lathen Vallor, Sky's only legitimate heir and the sole caretaker of the most powerfully insane Olvasho alive."

Morgan lifts her chin, looking him in the eye with determination as her tears continue to fall. She swallows. "I won't make excuses for Patrick, but I will tell you he's paying for his past. He's self-destructive, tormented by it. It keeps him up at night, and I believe Emily is the only reason he keeps going. He feels like if he can save her, then it might make amends for some of his wrongdoing. I don't know the details of his past, and I don't want to know. I don't blame you for wanting to hurt me to get back at him, but you said you're a caretaker, a nurturer. If that's true, then harming me will only hurt you more."

Lathe leans down, a hand wrapping around her throat. "You don't know me."

"And you don't know me," she warns before kicking out, jamming her knee into his thigh. When his grip loosens, she knocks his hand away and runs for the exit. She opens the door only for a torrent of wind to slam it shut. The force of it pushes her body against the door, and she closes her eyes as her long hair whips around her.

Even after the wind dies down, she can't move, held against the door by invisible shackles. She feels Lathe's body press against her back. "You think it's that easy to escape?"

She struggles to move her body, trying to break free, trying to fight. When Lathe scoffs, she throws her head back, slamming it into his face.

"Shit!" Lathe says as blood pours from his nose.

Whatever was holding her in place breaks, and she pushes away from the door, running for her mace on the kitchen counter. She grabs it along with the biggest knife in reach. Spinning back to Lathe, Morgan prepares to fight her way out.

Lathe is still by the apartment door, the trickle of blood slowing as he pinches his nose. When he catches sight of her in the kitchen, preparing for battle, he laughs through the blood dripping down his face.

Morgan tightens her grip on the knife, saying, "I won't make it easy for you to kill me."

He shakes his head with a bloody smile. "You can't beat me, Morgan."

"I guess we'll see," she says, her body vibrating with adrenaline.

"What happened to the sweet nurturing Morgan?"

"She learned that sweet doesn't always cut it. Sometimes you need to grow teeth and claws and fight your way out."

He shakes his head, his hand still holding his nose. "I have to hand it to you, Morgan. I didn't expect you to fight back, but you successfully broke my nose." With a crack, he snaps it back in place. Lowering his hand, he moves toward her. "How far do you think you'll go to save yourself?"

"I'll do what I have to."

"You think so." He takes a few more steps and Morgan shifts, moving into the living room and holding out her pepper spray.

"If you spray that, I'll blow it back in your face. You know I can." He flicks his wrist and a sudden breeze lifts the hair from her neck. It disappears just as quickly, sending a chill through Morgan.

She knows she's way out of her depth, but still, she asks, "How are you doing that?"

He smirks. "Family secret."

He moves forward, cornering her. She swings the knife, but Lathe catches her wrist. He looks her in the eye as he lifts her hand, touching the blade to his throat. He takes a step forward, leaning into it until beads of blood begin to form. Morgan tries to pull the knife away, but his grip is too firm around her wrist. Her eyes show fear as the blade continues to cut deeper into his neck. She opens her fingers, letting the knife fall to the floor between them, but he still doesn't let go of her.

"You were never going to kill me, Morgan, just like I was never going to kill you. Patrick is guilty, not you, and if I killed you, then I'd be no better than him."

As he releases his grip, Morgan asks, "Is this how you treated Ashley?"

At the mention of Ashley, Lathe flinches. To hide his reaction, he spins toward the kitchen, going to the sink to clean the blood from his face and neck. By the time he turns back around, Morgan is standing at the kitchen counter, the knife laid out before her.

"If you weren't going to hurt me, then why did you grab my throat?"

"I wanted you to shut up. The more you pretend to know me, the angrier I get. And it's not like I squeezed."

"Do all Olvasho have terrible interpersonal skills?"

"We have our own set of social rules."

"So, why are you here?"

"I need to talk to Patrick."

"He's not here, and he won't be home anytime soon. He won't come back without Emily."

Morgan's phone begins ringing, and Lathe pulls it out of his pocket to find Ashley's face lighting the screen.

Morgan peeks at the phone and says, "She remembers you, you know. Ben doesn't, but Ashley does. Why didn't you wipe her memories?"

He narrows his eyes. "I did."

"Not very well. She keeps asking me about you."

He doesn't believe her and to prove her wrong, he answers the ringing phone. "Hello, Ashley."

He's met with silence before a tentative voice steals his breath. "Lathe?"

Lathe's eyes dart to Morgan as his thoughts run wild. How can she remember him? He wiped her memory. He is flawless in deleting himself from people's minds. Had he messed up or is something wrong with her?

"Lathe, is that you?" Ashley asks.

She not only remembered him, but she recognized his voice, but how?

"It's Preston," Lathe responds. "Morgan's in the shower. I'll have her call you back."

"Wait! Don't hang up!" she says frantically.

Against his better judgment, he doesn't hang up.

In a shy voice, Ashley asks, "Are you at the apartment?"

"Yeah, Morgan and I are just about to go out on a date."

"Cut the shit. I know this isn't Preston," she says.

When Lathe doesn't respond, Ashley says, "Fine, whatever, just tell Morgan I'm going out with that guy tonight, so I need her to call me at nine."

A streak of anger runs through Lathe, but he buries it because the feeling is unfounded. "I'll pass it along."

Ashley responds with, "Out of my way, dickweed!"

"What?"

"Nothing. I'm driving."

Lathe smiles as she shouts, "Gas is on the right, sweetheart!" More calmly, she says, "Okay, Lathe—I mean Preston, I'll let you go. On second thought, have Morgan call me when she's out of the shower."

"Sure."

"Sure," she says, hanging up on him.

PATRICK IS behind the wheel again. It's been twenty-four hours since he got Emily back, although that may be a stretch. The girl in the back of the van is hardly a person at all. She goes back and forth between catatonia and hysteria. He has to pull over every time the hysterics come. At this rate, their trip is going to take forever. He hasn't slept except for those twenty minutes while he held her early this morning.

The mess Adelaide left rivaled Sky. While she hadn't killed anyone, she had manipulated all those people back at the hotel. Patrick didn't have time to deal with the victims, so he called in an anonymous tip to the Olvasho council. Handling such a matter is one of the things the council was created to do, and for once he was happy to let them do their job.

He pulls over at the next motel in order to get some sleep. He needs rest if he plans to survive this.

He parks outside of the shady motel lobby, but before getting out, he turns toward the back of the van and says, "Emily, stay here. I'm going to get a room."

Emily is sitting up, her back resting against the side of the van. Her eyes are open, but unseeing, staring blankly at the van wall. She doesn't seem to register his words or the fact that the van is no longer moving.

Patrick takes a breath before turning forward and exiting the van. He is sure to get a room at the end, furthest away from everyone else, just in case Emily begins screaming at random. So far, she hasn't used any of her Olvasho abilities, which Patrick is incredibly thankful for.

As he exits the lobby, he stops cold. Dozens of deer are

wandering around the parking lot, making a ring around the van. Come to think of it; he has been seeing a lot of deer today. He thought it was unusual, but now it makes sense. Emily was stirring something in them. They've been following her. This means she has been using her abilities all day, whether she was aware of it or not. He knows he needs to go to Morgan's plan B.

He shoos the deer away from the van and drives down to their room. He unloads their items and slips plan B into his pocket. The deer crowd his way as he heads to the back of the van. Mentally, he tries to push them away, but it has no effect because Emily's pull is too strong.

He slips into the van and says, "Emily, we are stopping for the night."

She doesn't hear because she's in a catatonic state.

He slips her sweater off her shoulder and removes the syringe from his pocket. He uses his teeth to remove the cap and plunges the needle into her bicep. Her head pivots and angry green eyes awaken. She shoves him away with more strength than he thought her capable.

"I'm trying to help you, Emily!"

She looks to the syringe still sticking out of her arm and then back to him. Her eyes become heavy and the anger melts as her body slumps to the side. Patrick pulls the needle from her arm, saying, "I'm sorry," as he lowers her onto the mattress. "It's the only way."

When her eyes close, he opens the van door. "Go!" he yells toward the herd of deer.

He watches as they scatter, leaping away now that they no longer feel the pull toward Emily. Relieved, Patrick gathers Emily in his arms and carries her into the rundown motel room.

Once inside, he lies her on one of the queen beds and pulls out his phone to call Morgan.

A masculine voice answers, "Hello, Patrick."

"Lathe?"

"Yes, I'm here with Morgan who is worried sick about you. You're still alive, so I presume you haven't found her."

Patrick looks over to Emily lying unconscious on the bed, saying, "I found her. I just need to find a way to reach her."

"That was her in Chicago, wasn't it? Some of those people lost months of their lives."

Patrick grins, pleased the council didn't kill anyone. "I'm sure I don't know what you're talking about, Lathe. Although, it sounds to me like losing a couple of months isn't the most unfortunate outcome. It's far better than losing their lives."

"So, I suppose you're the one who made the anonymous call."

"Again, Lathe, this sounds like council business. I'm not sure why you're involving me."

Lathe sighs. "Mother was asking about Adelaide."

Patrick looks at Emily again. Checking to see her necklace firmly in place, he questions, "What does she know about Adelaide?"

"You know Mother is not much for explaining herself, but I'd be happy to set up a meeting for the two of you to go over things."

"I'm going to have to take a rain check on meeting with mommy dearest." Patrick blows out a breath. "Lathe, let me talk to my cousin."

"Can I count on you to bring Adelaide to the meeting on Sunday?"

A crude laugh escapes Patrick. "You have no idea what you're asking, do you? Tell Morgan I said hello and I'll be in touch."

Patrick hangs up, wondering what the hell Lathe is thinking. He knows Lathe won't knowingly hurt his cousin, but the council would. The question is how much Lathe revealed to the council. Patrick knows the council will always be a problem, so he isn't sure how, but he will find a way to get to the meeting, and Adelaide will be going with him.

His phone rings and he picks it up.

"Lathe?"

"No, it's me," Morgan says. "Lathe just left. He didn't hurt me. He actually seems like a decent guy. He picked me up from class yesterday and brought me back to our apartment. I think he just wanted to talk to you. I told my dad I was staying with Ashley. You never checked in after going into the hotel yesterday. I was worried sick. Did you find her?"

"Technically, I found her but getting to her is more complicated than I anticipated."

"Where are you now?"

He opens the curtain and looks out over the flat farm landscape along the interstate. They were a five-hour drive from home, but now they would be taking a detour. "I'm still in Chicago," he lies. "And Morgan, I knew he wouldn't hurt you."

"Patrick," she says tentatively, "who is Katie?"

His eyelids close, trying and failing to block Katie from his memory. He knows he will have to tell Morgan eventually, but not yet. "Morgan, I really need to get some sleep. I'll be in touch soon, okay?"

"Sleep safe, Patrick," she says. "I'll talk to you later."

He turns the phone off as soon as he hangs up. He tosses it to the empty bed and sits down next to Emily's comatose body. He lies down next to her, wanting to be close in case she wakes up. And if he's being honest, he needs to feel her next to him, so he knows she's really there.

PATRICK WAKES to the sound of the shower running. He left one of the bedside lamps on the night before, but now the light is out, and the room is dark aside from the red neon glow from the clock next to the bed. It reads seven forty-six. Patrick gets out of the now empty bed and goes over to the curtains, cracking them enough for light to spill in, creating a harsh beam of light that divides the room. Patrick didn't hear her get up. He thought the tranquilizer would work longer, but then again, they slept for nearly twelve hours.

Soon the shower turns off and there is rustling in the bathroom before the door opens and Emily walks out wrapped in a towel. "You're awake," she notes, coming into the room.

Patrick looks to the bathroom and back to her. "Did you shower in the dark?"

She looks behind her and then back to Patrick. "Yes." She walks past him and goes to her suitcase on the other side of the room as if everything is normal. Only, normal people didn't shower with the lights off.

At least she is talking. "I prefer the dark. That way my eyes can't tell me one thing when my mind tells me another."

"You're still seeing things?"

"Sort of, my mind is a little clearer since I slept. What did you inject me with?"

"A sedative."

"Thanks, I needed the sleep. I suppose you did, too."

"You seem a lot better," Patrick says, eyeing her carefully.

"It comes in waves." She holds her clothes in one hand and her other hand holds the towel wrapped around her. "How's my dad doing?"

"He's in a coma. His physical injuries have healed, but his mind is not good."

"Why haven't you healed him?"

He looks to the floor, wishing he had better news. "My Uncle Tom and I have both tried." He lifts his eyes to her. "Some afflictions are beyond repair, but we won't stop trying."

Her face is blank as if she's no longer processing emotions. She asks, "How's Sam?"

"She's struggling, but I eased her mind a little, persuading her to continue with wedding plans and that everything would be okay."

"Thank you. What about Ben? Adelaide almost killed him."

"He knows that wasn't you in Grand Rapids. He's worried about you and he misses you, but he's accepted most of this Olvasho business very well."

She nods. "Anything else I should know?"

"You didn't ask about Morgan."

"Because she's stronger than all of us. She's probably upset, but otherwise, she's okay, isn't she?"

It's his turn to nod.

She asks, "When do we leave?"

"Check out is at eleven. We can stay another night if you'd like."

She walks back toward the bathroom, taking in the room. "In this shit hole? You sure do like to spoil me."

Emily is glad Patrick thought to pack some of her old

clothes. Adelaide wore dresses and heels every day, so it's a relief to slip into a pair of jeans and tennis shoes.

Once they are both showered and dressed, they head out to the van. For the first time, Emily sits up front as they drive. They stop for breakfast and then jump on the interstate. After a while, Emily starts paying attention to the signs and asks, "Why are we going this way?"

"I took a little detour. There is somewhere we need to stop on the way back."

She observes him. "Patrick, what are you up to?"

He sighs. "There is an Olvasho council meeting we need to attend the day after tomorrow. I know the timing could be better, but it's the first time they've convened since Sky died. If we don't make an appearance, some individuals will be all too happy to turn the whole group against us."

"Aren't they already against us? I really don't give a shit if they're against me."

"The Council hasn't learned the identity of the Valla blood, but it's only a matter of time. The last thing we need is a target painted on the backs of our loved ones. A show of strength and solidarity will go a long way in protecting ourselves and the people we care about. We need to know what we're up against."

"Are you sure that's such a good idea, Patrick? I'm not well. What if I have an episode while we're there? They already fear me because I'm a descendant of Valla. Do you want them to know I've lost my mind as well?"

He shrugs. "We have roughly forty-eight hours to prepare."

She whips her head toward Patrick, her hair falling in her face. "Forty . . . forty-eight hours?" She pushes her hair back and grabs the hair tie from her wrist. "You think you can fix me in forty-eight hours?"

"No, but we can work on concealing your fragile condition."

"And what if I have a meltdown there and they decide to kill us both?" she questions, as she puts her hair up into a ponytail.

"I won't let that happen and neither will you."

"Okay, then what if I have a meltdown and kill everyone there?"

He turns to look at her, saying, "That's not going to happen."

"Patrick . . ."

"Emily, I need you to trust me," he says, reaching out to squeeze her hand.

Relenting, she says, "I trust you, but I don't trust me!"

"I promise. I won't let anything happen."

"You can't make that promise, Patrick." She unbuckles her seatbelt and goes to the back of the van, ending their conversation.

Patrick can feel her mind weakening as the day goes on. Twice he's seen her rocking back and forth on the mattress.

As they pull into Fort Wayne, Emily breaks the silence, asking, "Do you have any more of that sedative, Patrick?"

He looks at her in his rearview mirror. "You think you need it?"

She's nodding her head before he's finished asking the question. "Yes, please. Now would be good." She grabs at the sides of her head and curls up in the fetal position.

He pulls the van over to prepare the injection for her while she pulls up her sleeve with a trembling hand. After the injection, her body slowly uncurls from the corner of the mattress and she sleeps while Patrick weaves his way through traffic until he finds a hotel.

He makes sure this hotel is nicer than the last one. He also rents all the surrounding rooms just to be safe. The beds are huge and lush. As he lays Emily down, she is almost swallowed whole by the soft white duvet and fluffy pillows.

A few hours later, Emily wakes.

"Did you give me a smaller dose?" she asks, startling Patrick.

He shakes his head, concern in his eyes. "No, I wasn't expecting you to wake until morning."

Her eyebrows scrunch and Patrick leans over to feel her forehead. "I think it's your body burning through the medicine. You've been running really warm. How are you feeling?"

The concern is still etched in her features as she answers, "Better than earlier, but I eh, I don't know how long this clarity will last."

"What do you feel?" Patrick asks.

"Right now, it's not so bad. It's like there is this annoying ringing in my ears. The longer I ignore it, the louder it gets, until eventually, it's all I hear. And once it's all I hear, the ringing becomes something else. It becomes words, Adelaide's words, and the words become thoughts, and the thoughts become hallucinations, and those hallucinations provoke all sorts of emotions. And those emotions elicit the extreme reactions you've seen. It's a cycle and without you there to calm me down and take the brunt of my reaction, or drug me, I could be much more violent and dangerous."

"You say it turns into words. What does she say?"

"Anything to get a reaction. She knows everything about me, all my mistakes, my weaknesses. She knows what to twist and how to make it believable and how to get me to second guess myself. She uses my attraction to you to screw with my head; that's why you can't let anything happen between us, Patrick. No matter what I do. These emotions are so tangled, and you are a weakness for me. Adelaide already told you as much. You gave into her once, but you can't let it happen again. If you let your guard down, I might kill you, and I really don't want to kill you, Patrick. You just . . . you can't trust me."

Emily feels Adelaide at the corners of her subconscious trying to break through. Looking to the clock, she says, "Shit, it's only been a few minutes and she's already back."

"Come here." Patrick moves closer to her, extending soothing waves to lap against Emily subconscious. She relaxes against him, basking in the calm waters. He tries his best to help Emily collect her thoughts and gain control over her psyche.

A NIBBLE at his ear wakes Patrick. It takes him a moment to remember where he is and what's happening. He pulls away from Emily. Voice groggy, he says, "You have to stop."

Her voice is low and pleading. "I don't want to stop."

Patrick sits up and turns on the light, thanking God she isn't naked, but dammit, she's tempting.

She reaches for the hem of her shirt to pull it over her head, but Patrick stops her. "No, Emily, wait!"

"I don't want to wait." She writhes against him.

As he stands from the bed, she locks her legs around him and continues to move and grind.

"Shit, love. Hold on."

She's trying to kiss his lips, but he tilts his face, so she goes for his neck. With her legs locked around his hips, he carries her to the bathroom. He tries to put her down, but she won't let go.

He reaches to turn on the shower and in a breathy moan, he says, "Emily, I need you to stand for a moment so I can see you."

She obliges, standing to remove her shirt, but while her arms are tangled above her head, he picks her up and positions her in the shower under the cold stream of water.

She shrieks against the assault while Patrick shuts the shower curtain. He walks out of the bathroom, so he's not tempted to do anything stupid. He closes the door and slides down it, keeping as many barriers between them as possible. If it weren't so dangerous, he would be sleeping in his own room. But he can't leave her alone right now.

After several minutes pass, the shower turns off, and he hears her soft footfalls against the tile floor. Emily slides down the opposite side of the door, whispering, "I'm sorry, Patrick. Thank you."

There is nothing he can say. She has no idea how hard it is for him to resist her, and as much as he wants to pull her into his body and feel her lips against his neck—No! He can't go there!

He jumps up to gather a blanket, pillow, and some pajamas for Emily and taps on the bathroom door. "I think you should sleep in there tonight," he says. "I'll be right out here."

"Fair enough," she mumbles as she takes the items from him before closing the door. "I'm sorry, Patrick."

Not as sorry as he is. "It's okay, love." He rests his head against the door, saying, "It's nothing to worry about."

Nothing to worry about, *riiight* . . . that's why he's making her sleep in the bathroom. Tomorrow night he'll be giving her a double dose of the sedative.

CHAPTER THIRTY-ONE ~

T HEY ARRIVE an hour before the Olvasho council meeting,
parking down the street. Patrick points out the gated mansion as
he takes Emily down the perimeter of the yard, keeping them
hidden from sight behind a seven-foot wall of hedges.

"So, what exactly is this place?" Emily asks.

"It belongs to one of the families Sky destroyed. He stayed
here sometimes. It was just one of the many residencies he
inhabited. It became the official meeting place for the Olvasho
council. The council is made up of twelve members and their
primary job is to help govern the Olvasho, to keep them in order
and to keep them safe from discovery. It was initially set up to
run like a democracy, but it became corrupt years ago." He
pauses. "We will need to disguise ourselves, so they don't know
we're here."

"I thought you wanted them to know we're here."

"Yes, but not until we have observed them from a safe
distance. I want to know what they say about us when they think
we aren't listening."

"There's the manipulative Patrick I know and love," she
jokes, and Patrick feels relief that she has a clear head today. The

sedative the night before along with all the work they put in yesterday appears to be paying off.

Emily goes first, throwing up a shield around her mind, completely cloaking her essence. Patrick cloaks himself only after he loses the connection with her. They will be able to feel the Olvasho present at the meeting, but as long as Patrick and Emily stay out of sight, their presence will be completely hidden from everyone in attendance.

They walk along the hedges until they reach a stone wall. Patrick shifts some of the crumbling stones out of the way to reveal an opening. They climb through the narrow entrance, and Patrick leads Emily through a passageway underground. Behind another hidden door, the tunnel opens into a basement maze. They climb several flights of stairs, ducking out of sight when anyone comes near.

Emily whispers, "How do you know where we're going?"

"I lived here with Sky for almost a year. I know all the ways in and out." He opens yet another hidden door where the two of them enter a passageway between walls. "They'll be getting ready for the meeting soon. We should be able to watch uninterrupted from the balcony, just through here." He presses a hidden lever and a grandfather clock slides to the side, revealing a balcony that overlooks the ballroom below.

They step out and crouch to stay out of view. Below, hundreds of chairs are lined up facing away from the balcony. With their thoughts guarded, they watch and listen as the room fills up.

Soon a solitary voice speaks above the others. "Welcome," a middle-aged man greets from the podium, silencing the lingering conversations. "We will commence our first Olvasho meeting since the passing of our appointed leader, Sky Vallor, of the Leona bloodline."

"Appointed leader?" Emily whispers to Patrick, not bothering to hide the accusation in her voice, "You guys appointed that psycho?"

Patrick shrugs. "Politics are messy."

"Messy? He believed in genocide! He almost wiped out my entire bloodline." She shakes her head, repeating, "Messy?"

"Shhh! We're missing it."

Emily leans back, silent but furious.

The man below says, ". . . of the leader. Every Olvasho within fifty miles felt the pull in their blood the night Sky died, which confirms the Valla bloodline we once thought to be extinct was just another deception. We know now that a descendant of Valla is responsible for the death of Sky and five other Olvasho from that night back in August. We believe she has been lying low these past few months. That is until the other day when an anonymous tip led us to sixty-two people the Valla blood mentally manipulated requiring us to clean up and cover the situation. Although she has not come out with any demands, it is safe to assume she has made her motives clear. If history has taught us one thing about the Valla bloodline, it is that the mind slaves and deaths will only multiply from here.

"We have reason to believe she is not working alone. This descendant of Valla has another Olvasho helping her. We need to stand together against this enemy and the best way to do this is with a leader strong enough to unite us. Some have volunteered for this position, and we will be hearing from them in a moment. By the close of tonight's meeting, we hope to have appointed new leadership to guide and protect our Olvasho community.

"So those of you who wish to be considered, please step to the side over here and you will each have a chance to speak and explain why you believe you are fit to lead our people."

"I believe that's my cue," Patrick whispers, as he pulls Emily face to face, resting his forehead against hers. "Remember, no matter what you see or what happens, don't react with fear. You can do this."

She nods, but self-doubt is heavy in her thoughts. Patrick kisses her temple and walks toward the stairs. She peeks down at the people below, feeling their fear, their loss, their hatred.

Perhaps what they say is true; maybe her blood is too powerful. The outreaching affect her blood has on Olvasho was evident at the compound when she fought Sky. Without realizing what she was doing, she had turned Sky's men into weapons against each other.

It hurts to know she is the reason those men are dead, but she can't think about that now. She must remain calm, no matter what happens.

PATRICK STROLLS CALMLY into the room even as he mentally prepares himself to be greeted with hostility. He knows nothing can erase the crimes he committed against humanity when he was with Sky. He is prepared to take his punishment in whatever form it comes because they deserve to hate him. Unlike Emily, he earned their loathing.

"You will each have eight minutes to . . ." The speaker, who Patrick knows as Keith, loses his words when he spots Patrick swaggering onto the low stage. Patrick knows Keith is a manipulative bastard, always sucking up to the people who can give him power. He was after Patrick's position with Sky for years, a position Patrick never asked for or wanted. Seeing Keith on stage gets under Patrick's skin.

Patrick fills the silence, "Please don't stop on my account, Keith."

The mood in the room turns hostile. Some shout curses, other's bombard Patrick with mental assaults, while a few blood-thirsty men approach the stage. Keith holds a hand out, warning them to wait, as he says, "Are you lost, Patrick?"

"I figured my invite got lost in the mail. Appointing a new leader without *my* vote would be unethical. I know how important ethics are to you."

"Oh, and I suppose you'd like to put your name on the ballot." Keith sneers, basking in his temporary power.

"On the contrary, I have someone else I would very much like to nominate."

"You found another master to serve?"

"I found someone to believe in," Patrick corrects, as the curses continue.

"So quickly?"

"Quickly, no, however, I suppose you gave me enough time. Tell me, why did it take you so long to pull this gathering together? Sky has been dead for months."

"Many died that day. As his second in command, you surprisingly lived. How is it possible that you walked away unscathed when so many others died?" The crowd is silent once again, listening for his answer.

With a shrug, he says, "What can I say? I'm just lucky, I guess." Patrick can't help but use sarcasm, even knowing he is only making them hate him more.

Keith sneers. "You're lucky enough to find another individual's power to leach off."

"Actually, I found her before Sky's death."

"How convenient," Keith says with false excitement. "So, tell me, who is she?"

"Her name is Emily, but you probably know her as the descendant of Valla."

There is a collective gasp from the crowd. Only three months ago, most believed the Valla bloodline had been extinct for hundreds of years. By now everyone knew the bloodline lived on. It was one of the reasons it took so long to organize a gathering. Many were too afraid a meeting like this would draw out the Valla blood.

"Even you, Patrick Glenn, are not that stupid," Keith condescends.

Men rush the stage. Keith pretends to object but does nothing to stop the men from pummeling Patrick to the floor.

"She's with me," Patrick chokes out, and they pause their attack.

"You're bluffing!" Keith says, but the men back away, waiting for Patrick to continue.

Rolling to his side, Patrick wheezes, "Why else would I come?"

"You brought her here?"

Patrick struggles to stand. "She's our best bet."

"You idiot!" Keith's smooth veneer melts into fear. "You may have a death wish, but are you so determined to bring us all down with you?"

Chaos ensues. The Olvasho begin shouting.

Patrick's pain has the room spinning and nausea hangs heavy in his throat, so he stays on the floor, holding his ribs. Wincing, he says, "We've contained Valla."

"Valla cannot be contained!" Keith shouts. "That is why they killed them off!"

Patrick wheezes, "But they didn't kill them off, did they?"

"And so you led her here to slaughter us!"

The crowd begins to scramble, hurrying to exit the building.

"She—" It's all Patrick gets out before they begin pummeling him, again.

People are struggling with the doors, but they cannot escape. The doors are locked. Patrick made sure of that.

Emily releases the shield concealing her mind as she steps down from the winding balcony staircase. The few people attempting to escape that way, stumble and trip over themselves. The silence Patrick couldn't attain fills the room like an explosion. Even the crying infant becomes quiet as Valla's power permeates the room. All eyes fall on her.

Emily ignores the looks, but it's difficult to ignore the shock and horror registering in every mind. It puts her senses on edge, and Adelaide's cruel laughter fills her mind.

Someone in the crowd whispers, "She's so young."

"Remember to breathe slowly," Patrick had told her. *"Don't react with terror, no matter what you see or feel."*

Registering his severe pain, Emily walks to where Patrick is lying on the floor. The people surrounding him back away. Emily finds him clutching the right side of his chest and struggling to breathe. His lips are turning blue. She kneels next to him, placing her palm against his chest. A broken rib has punctured one of his lungs. With the physical connection, Emily heals his injuries.

"How sweet of you to show up," he says softly, attempting a cocky grin as he wipes the blood from his lips.

"Why did you let them do this to you?"

His smile fades. "Because I deserve it."

She stands, offering him a hand. There is an audible reaction from the crowd as she helps him from the floor. Although most are too shocked or scared to react, a few brave souls launch mental assaults at both of them. Emily easily blocks the attacks and turns to one individual in the crowd who is trying to incapacitate her. She pins him with her emerald eyes, and although he's frightened, he doesn't stand down. She respects his courage which is why she doesn't knock him out.

Emily says, "If Valla were in charge, you'd already be dead. Rest assured. I'm one of you."

"Is it true?" a woman says from the crowd.

"You'll never be one of us," someone else replies.

"What kind of trick is this?" another shouts.

Patrick stands by her side, helping to fend off the assaults.

Emily stares at the man who is flinging mental assaults at her. He stops his attack when she makes eye contact with him. She proceeds to fill his head with images and memories.

Using her gifts triggers Adelaide and soon Emily hears her whispering into her subconscious, *Show them what your power can do. Kill him and feed on his soul. Come on, Emily, show them why they should fear you.*

Emily keeps eye contact with the man. He groans, grabbing at his head. Everyone in the room is tense as they helplessly watch.

"Enough!" A deep voice cuts through the crowd, and once again, silence takes the room.

"Lathe, what a pleasant surprise," Patrick says, with a resigned lack of enthusiasm.

"What is she doing to Walter?" Lathe demands.

Patrick continues his calm posture, but it's a front. He's worried. He trusts Emily, but he knows she is unstable. Patrick replies, "She's showing him the truth."

Lathe steps forward to put a stop to it when Walter—overcome with Emily's power—goes limp and falls to the floor. The people near him cushion his fall.

Emily shifts her attention to the man Patrick calls Lathe. She can feel the crowd both fear and respect him. She imagined someone who held so much influence would be older and more put together, but he is unlike any Olvasho she has seen.

He wears a loose hoodie, hood up, covering part of his noticeably scarred face. The scars themselves are intimidating, making him look tough. Pairing his face with his height and his glare, Emily can see why they fear him, but she is more interested in why they respect him.

His clear blue eyes remind her of Sky, but there is conflict in these eyes she hadn't seen in Sky's. With one hand he pushes his hood back, revealing the severity of the burns to the left side of his face and scalp, while the right side remains unblemished, a reminder of how beautiful he once was.

Lathe steps forward, and Emily looks to Patrick. "Care to introduce me to your friend, Patrick?"

"Patrick doesn't have any friends here," Lathe corrects. "He killed his mother to help an evil man."

Emily shakes her head. "I'm Patrick's friend and without Patrick, Sky would still be controlling you."

"He couldn't control me," he corrects.

"No?" Emily steps forward. "So, if he held no power over you, then why didn't you stop him?"

Lathe narrows his eyes and Patrick steps toward Emily, gently placing a hand on her shoulder. "Emily, careful what you say."

She shrugs out of his hold and continues, "It's time you all cut Patrick some slack. He was fifteen and without his powers when his mom died. Alessandra saved my life, and in doing so, she damned her own. Sky was an experienced serial killer who used Alessandra's son as a weapon to destroy her. It doesn't take a genius to figure it out, and yet, you blame him." She motions to Patrick.

Lathe states, "Every person in this room has suffered Sky's wrath one way or another. I could tell you each and every story, most of them involving Patrick. He may have been without powers when he met Sky, but even after his mother died, he stayed, willingly taking part in hundreds of malicious acts of violence. Patrick was Sky's loyal accomplice."

"Sky, the man you geniuses appointed as your leader? Yes, Patrick was loyal out of necessity to save his own life. He was biding his time until he found me, protected me, trained me, and brought me in to destroy Sky."

Lathe flicks his eyes to Patrick. "From one master to another, Patrick? Was it worth the sacrifice?"

"It will never be worth the sacrifice, but he had no choice," Emily seethes.

Lathe snorts in disgust. "I see she speaks for you, too."

Emily steps forward. "Patrick's better at controlling his temper than I am. If I were you, I'd be careful."

"Are you here to intimidate us?" Lathe mocks.

"I'm here to make sure no one plans to cause my family or me any more pain."

"You are Valla," someone in the crowd shouts. "You are pain!"

With an eye roll, she shakes her head and looks towards the crowd, saying, "Am I? Everyone thinks they know who I am." She turns back to Lathe. "Do you know how frustrating that is? I'm sure you've done your research, but a man like you must know everything you hear is not the truth."

"Enlighten us," Lathe says. "We're all ears. Personally, I'd like to know how you killed the unkillable man."

Emily vocalizes, "I was twelve when I watched the Olvasho murder my mother. Sky held her soul captive inside his mind so he could leach off the power and keep himself young. He was over two-hundred years old. Didn't any of you wonder why he never aged? He bragged to me that he'd killed so many from the Valla bloodline that he only needed to take one life a year to prevent him from aging. He would've killed me too if I hadn't been his daughter."

There is a collective gasp and mumbling in the crowd.

Emily continues, "He thought he could control me and the future Valla bloodline. He was wrong. I set his hostages free and watched him disintegrate before my eyes."

Stone-faced, Lathe asks, "Sky was your father?"

"Sky was the man who raped my mother. I might share his blood, but I have no desire to give him that title."

"And you expect us to believe you freed those souls? No one can do that. It would've killed you," he accuses.

Emily wishes she was strong enough to show the whole room what she went through, but she has neither the strength nor control to pull that off right now, so she says, "Ask your friend over there." Emily nods to Walter, who is once again on his feet.

Walter clears his throat and announces, "It's the truth. She fought her father and won with help from the spirits of our loved ones. She offered them freedom and they escaped Sky's mind. Sky crumbled without the source of his power. She grew stronger until the power nearly consumed her, but she fought against it and freed the souls Sky had consumed." Tears fill his eyes. "She freed my Danielle. I saw her." He looks at Emily, with gratitude and great loss. "You saved my wife from Sky's eternal hold. How can I ever repay you?"

"You can start by believing I'm not your enemy."

He continues, "You aren't our enemy. You're our savior." He turns to face the crowd. "She is our savior! The Valla blood has awakened, but she's . . . she's controlling it somehow." He shakes his head with amazement.

The crowd is riled, everyone talking at once. "The prophecy!" someone gasps, while another shouts, "She's born from Valla and Leona!"

Walter speaks over the crowd. "You are the one prophesied."

"The who?" she asks.

He begins in a low voice and others join in.

"Bred to be orphaned, pursued but not found,
The weak build the strong to find light underground.
Rising from nothing to fight for a cause
A victim, a killer, an innocent one.
Finding freedom for souls, we believe to be lost,
By crossing lines that cannot be crossed.
Fear breeds allegiance that is easily broken,
While love builds loyalties that remain unspoken.
Rising from evil, from death, from ash
To encompass abilities no other can have.
Garnering gifts from mother and father alike,
Her blood will awaken three sisters to fight.
Saving us all, for it is fated,
Unless she befalls, incinerated."

Next to Emily, Patrick sucks in air. Over the years, he paid no attention to the stupid prophecy. He never believed in fortune telling, but hearing the words now, he believes, and he knows Walter is correct. It is about her.

Emily has heard some of this before, but where? She recalls the ghost of a woman with crazy hair. She wore a nightgown and snow boots the first time Emily had seen her. She continued to show up, repeating little rhymes each time, but Emily hadn't seen her since Adelaide took over her body.

"It's her." Walter points to Emily and says, "You are the one we've been waiting for."

Lathe moves closer to Emily to be heard. "I'm sorry for what's about to happen. Just go with it." Then he and everyone else get down on a knee and bow, all except for Patrick who is watching with his warmest smirk.

"Are you kidding me?" Emily shouts, "Stand up! One minute you plot to kill me and the next you're bowing. I'm not a damn prophecy! I am not a monster, either. I just want to live my life in peace. And I want you to choose a better leader this time. And stop hunting my family. If you ever come after someone I care about; I will make you wish you were dead."

Patrick wraps a hand around her arm in warning, but Emily continues, "Valla blood is contained, but—"

Patrick talks over her, "But, she is powerful enough without Valla." Emily glares at him, as he continues, "She is a prophecy. She has been on the losing side all of her life, but through her own sheer willpower, she has defeated the man who oppressed us for years! She set us free. She has conquered Valla, and you heard her, all she asks for is peace. She is the perfect candidate."

She grabs his wrist, warning, "Patrick."

Someone shouts, "You have my vote!"

"No!" Emily shakes her head.

Patrick turns to face Emily while he speaks through their mental link. *"Emily, I know you weren't expecting this, but even you have to admit you would be perfect."*

"No, Patrick!"

"If you don't take it, then someone like Sky, who is hungry for power, will."

"Patrick, I hear voices in my head, and you want me to lead an army. Are you crazy?"

"It's not an army. The only reason we appoint someone is so they can regulate and keep the Olvasho in line."

"You're not hearing me."

"I am, and I know you're scared, but if you really want peace, this is the only way to secure it."

Emily grits her teeth. "You made me sound like a hero in that little speech of yours, Patrick. I almost killed you. I'm the reason so many died that night with Sky. I had a hotel full of people I manipulated and worse, mind slaves. I almost killed everyone. I still might. It's not safe for me to be in charge of myself, let alone an entire group of people with powers that have the potential to kill off the human race. Even if I am the prophecy, did you hear the last little bit? I'll save us all or be incinerated. Sounds like a fifty-fifty chance at best. These people—you included—have way too much faith in me."

"I've seen too much good in you to believe you're capable of murdering the innocent."

"Are you forgetting that I almost killed Morgan and Ben?" Then out loud, she says, "Patrick, no! My answer is *no!*"

Patrick counters, "She doesn't want the power, which is exactly why she would make a great leader."

The crowd is murmuring among themselves when Lathe questions, "Is this your perverse way of making her suffer more?"

Patrick turns to Lathe. "And I suppose you think we should get her grief counseling and lock her away in a basement."

"I think we should have this discussion in private," Lathe says, stepping back. To the room, he announces, "Then it is decided. We will go ahead with candidate speeches tonight and reconvene in a month to put it to a vote. In that time, Emily can decide if she wants to run. Keith, if you would take over, I'm going to see them out."

Keith steps back up to the podium, completely deflated.

To Patrick and Emily, Lathe instructs, "Come with me."

Lathe pulls a key from his pocket to unlock a door, leading the way out of the room and down the hall. This part of the mansion has been modernized, but the Victorian style resonates throughout. The walls are lighter and more simplistic here, but the architecture is elaborate and the paintings on the walls are eclectic.

As they travel the maze of corridors, Emily comments, "Lathe, why don't you take leadership? They seem to respect and listen to you."

"I have a different role that keeps me from leadership."

They enter an office with three walls of built-in bookshelves, overflowing with books. A large desk covered in globes sits in the center of the room. As Emily takes a closer look at the collection of globes, Patrick closes the door behind them.

Lathe steps in front of Emily and with kind eyes, he says, "Let me start by saying thank you. Thank you for killing the man I couldn't kill."

"I didn't kill him," she notes, because the distinction is important to her. "I disempowered him, and I didn't do it alone."

"So you've said."

Patrick comes to Emily's side. "Lathe is your half-brother. He's Sky's son."

Emily stares at Lathe. "You have his eyes."

"I am nothing like him."

"Neither am I, Brother."

"Half," Lathe corrects. "One of many, though the others are much older. You weren't Sky's only project. My mother is from the Leona bloodline. Sky had many children, though he still preferred Patrick to any of his offspring."

"He preferred you," Patrick corrects. "I was just his contingency plan."

"He knew I would never give him the kind of affection and pleasure you could."

Emily steps between them. "We're all victims, but we're alive and he isn't so how about we stop letting him win," Emily comments, trying to ignore the growing sounds in her head.

"Sure, Sky is gone, but Patrick isn't," Lathe says. "He is dirty, and nothing you say will change my mind." He eyes her with worry. "You on the other hand . . . are a mess. You should sit down before you fall over."

The crackling sound started when she entered the room, but it continues to grow in Emily's mind. She sits in a wingback chair ignoring the increasing sound.

Patrick says, "Remember when you told me to bring Adelaide?"

Lathe nods.

Patrick motions to Emily. "After she nearly died fighting Sky, Valla saved her by bonding their souls together. But along with Valla came Adelaide. They appear to be a packaged deal. Where Valla is powerful, she isn't malevolent. However, Adelaide wants revenge against the entire world."

Lathe thinks on that for a moment before saying, "How are they a packaged deal? Why have I never heard this before?"

With her head in her hands, Emily answers, "Because everyone who knew the truth died. Queen Adelaide made sure of that."

Patrick continues, "The story we were taught isn't as true as we were led to believe. The queen was far from innocent, and Isa and Leona weren't even the queen's biological children."

"She—" Emily looks up to tell the real story but stops short as Lathe's body slowly catches fire.

"No!" She jumps up from her chair, inching backward until she runs into Patrick.

Lathe looks leery of her, but he doesn't seem bothered by the flames. His skin begins melting, and Emily gasps, closing her eyes tight because what she's seeing can't be real. She leans back against Patrick and his arms surround her, holding her to him. "Shhh," he reassures. "You're safe, love. I'm right here. What you're seeing isn't real. Emily, just breathe."

She breathes in and chokes on the smoke in the room. Hysteria has her opening her eyes and what she sees is fire. Heat scorches her face while flames devour Lathe right in front of her. Bloodcurdling screams pierce her brain while she looks around, frantic to find Patrick. But he isn't here—he left them here to die. Her lungs ache and she can't catch her breath. *Who is screaming?* Someone's hand is covering her mouth. She makes an effort to pull away, but the hold on her is too tight.

Everything goes quiet as she is submerged in cool water. It

soothes her warm skin and calms her mind, so she stays submerged underwater until she can breathe again.

"Emily?" Patrick calls into the water.

She opens her eyes and reality returns. They are in the room with Lathe, only instead of standing and talking, Emily is on the floor with Patrick's body wrapped around her.

"Is it over?" he asks.

She nods her answer, and he hesitantly moves the hand covering her mouth. When she doesn't scream, his body eases away and they both sit up.

A few feet away, Lathe leans against the desk watching them. With folded arms and a furrowed brow, he crosses one ankle over the other.

Patrick looks to Lathe and warns, "You tell anyone about this and—"

"And what, I'll end up like Katie?" Lathe finishes.

"Katie was an accident. It wasn't supposed to end like that. I didn't . . . I didn't know. I'm sorry."

Lathe's ankles uncross and his hands land on his thighs as he leans forward. "Your apology is worthless, Patrick." He gestures toward Emily. "What's wrong with her?"

"She's been traumatized one too many times. Her mind is still recovering, but she's improving."

"No, I'm not, Patrick. This is a great example of why I shouldn't take charge of anyone," Emily says on her hands and knees, debating whether she can stand or not. "It's not getting better. I could've hurt someone," she finishes, deciding to stay on the floor.

Lathe snorts with laughter and Patrick shoots him a death glare.

"Is this your penance, Patrick? Letting her—"

"Quiet," Patrick demands.

"—torture you, or do you get a sick pleasure from it?"

Patrick glares at him. "You, better than most, should understand taking care of someone after their mind has been displaced."

Lathe stands from the desk and offers Emily his hand. She takes it and he helps her to her feet. "Emily, I'm glad to meet you. What happened here will stay between us, and whenever you're feeling up to another visit, my mother is dying to meet you. Speaking of," he pauses and heads toward the door, "I'm sure she felt whatever the hell that was." He waves his hand toward them. "I need to go check on her. She'll probably need to be calmed down. Patrick, I'll be in touch. Emily, you have loyal friends, and that says a lot about a person. I trust you'll figure out how to fix your situation. Call if you decide you'd rather have my help instead of Patrick's."

He's out the door before they can respond. Emily looks at Patrick. "I messed up."

"We knew this might happen. It's okay, Lathe will keep your secret."

"How can you say that? He hates you."

"He hates me, but you remind him of his mother."

"How do you know?"

"It's a long story, but lucky for us, we have a long car ride ahead of us, so I can fill you in."

As they head for the door, Emily asks, "Did Sky do that to his face?"

"He did it to himself." Patrick cracks the door to see if anyone is awaiting them in the hallway. Seeing the coast is clear, he says, "We'll go out the way we came in, but we need to hurry before they corner us." He grabs Emily's hand and they take off down the hall.

CHAPTER THIRTY-TWO ~

FROM THE DRIVER'S SEAT, Patrick says, "Lathe's mom is one of the strongest of the Leona bloodline, maybe the strongest now that Sky is dead. The rumor is she can see glimpses into the future, which I guess was confirmed tonight. She is the one who revealed the prophecy."

"Patrick," she says hesitantly. "Do you know what she looks like? Lathe's mom?"

"Her name is Evelyn. I've seen pictures of her before she lost her mind, but no one except for Lathe has had any contact with her in the last ten years."

"That may not be entirely true. I think I might've seen her."

His head jerks in her direction.

She continues, "She started showing up around the time you came into my life. She would show up at random, spew out a rhyme and disappear."

Patrick looks at her with a troubled expression. "Be careful of her, love. There is a reason she's locked away. She is dangerous, despite her incredibly accurate visions."

"You think the prophecy is accurate? How do you figure?"

"'Bred to be orphaned.' Your parents didn't really conceive you so much as Sky bred you, then he killed your mother and died when you took his power. 'Pursued but not found.' Sky had people searching for you."

"Yeah, but you did find me."

"That's why the next part is so interesting. Because I found you, but I didn't turn you over to Sky until after the next line. 'The weak builds the strong and finds light underground.' Emily, I'm the weak. I found you and I trained you to build your strength, and in return, you showed me light and love when we were in that underground lair.

"'Rising from nothing to fight for a cause, a victim, a killer, an innocent one.' So, you rose from nothing, you didn't know your heritage, or of what you were capable. You are the victim and the innocent one. Sky is the killer."

"I think you have that wrong," Emily interrupts. "I think you are the victim. Sky is the killer and I hardly feel innocent, but among you and Sky, I guess that makes sense."

"So, I am weak and a victim. Should I add this to my dating profile?"

Emily gives a short laugh and shakes her head.

"Continuing on, then," Patrick says. "'Finding freedom for souls, we believe to be lost, by crossing lines that cannot be crossed.' You freed the souls, which everyone thought impossible, and in the process, you died, crossing lines. 'Fear breeds allegiance that is easily broken, while love builds loyalties that remain unspoken.' People were only loyal to Sky because of fear, but our loyalty to you isn't as easily broken, because love is stronger than fear. 'Rising from evil, from death, from ash to encompass abilities no other can have.' You beat Sky and you will beat Adelaide. You came back from death and awakened the fire in your Valla blood. 'Garnering gifts from mother and father alike.' You have gifts from Leona and Valla bloodlines. 'Her blood will awaken three sisters to fight.' This part I haven't figured out yet, but I'm guessing involves Isa, Leona, and Valla. 'Saving us all, for it is fated.' I believe you will save us all. It *is* fated."

Emily chimes in, "Or I fail and am reduced to ash. You know, it could go either way. I don't know what to think about that, Patrick."

"Prophecy or no prophecy, it doesn't change the path we're already on."

She takes a breath and sighs. "So, what else does Lathe's mother do, other than reveal herself in visions and prophecies?"

"Other than her mental ability, she also had the physical ability to move things with her mind. I don't know how many of the stories are actually true, but she was a big enough deal that she caught Sky's attention. She was beautiful, even by Olvasho standards. There was something magical about her. She was in her early twenties when Sky decided she would be his. They even got married, but he was only using her for her capabilities, forcing her to look into the future. When Lathe was young, maybe four or five, Sky had demanded so much of her, she could no longer tell the future from the present or what was real and what wasn't. She had been using her telekinetic powers so much that Sky locked her away so he could keep an eye on her. The more unpredictable she became, the less interest he had in her. To this day, Lathe is the only one to have contact with her. Without Lathe, she would have been murdered by Olvasho years ago."

"What did he mean when he invited me to meet her?"

"You killed the man who made her crazy and the episode Lathe witnessed back there reminded him of his mother. Lathe can relate to you because you were just as much a victim of Sky as they were. You still shouldn't go. As innocent as she may appear, she is not well and will likely try to kill you."

"Lathe's scars? You said he did it to himself?"

Patrick nods. "Lathe also made an impression on Sky. Just like his mother, there was something almost magical about him. When Lathe was in his early teens, Sky started grooming him to be his second in command. Lathe didn't want that honor. He hated Sky, and he also knew the Olvasho would murder his mother if he were not there to protect her. He knew Sky couldn't have his second in command looking like a monster, so he burned his face to make himself ugly.

"Of course, we didn't find out it was self-inflicted until much later. He staged it very convincingly to look like an accident. The owner of the restaurant where Lathe was burned was in the United States illegally and fled after the squad arrived to take Lathe. Lathe's mother was his emergency contact and they couldn't reach her because she was locked away.

"By the time the Olvasho heard about his injuries, it was a week later, and the natural healing process had already started. Olvasho healers did the best they could, and the Lathe you met today looks ten times better than the Lathe he was right after the incident. They were able to repair his left eye and the movement to his neck, but in the week it took to find him, Lathe's scar tissue had already started forming. Once formed, the scar tissue cannot be restored to its original state, which means Lathe was already permanently disfigured by the time they got to him."

"Wasn't Sky pissed?"

"Yes, but he didn't know until much later that it was self-inflicted."

"How did he find out?"

"I told him."

"Patrick, you . . . you . . ."

He turns to look at her. "Emily, what Lathe said is true. They have every right to hate me."

She shakes her head. "Maybe they do, but I know you Patrick, and I don't hate you." She lays a hand on his arm for a moment before asking, "Who is Katie?"

A look of pain crosses his face and he swallows before saying, "I promise I will tell you, but I'd rather not talk about Katie while I'm driving."

"Another time then."

Silence drags on and she studies the road signs as they pass by in the dark. She's worried about going home and concerned about her losing touch with reality. "Patrick, what if it doesn't get better and I end up like Lathe's mother?"

"That won't happen. You've already shown improvement."

"What did I do to you when I freaked out? Lathe said I tortured you."

"He was only saying that to get to me."

"But it's true, isn't it?" she says, "I'm hurting you."

"No more than I deserve."

"You don't deserve any of it." She looks out the window. That's when she begins to see them. Deer. A herd of them are running alongside the road. Their numbers seem to multiply.

"Patrick! It's happening again. I'm seeing things."

He lets off the gas. "What do you see?"

"Deer! Lots of them running next to us."

He accelerates, explaining, "I see them too. They've been doing that on and off for the last few days."

"They have? There must be twenty or thirty of them. Some of them have huge antlers."

"Once we pick up speed, we'll lose them."

"Why are they following us?"

"They're attracted to your power for whatever reason."

"Nothing is going to be the same, is it? I'm hallucinating about blood that isn't there and fire that doesn't exist, but the herd of horned animals, those are real."

"We can remedy the deer issue. And we'll work on getting rid of the hallucinations. We've got this. You have some very anxious people waiting for you to come home."

"Do they know I'm coming?"

"I thought I'd let them see for themselves. Where do you want to go first?"

CHAPTER THIRTY-THREE

THE HOSPITAL SMELLS PRECISELY the way Emily remembers, part antiseptic, part desperation. The smell of the hospital brings back painful memories of her stay in the psych ward after her mom died. She hates the sterile white hallways and the buzzing glow of fluorescent lighting. Her nerves are on edge. This is the last place she wants to be, but it's the first place she chooses to go.

The elevator opens into another sterile hallway and the smell of antiseptic is stronger on this floor. Emily follows Patrick in a daze, thankful he's with her. He doesn't hesitate to enter room 407, but she does. She looks around to see where all the nurses are. Taking a deep breath, she steps into the dark room and cringes at the smell of her father's comatose body. It is a mix of stagnant body and hospital soap. Patrick flips on a light and there in the center of the room, in the hospital bed is a man she barely recognizes. She steps up to him slowly, reminding herself to breathe. Even though she knew he was sick, and even though the last time she saw him he was dying, she still expected to see her big strong, intelligent father. Instead, there is a shell of a man lying before her. His grayish skin is hanging off his bones and his mouth is slack, hanging open with a tube sandwiched between dry, chapped lips. Emily would think he was dead if it weren't for all the tubes and the repetitive beeping on the monitor.

"That wasn't there before," Patrick comments, pointing to the tube going down his throat. "Something must have happened."

"I left him like this." The regret in Emily's voice is unmistakable.

"You didn't have a choice. Besides, if you want to blame someone, blame me. I'm the reason he's here."

For a moment she's angry at Patrick because he is partly to blame. If he hadn't told Sky where to find her dad, then this never would have happened. Patrick made a choice that led to her dad getting kidnapped and beaten, but Patrick also saved him. Her dad would have died in that cell if it hadn't been for Patrick keeping him alive, then later taking him to the hospital.

With more determination, she says, "Sky is the reason he's here. I know you and Tom have worked on him, but maybe . . . maybe I can help."

"I knew you would want to try."

She lays a hand on her dad's arm and the other against his cheek. She focuses, putting all of her strength into healing him. She feels the heat come. It builds in her chest, moves down her arms, and out through her hands.

"Emily, stop!" Patrick's voice is frantic. "Stop!" He grabs her and pulls her away, moving between her and Mark. Patrick's hands cover the new burns across Mark's skin. The blistered skin begins healing in rapid motion as Patrick uses his abilities to fix the damage Emily caused.

Emily stands back, looking between her hands and her dad. She could've killed him. While she stands there in shock, Patrick spends several minutes fixing the broken parts of Mark. By the time Patrick pulls away, his eyes have faded to misty blue, and his skin is pale.

Emily stutters, "I didn't . . . I'm . . . I don't . . ."

Patrick wraps his arms around her. "It's my fault. It's way too soon to try this. We can come back later after you've recovered. You need more time."

"I didn't know that could happen," she whispers.

"Look, Emily. He's better than when we first came in. We'll come back to heal his mind another day. Come on, let's go."

Emily is in a daze as they leave the hospital. "How did I do that?" she asks, as they climb into the van.

From the driver's seat, he says, "It's your powers manifesting into physical form. Very few Olvasho have that gift. Lathe's mom does, and I know Sky could do little tricks with the air, but only in small controlled environments. There are rumors of a man named Sebastian who could manipulate water, but he's been dead for nearly a hundred years now."

He pulls out of the parking lot. "I'm not surprised your powers are showing physically. We'll figure it out just like we did with your other gifts. Give it time and you'll learn to control it. Then it won't seem so overwhelming."

While Emily absorbs the new information, Patrick pulls onto the highway and asks, "Do you still want to go see Ben?"

Emily nods, hoping her reunion with Ben will go better than it did with her dad.

Patrick hesitates, suggesting, "It can wait, if you're not feeling up to it."

"Please just go, Patrick. I'm fine and I need to see Ben." He always went to the dojo on Monday evenings, and she's hoping that hasn't changed. She realizes she should've been asking more questions, but there is only so much she can handle right now.

Patrick drops her off at the dojo twenty minutes later. He wants to come with her, but she talks him into staying in the car. According to the banner out front, there is some sort of community open house tonight. The place is filled with curious kids, questioning parents, and loitering teens.

She finds Ben in the middle of the chaos. It's surreal seeing him just across the room. It's like she can breathe for the first time in almost four months. She watches him for a while, enjoying the carefree smiles of the man who stole her heart. The thought of him kept her going so many times when she wanted to give up. He has always been her home. She can't figure out why it took her so long to realize she was in love with him. She pulls herself from the puddle she's melted into and moves closer.

Ben begins chatting with the man next to him when his eyes glance past hers. Quickly, his gaze flicks back, finding her across the crowded room. His lips freeze mid-sentence, his smile abruptly fades, and his expression is one of disbelief.

Emily expects him to snap out of it. She waits for his expression to change, to become warm. She expects him to rush over to her and wrap her up in those solid arms. She can't wait to melt into him, but he still hasn't unfrozen from his stance. His brows fall and his face changes, looking wary. He's staring at her like she's a ghost. Maybe that's all she has become to him.

A war is taking place inside his head and she realizes she's been a fool. He gave her his heart and she tore it out, burned it to ash, and shoved the charred remains back in his chest, expecting him to figure it out while she disappeared without a word. Judging by the look of him, he hasn't figured it out, and she senses it's more than just her. He's been through hell and she wasn't there for him the way he's always been there for her.

She wants to be there for him now, but what claim does she have? The fire she used to see in his eyes is gone; replaced by an untrusting stare. She ruined him. She looks away trying to forget the promise she'd made to him. She tries not to think of the words, but they are there like little demons dancing inside her head, taunting her . . . *And when you realize I'm too great a burden, I will absolve you of your promise and walk away a better person having known you.* She wants to rewrite history. She should never have gotten him involved.

Ben heads her way. It feels like a millennia passes in the time it takes for him to cross the room. It's enough time for Emily's thoughts to run wild.

Ben stops just feet from her, but it's too far away. The distance is taunting. He's right there, so close, but completely unreachable. They stare at each other, neither of them knowing what to say or liking the way this feels.

Bypassing the expected greeting, he says, "Did Patrick bring you here?"

Emily nods, unable to trust her voice. She spoke in front of an army of Olvasho, but she can't speak to the other half of her heart.

He runs a hand through his hair and then as if realizing that's too much of a tell, he buries his hands in his pockets. "It's surreal seeing you."

She's dying for him to step forward and hug her. She resists the urge to draw herself into him. Her abilities—her pull—will only distort his true feelings, and she needs to know what is real and what is not. Holding herself in place, she breathes, "It's weird for me too."

"I was so worried about you," he confesses.

"I know," she whispers, feeling guilty.

"I didn't even know if you were alive."

"I know," she whispers again, holding back tears.

"You know?" He sounds angry. "We were all so worried something terrible had happened to you and now you just show up here and say you know."

Emily stares at him, at a loss for words.

"The last time I saw you, you almost killed me. If you're you again then why didn't you call, or send a text, an email, anything to let us know you were okay?"

"It's not that simple, Ben."

He takes a step back, grumbling, "It never is." He looks around the room as if remembering where he is. "I'm glad you're okay, but I can't do this right now. I've gotta get back. I'm sure I'll see you later."

He walks away, and Emily stands there for a moment feeling completely hollow. He just walked away. She turns, leaving the room as slowly as her legs will allow, but as soon as she's outside, she runs. Patrick catches her body in a collision that stops her as she rounds the corner of the building. He wraps his arms around her and holds her to him.

"It'll be okay, Emily," he reassures as if he'd been watching. She pushes him away with force because she would rather be angry than vulnerable. All she's been lately is vulnerable, and she's sick of it.

"I defeated Sky!" she snaps, pushing him away. "I freed hundreds of souls! I contained Adelaide! I can crush you! I don't need your sympathy!" She strides away from him, away from the van.

"Emily," he calls after her.

Without looking back, she yells, "Don't follow me, Patrick! I need time. I need a moment to breathe without you hovering."

"That's not safe! Where're you going?"

She spins around to face him, voice grave, "Nothing in this world is safe, Patrick. I'll find you when I need you." With that parting line, she jogs away and quickly realizes December isn't a great time for jogging. She can't wait to get to her house. She can't wait to crawl under her covers and pretend this nightmare isn't her life. It's not that she's in denial, she just wants a break. She knows she'll soon need to let Patrick know where she is. She may have been dramatic back there, but he was right about it not being safe for her to be alone right now.

Her street is well lit despite the dark evening. She wonders if Chris still has eyes on her house. Surely, he'll tell Patrick where she is, but at least she'll be home. Finally home after so many months.

She's about five houses down when she realizes something isn't right. The street light by their house is out, leaving everything sheathed in darkness. She continues walking, hoping her eyes are playing tricks on her, but the closer she gets, the clearer the picture. She sinks to her knees there on the sidewalk, covering her face with both hands. She peeks through her fingers, double checking this isn't one of her hallucinations. Yellow caution tape flaps in the wind. Her eyes lift to the charred beams and exposed brick of the foundation. The house is gone, burned to the ground, along with everything she once owned. All of it—gone—along with her old life.

A chilling breeze barrels into her. She stands, wiping the tears from her face and hugs her arms tighter around herself as she drifts away from the rubble. There is only one place close by, so she heads in that direction.

A few minutes later, Alec opens the door and looks down at Emily. "Holy shit! Where the hell have you been, Burk?" He steps back, inviting her in. "What happened?"

She walks past him, saying, "I just need to shower, then I'll be out of your hair."

He reaches for her. "Wait, Em, where have you been?"

"Alec, I just need a hot shower, okay?"

"Okay," he mutters.

Emily enters the bathroom and strips down. She turns the faucet and freezing water sprays out of the shower head. Once the water warms up, she steps in, realizing she's going to have to use Alec's masculine scented body wash. What she didn't expect was for it to smell so much like Ben, like he's wrapped all around her. It's the last straw. Like an overfilled balloon, her body rejects the pain she's trying to swallow, and emotions burst out of her in a disgusting display of tears and snot. She cries alone in the shower, letting her demons out against the spray of water. Then the whispers start, drowned out only by the crackle of fire. She smells smoke before she notices the flames licking their way up to the ceiling.

CHAPTER THIRTY-FOUR ~

Morgan is helping the patient in room 308 back from the bathroom when her phone vibrates in the pocket of her scrubs. She ignores it as she helps her patient pivot her walker until the backs of her legs are against the bed. Then Morgan helps her sit on the side of the mattress to catch her breath before laying her down. Once the patient is comfortable and covered, Morgan leaves her with the call light and hits up the hand sanitizer on her way out of the room.

She pulls her phone from her pocket to see she missed a call from Alec. She shakes her head, drops her phone back into her pocket, and walks down the hall to help another patient. She makes it four steps before Alec calls again. She presses ignore as she knocks on room 314.

She enters the room slowly after hearing no response. The television is blaring inside and as soon as the man in the hospital bed sees her, he shouts, "It's about time! Where's my water?"

"I'm sorry, Mr. Brown, you can't have anything to drink until after your surgery."

"Don't you tell me what I'm allowed to have! I'm seventy-three years old and I want some damn water!"

"They should be coming to take you down any minute," Morgan reassures him as her phone buzzes in her pocket.

The man continues to yell at her until a knock comes at the door.

"Thank God," Morgan mumbles and then more loudly says, "It's transport. They are here to take you to surgery."

She helps load up the very uncooperative man. He continues his complaints out into the hall and down the corridor until the elevator doors close.

Morgan's phone goes off again. Squeezing more hand sanitizer into her palm, she heads into the staff bathroom.

She pulls out her phone to see three missed calls and a text from Alec. She reads his message.

Alec: **Where are you?**

Morgan: **I'm at work.**

His response is immediate.

Alec: **I need you!**

I need you! Her breathing halts and her chest hurts. *He needs me.* "Get a grip, Morgan," she whispers to herself just as her phone vibrates.

Alec: **Please! Emily is here.**

Morgan blinks and thoughts of Alec fall to the background. She dials him and holds her breath as it rings.

"Fletch, thank God!" Alec answers.

"What do you mean, Emily is there?"

"She just showed up on my doorstep out of the blue looking like death. She's been missing for how long? I didn't know what to do. She won't talk to me; said she just needed a hot shower then she'd be out of my hair. She's been in there forever. I mean, I know girls take long showers, but it's been over an hour. I don't know what to do."

A thousand thoughts flood her head. "Did you knock?"

"Yeah, she's not answering, and the door is locked."

"I'll be right there," Morgan says.

"I have the key. Should I try to go in?" He sounds like he would rather stick the key in his eye than unlock the door.

"Wait for me."

"Morgan, she's a mess," he hesitates. "I think she's on something. She's too skinny and looks like she hasn't slept in forever."

"Just wait for me before you do anything. I'm already on my way." She hangs up as she rushes out of the bathroom. She goes straight to the nurse's station to find her nurse supervisor.

"Denise, I'm really sorry. There's a family emergency. I need to leave."

Denise stands, looking worried. "Of course, we'll cover you. Are you okay, honey? Do you need someone to pick you up? You look pale."

"I'll be okay. Thanks, Denise." Morgan hurries down the hall to the break room to grab her things, and on her jog out of the hospital she pulls her phone out to call Patrick. The parking lot is brutally cold as the wind sweeps between buildings.

Patrick answers on the fourth ring. "Morgan, to what do I owe the pleasure?"

"Oh, your phone works. Thanks for letting me know you're back! You brought her back and didn't even bother to tell me!"

"I was planning to call you tomorrow."

"Why?" Morgan shouts, unlocking her car. "Why wait until tomorrow? How long has it been?"

"Things are complicated, Morgan. I didn't want to get your hopes up before I knew she was . . . herself again." He exhales. "Are you with her now?"

"I'll let you know tomorrow!" She hangs up on him. She knows it's childish, but at the moment it's satisfying.

Patrick calls back immediately and Morgan ignores the first few calls, but when he keeps calling, she finally answers, "Yeah?"

"Is she okay?" he asks with a nervous edge.

Morgan is still angry. "I don't know. I'm not with her," she snaps, "but it doesn't sound like it. What happened, Patrick?"

"She ran. She wouldn't let me follow her or I would have."

"Why did she run?"

"Morgan, where is she?"

"I'll let you know when I get there."

"Morgan?" he chides.

She lets out an exasperated sigh. "You know I worry about her every day. I was worried about both of you! How long have you kept her a secret, Patrick?"

He's quiet. "I had to make sure it was safe to bring her back."

"And?"

"It's more complicated than we originally thought. We contained Valla, but Emily is quite unstable. Morgan, it's not safe to be around her right now," Patrick urges. "Where is she?"

"She won't hurt me."

"Did you not learn your lesson from the trip to Grand Rapids?"

When she doesn't respond, Patrick sighs, saying, "Look, she's doing better every day, but being back here hasn't gone so well and I'd rather not risk your safety."

Morgan says, "Patrick, I'll call you if I need you." She hangs up and wonders why, out of all the places Emily could've gone, did she go to Alec's.

MORGAN ARRIVES at Alec's house a few minutes later. She knocks on the front door before walking in and making her way to the bathroom. She finds an anxious Alec standing in the hall. Seeing him sends a fresh wave of pain over her. She wishes he didn't affect her so much, but that doesn't stop her heart from turning into a balloon animal when she's near him.

"Hey, Fletch." He starts toward her but stops himself before hugging her.

She pretends not to feel the sting.

Alec continues, "I unlocked the door but didn't go in. She's been in there for an hour and a half now, and she's not answering when I knock."

"It's okay," Morgan says, wondering who she's trying to reassure more. She drops her purse and coat in the hall and turns the knob to the bathroom door. She enters carefully, scared of what she might find on the other side.

The steam in the bathroom is thick and the shower head is still on full blast. Her skin prickles and crawls at the dark, unsettling feeling inside the room. On stiff legs, she moves to the shower curtain.

"Emily, it's Morgan. Are you okay?" She holds her breath, feeling her own heartbeat thrum rapidly as she waits for a response that doesn't come.

"Emily, I'm going to open the curtain, okay?"

Morgan's body turns cold at what she finds when she pushes the shower curtain aside. She turns the freezing water off and steps inside to wrap her arms around Emily who is huddled stark naked on the shower floor. Her eyes are glazed over as she rocks back and forth. At first, Emily doesn't notice Morgan who reaches up to grab a towel. She covers Emily the best she can.

"Emily, shh," Morgan soothes, running hands through Emily's dripping hair. "Shh."

Emily finally looks at Morgan with startling green eyes that begin to focus. Her lips tremble and Morgan pulls her closer. In return, Emily claws at Morgan's arms like she's the only thing keeping Emily from death. Great racking sobs break from Emily's throat and her body shudders. Morgan can't help but cry with her.

After a while, Alec knocks on the door. "Is everything okay?"

Morgan wonders how to respond. She pivots her head to answer, but Emily clings tighter to her, so Morgan clings back and leaves Alec to worry.

Morgan holds her for a long time before the bathroom door opens. Emily's tears have softened, and her body relaxes, even though she's still holding tight to Morgan. Alec is hovering behind Patrick in the doorway and pales when he sees them huddled together on the floor of the shower.

Patrick's presence wafts into the room, soothing like a Xanax-scented candle. Emily loosens her firm grip on Morgan as her anxiety melts away. She gazes up at Patrick with a look that speaks more emotions than any words could say. Gratitude, fear, and pain show before shame and embarrassment take over. Her eyes shift to Morgan and she drops her arms and scoots away.

Patrick lifts Morgan from the shower floor and gently settles her on her feet by the bathroom door. He gives her a hug, kisses her temple, and says, "Leave us for a moment."

Morgan hesitates, looking to Emily who is wrapping the towel more securely around herself. A hand on Morgan's shoulder guides her out of the bathroom. She goes with it, feeling too many emotions to comprehend a single one. The bathroom door shuts, and it's just Morgan and Alec standing in the hall with his arm around her shoulder.

Morgan is emotionally raw which makes this the worst place for her. Alec's touch is torture—giving her a taste of what she wants only to tear it away. She's a rip the Band-Aid-off-quickly kind of girl, so she pulls away from him. The problem is, he's not a Band-Aid, so even after they have five feet between them, she feels him in the way her pulse reacts. It's screaming at her to step back into those arms and let him give her the comfort she so desperately needs.

She feels before she sees his hazel eyes watching her, constricting her chest, leaving her breathless. She slides down the wall and buries her face in her knees.

Rather than leaving, Alec kneels beside her, strokes her back, and whispers, "It's okay, Morgan."

He called her Morgan. He rarely calls her by her given name; it's usually Fletcher or Fletch or any of the assorted nicknames he's given her over the years.

Morgan brings her head out of her knees. She finds his face even closer than she'd imagined. His fingers brush the hair from her eyes and his palm rests gently on her jaw. His eyes stay steady on hers for a moment before they dip to gaze at her lips. Morgan stops breathing, preparing for what might happen next. She's watching him closely, so she notices the second he realizes this isn't right. He closes his eyes and pulls away, breaking all contact. He hangs his head for a moment before standing up and walking away.

He wanted to kiss her; she was sure of it. He was so tempted to kiss her that he had to leave. Morgan has never seen him use so much restraint. Why did he have to use it now?

"Oh, right, he's using restraint because he loves his pregnant girlfriend," Morgan mumbles. She tries to be happy for him because that's good news, but she feels cheated.

She hates that her feelings for him are turning her into an ugly person. She wants him to be happy. She does, doesn't she? If being happy means staying with his girlfriend and their child, that's great. She just can't be around to see it. Then she remembers Preston. *Oh my God, Preston!* She hadn't thought about him once since Alec's text earlier. She hits her head against the wall, feeling terrible.

Morgan remains on the floor against the wall, dripping wet and cold for several minutes before getting up and grabbing her phone to call Ben. She pulls away from the wall and wanders down the hall as the phone rings.

"Hey, Morgan."

"Hey, Ben," she croaks, her voice sounding lost.

"What's wrong?"

She hesitates, before saying it outright. "Emily is back."

"I know."

"What do you mean, you know?" Morgan enters the kitchen, her clothes dripping on the wood floor.

"I saw her earlier. She came to see me at the dojo."

"What?" she says, grabbing a towel from the counter and trying to ring out the bottom of her pants. "Why didn't anyone bother to tell me? I had to hear from Alec."

"Alec?"

"Yeah, apparently you and Patrick couldn't spare a second out of your day to send me a text or God forbid, a phone call. I had to hear from Alec, who called me at work begging for help." She goes back to drying herself.

"What did he need help with?" he asks.

"With Emily. He needed help with Emily." Morgan repeats just as Alec walks into the kitchen. She tries to ignore him as she continues, "Ben, how was she when you saw her earlier?"

"She was fine. Completely fine."

"Yeah, well she—"

Alec interrupts, "You're shivering. You should change."

She looks up to see the pile of clothes he's offering her—his clothes. Her body starts making balloon animals out of her heart again, squeezing and twisting. It's agony, but at the same time, her hands reach for the clothes unable to deny them.

She realizes belatedly that Ben is still talking in her ear.

"Ben, I'm gonna hand you to Alec for a minute, K?"

She hands the phone over to Alec before he can respond. She's careful to avoid his eyes as she heads for the half bathroom off the kitchen.

Morgan peels off her wet clothes and pulls on the sweats, t-shirt, and hoodie he offered. She is swimming in his clothes, but the drawstring holds the pants on her hips. She pulls her wet hair back and studiously ignores Alec's scent draped all around her, tempting her, teasing her, helping her forget all about Preston. She knows she's playing a dangerous game. She folds her wet clothes in a little pile and leaves the bathroom.

Alec is there waiting for her. "You shouldn't have called Ben," he says, setting her phone on the kitchen island.

Her eyebrows go up. "Why not?"

"His head is already screwed up over this shit."

"He has a right to know what's going on. Wouldn't you want to know if you were him?"

"Hell, no!"

She throws her hands out. "How can you say that?"

"Okay, maybe I would, but damn it, Fletch, she's bad news for his mental state."

She notes that he's back to calling her Fletch.

He rubs his hands together like maybe he's trying to rub off a layer of skin or start a fire between his palms. "Look," he says, coming closer, "I like Emily, but what she's doing to him, to herself, I don't get it."

"You're right. You don't get it," Morgan says, grabbing her phone from the counter and walking away.

"Morgan," he says, killing her slowly by using her name . . . again.

"I don't expect you to understand, Alec," she says over her shoulder.

"Why are you avoiding me?" he asks, "We're still friends, aren't we?"

She takes a breath as she spins. "I'm here, aren't I?"

"Yeah, but not usually. You only came because of Emily."

"Alec, your girlfriend hates me!"

"She doesn't know you. If you'd hang out with us, she'd see you're like one of the guys."

Morgan sucks in a breath then slowly closes her eyes, trying not to feel hurt by his words. "One of the guys," she whispers, the pain clear in her voice. She could've sworn he wanted to kiss her earlier and now she's just one of the guys. Morgan glares at him. "I'd rather drill a hole in my head than spend time with you and your girlfriend."

A look of shock crosses his face. Morgan turns and continues down the hall to the bathroom door. It's cracked and when she approaches, Patrick pulls it open the rest of the way.

"Ouch," he mouths, making a face, tuned in to her conversation with Alec.

Morgan crosses her arms, ignores his comment, and looks behind him to find Emily wrapped in a dry towel sitting on a stool next to the shower. Emily doesn't look up. Her face is blank and pale with glazed eyes.

As worry consumes Morgan's mind, the anger slips out of her. "How's she doing?"

"She'll be okay. She just needs to sleep."

Alec comes from behind Morgan, looking pissed. "She can sleep in my room. I'll crash on the couch." Despite his hostile tone, his offer is genuine.

Morgan knows Patrick would normally decline, but he looks as if he's about to collapse from exhaustion. He was right when he told Morgan that Emily isn't the same. She isn't. But it looks like the harder he tries to hold her together, the more he falls apart.

"Patrick," Morgan whispers, reaching out a hand to console him.

His tired, pale irises meet hers knowingly and he doesn't hide any of it. Looking to Alec, he says, "Thank you, Alec. I'm going to stay with her to keep an eye on her."

"Yeah, whatever," Alec says, before walking away.

"Do you need help?" Morgan offers.

"Yes, please, and do you think you can watch Maggie a little longer, too?"

"Of course."

CHAPTER THIRTY-FIVE ~

Emily opens her eyes to glare at the petulant woman scream-ing. Under another circumstance, Emily might say she was cute, but right now, the woman is exuding too much bitchiness to be attractive. Patrick sits up in bed next to Emily, and the eyes of the yelling woman go wide when she sees him.

"Where's Alec?" the girl demands.

Alec comes through the door before either of them answer.

"Sadie, what are you doing here?"

She spins to face him with hands on her hips. "Who's this tramp sleeping in your bed? God, Alec, I thought you'd changed, but you're sleeping with some whore! Look at her! She looks all strung out! Is that what you want?"

Alec is biting his tongue as he stalks forward. "Dammit, Sadie, calm down! Think for a second!"

"You think you can screw around on me, Alec!"

"I'm not screwing around on you! Open your eyes, woman! I slept on the damn couch!"

"Don't yell at me!" she screams.

"Stop acting crazy, and I'll stop yelling!"

276

"I'm hormonal Alec, God! Is this what it's going to be like when the baby comes?" She places both hands on her flat belly.

Patrick laughs outright, looking far too happy for the situation.

Sadie glares at Emily. "Yeah, that's right. I'm pregnant! What, he didn't tell you when he was screwing you?"

"Oh my God," Emily breathes, discerning the truth. She looks to Patrick and watches his grin melt away, replaced by look of disgust.

Emily opens her mouth to speak, but Patrick interrupts, "Sadie, tell Alec the truth. You want to tell him the truth."

She sneers at Patrick and then, as if a switch flips, her whole demeanor changes and she faces Alec, confessing, "I'm not pregnant."

"What?" His anger disappears as concern floods him. "Did something happen?"

"I was never pregnant," she confesses.

"I don't understand." He shakes his head. "I saw the ultrasound pictures."

"I pulled them off the internet and altered them." She pulls the bag from her shoulder and unzips a compartment, containing birth control pills. Alec stands frozen and numb as she shows him her half-empty case of birth control pills. He brings his eyes up to glare at her.

"I didn't want to lose you," she says, reaching out to him.

Alec brushes her off. "Lose me? You didn't want to lose me? And you thought pretending you were pregnant would keep us together!"

"I only . . . I just wanted you to settle down a little, show you how good this could be."

"Good?" His face contorts with revulsion. "Babe, the only good thing between us was a fucking lie. Now get the hell out of my house!"

Tears prick her eyes as she moves toward him. "Baby?"

He backs away. "Don't touch me, Sadie! Get out!"

"You're making a mistake, Alec."

His laugh is cruel. "Honey, you were the mistake!"

"But, baby—"

"Sadie, you need to leave," Patrick says.

She drops her birth control pills back in her purse and exits without another word.

Alec hides his face in his hands for a moment before pulling away with a toothy grin. "I am done! Done with that crazy bitch! Done with crazy women!"

"You've said that before," Emily mumbles.

Alec eyes Patrick, "How'd you know she was lying?"

Patrick shrugs. "Just a hunch."

Alec doesn't believe it for a second, but he nods anyway. "Hell of a hunch," he says on his way out.

"So, there is no way we can meet up later?" Morgan asks into the phone, sounding desperate.

"I'm sorry," Preston answers. "I know it's been weeks, but this project is due tomorrow and I'll be up all night just to complete it."

"Why did you procrastinate?" she complains.

"I didn't. It's a huge project and a critical part of my grade. If I do well, it could be nominated for a regional contest and that could open up a lot of doors for me. I'm sorry, Morgan."

She sighs, "It's okay. I just miss spending time with you."

"Winter break starts in ten days. In ten days, I'll be all yours."

Morgan smiles. "I guess I can wait ten days."

Morgan's phone beeps with another call and she peeks at the screen. "Oh, Ben is calling me. Will you hold on a minute?"

"I've gotta go anyway, so I'll just talk to you later."

"Oh, okay," she says with disappointment.

Preston reminds her, "Ten days, Morgan."

She repeats, "Ten days." Then she switches over to Ben, saying, "Hey."

"Morgan, I've been going over it in my head since we talked last night and something isn't right. You said she was upset, but she . . ." Ben pauses and belatedly says, "I'm sorry, do you have a minute?"

"Of course," she says, with a sigh, because that's what you're supposed to do when someone is important. You make time, yet her boyfriend can't do that for her.

"Will you meet me at the coffee shop? I have a couple of hours between things and I can get us free drinks."

"Sure. I'll be there in twenty minutes."

AT THE COFFEE SHOP, Ben looks weary. His hair is all over the place like his hands had done a number on it. He isn't acting like himself either. Usually, he would have spotted Morgan the second she walked through the door, but today she sits down across from him and watches him doodle on a napkin for almost a full minute before he notices her.

He jumps. "Oh, Morgan." He looks to the door. "When did you get here?"

"What's going on with you, Ben? You don't look so good."

He points to the drink sitting in front of her on the table. "I got you a skinny vanilla latte."

"My favorite."

"At least I got something right." He leans back in his chair. "Last night keeps playing through my head. Morgan, she was just a shell of a person. The Emily I saw last night was the same one who froze my body so she could escape four months ago. I'm telling you, her eyes were vacant. She had no expression or emotion. She was like a fucking robot. I don't understand how she could go from that to what you described in a matter of hours." He takes a breath, before continuing, "I stopped over at Alec's this morning, but he said they were already gone. And that's another thing. Alec said Patrick stayed with Emily. They slept in the same bed and now they've run off together."

"Run off?"

"Yeah, they aren't at his apartment. I checked and he's not answering his phone. She doesn't have a phone, or does she? There is just so much I don't understand, and I fucking miss her, yet she was right there in front of me and I told her to go away because it . . . it wasn't her. She was right there, but completely absent."

Morgan lays a comforting hand on Ben's, saying softly, "Under the circumstances, I think it's normal to question everything. I wouldn't be okay if my boyfriend slept in the same bed with some girl, but Ben, have you ever . . . Shoot, I don't know how to ask this. Have you ever felt Patrick's mind? Or really it's more like his essence or something."

He raises a brow. "I don't even know what that means."

"Yeah, that's because it sounds crazy, but he has some kind of calming aura or something. It's one of his gifts, so with Emily the way she was last night, being close to Patrick was like taking a Xanax. It's kind of like how Emily healed your hand, only he's soothing her mind. From what I saw last night, it didn't look like Patrick was getting any pleasure out of what was going on. He's fixing her, so she can be the Emily we remember. And as far as seeing her at the dojo, maybe her emotions were all out of whack. Patrick said she wasn't in her right mind and that she was unstable."

"Patrick's in love with her. What if she . . . ." He can't bring himself to finish the sentence.

"He might be in love with her, but she chose to come see you."

Ben cringes, looking down at the table. "And I basically told her to go away."

"It's not simple, is it?"

"I need to see her again," he says, "Will you call Patrick? Maybe he's not answering because it's me who's calling."

"I'll try, but he keeps turning off his phone." She picks up her phone to call Patrick, but it goes straight to voicemail. "Still off."

LATHE SITS ON THE SOFA, watching his mother eat. Since Sky died, she has lost another ten pounds, bringing her total weight to a whopping ninety-five pounds. In the last week, he's been mixing protein powder into anything he can.

She looks so proper and full of grace as she eats, proof she hasn't always been locked in a basement destined to live a life of solitude. She was raised in a wealthy home with a proper upbringing. She excelled in her lessons and her gifts were something to talk about. And talk they did. The Olvasho were all interested in her. She was a beauty like no other and Sky ripped it all away from her.

She looks over to Lathe and motions for him to come to sit with her. As he lowers himself onto the seat next to her, she asks, "Why haven't you brought Katie by to see me? She's such a sweet girl. Tell me the two of you didn't break up."

Her mind has reverted to the past again, and Lathe is forced to tell her lies, so she doesn't get upset. He hates this conversation. "Katie and I didn't break up. I'll invite her over when she comes back from visiting her grandparents."

Of all times for clarity to hit, why did it have to be now? Lathe watches the change in her. Gone is the prim lady eating soup, replaced by slouching shoulders and wilted eyes that speak volumes. She drops her spoon and reaches out to him, placing her hand on his cheek. "My son, you waste so much time on me. You shouldn't throw your life away to be with someone who can't remember her own name."

"I'll never give up on you, Mother," he says, his hand covering hers.

"Lathen, what happened to Katie?" His mother loved Katie. He did too, and to lie about her feels wrong. It's one thing to lie when she's not clear-headed, but with her crystal blue eyes watching him, he breaks down and tells her the truth.

"She died."

Her breath catches and her face melts into a mask of sympathy. "I'm so sorry, Lathen. Oh, my poor boy."

"It's okay. It's been a while."

"Do you have anyone you can talk to? Anyone you call a friend?"

"I have you," he says with a grin.

"Lathen, no one has me. I barely exist. You need someone else, someone you can talk to. Someone you can be yourself around. There has to be someone."

A certain platinum blond with long legs, sinfully dark eyes, and a knack for trouble pops to the forefront of his mind, but he pushes that thought right back out. *Not in this lifetime.*

His mother continues, suggesting, "Maybe your sister? I could feel her when she was here. There is a sinister spirit inside of her, and her powers rival yours. I wish I could've met her."

He laughs. "Maybe someday you can, but Emily isn't in any kind of shape to come see you now, especially with this sinister thing inside of her."

"Maybe she needs your help."

"She has plenty of help," he says, thinking of Patrick.

"Maybe she needs the kind of help only you can give."

He'd be lying if he said he didn't think about it. "It's too dangerous."

She places her hand on his shoulder. "You have so much to give. Your gifts are wasted here. You can't sort me out, Lathen, but maybe you can help someone . . ." her words fade, and Lathe realizes she's gone. Her hand falls from his shoulder and she picks up her spoon.

Lathe wonders if she's right. Are his gifts being wasted here? Things are changing now that Sky is gone and as much as he doesn't want to be a part of the change, he can't stand for things to stay as they are. He needs Emily to take leadership of the Olvasho. He knows she is capable, and she will keep the corruption at bay. But he will have to find a way to persuade her, and then he will have to monitor her to make sure the evil inside her doesn't take over.

CHAPTER THIRTY-SIX ~

EMILY FLIPS up the hood on her overstuffed coat to help conceal her identity. It's not public knowledge that she's back in town and she doesn't want anyone from her father's office building to recognize her. She and Patrick enter the glass doors, and Emily takes a seat while Patrick walks up to the receptionist, claiming to have an appointment with Chris.

Emily slumps in the lobby chair, completely drained. She rubs at her temples, trying to will away the fuzz coating her brain.

Not only did she get an early morning wakeup call, but she also had trouble falling asleep last night. It took a few hours, but eventually, she was able to let the ocean in Patrick's head carry her away. She wasn't surprised that Patrick fell asleep before she did. She'd drained him emotionally, mentally, and physically, taking what he so willingly offered. Once again, she used him up like a battery, bringing him close to death in the process. It takes an incredible amount of energy to force calm into someone else's mind when they are mid-freak-out. Nobody else would have risked it with a Valla blood. Patrick feels like it's his penance and Emily wishes she didn't need him the way she does.

She knew running away from him was stupid. It was

dangerous for everyone because Patrick is the pin in her grenade, the only thing keeping her from detonating. Without him, she was an explosion waiting to happen, but she really doesn't want to need him as much as she does.

"Emily," Patrick calls to her and she stands to follow him.

They meet Chris in Mark's office. Patrick closes the door behind them, and Emily immediately collapses onto the loveseat. The hallucinations have returned and though she knows what she's seeing isn't real, her body reacts to the chaos, anyway.

"What's wrong with her?" Chris asks, standing behind her father's desk. Patrick called him the day before to tell him Emily was back, and they would be over soon to pick up some of her belongings from the underground bunker.

Patrick falls into the chair next to her, saying, "It's a long story."

"You guys look awful."

Patrick looks up at Chris. "Is this office soundproof?"

Chris looks concerned and hesitates before answering, "No .. . why?"

"You wouldn't happen to have a fast-acting sedative or tranquilizer, would you?"

Emily begins groaning from the loveseat, her face buried in the cushions. Chris looks at her, then back to Patrick.

Patrick offers, "She's having a rough time adjusting back into her life. It could get rather loud."

Chris nods. "So, is that why you look so exhausted?"

"It's exhausting trying to keep her and everyone around us alive. So, again, any sedatives, tranquilizers?"

"You're serious?" Chris questions.

Patrick nods.

"I have something downstairs that might help," Chris says, his paramedic background coming in handy once more. He goes to the bookcase and swinging it open to reveal the stairs below.

Patrick reluctantly stands, his body heavy on his feet. He lifts Emily into his arms, whispering, "Shh, keep your eyes closed and listen to my voice, Emily." He carries her down the stairs and Chris opens the basement stairwell to let them into the bunker. The whole time, Patrick is soothing Emily. "I'm taking you somewhere safe. Somewhere private. Keep your eyes closed. We'll turn the lights off soon."

He carries her into the bedroom she used to sleep in, while Chris disappears into a different room. Patrick strips her of her down coat and pulls a throw blanket over her.

Soon Chris comes in with IV equipment, saying, "I know there's more going on here than you're willing to tell me, but she looks like she needs help."

Patrick points to the open door and they walk out into the hall before he explains, "She does, but unfortunately she likely won't cooperate with you right now."

"What have you been giving her?"

Patrick pulls out the empty vial of medication from his coat pocket and hands it to Chris.

He reads it and looks back to Patrick. "How much have you been giving and how often?"

"It seems to be less effective each time, so I've been doubling the recommended dose."

Chris's eyes go wide, and he looks into the room. In a hushed angry voice, he scolds, "She's lucky to be alive!"

"You have no idea, but don't worry. It's not hurting her. I think her body temperature is messing with it. Her temperature is running warm, which isn't a fever, it's just one of those things we can't talk about. She's burning through the medication."

"That is not how this medication works."

Patrick shrugs. "Okay, so what do we do?"

"I'm not a doctor, but I think if we give her a sedative first and then start an IV of fluids, we can filter in some longer acting sedatives."

"Do you have access to all of that?"

"Not here, but I can get it. Will she be okay for a couple of hours?"

Patrick groans, "Yeah, just keep me informed and do me a favor. Lock us in here when you leave, and when you return, call me before coming down. If I don't answer, leave us locked in. I don't care what she says to you. Do *not* let her talk you into opening it for her."

Chris narrows his eyes, "Should I be worried?"

"Just hurry."

He nods and walks out.

AFTER THE COFFEE SHOP, Morgan decides to go to Patrick's apartment instead of her parent's house. Patrick sent her a text a few hours earlier to inform her that he and Emily would be gone for a few days and not to worry, that everything was under control. Morgan trusts Patrick to take care of Emily, but she worries about him.

Sitting on the sofa with a mug of hot cocoa in one hand and the other hand wrapped around a remote, she scrolls through Netflix. She chews on her bottom lip, worrying when a knock at the door startles her. She jumps, almost spilling her drink in her lap. She sets her mug on the coffee table and runs for her pepper spray. Peaking at her unexpected guest through the peephole, she sighs in relief when she sees it's Preston. She discards her pepper spray and opens the door, asking, "What are you doing here?"

Preston's smile lights up his whole face. "I had to see you."

"But your project?"

"My project will still be there when I get back. I just . . . I couldn't wait another minute. I missed you and couldn't wait."

Her smile is interrupted as he swoops in and crushes her lips with his. She wraps her arms around him and pulls him into the apartment while he closes the door, never breaking their kiss. His hands tangle in her silky brown hair while she cradles his face, noting the day-old stubble.

He pulls away after a moment, taking in the apartment and asking, "Is your cousin here?"

She shakes her head. "He's out of town. It's just me, my cocoa, and Netflix. How long can you stay?"

"Only a little bit." His eyes drag over her. "You are gorgeous."

She looks down at her sweatpants and tank, saying, "It's not exactly a little black dress."

His lips quirk into a sensual smile as he gestures toward her attire. "No, but this is sexy. *You* are sexy." He moves in closer, meaning every word. "You don't have to try to be beautiful. You just are. With you in front of me, it's hard to care about anything else." He pulls her in for another kiss.

She pushes against his solid chest, saying, "Seriously, what about your project?"

"It's hard to care about my project right now."

She gives him a grin, laces her fingers through his, and pulls him into the living room. "Maybe a distraction is exactly what you need."

She thinks he's going to kiss her, but he doesn't. Instead, he looks down at her in awe and asks, "How did I get so lucky?" He pulls her down on the sofa next to him and continues, "I thought if I didn't see you, these feelings would fade, and I'd be able to focus on school and my career, but the longer I'm away from you, the harder it is to concentrate on anything else."

He presses a kiss to the tip of her nose, then against her cheek, and one against her jaw. "I think I've completely fallen for you," he whispers into her ear as he nuzzles against her. She closes her eyes, and they fall back onto the sofa. Preston kisses her neck as he shifts his body over hers.

The second she feels the pressure of his body; she feels pinned down and the feelings from the night of her attack overwhelm her. Panic seizes her mind, and she reacts the way Ben taught her, keeping good on his promise to teach her self-defense.

It happens so quickly. Morgan tilts, pulls his shoulders, pins his ankle and flips him onto the floor. Morgan is on her feet across the room before she realizes what she's done. She turns back to him, covering her mouth with both hands as she creeps forward, saying, "Oh, Preston, I'm so sorry."

He's lying on the floor, looking bewildered, as he watches her take tentative steps forward. She sinks down onto the furthest edge of the sofa while he sits up.

"Morgan?" he says, keeping his distance.

"I'm so sorry," she pleads. "I didn't . . . I didn't mean to do that."

"Did I make you uncomfortable?" he questions, trying to make sense of what just happened.

"No, no . . . well sort of, but it wasn't you. It's me. I . . ." A tear leaks from her eye and she swipes it away, but more follow.

Preston moves forward cautiously as if any sudden movement might scare her away. He kneels on the floor in front of her and wipes away her tears. "I'm sorry, Morgan. I never want to make you uncomfortable."

"It wasn't you. I promise it wasn't. Everything we did, I wanted. It's just . . . I felt pinned and I freaked out. I'm sorry. Maybe, for now, can we move a little slower?"

He nods. "Of course."

She gives him a sad smile. "I really am sorry."

"Stop apologizing. I'm fine." He moves to sit next to her. "Maybe we can watch something together."

She nods, but neither makes a move for the remote; instead, they sit in a heavy silence. After a moment, Morgan scoots closer to him and he cautiously wraps an arm around her, asking, "Is this okay?"

She nods and leans into him.

He kisses the top of her head and gently asks, "What happened to you, Morgan? That extreme reaction doesn't happen for no reason."

He said he was falling for her. He came here to be with her tonight when she knew he would normally be obsessing over and perfecting his project. And he is still here after she flipped him off the sofa for no reason.

After a deep breath, she explains, "When I lived in Florida, two guys from my dorm forced their way into my room one night. They . . . they were drunk, and at first, I thought they were harmless, so I let my guard down. They became demanding and overpowered me. I fought them, I gave one a bloody nose and the other might have trouble having kids someday, but nothing I did seemed to matter. The alcohol made them numb to the pain I inflicted."

She is wringing her fingers, uncomfortable in her own skin, as she reveals the worst part. "They ripped off my clothes. The one with the bloody nose bled all over me while I screamed and fought. My roommate walked in just as nosebleed put on a condom."

She bites her lip, trying to hold herself together. "We called the police, but nosebleed's lawyer-father showed up first. He threatened to charge me with assault because of the injuries I inflicted trying to defend myself. I knew it didn't sound right, but I just wanted it to be over. I wanted to shower and wash the blood off of my skin. I wanted to burn my sheets and clothes, and I never wanted to see that dorm room again.

"My parents complained to the administrators and told them what happened, but by then the evidence was gone, and it was my word against theirs. The guys were given a warning, and I moved back home. I always thought if something like that happened to me, I would be strong and do whatever it took to bring them down, but I've never been more scared and felt so weak in my life."

He holds onto her, suppressing the urge to pull her into his lap. "My God, Morgan. Why didn't you tell me this sooner?"

"You haven't exactly been around. And besides, it's not something one brings up on a first date. I thought I had moved past it. I was feeling empowered after Ben taught me some self-defense moves."

"This isn't something you just get over after a few months, no matter how many moves you know," he says, before insisting, "Come home with me."

"What?" Morgan asks, pushing away to look at him.

"I don't want you staying here alone. I can drop you at your parent's house if you'd rather."

"I'm fine here," she defends, refusing to let fear control her.

He sighs, looking contemplative for a moment before saying, "If I leave you here tonight, I'm going to have trouble sleeping. I know you are a grown woman who can handle herself, but I'll feel better if you aren't alone. I hate the idea that I won't be here to comfort you if you're scared. I want to hold you and make you smile instead of feeling afraid. I understand if you're not comfortable coming home with me, but please don't make me worry that you're alone."

Her heart feels full. Preston doesn't tell her she's weak or look at her like she's a victim that needs his protection. He doesn't look at her like she's his little sister or one of the guys. He looks at her with adoration and Morgan's eyes well with happy tears.

A look of concern crosses his face. "Wait, why are you upset? I didn't mean—"

She interrupts him with a kiss, pushing against his chest until he falls back onto the cushions. She follows him down, straddling him as she lands on top of him.

After a long make-out session, Morgan follows Preston back to his place where she watches him work and he explains his project to her.

Eventually, her eyes fall closed and she briefly wakes as Preston carries her to bed. She falls asleep against his pillow and awakens the next morning with him lying beside her. She smiles to herself as the sun makes its ascent into the sky.

EMILY IS SLEEPING SOUNDLY as Chris changes the bag of IV fluids. She slept through the night with the different medications circulating in her system and even her temperature is down this morning. Patrick walks into the room as Chris finishes.

"Thank you, Chris," Patrick says. "Do you mind if we stay another day?"

"Stay as long as you need. We have enough to keep her sedated for a couple more days if necessary. You're looking better this morning, but you still don't look good."

When Chris came back with the medication the evening before, Patrick looked half-dead. Chris knows there are things he doesn't understand, but he could feel an ocean of calming waves pour over him when he walked into the room with Emily and Patrick last night. Patrick was doing something to sedate her that Chris couldn't comprehend. As soon as Chris inserted the IV and pushed the sedative through, Patrick collapsed, and the ocean disappeared. Chris checked his vitals and ended up dragging him into the next room and hooking him up with his own IV.

Patrick came to in the middle of the night, and Chris forced him back to bed, but here he is again, checking on Emily.

Patrick yawns. "If you're able to keep an eye on her, I'll go back to bed."

"I'll call you if there are any problems."

"Thank you," Patrick says, before going to his room.

CHAPTER THIRTY-SEVEN

TWO DAYS of rest and recuperation later, Patrick and Emily pack up to leave the bunker. She's feeling more like herself and Patrick has renewed energy. They stop in Mark's office to talk to Chris before leaving.

"Your house was destroyed by a fire two weeks after your dad was hospitalized." Chris explains to Emily, "The police investigation proves it was arson, but they suspect your involvement in setting the fire. I have video footage of the real perp but didn't want to hand it over until I spoke to Mark. Since that hasn't been possible, I showed it to Patrick a few months back. We came to the agreement that it was in our best interest to hold onto the video and do our own investigation until you showed up. Now, of course, I'll turn it in so we can clear your name."

She asks, "What did you find?"

He pulls up a snippet of the footage and zooms in on the dark-haired man setting the fire. "Have you seen this man before?"

Emily shakes her head. "No, do you know who he is?"

"We haven't been able to identify him, but the way he set the fire matches several other unsolved cases around the area," Chris says.

She looks to Patrick. "Do you think—"

"It's not Olvasho related. This isn't how they would get your attention, and they didn't know your identity four months ago. Also, I don't recognize that man." Patrick nods his head at the photo. "Clearly not one of us. The face tattoo would stand out."

"Why would someone burn down our house?"

Chris answers, "Your father's line of work could make some people very unhappy. Right now, we think they knew the house was empty and were sending a message. It fits with the other unsolved cases as well."

"So, it's not because of me?"

Chris leans forward. "We don't believe so."

Patrick says, "Let the police figure it out. I don't think this has to do with us and we have enough to deal with right now."

Since Morgan has been staying with Preston, Emily gets settled into the guest bedroom at Patrick's apartment. She wants to see Samantha, but she is waiting until her mind is more stable. No need for her sister to catch a glimpse of the mess Morgan witnessed a few nights ago.

In the afternoon, Morgan comes by to drop Maggie off and to check on everyone. As soon as Emily feels Morgan pull up with Maggie, she stands and walks to the door. She misses her dog. She remembers the day she sent her to find Patrick. She was so worried about her, but she knew Maggie could do it. She knew Maggie would save her.

As soon as the door opens, Maggie bursts through and Emily drops to the floor to embrace the best damn dog in the world. Maggie jumps into her arms, wiggling and spinning and licking.

"I swear, the deer around here are getting bold," Morgan says from the door, looking out at the small yard.

"Is that so?" Patrick smirks, looking to Emily.

Morgan closes the door and turns to them. "They were all

over the place last night too, but today they're right outside the apartment. Do you think they're rabid?"

Patrick laughs. "They aren't rabid. They *are*, however, very interested in Emily. They were following us while we were driving, too."

Emily's head shoots up, defending, "I'm controlling it a little better. At least they aren't all at the door like at the motel."

Morgan offers, "Maybe the deer is your Patronus, like in Harry Potter."

"Nerd!" Patrick calls out.

"Okay, but really in all seriousness, maybe they are protecting you. You obviously have a connection to animals. Patrick said you had tigers, and Maggie would die for you. So why wouldn't hordes of deer be protecting you? They can be scary with their giant antlers."

Patrick singsongs, "Deer and tigers and dogs. Oh my!"

"Shut up, Patrick. I'm serious."

Patrick surrenders, admitting, "I'm not necessarily disagreeing with you."

Emily kisses Maggie's head one more time before standing to say, "So the deer are protecting me, huh?"

"Maybe." Morgan shrugs. "You seem to be doing a lot better today?"

Emily moves forward to embrace her friend. "I didn't mean for you to see me like that. It's hard for me to know what's real and what is in my head. Being back here and seeing my dad and my house and Ben . . . it was all too much." She steps back. "Honestly, everything is too much. I don't exactly have the best control over my psyche right now."

Patrick says, "Hopefully, Maggie's presence will help."

"Is there anything I can do?" Morgan asks.

Emily snorts. "No. I need to practice my healing skills, but you can't help with that. It's way too dangerous. The last time I tried, I gave my dad second degree burns and Patrick had to heal him for me."

Morgan takes off her coat. "I can be your guinea pig."

Emily shakes her head no, while Patrick responds, "Absolutely not."

"Why not?" Morgan complains.

Emily's head comes up, looking toward the front door while Patrick and Morgan continue arguing like siblings. Without a second thought, Emily moves toward the entry. Patrick is clued-in to what's going on while Morgan watches curiously, witnessing the change as Emily's face goes blank and her body stiffens. With her chin up, Emily opens the door.

Ben is standing just outside, looking unsure about knocking. When he sees Emily opening the door, relief floods him. He stares at her for a moment, wondering if she'll ask him to leave, but she just stares at him with the same vacant expression she wore the last time he saw her.

In a small voice, she asks, "What are you doing here, Ben?"

He stares at her, taking in every new detail. In the months she's been gone, her hair has grown longer and lighter and she's wafer thin. She disappeared four months ago, and he feared he would never see her again. Now she's standing here, right in front of him.

He still feels a connection to her, but it's buried under layers of doubt and fear and something else that he can't quite pinpoint. He stands in the open door, letting the cold breeze sweep her hair from her shoulder. She folds her arms across her chest, protecting herself from the cold and from him. She's hiding from him, and he can't figure out why.

He's not backing down this time. Ben takes a step forward, and the movement incites a reaction from her. She lets out a breath and her mask slips a little, showing emotions he's been waiting to see.

He takes another step and she tilts her face up to him. There is a depth in her eyes he didn't see the other day, and best of all, she's not backing away or slamming the door in his face.

He closes the gap between them by enveloping her in a hug.

Returning his embrace, she closes her eyes. He buries his face in her hair, taking in her scent, her feel, her desperation as her hands cling to him.

Into her ear, he whispers, "I'm sorry, Emily. God, I'm so sorry."

She pulls back, her blank expression gone, replaced by so much hope her emerald eyes are shining with unshed emotion. She begins to smile, but he interrupts her with a kiss. His lips press against hers while she wraps her arms around his neck, returning the kiss with so much passion, the freezing air doesn't seem to touch either of them.

Wrapped in this kiss are all of their hopes and dreams and plans for a future they didn't think they would ever experience. She parts her lips and his tongue finds hers. He bends forward to scoop her up. Her legs wrap around him as he carries her forward without direction, without caring where they end up as long as they are together.

The heat from their kiss spreads through Ben, encasing him in loving warmth. The temperature increases until his neck begins to burn. He breaks their kiss realizing something isn't right as searing pain radiates down through his neck and shoulders. There are sparks and the scent of burning flesh. Emily lets go of him, quickly finding her feet and stepping away as Ben grimaces in pain. Emily covers her mouth with trembling hands, on the verge of full-blown panic.

Patrick, who was silently sitting with Morgan at the dining table, takes control of the escalating situation. He stands with his half-empty glass of water and throws it at Ben's back to put out his singed shirt. Ben swings around, only now realizing Patrick and Morgan are present while Patrick shuts the apartment door.

Before Ben can speak, Patrick commands, "Ben, take off your shirt and sit down at the table."

Patrick steps over to Emily who is visibly shaking. She stares at her hands afraid to touch anything. She lost control with Ben, forgetting how badly she could hurt him.

Patrick grabs her hands in between his in order to get her attention. When her eyes meet him, he says, "Pull it together, Emily. You don't get to feel sorry for yourself. Not right now. We are fixing this. Either you fix it, or I will, but I know you want to learn to control it, so stop spinning out and let's go over there and figure it out together."

She blinks and her fear turns into determination. God, she's thankful Patrick calls her on her shit and reminds her of the big picture. They move to the table where Morgan is tending to Ben by putting a cool rag against the second and third-degree burns. Ben is grimacing with his head down and his fists clenched, barely containing the groans that are begging to rip from his chest. Morgan steps aside as Patrick and Emily step forward.

Patrick removes the wet cloth to get a good look at the mirrored handprint burns etched into his skin. Patrick says, "I'm going to start the healing, so he's not in so much pain, but you can break in whenever you feel comfortable."

Emily swallows her tears and watches Patrick. She imitates what he's doing, and soon enough Emily pushes Patrick out of the way and continues to use her lethal hands to heal the burns she caused.

After ten minutes, Emily finishes healing Ben's skin, Patrick provides Ben with a new shirt, and the four of them sit around the dining table speechless.

Patrick addresses the elephant in the room, saying, "So, as you can see, Emily has developed the ability to manipulate physical elements. We stopped at the hospital the other day to see Mark and the same thing happened when she tried to heal him."

Looking to Emily, Morgan asks, "But you're feeling better, right?"

"I'm feeling more like myself, and I'm not having delusions."

"That's a good sign," Morgan says, "and look how she healed him."

Ben reaches out to the hand Emily has rested on the table. She begins to pull back, but he captures her hand and says, "Why did you pretend everything was fine the other day?"

Emily asks, "What are you talking about?"

"At the Dojo, when I saw you. You looked like you were completely fine, like none of this fazed you. Like you were coming back, well rested and emotionless."

Patrick snickers while Morgan looks at him incredulously, but it's Emily who says, "I didn't want to influence your perspective, so I cloaked my emotions the way Patrick taught me. I didn't want my strong feelings to overwhelm you or make your decision for you. The last time I saw you, I was a stranger, and I almost killed you. Months have gone by, Ben. I couldn't just assume you still felt the same way about me. And then I saw you at the dojo looking amazing, but when you looked at me, you flinched. I didn't want to persuade you into something you didn't want, so I masked everything."

Ben is shaking his head. "Don't ever do that again. I'd rather see or feel what you're feeling. Not that blank person. I didn't even know if it was really you in there."

Morgan cuts in, "Speaking of, I'm missing pieces. What actually happened in Chicago? Is Valla gone?"

Emily and Patrick look at one another, and Patrick says, "Essentially Valla latched onto Emily's soul and she is still living inside of Emily unable to regain control unless the necklace Emily is wearing is removed."

"Do we need to get a stronger chain?" Ben asks.

Morgan suggests, "Maybe something made of steel."

"The necklace is plenty strong, but it's not Valla we need to concern ourselves with," Patrick says, while Emily squirms in her seat. "It's Adelaide."

Patrick and Emily explain what happened after Patrick found her. From the bar in Chicago to the Olvasho meeting, to the stay at the bunker; they tell everything, glazing over the more sensual details.

Ben volunteers to be Emily's guinea pig so she can keep practicing. While she adamantly refuses, Patrick leans back toward the kitchen counter. He picks up a letter opener and swiftly stabs it through the hand Ben has rested on the table.

Morgan screams, Emily gasps, and Ben shouts in pain as much as surprise. Patrick looks all too happy to oblige in causing Ben pain, but Ben's shout turns to laughter as soon as he realizes what's happening.

"Thanks," he says to Patrick as he rips the letter opener from his hand and offers his bleeding palm to Emily.

Closing her hands around Ben's bloody wound, she decides to deal with Patrick later and focuses on healing Ben's injury.

LATER THAT EVENING, Emily is cuddling on the couch with Ben, alternating between watching TV and kissing. Emily has remained in control of her abilities all day, though Patrick is keeping a close eye on her from the dining table where he sits next to Morgan.

While Patrick tries to gain knowledge of Adelaide by reading through the red book written in the Olvasho language, Morgan is simultaneously working on homework and texting Preston.

Sighing, Patrick closes the book. "She's not mentioned in any of these. Did nobody know the real story?"

Morgan sets her phone down next to her laptop. She hates to see Patrick looking so defeated. "Didn't she tell you that everyone who knew the truth was either dead or too afraid to speak?"

"I suppose." He sighs again, his eyes wandering toward the living room before they flick back to Morgan.

She snorts, then whispers, "You're being obvious."

Patrick tilts his head, offering, "Almost as obvious as you were a couple of nights ago."

Morgan looks at the table, feeling guilty. Here she is texting her boyfriend when she had wanted Alec to kiss her. Morgan leans forward, more serious now, asking, "How can you be around them when they're together?"

Patrick gives her an encouraging smile. "I would think if anyone understood, it would be you. Alec philandered around right before your eyes for years. All the while, you loved him."

"Yeah, but—"

He glances toward Emily and Ben on the couch. The TV is turned up loud enough to keep the happy couple from hearing their conversation. "He doesn't love her like I love her."

"They love each other, Patrick. They're just beginning to rebuild their relationship. I wouldn't want you to—"

Patrick's eyes swing back to her. "I won't get between them, Morgan. I'm not trying to ruin what they have. I want what's best for Emily, and I may love her more than he does, but it doesn't mean I'm the best option for her. Just like you and Alec. He's single now, but it doesn't mean he's right for you."

CHAPTER THIRTY-EIGHT ~

THE FOLLOWING EVENING . . .

THIS TIME of night Emily expects the hospital to be empty, but a few people are scattered around the lobby. One man is curled up in a lounge chair sleeping. They walk past the sleeping man and follow the sterile white hallway down to the bank of elevators. Patrick hits the button, and as they wait, two women in scrubs exit a room down the hall. Their laughter is loud and incongruous with Emily's perception of a hospital. They walk off in the opposite direction, but their conversation and laughter echo down the hall, putting her on edge.

An elevator opens and they step in. Patrick hits the number while Emily fights the feeling of déjà vu. It's been five days since she was here last and tonight, she is feeling more confident.

The floor is silent this evening, as most of the patients are sleeping. She doesn't need Patrick to guide her this time. She enters room 407 without hesitation. She flips on the lights in his room and walks up to his bedside, noting the improvement in his condition since her last visit. The tube is out of his throat and he is breathing steadily through the same chapped lips and gray skin. His boney, skeletal body reminds her of the demon version of Sky, and that sends an unpleasant shiver through her.

"I'm going to try," Emily tells Patrick.

"I'm here to back you up."

Emily wonders what people in comas dream about or if they dream at all. She wonders if they make up their own world inside their head. If someone lived in a coma long enough, would they want to wake up?

If her dad is dreaming, she isn't seeing what he sees. His mind is a muddled mess, like a math problem gone wrong. It's nonsense, like his thoughts and memories and normal brain functions were chopped up and run through a blender. She tries to piece his mind back together, but nothing stays in its place. There is nothing concrete enough to hold. He is too broken.

Patrick and his uncle could not heal him, but Emily has Valla blood. She thought she had enough power to beat the odds. After all, she had beaten Sky, the unbeatable man. But despite her extraordinary blood and capabilities, even she is not infallible.

PATRICK WATCHES Emily as she tries and fails to make any progress with Mark. The skin between her eyebrows keeps bunching as she struggles to make an impact. Her eyes remain closed even as grief overwhelms her and tears trickle down her angelic face. Patrick's heart breaks for her as he realizes that Mark is likely beyond repair.

After a while, her chin comes up and her eyes open. "Patrick," she says, voice filled with regret, "it's the only way to save him." There is a glint in her emerald-green eyes as she reaches behind her neck. "I'm sorry," she whispers, just before unclasping the delicate chain.

"Emily, no!" He reaches for her, but it's too late. She drops the necklace on the bed and the moment it leaves her hand a warm breeze sweeps the room, forcing him a step back.

Her voice is powerful, as she demands, "This will go more smoothly if you do what I say and don't get in my way."

"Valla?"

She smirks. "Emily is stronger now. You've done well with her."

The door to the room closes with a little help from Valla, and to Patrick's surprise, she places a hand over Mark's head and heart. The breeze turns soft and the room gets warmer. The beeping on the monitor leaps and then continues at a faster pace. Patrick reaches for the necklace, careful to avoid the pendant.

While Valla is focusing on Mark, Patrick comes up behind her, holding the necklace, ready to clasp it around her neck the second she's finished with Mark. Mark's body begins to shake, and his monitors jump around, sounding an alarm.

"People are coming," Valla warns. "Barricade the door or deal with them. This will take all of my focus."

Patrick hesitates until the door begins to open, then he drops the pendant and spins away from Valla to deal with the nurses trying to enter. With a little mental persuasion, the nurses turn off the alarms and are on their way back out the door none the wiser.

Patrick closes the door behind them and gets back to Valla. Mark's body has stopped shaking and his cheeks have a little more color.

Eventually, the monitors continue their normal relaxed rhythm and Mark has a new glow. When Valla removes her hands from Mark, she is trembling. Patrick reaches up to reattach the necklace when her hand grabs his wrist, burning his skin.

"Give us a minute longer, Patrick. She needs me to help her recover from this."

He pulls his wrist away and shakes his head. "I'll help her."

"You can't survive the kind of help she needs right now."

"I'll make do."

"But she won't," Valla says. "She needs me, Patrick. I can help her better than you can."

Ignoring her, he clasps the necklace and lets it fall against her skin. Emily begins to fall and Patrick scrambles to catch her. She whimpers against his touch and although he tries to heal her, she takes too much, just as Valla said.

They sink to the floor as she drains him. When he tries to pull away, she holds on tighter just like it happened in the boat so long ago. She's killing him.

He reaches out, wrapping his arms around her. He unclasps the necklace and feels it slide from its place around her neck.

The instant it falls away, Valla wraps her energy around Emily while Patrick slides the rest of the way to the floor, completely drained and half-dead. Valla leans forward, her lips touching his ear as she says, "Say hello to my sister for me, Patrick."

He tries to reach out, but everything becomes dark and the beeping of the monitors fade until Patrick can hear nothing but the ocean tide. His body relaxes into the cool sand. He sits up, looking out toward the water before coming to a stand. His bare feet carry him forward, to the shoreline.

With each wave, the ocean water reaches out to caress his feet as if to say hello, dear friend. He looks out across the vastness of the ocean. The moonless night shrouds everything in darkness, but hundreds of stars glisten, sparkling brightly across the sky, looking like a meadow full of fireflies in the middle of summer. Patrick takes a deep breath, inhaling the warm salty breeze and relaxes at the familiarity of it all.

"Patrick," a voice calls, and he looks out to the ocean. A woman is wading out into knee-high water with her hair flowing down to her hips in blond waves. She continues to move out into the sea, the water to her thighs before Patrick thinks to respond.

"Hey," he calls out to her.

She pauses and turns her head to give him a glimpse of her profile before continuing her journey deeper into the waves. The water is up to her waist and her hands caress the small ripples at her sides.

"Wait!" Patrick calls, stepping forward. "Who are you?"

She keeps moving away, so Patrick steps into the water. "Stop." He means it as a command, but his voice is weak.

"Join me, Patrick," she calls. The water is up to her chest and her long hair floats out around her.

"Who are you?" The calm waves lap at his knees as he continues forward.

The water is to her shoulders when she finally turns to face him. Her pale face and crystal blue eyes shine through the darkness. "I've been waiting for you, Patrick," she says, before diving into the water.

Frantic, Patrick races into the waves. Once deep enough, he dives in after her, swimming with no direction. He doesn't know how to find her, so he keeps paddling deeper until his lungs burn and the current pulls him downward. He begins to suffocate in the cold water, but as a jolt penetrates his brain, he remembers his promise to Morgan. He said he wouldn't do this again. Just when he's about to go up for air, something wraps around his ankle and just as quickly releases its hold.

Patrick spins around to find her there. Her blond locks float around her face emphasizing her angelic features while her naked body shimmers with translucent light in the deep waters. She is a goddess, and he no longer cares that he can't get the oxygen his body needs. This is the closest he's ever come to the enchantress in his dreams.

"Breathe," she says into his mind.

He fights because he doesn't want to wake up, but ultimately his body makes the decision for him, and he inhales deeply. Only, he doesn't wake up. Instead of the water burning his lungs, it soothes like the touch of velvet on skin. He fills his lungs to capacity, and tranquil relief chases away the dizziness he felt a moment ago.

"I didn't wake up," he speaks through his mind.

A pleasant smile takes the enchantress's face and she says, "You are no longer dreaming."

"Am I dead?" he asks.

A devious laugh curls her lips. "Oh, Patrick, you have been taught so little about your heritage."

"How do you know me?"

"I've known you your whole life. I've waited a very long time to meet you."

Patrick looks around the dark waters wondering what she's talking about. "You've been haunting my dreams."

Her smile is warm. "Yes."

"Why am I here?"

"You called on me for help. I am unable to help you until you free me from this place."

"This place? Where are we?"

"My eternity," she says, spreading her arms as if to show Patrick her surroundings. "Eternal darkness, eternally alone, eternally cursed. Until you."

"You're Princess Isa?"

"Yes," she says. "I'm here because my stepmother, Adelaide, cursed us. We didn't know until we died that we would never be free. She stole our happiness even in death and traded us her fate. The three of us, Valla, Leona, and I are bound by the blood of our progeny. The Olvasho continue to kill each other and once the last of my bloodline dies, I will forever be stuck here."

She continue, "For generations, the Olvasho have fought over power. Others have called on me, but they've never made it as far as you have, Patrick Glenn. They drown in their sleep trying to reach me. You are the first to make it here alive, though by the narrowest of margins. You were on the brink of death before coming here. Perhaps that's how you made it this far."

With her words, Patrick remembers Emily and how he left her. "I have to get back."

"You cannot save the girl. Not in the shape you are in. If you keep sacrificing yourself, she will kill you. You must let Valla help her."

"Valla won't help her. Adelaide will take over."

"Emily and Valla must form trust and learn to work together. That will not happen with you keeping them apart. Valla has already had the opportunity to take Emily's body, but if you'll remember, she forced Emily to take control."

"But—"

"Patrick Glenn, I will hear no more!" Her voice is thunderous in his head and reverberates through his body. She continues in a much calmer tone, "Now allow me to heal your body and we will return together."

EMILY KNEELS on the floor of the hospital room. She is unable to move with Valla controlling her. She knows Valla is healing her body, but she is more concerned about Patrick lying unmoving on the floor. He hasn't taken a breath in at least five minutes, and Emily fights for control over her mind so she can help him.

"Be still," Valla commands in their shared mind.

"We have to help him," Emily argues.

"We need to take care of you first, Emily."

"He's turning blue."

"Emily, there is nothing we can do for him. Either my sister will help him, or she won't, but if you continue to drain yourself, then Adelaide will regain control and that is far more dangerous."

"I can't just let him die," Emily argues.

Valla's mind shifts focus and urgently says, "Emily, she's coming. We need to hide."

Samantha was relieved to get the call that her dad was breathing on his own again. The last week was a nightmare with all the ups and downs. Six days ago, the doctors told her to prepare for the worst. They said his body had finally given up. Then his miraculous overnight recovery stunned them all.

The elevator doors open and she steps out onto the fourth floor of the north hospital wing. She breathes in the familiar smells and sounds as she walks to her father's room, noting the silence punctuated only by the faint beeping of monitors. This is how Samantha prefers it. She is tired of the nurses giving her sorrowful looks. She refuses to stop hoping and the more she sees his nurses, the harder it is to keep up the positive thinking. To avoid them she's started coming in the late evenings to do his exercises.

She taps the hand sanitizer in the hall right before entering her dad's room. "His door is never closed," she grumbles to herself, thinking the staff has given up on him. She opens the door, saying, "Hey Dad, ready for your exercises?" She sets her things in the chair next to his bed and moves towards him. She inhales quickly and leans forward to place a palm against his pink cheek. He looks like he is sleeping, not dying. "Look at you. You're so much warmer today. But the nurses say . . . "

"Forget what they say. You're getting better. They said you wouldn't but look at you, handsome as ever. Hold on just a minute, Daddy. Let me grab the nurse. She's gotta see this."

Samantha quickly exits the room, leaving the door open.

From the bathroom, Patrick gasps, coming awake. He finds himself lying on the bathroom floor. The lights are out, and Emily is peeking through the cracked door, looking out into Mark's hospital room.

"Emily?" he says.

She turns to face him in a daze. Patrick notices the pendant hanging from its chain in Emily's hand.

"What happened?" he says, picking himself up off the floor with more energy than he's felt in months.

"Thank God you're alive," she says with relief, but her movements are stiff, and she turns back to spy through the crack in the bathroom door.

Patrick peeks into the room with her. Everything appears to be fine with Mark gently breathing in his hospital bed. Then he notices the purse on the side table—Samantha's purse.

"Come on." He nudges her. "We have to get out of here before she comes back."

Emily makes no indication she hears him, so Patrick slides the door open and pulls her from her hiding spot. They make it out of his room and down the hall, ducking into an empty room when they hear footsteps approach from around the corner.

"He's so much better!" Samantha says to the woman in scrubs walking next to her. "You won't believe how much better he looks."

Emily steps forward to get a better look at her sister, but Patrick holds her back. As soon as the danger passes, he takes the necklace from Emily, afraid she'll drop it and he pulls a dazed Emily alongside him all the way to the car. Patrick opens the door for her, and she snaps out of her trance.

"I got it," she tells him, sitting in her seat unprovoked.

When he gets in, he says, "It must be difficult keeping this from your sister."

"It's not that. I'd rather Sam hate me than to know the truth. It's just that even now, even not knowing; she's still changed so much."

"You and your father are the only family she has, and she lost both of you. That changes a person."

"Is it wrong to keep it from her? I'm doing to her what my dad did to me."

"I don't think it's wrong, but maybe you should consult else-where. I'm not the right person to advise on ethics," he says, handing her the necklace. "Put this on."

She does as he says while he starts the car.

Changing the subject, Emily suggests, "We should probably talk about the other things that happened up there."

Patrick smirks. "You almost killed me, again."

CHAPTER THIRTY-NINE ~

THE COMPUTER IS bright in the dark room where Morgan charts on her patient. She hates to wake patients to get their vitals, but Mrs. Miller was to have her blood pressure checked every hour. Morgan finishes her charting and leaves her patient to sleep for another hour.

As she walks down the hall, she notices commotion around the nurse's station. She almost shrugs it off, but she hears her name. Entering the group of hospital employees, she hears first-hand about the man on the fourth floor. They believed he was brain dead, but he just woke up out of a four-month coma.

"Morgan, isn't that the guy you've been checking up on?" asks a coworker.

Morgan smiles. "It's my friend's dad."

"Well, maybe you ought to go check up on that friend."

As Morgan walks away, she pulls out her phone and shoots a text to Patrick. **Visited the hospital lately?**

Patrick still hasn't responded by the time Morgan gives her report to the next staff member. She makes her way down to the fourth floor and knocks softly at the opened door as she enters Mark's room.

Samantha wraps her in a big hug. "He's awake! I told

everyone he was going to wake up, but no one believed me, except for you."

Morgan smiles and pulls back. "I knew it was just a matter of time."

"Come say *hi* to him," Samantha says while ushering her over to the bed.

Mark is sitting up, looking too thin but otherwise healthy. It is a drastic difference from what he was a week ago. "Mr. Burk, I'm so happy you're awake."

Mark smiles, "I heard you've been checking in on me."

"The nurses couldn't keep me away," she teases.

"Samantha says that cousin of yours has been looking for Emily. Has he had any luck?"

Morgan's eyes flick to Samantha and back before she says, "Patrick isn't good at keeping me informed, but I asked him for an update earlier, and I haven't heard anything back yet. I think he had a very busy day today. I'll let you know what I hear."

Samantha's phone begins ringing and she smiles down at it. "Oh, it's Dan's mom!" She walks to the other end of the room as she answers the call. "Hi, Judy."

Morgan listens to her tell Judy that Mark is awake. When Morgan turns back to Mark, he's watching her. "Thank you, Morgan. Samantha tells me you've been keeping her company and checking in on me . . . and her. I really appreciate what you've done for us."

A small grin tugs her lips as she whispers, "Of course. I'm so happy to see Emily and Patrick pull this off. Samantha doesn't know she's back yet. Emily wants to be entirely in control of her mind before she sees Samantha."

His face changes. "You said Emily and Patrick?"

She nods.

"He's double-crossing her. He betrayed us both."

Morgan realizes how much he's missed, placing a hand on his shoulder to reassure him. "They worked it out. Patrick saved her life. He saved both of you. His loyalty has changed."

Mark's face shows skepticism.

"I promise you; no one has tried harder to make amends for the wrong they've done. Patrick loves Emily. He'd do anything for her."

"What happened to Sky?"

Morgan glances over to Samantha who is still prattling away on her phone. To Mark, she says, "Sky is dead. There is a lot to explain, but for now, everyone is safe. Emily will explain everything soon."

"Knock, knock," a male voice calls from the door. Morgan turns to find a dark-haired man in his thirties entering the room.

Mark greets, "Hey, Chris. You made it here so quickly. I didn't expect you to come tonight."

Chris approaches the bed. "Are you kidding? I've been waiting for this call for four long months. Did you have a good nap?"

Mark nods, "Best of my life."

Chris looks at Morgan still in her scrubs, "Are you his nurse?"

Mark cuts in, "This is Morgan. She's a friend of my girls and has been checking up on me.

Samantha hangs up and joins the conversation. "Chris, you made it." She gives him a quick hug.

"Thanks for the call," he says. "Do you mind if I have a few minutes alone with him?"

"You better not talk about work."

"Promise I'm not," Chris placates.

"Okay." She turns to Morgan. "Want to venture down to the cafeteria with me?"

Once the two of them are gone, Chris closes the door and gets down to business. "Mark, I'm sorry to do this while you're in—"

"Just get on with it, Chris."

"Business is good. I've kept the place up and running. There are a few things I could use your help with, but for the most part, things are good. With that said, I want to tell you I did everything I could for your daughter and Patrick. I even took care of that dog that hates me. Some of the things I've seen them do, can't be unseen, yet I can't comprehend them. They said the less I know, the better, but it's hard to prepare when I don't know what I'm dealing with."

Chris continues, "They both should be dead. I've witnessed Emily heal an arterial wound and I've seen Patrick . . . I don't even know what I saw. I doubt it's a coincidence they came back just before you woke up feeling one-hundred percent."

"Mmm, let's make that eighty. My muscles still need some work."

"Still the most miraculous recovery I've ever seen!" Chris exclaims. "Last week they gave you days to live. Multiple organs were failing. The machine was breathing for you and now, this." He waves a hand at Mark.

With a humble grin, he responds, "Thank you, Chris, for everything you've done and for your discretion."

"I'm afraid I do have some bad news." Chris frowns. "Someone torched your house a couple of weeks into your coma. I've got the guy on camera. I was waiting to turn it in, but now that the police suspect Emily, I was going to hand it over. I was just waiting until Emily came out of hiding."

"Don't turn it in. I need you to destroy it."

"What? Don't you even want to look at it first? It'll clear Emily."

"Did he have a tattooed face?"

Chris narrows his eyes. "Do you know him?"

"Destroy the tapes. Emily will be fine."

"I don't know how to react." He shakes his head. "Good thing I trust you."

Instead of discussing their near-death experiences, Patrick and Emily ride in silence back to the apartment, both engrossed in introspection. They understand they should both be dead several times over, yet here they are, alive and stronger than ever.

Isa brought Patrick back to life, just as Valla tugged Emily out of the afterlife all those months ago. Their job here isn't done yet, and death won't have either of them today.

Patrick feels strong. He can feel Isa swimming through his subconscious, sharing his vessel. She is a benign presence, but the energy and life force she carries with her is heaven on earth. His body and mind feel whole for the first time since Sky's men forced him into that jail cell six years ago. Possessing Isa's strength doesn't erase his past, but he feels ready for the future. He's strong enough to make things right.

Emily stares out the window, her necklace in place. She wonders how she can make things right with her sister. It feels impossible, but at least her dad is awake. She regrets that she didn't get to spend time with him before fleeing the hospital.

They pull up to Patrick's apartment without breaking the silence. It isn't until the apartment door closes behind them that all the words catch up, and Patrick says, "Isa told me what we need to do to get rid of Adelaide. Awaken three sisters to fight. That part of the prophecy makes sense now."

"Valla showed me the same. I know I am Leona's descendant, but Patrick, I can't do it. I can't take on another entity."

"Of course, you can't," Patrick laughs. "Emily, you aren't alone in this. In fact, you have a brother who fits the specs."

"A half-brother who also hates you. And it's a huge risk. It's not safe for him."

"Safe? Emily, nothing in Lathe's life is safe. He spends his time with the most violent woman on this planet. Ten years ago, she killed three people with the wave of her hand. She crushed their bones with a single flick of her wrist. They looked like they'd been hit by a bus. Their bodies remained stuck in the room with her for two days before she finally calmed down. Lathe was twelve when he went in to clear out the bodies that his mother decimated. Since those deaths, no one except for

Lathe has had contact with her. So, when I tell you Lathe will take the risk, I mean it."

Emily's eyes are wide even as she justifies, "Yeah, but he loves his mom. Why would he risk it for this—for me?"

"First, because it's in his character. Second, because you're his sister. And third, because we are changing Olvasho history. There is so much corruption. Very few hate the corruption as much as Lathe."

"But it's dangerous. If it doesn't work and he dies, then he'd be leaving his mother to die."

Patrick sighs, "I guess we'll just have to ask him."

"How do you ask something like this? Hey, brother I've only met once, would you go to the brink of death to let your super-great-grandmother—who is also a princess and a legend—possess your body?"

"That sounds like a good place to start," Patrick says, pulling out his phone.

Emily covers the screen with her hand. She looks more serious as she asks, "How are you feeling? Honestly, are you having trouble adjusting to your visitor?"

"The truth is, I feel good, better than I've felt in a long time."

"That's good to hear." She removes her hand, saying, "I think we should ask him in person."

Patrick puts down his phone. "Perhaps you're right. Are you down for a quick road trip in the morning?"

THE THREE-HOUR DRIVE to the Fort Wayne mansion goes by in a flash. Emily is nervous to ask Lathe to take on such a burden. Patrick, on the other hand, knows Lathe will never forgive him, but he hopes it won't keep him from doing the right thing.

They arrive at the mansion at two o'clock the next day.

Patrick rings the doorbell, and after a long wait, Emily tries the doorknob. It's unlocked, so they enter.

As Patrick leads Emily through the mansion, she asks, "Where is everyone? Last time we were here, this place was crawling with people."

Patrick says, "Only Lathe and his mother live here full time. Technically, Evelyn still owns the estate. Others will stop in and stay for a while. It's where the council meets, but when nothing is going on, it's usually pretty quiet."

She looks him over as he leads her into a billiard room. She can't help but feel like this mansion is fitting for him. Even now, he's wearing a suit without the jacket while she's in jeans and a sweatshirt. There was no reason to dress nice today, but she's only seen him dress down a hand full of times. "You used to live here?"

"On and off," he answers, going directly to the bar where he makes himself a drink. He offers one to her, but she waves it away.

Patrick takes a seat in one of the leather chairs while Emily leans against the pool table, asking, "Should we call Lathe to let him know we're here?"

Patrick finishes his drink in one go and gets up to make another. With his back turned, he says, "No, he'll find us here."

Ten minutes later, Emily is knocking balls around the pool table when Lathe appears in the doorway without a sound.

"What's so important you need to see me in person?" He looks at Emily. "Have you decided to lead the Olvasho?"

Emily shakes her head. "No, but we have other Olvasho matters to discuss."

Lathe raises an eyebrow. "Yeah?"

Patrick downs his second drink and says, "We found out how to get rid of Adelaide, but we need someone from the Leona bloodline to help us."

Stone-faced, Lathe points out the obvious. "Emily is from the Leona bloodline."

"Yes," Patrick tips his chin toward Emily, "but you've seen the toll it takes for her to contain two entities. Adding a third will kill her."

Emily chimes in. "To get rid of Adelaide, we need to awaken Princess Leona. In order to do that, we need you."

Patrick clarifies, "Not you specifically. We need a strong and willing participant from the Leona bloodline."

Lathe's eyebrows furrow. "What makes you think that's possible?"

"Princess Isa showed me, the same way Valla showed Emily."

With outrage, Lathe growls, "You're joking! Isa chose *you?*"

Patrick leans back against the bar ignoring Lathe's question. "There is some risk involved. To obtain Princess Leona, you will have to reach the brink of death and her spirit will guide you back. Emily and I are the only two who have survived it, but I'm sure with our help, you will most assuredly survive."

Lathe chokes, "You're serious?"

Emily interjects, "We understand you may need time to think it over."

Lathe turns to her, his anger stirring the air around him into a vivid red. "When I refuse, who will you go to?"

"We don't anticipate your refusal," Patrick admits, pushing away from the bar to move next to Emily. "I suppose we would find someone willing to risk it, but we'd rather it be you."

Lathe's glacier eyes focus on Patrick. "I understand Valla choosing Emily, but how could Isa choose you? You have so much blood on your hands."

Patrick feels Isa rise up within him, whispering into his mind, her words like silk. *It will not be easy atoning for your sins, Patrick Glenn, but let your history remind you of the man you want to be, instead of the man you once were. Though you did not gain pleasure from the vile acts you participated in with Sky, you cannot negate your past completely. Instead of hiding from your memories, confront them, so they hold no power over you.*

A shiver runs through Patrick and Emily catches him as he

staggers. Isa riffles through his memories until she finds the one he's been trying to bury.

Katie turned over in bed with her blond hair spread out on the pillow. "I think I'm falling in love with you," she said softly, draping her arm over Patrick's bare chest.

He pushed the hair out of her face. "I thought you were in love with Lathe."

Her hair tickled across his chest as she leaned over to place a kiss over his heart. "That was before I met you."

More like she was in love with power. At first, Patrick wanted to seduce her to get back at Lathe, but then Patrick realized she was working her way up the Olvasho chain of command. He noticed the way she watched Sky. She was waiting for her opportunity, which would never happen because Sky's preferences tended toward the male variety.

She pressed kisses down his chest and abdomen, moving south. Patrick closed his eyes, expectantly. She was almost there when the door flew open. Katie sat up and Patrick watched Sky prowl into the room wearing nothing but his silky black robe.

Sky was possessive of Patrick, and though Patrick was allowed to have playthings, Sky liked to remind him of who was in charge and who he belonged to. Sky angrily waved his hand at Katie, demanding, "Who is this?"

Patrick realized his mistake too late. Katie may not mean anything to him, but she meant something to Lathe, and Sky also wanted to destroy the son who betrayed him. Patrick knew it would do no good to lie, as he suspected Sky already knew who Katie was and what he was going to do to her.

Patrick sat up, shutting out his human side as he pealed the girl from his body and answered, "This is Katie. She's a very enthusiastic plaything. She belonged to Lathe before his accident, but Katie loves power, and as Lathe lost his power along with his looks, she's seeking bigger fish."

Katie looked as if he'd slapped her, but Patrick knew it was the truth and it was far better for her to have feelings for power than it was for them to have feelings for each other. Sky killed anyone who meant something to Patrick, and this girl was likely to meet the same fate.

Sky scrutinized Katie, before asking, "Are you working with Lathe?"

Katie looked shocked, still recovering from Patrick's words. She stuttered, "Eh' he umm . . ."

Sky took another step forward and touched a finger to her chin, tilting her face to his. "He doesn't know you are here, does he?"

She looked down, embarrassment coloring her pale cheeks to a bright rose. "Lathe and I aren't together."

A smile blossomed across Sky's face. "But you're still sleeping with him, you harlot."

She had the audacity to look offended. She may have wanted power, but she didn't understand the danger she put herself in to achieve it. Sky would strip her of her dignity without blinking.

"Patrick tells me that Lathen sabotaged his face on purpose. What do you say?"

She looked him in the eye, a brazen move. "Yes, he . . . he did it to himself. He didn't want to leave his mother." She batted her lashes. "I don't understand why he'd give all this up to stay with her."

Sky stepped back, demanding, "Stand up!"

She did as instructed, believing he would be lenient with her. Patrick wanted to warn her, but she willingly walked into a lion's den and now she was stretching out on the dinner table. How could she not understand what was about to happen?

With a cunning smile, Sky inquired, "Does Lathen love you?"

She moved forward and ran a finger down his exposed chest to the belt of his silky robe, purring, "Yes."

"Katie, did you know we have video cameras in every room? What would you think if we sent Lathen this particular video?"

Her eyes jerked up to the ceiling, searching. Her hands folded over her heart as fear broke through her bravado. She belatedly realized she was no match for this lion. In fact, she was not a lioness at all.

Patrick stood to pull on his sweatpants while Sky instructed Katie to get to her knees. Sky jerked his chin toward the nightstand indicating for Patrick to get the gun hidden there. Katie kneeled to the floor, tears streaming down her face, as she realized there was no escape.

Patrick offered the gun to Sky, but he refused, saying, "You brought her here. You will be the one to finish her."

Katie's fight or flight reflex finally kicked in. She struggled to stand and realized Sky was holding her in place with his mind manipulation. Her terror escalated, and she pleaded, "Patrick, don't do this! Please, I'll do anything!"

A stronger man would've listened to her, but when Sky sensed Patrick's hesitation, he reassured him by saying, "You are the son I always wanted. I may have sired Lathen, but you are my legacy."

Even as Patrick's humanity begged to be heard, he shoved it down and aimed the gun at Katie's head. Her horrified words echoed throughout the room. "Lathe will kill you for this! He'll kill you!"

He never meant for it to go this far. He wanted to hurt Lathe, because if Lathe hadn't destroyed his face, Patrick wouldn't be stuck with Sky. The human part of Patrick knew Lathe was just as much of a victim as the rest of them. Lathe took extreme measures to protect himself and wasn't Patrick doing precisely the same.

If he made Sky angry things would only get worse for him, and there was no way Katie would make it out of here alive, so why was he hesitating? He had a job to do. Sky had trained him for this, and Sky would question his loyalty if he delayed any longer.

The shot resounded through the room. One bullet—one fraction of a second—was all it took to pierce a hole in Katie's head and blacken his wretched soul. Her sobs cut short as she fell to the floor.

"Well done, Son." Sky clapped Patrick on the back. "Once you get this cleaned up, come see me in the study. We have a movie to send."

Sky went to collect the video footage while Patrick cleaned up his mess.

As the vision ends, Emily deposits a despondent Patrick in a nearby chair. Patrick slumps in his seat hating that Isa just drudged up the painful memory to share with not only him, but also Emily and Lathe.

Emily knows by glancing at Lathe that he received Sky's home movie. There is no shock, only anger. He is seething, his aura a flaming crimson, as he takes a menacing step towards an incapacitated Patrick.

Emily steps between them.

"Why are you protecting him?" Lathe snarls.

"Because I love him."

A look of disgust curls his lips and he motions toward Patrick. "How can you love that?"

In a sorrowful voice, she says, "Katie wasn't perfect and you loved her. If you'd been in Patrick's situation, what would you have done?"

"I would have shot Sky."

"You know he wouldn't let that happen."

"Then I would have shot myself."

"And left Katie to suffer."

Lathe rubs at his scars.

Emily moves closer. "I'm not saying what Patrick did was right. He is still torn up about her. He made a mistake, but killing her was the most humane thing he could've done. Had he tried to save her, Sky would have prolonged her death and made Patrick watch her suffer. I'm sorry, Lathe, for the video, for Katie, for the way you were raised. None of it was fair, but now you get to decide which path you take. Isa chose Patrick because of his heart and his desire to make amends no matter the cost. Honestly, Lathe, I don't know if Leona will accept you, because you're so full of bitterness. I'm not trying to be insensitive, but you're the only one who can change your attitude." She pauses with a sigh. "We want your help, but we'll find a way with or without you."

Lathe's biting huff is followed up with bitter words. "Don't pretend to know what my life has been. While your parents put you in dresses and sent you to kindergarten, my son-of-a-bitch father sent me into a basement to keep my mentally deranged mother alive."

"I don't pretend—"

Lathe cuts her off. "I hope you make your decision to lead

the council soon. I'd hate for something to happen to someone you care about just because you decline."

He leaves the room before she can respond. Only once he's reached the basement does he realize his last statement sounded like a threat, but he isn't going to go back to clarify. *Let her think whatever she wants.*

Lathe paces through the maze of basement corridors. His anger grabs hold of him and unable to contain it; he punches the wall.

"Shit!" he yells, pulling his fist back as pain radiates through his broken knuckles. He should have chosen a different wall. The rough concrete surface leaves his hand bleeding.

Over the years, Lathe has put a lot of time into learning how to heal in hopes of fixing his mother. What he discovered was he has an exceptional ability to heal himself, which is an incredibly rare gift for an Olvasho. It was also essential to his survival when his mother got into one of her more violent moods. Clenching his busted knuckles, he begins healing the broken skin and bones. To date, Lathe has mended forty-six of his bones, some more than once and on one particular occasion, he repaired his liver and spleen. He could heal almost anything, except for his mother's condition and his broken heart after Katie died.

PATRICK FINALLY REGAINS himself to find Emily sitting in front of him, a look of sympathy coating her features. He moves to the bar in an attempt to avoid the inevitable heart-to-heart.

From her seat, Emily says, "When I was imprisoned at the compound, you allowed me in your head, and I saw so many fragments of your life. I saw you pull the trigger. I didn't know her name back then, but I know she isn't the only one."

He often forgets she's seen the worst pieces of him because she doesn't treat him with animosity like the other Olvasho. He almost wants her to look at him with disgust, the way he feels he deserves.

She crosses the room to him, saying, "Katie was innocent, albeit a little greedy. It still doesn't change the way I see you." His blue eyes find hers and she places a hand over his heart. "I see what's in here. Your soul may feel black, but your heart is full of light and it's all I choose to see."

He holds himself perfectly still because if he moves, it will be to wrap her in his arms and devour her.

Love means something different to everyone. To Patrick, love is this woman. She is so incredibly beautiful and present, yet so frustratingly off limits. His affection for her is obvious, and he wonders if she comprehends the depth of his love for her.

She doesn't look away or move her hand, and it feels like a challenge, but he doesn't act on it. He'll never act on it because he wants what's best for her and she deserves so much more than him.

CHAPTER FORTY

EMILY TAKES A STEADYING breath and lifts her hand to knock. She knows she's delayed this visit long enough. After knocking, she steps back from the door to wait. She goes over the words she had rehearsed on the way over here and the entire morning, and the last three days, basically, ever since she saw Samantha at the hospital. She looks down at the welcome mat and takes more of those steadying breaths.

After a moment, the door swings open and Emily braces herself as she lifts her chin. Only it isn't Samantha staring back at her. It's Dan.

He glares at Emily, his mind moving a million thoughts per second. Surprise mixes with relief, which is overshadowed by anger and the need to protect Samantha. After a long pause, he finally asks, "Where have you been? Do you know what you've done to your sister?"

"I'm here to talk to Sam." Emily's voice is hard, a diamond blade cutting through Dan.

But he stands strong. "How could you do this to her?"

She marvels at his perseverance. The force she put behind her words should've left no room for argument, yet his desire to protect Sam is stronger than Emily's half-hearted attempt to get past him as quickly as possible.

"Dan, I'm sorry for what I've put you through, for what I've put Sam through. I didn't leave because I wanted to abandon my family. I left because of my mental state. I really want to make things right. So please, will you let me in to talk to Sam?"

After a relenting sigh, he steps back to allow her entry and gestures to the living room couch. "Have a seat. I'll get Sam. She's helping your dad with his exercises."

He disappears down a hall and despite her nervousness, Emily sighs in relief. She is finally going to see her sister again. Emily doesn't sit down. How can she? Her nerves have her wrapped so tightly she can barely move, let alone sit. Instead, she looks around the new place Samantha and her fiancé share. It is their first home. Judging by the decorations hanging on the walls and every piece of furniture in its designated place, they have been here a while. It has all the personal touches a home should have, very unlike their house growing up. She picks up an engagement photo of Samantha and Dan. Her sister always insisted on having photos taken for every event.

Her sister . . . Emily feels a wave of grief that they share no blood. They were raised as sisters despite having no genetic connection. Emily won't ever call Sam her stepsister because it sounds ugly and wrong. They are sisters and Samantha is never going to know otherwise. What did blood matter, anyway?

"Emily . . ." a soft voice comes from behind her. Samantha stands in the mouth of the hall, staring as if terrified to make any sudden movements for fear Emily will disappear.

Emily sets the photo back in its place and walks to Samantha, coming to a stop in front of her. Samantha gently places a trembling hand to Emily's cheek, whispering nonsensical gibberish. Then without warning, she pulls Emily in, wrapping her arms tight around her sister. She tucks her face into the crook of Emily's neck, where she begins sobbing.

Emily takes the olive branch, shit, the whole olive tree that her sister extends and embraces her back and embarrassingly enough even joins in with tears of her own.

"Sam, I'm so sorry."

Samantha pulls back, wiping her eyes. "I never should've said all of those terrible things to you. I never should've yelled at you. I didn't know. I didn't . . ."

"It's not your fault, Sam. I just . . . I just lost my mind a bit. Like amnesia, I couldn't remember who I was. It wasn't until Patrick helped me that I remembered my life. I didn't mean to leave you alone to pick up the pieces. I didn't mean to leave you with everything that's happened."

"You're staying, right? You're not leaving again?"

Emily nods, "I'm not going anywhere."

"Will you still be in my wedding?"

Emily is shocked. She didn't expect her sister to welcome her back with open arms. "Yes, of course I'll be in your wedding. If you'll still have me."

"Yes! I have your dress in my closet. It came in months ago," she says, walking back to her room.

Emily follows hesitantly, and in a low voice, she says, "Sam, Dan said Dad is here."

Samantha's eyes widen and she hits herself in the forehead. "Of course, you want to see him. I'm sorry. I'm just so out of . . . I wasn't expecting you." She switches direction. "He's this way."

Emily follows her down a hall to a half-open door. Samantha knocks as she slowly enters with Emily on her heels. It all feels so surreal. Dan is standing next to the bed talking with Mark, who is propped up with pillows, his muscles still too weak to do much more than sit.

Emily smiles a hopeful smile as she looks at her dad. Mark looks back at her with the same soft expression he usually reserves for Sam, and says, "Will you guys give me a minute alone with Emily?"

Emily stays frozen to the spot as Dan and Samantha leave the room. Once the door closes behind them, Emily rushes forward and crushes her dad with a hug, whispering a heartfelt, "Dad."

Mark wraps his arms around his adopted daughter, whom he raised as his own. "Emily, I'm so glad you're okay." Those words feel terribly inadequate, but he doesn't know how to put into words all that he feels.

"There is so much I need to tell you," she whispers against him.

"You can start by telling me what happened at the compound. Morgan said Patrick saved us."

An hour into catching up, Emily learns her dad is responsible for their house burning down. "Why did you burn down our house?"

Mark shrugs. "It was one of those precautions I put in place in case we were ever compromised. Chris didn't know about it, and I was in a coma so I couldn't stop it."

"So you just had a guy on standby for that?" she asks but doesn't get the answer as Samantha knocks on the door.

Peeking her head in, she says, "Sorry to interrupt, I just wanted to let you know I'm heading out for a bit. I have my final dress fitting, but I'll be back afterward. I was hoping we could all have dinner together tonight."

"That sounds wonderful," Mark agrees, and they both look to Emily.

"Yes, dinner as a family. How long has it been?"

Samantha answers, "Too long."

She begins to leave when Emily stops her. "Wait, Sam!"

Samantha turns around in the doorway.

"Is it okay if I go with you? I'd love to see you in your dress again." She cannot believe the words coming out of her own mouth, mostly because they are true. The last time she was in the bridal store she couldn't wait to escape, and now she is asking to tag along.

"Of course."

Emily smiles and kisses her dad on the cheek before hopping off the bed.

Samantha says, "How about we bring your dress and see if she can squeeze you in for a fitting, too?"

"Sure," Emily agrees.

PERHAPS THINGS SHOULD FEEL a bit stranger, but Emily is enjoying the time with her sister. Samantha's valley-girl attitude is noticeably absent, her sharp edges buffed out by a brutal four months.

Even with Samantha's weight loss from stress, her sparkly white princess dress is the perfect fit. Emily's black halter dress will need a tuck here and there, but it is better than she remembered. The silky halter hugs Emily's curves and seductively dips between her cleavage. The halter strap is thin around her neck, and the back of the gown dips to expose her lower back. The previous time she wore this dress, she wanted to hide but now feels a confidence she didn't have before. Her journey over the recent months has exposed her to so much that the little things don't have the power to lock her up like they used to.

CHAPTER FORTY-ONE ~

Ashley was relieved to find out that Emily had returned and glad to hear her father is out of his coma. Ashley still has not seen Emily, so she talked Morgan and Emily into a girl's night.

When Ashley arrives at Patrick's apartment, he opens the door and welcomes her in, saying, "Emily and Morgan aren't here, yet."

"Figures. That's okay, I'll wait." She closes the door behind her and follows Patrick into the kitchen. Ashley pops her ass up onto the kitchen counter as she pesters Patrick. "So, Morgan told me Emily and Ben are still together; have you told Emily how you feel?"

Patrick goes about making his sandwich. "She knows how I feel, but she's happy with Ben."

Ashley leans back, thunking the back of her head dramatically against the cabinet doors. "Then you need to move on." She scoots closer and taps him with her leg. "You know, I'm still available. Shocking, I know, but I don't let just anyone tie me down, well, you know, like in a relationship. I'm not saying I'm opposed to restraints." She lifts a brow. "Maybe you just need a rebound."

Patrick smirks. "Ashley, are you looking for a rebound for *me* or *you*?"

Her face shows confusion because surely he can't know she's been thinking about that guy from the bar. She hadn't even kissed his scarred lips, but her mind keeps drifting back to him.

"Patrick," Ashley whines, "I haven't even been on a serious date for, like months." She waggles her eyebrows. "Maybe we can help each other."

Patrick laughs. "Ashley, you can put that out of your dirty little mind. I'd hate for us to ruin our friendship over sex."

"You think this is a friendship?" Ashley scoffs. "Let's be real. You only put up with me because of Morgan and Em."

"That may have been true in the beginning, but you've grown on me."

"Really?" she says, scooting even closer.

He turns and puts a hand on her knee, only to push it out of the way so he can open the drawer below her for a knife. Closing the drawer, he says. "You deserve better than me, Ashley."

Ashley clunks her head back again, complaining, "Why am I surrounded by gorgeous, insightful men and not a damn one will give me the time of day? Everyone is too busy being in love with someone else. It's disgusting!"

A knock at the front door saves Patrick from having to respond. He picks up his sandwich and walks to the door. He already knows who it is, so he opens without checking the peephole.

"Alec," he greets. "Morgan isn't here yet, but you're welcome to keep Ashley company. She's waiting in the kitchen." Alec enters the apartment and Patrick points toward the counter where Ashley is seated before slinking off to hide in his room.

"Hey, Alec," Ashley calls, hopping off the counter.

"What're you doing here?" he asks.

"We were supposed to have a girl's night, but I think I might be getting stood up." She pulls out her phone to text Morgan and Emily.

"Do you know when they'll be here?" he asks, looking uncomfortable as he fiddles with the zipper on his coat.

"They?" She folds her arms over her chest. "You mean Morgan, right? I know why you're here, Alec."

His eyebrows arch in surprise, but he doesn't say anything.

"Oh, come on! You love her." Ashley rolls her eyes. He opens his mouth to speak, but she stops him. "Before you deny it, remember why you came here. If you can't even be honest with me, like, how are you supposed to convince her?"

He closes his mouth and looks to the floor.

Ashley shakes her head. "You're hopeless." Looking to the ceiling, she says, "God, help me." She takes a photo off the refrigerator and sets it on the counter in front of him, pointing at the child in the picture. "Do you know who this is?"

Alec shakes his head.

"He's the kid Morgan has been sponsoring for the last four years. And this . . ." She places a Christmas card on the counter. "This is a card from the nursing home where Morgan volunteers to read to the elderly."

He searches the picture, brows pinched in confusion.

"Alec, do you know why I'm showing this to you?"

A long pause makes the silence feel heavy. When he finally speaks, his voice is low. "To prove she's too good for me. You think she's better off with Preston."

She shakes her head. "Preston is boring. He makes her happy for now, but he's all statistics, and he's way too worried about his status. I'm trying to help you by showing you the real Morgan. The one you haven't taken the time to really know."

His chin jerks up. "Why would you help me?"

"The question is why would I stop you?" She taps her manicured nails on the counter, waiting for him to explain himself.

"I'm not good enough for her. She's fuckin' perfect and she can't even stand to look at me anymore." He looks stunned by his own words. He shakes his head. "I don't know why I'm here." He moves to leave.

"She's already in love with you, Alec."

He stops and turns back.

She continues, "She can't look at you because you've chosen easy girls over her *so* many times. You broke her heart, Alec, so of course, she doesn't trust you. You've shown her enough reasons to doubt you."

"I can't fix that, so what am I supposed to do? Give up?"

"Show her! Be the guy she deserves. You can't just come here and tell her that you're interested now that your last fling fell through. She won't believe you. And she won't give up Preston for empty words. You need to show her. Give her a reason to have faith in you. Prove to Morgan that she's more than just your flavor of the week."

"How?"

"Keep your dick in your pants! And get off the damn fence, Alec! Either be that person she deserves or walk away! She's what you've always wanted, so get your shit together."

"Damn, Ashley."

"She's my best friend. I'm helping you because I want her to be happy and she'll be happy when you get your shit together."

Ashley's phone chimes and she looks down at the incoming text. "Damn it!"

"What?"

"Morgan's staying at work to cover half the next shift, and Emily's insurance came through from the fire, so she's shopping for a new car." She sighs heavily, then peeks at Alec. "How old are you?"

"Twenty."

"Why do I hang out with babies?" Deciding it doesn't matter, Ashley grabs his arm and her purse. "Let's go."

Alec pulls back. "Where are we going?"

"There's a bar I know that doesn't ask to see your ID."

"I don't have any money, and even if I did, you shouldn't be encouraging me to drink after you just yelled at me to get my shit together."

Ashley pulls at his arm again, saying, "Oh, please. I'll drink cocktails while you drink whatever it is you drink, and it'll give us time to talk about getting your life together. Come on! I'm paying."

Alec laughs. "You're such a contradiction."

She shrugs. "What's your point?"

Alec laughs as they walk out the door. Turning back, Ashley calls, "Bye, Patrick! Let me know if you change your mind."

ASHLEY TAKES a seat on her side of the bar table, saying, "The last guy to check out my ass got a drunk beatdown from his crazy girlfriend."

Alec argues, "I doubt that was the last guy to check you out. He was just the last one to get caught."

Ashley smirks. "You're actually charming. I get why girls throw themselves at you. Sometimes when you smile, I want to like, lick your dimples."

Alec throws his head back and laughs.

"See!" Ashley shouts, "There they are again. Lickable!"

"How drunk are you?"

"I'm not drunk!"

"Yes, you are."

"Not even." She stands up and does a perfectly graceful pirouette.

A few people whistle and clap as she bows.

She takes her seat and grabs her glass, saying, "See, not drunk."

He chuckles. "That doesn't prove anything."

"I'd like to see you do one."

He shakes his head. "No fucking way. What are you, some sort of ballerina?"

Ashley plucks the cherry from her drink and twirls it around on the stem before popping it in her mouth. "Not anymore."

"Fine, you're not drunk. You do have a way of drawing atten-tion to yourself, though."

"Yet, it never seems to draw the right attention," she complains.

"What are you looking for?"

Ashley purses her lips as she thinks, twirling a strand of her platinum hair. Then as if coming to a conclusion, her dark eyes stop on his. "I want to be with someone who interests me every day instead of some shallow man who gets on my nerves after a day or two. I want someone who is as complex and genuine as they pretend to be. I want to look at them the way you look at Morgan, like you fall in love a little more each day."

"Damn, Ash."

She blows out a breath and shrugs. "In the meantime, I'll probably find some shallow asshole to take me home."

"Maybe we should work on getting your life together. You should listen to all the lectures you've given me and stop wasting your time with shallow assholes and make yourself better for the person who matters."

"Oh God, is that what I sound like? Gah, that's terrifying. You definitely shouldn't listen to me."

"I kinda questioned your advice when you brought me here."

"There is nothing wrong with here." Even as she says it, she knows she's wrong. It's a little run-down hole in the wall, but it's where she met *him*. She can't understand why thoughts of Lathe continue to skate through her mind. She only met him once and it was brief. She can't even remember half of their conversation. And his scars. She doesn't know what to make of it. Sure, he intrigued her, but she hasn't seen him since, so even if she wants to see him again, she doesn't know how, except for this bar.

Leaning forward, she says, "I'm gonna get another drink. Do you want anything?"

"No, I'm good."

She stands from her seat. "Don't leave with any sluts while I'm away."

"You're the only slut I'm leaving with tonight."

She swoons dramatically, putting her hands to her chest. "How charming."

Ashley searches the bar as she waits for her next cocktail. Lathe isn't here tonight. She wants to see him just once more so she can convince herself it is just a stupid crush. She can't even explain her attraction to him. His scars were ghastly, but he was beautiful.

Someone taps her on the shoulder, and she spins, hoping to find Lathe, but instead finds an ex-fling. His dark hair and cocky grin make her want to rip the stupid ring out of his lip. Brent towers over her, all dark and handsome. She thought he was as complex and genuine as he looked, but nope, she found out he's just a dick.

"Oh hey, Grant," she says.

"It's Brent."

"Oh, is it? My bad." She looks back at the bar, impatient for her drink. If she ordered a beer, it would be ready by now, but she had to order some fancy drink.

"Are you here with Alec?" Brent asks.

That brings Ashley's head around. "Um, yeah."

Brent gives her a condescending laugh. "Honey, you don't have to stoop so low."

"Excuse me?"

"He's a player. Everyone knows he's a player."

"How do you know Alec?" She crosses her arms over her chest and the movement pulls his eyes to her cleavage.

He answers while staring at her boobs. "The dumb shit was in the grade below me in high school. Just looking at his dick'll give you chlamydia."

Ashley is seeing red, but she isn't about to stoop to his level. Her drink finally plops down on the counter. She picks it up and turns to walk back to her table.

Brent continues after her. "Sugar, you don't have to settle for a second-rate dick! Your pussy ain't made of gold, but I'll fu—"

She spins, throwing all eight dollars of her new cocktail in his face.

He sputters, while she complains, "Damn it, I was really looking forward to that drink!"

He takes a menacing step forward while Ashley stands her ground. "I've seen what you're packing, Brent, and if I were you, I wouldn't go around bragging about that little caterpillar in your pants."

He lifts his arm to slap her, but a giant of a man nearing his forties grabs his arm. The man puts himself in front of Ashley. "I think it's time for you to leave," he growls at Brent.

"That bitch jus—"

The giant shakes his head. "Didn't ask for excuses." He tips his chin toward the door. "Out!"

Brent shoots daggers at Ashley, then turns to leave. Once he's out the door, the giant turns to face her. "You okay, darlin'?"

"Yes, thank you."

"What are you drinking? I'll buy you another," he offers.

"Thanks, but I think my friend and I are leaving anyway."

"You need me to walk you out? Make sure he's gone."

Alec walks over, carrying Ashley's purse, while she answers, "Nah, Brent's a pussy."

Alec snickers then turns to the giant. "Thanks, man. I couldn't get over here fast enough."

"Ya'll have a good night. Stay outta trouble," the giant says before going back to his bar stool.

Alec whispers, "I'm gonna start calling you trouble."

Ashley laughs, sets her empty glass on a table, and takes her purse as they set off toward the door.

In the car, Alec asks, "What did he say to you?"

"He saw us together and was jealous. We dated a while back."

Alec lets his head fall back on the headrest. "Oh, no, tell me you didn't?"

"In my defense. He's hot."

"Now I know what I sounded like all those times Emily asked me what I was thinking."

"Just like staring into a mirror, right?" Ashley says, then turning to him, questions, "You *are* sober, right?"

"Yes, against your wishes, I finished my one drink an hour and a half ago."

"You know, Alec. I think if you and Morgan don't figure this out by Samantha's wedding, you should be my plus one."

"You got an invitation to Sam's wedding?"

"Yes, people tend to like me."

"Why would you want me to go with you?"

"First, so you can at least get a dance in with Morgan and second because I don't want to go alone, but if someone wants to pick me up there, then I don't want to be tied down with a date."

Alec says, "I don't want to see her with him."

"Oh, man up! She dealt with seeing you with other girls for all these years. You can handle one night."

CHAPTER FORTY-TWO ~

MORGAN AND PRESTON walk out of spin class dripping with sweat.

Preston throws his arm over her shoulder, saying, "I beat my best today."

"That's awesome! I wasn't moving very fast today. I'm still sore from leg day."

Preston leans in to kiss her on the cheek. "Want to swim a few laps with me before we go?"

"Sure," Morgan says, "I'll meet you in there."

They go to their separate locker rooms to rinse off and change before entering the pool room. Preston is already swimming by the time Morgan walks in. She dives into the lane next to his and swims a lap.

When she comes up, Preston is waiting for her. "I know this isn't romantic, but I'm glad we get to spend time together."

She leans in to give him a sweet kiss, saying, "Romance is so overrated. You can bring me to the gym anytime."

After a few more laps, they call it quits.

As they walk to the locker rooms, Preston asks, "Do you want to hit up the smoothie bar on the way out?"

"No, I can't. I have to pick up a cake for my dad. We're celebrating his birthday tonight."

"Are you staying at your parent's tonight?"

"Yeah, I think so."

"You're welcome to stay at my place again."

Morgan says, "I kind of feel like I'm living out of my car, bouncing between your place, my parent's, and Patrick's."

"You can keep some things at my place if it's easier."

She can't believe how well things have been going between them. The last week showed Morgan how serious he is about her, but she's nervous they are moving too quickly, so she answers, "Maybe, but tonight I think I'll stay with my parents."

He pulls her against him, his hard muscles and smooth skin touching hers.

"Mmm," she moans against him. "Too bad we're in public right now."

He leans down and just before their lips meet, he mumbles, "Too bad."

Once Morgan is showered and changed, she runs out to her car through the freezing rain. She turns the heat on high as she pulls out of the parking lot. The storm doesn't give up the entire drive to Alec's house . . . well, Cindy's house. Alec's mom made good on her promise to make Morgan's dad a cake.

She parks on the street and runs through the downpour up to their house. Morgan knocks as she enters the house, the way she's always done. And as she walks toward the kitchen, her heart and body come to a screeching halt when she catches sight of Alec in the hall, coming out of the bathroom with only a towel around his hips.

As soon as he notices her, he stops. His brows shoot up in surprise, but he makes no move to walk away. Instead, he stares back at her.

Holy hell, her libido goes crazy. If she thought her time at the gym was heated, then this is—melt your insides—hot. And that's precisely what he's doing, melting her like he always does.

She can't peel her eyes from him. They're too busy taking in his exposed chest and abs, and that distinctive v shape that partially hides beneath his sagging towel. A little voice in the back of her head, taunts, *"He's single now."*

"No," she whispers, as Cindy shouts from the kitchen, "Alec, will you get the door. Morgan is stopping by. I thought she'd come on in, but—"

"Got it, Mom," Alec calls.

"Thanks, baby."

Her heart can't take it. Damn it, she thought she was over him, and here he stands, gutting her just by existing.

Alec throws a thumb over his shoulder, saying, "I'm gonna go put some clothes on. I guess she's expecting you."

Morgan snaps out of her stupor, responding, "Sure, yeah. I'm gonna . . ." She points toward the kitchen and lets her sentence drop as she heads that way, mumbling, "Smooth Morgan, real smooth."

She passes their adorable Christmas tree and her heart twists, wringing her out. All the hideous construction paper and stick ornaments Alec made over the years are proudly displayed on the front of the tree. There is no doubt this woman loves her son, despite his lack of artistic talent.

When Morgan walks into the kitchen, Cindy is bent over, taking cupcakes out of the oven. She sets them on the counter and spots the newcomer. "Morgan, oh my God, you're soaking wet!"

Morgan looks down and realizes her coat is dripping all over the floor. "Oh, I'm sorry," she says, stripping out of her coat.

"You must be freezing," Cindy says, slipping off her oven mitts.

"No, I'm really not." Alec warmed her right up the second she walked in. To get the attention off of herself, she gestures to the counter, "You're making cupcakes."

"Yes, they're for a two-year-old's birthday party. It's my good friend's son. I volunteered and think I stretched myself too thin," she says while hugging Morgan. "It's so good to see you. How're you doing?"

"I'm doing well. I just finished my exams and now I'm on winter break. I picked up a few more shifts at the hospital and I've been spending time with my boyfriend, Preston."

"Boyfriend?" Cindy perks up. "That's new! How did you meet?"

"We kept running into each other at the Campus Library, and one day he asked me out for lunch. We really hit it off."

Cindy gives her soft eyes. "That's sweet, honey. What's he like?"

Alec picks that exact moment to walk into the room. Morgan hesitates, before answering, "He's really driven. He'll be graduating with his bachelors in the spring, but he'll be going on for his masters. We've both been pretty busy lately, so it's hard to find time to see each other. We've actually been making gym dates; that way we still get our workout in and we get to spend time together."

"Is he as athletic as you are?" Cindy begins icing the cupcakes that have already cooled.

Morgan smiles. "Yeah, he was on the swim team, but it took up too much of his time, so now he just does it for fun."

Cindy says, "It sounds like things are going really great."

"Yeah." Morgan nods because it did feel like everything was going great until she came here.

Cindy turns to Alec who is glaring at the cupcakes. "What's wrong, sweetie?

Alec flicks his eyes up, realizing he's been caught. "Nothing."

Cindy puts a hand to her hip. "Alec Michael Garner, you *do not* have to work there! I don't know how many times I have to tell you that."

"Mom, it's fine. It hasn't even been a week. I'm fine."

"You *are not* fine." She points at him with the tube of icing. "This is not my son."

He walks over and pulls her into his side, resting his head on top of hers. "I told you I'm fine, Momma. Stop worrying about me." He kisses the top of her head and steals a cupcake, jumping away as she swats at him.

"Alec, those are for Henry's birthday!"

"He's two!" Alec justifies, "He doesn't need that much sugar."

Her glare is hardly intimidating as it slowly melts into a smile. "There he is. There's my boy."

Alec shakes his head and walks out of the room. Once he's gone, Cindy goes back to icing. Speaking softly, she says, "You know after what happened with Sadie, I thought maybe you and Alec would work things out, but it sounds like this Preston is quite a catch."

"He is, and I don't think Alec is all that interested in me anyway. We haven't talked since he and Sadie broke up, but I'm sure he'll move on soon enough." She tries to be flippant, but it's like shoving toothpicks under her fingernails.

Cindy shakes her head. "Sadie did a number on him. He hasn't been himself. He didn't move out, but he still went to work for his father. Don't get me wrong. I like that he's taking on more responsibility, but he's miserable working for *him*."

"What does he do there?"

"He won't give me details. He knows I hate Dave, so he won't give me any more ammunition." She looks at Morgan with hopeful eyes. "Maybe he'll talk to you."

Morgan bites her lip. "I don't think that will work."

"Maybe not," Cindy says, putting down her tube of icing. "So, do you want to see your dad's cake?"

"Yes!"

"I was taking photos of it, so it's in here," Cindy says, leading Morgan into the dining room. "I think it turned out perfect." There in the middle of the table is a gorgeous cake that looks like a replica of the rowboat Morgan's parents purchased this past summer.

"He's going to love this. I can't believe you got all that detail," Morgan gushes, leaning in to get a closer look.

"It was so much fun. I'm thinking of making this into a business. I enjoy it so much and if I could make enough baking, I'd rather be home. I could hire someone to help with my cleaning business."

"You're amazing, Cindy. I'll recommend you to everyone I know."

"Oh, you're sweet."

Cindy's phone rings from the kitchen and she rushes over to grab it. After a moment, she presses her hand over the speaker, and to Morgan says, "I'm sorry. Give me a few minutes."

Morgan hears sobbing through the phone and waves Cindy away. "You go do what you need to do."

"Thanks," Cindy mouths and walks toward her bedroom.

Morgan stands there for a moment, puzzling over what she's supposed to do. She can't just take the cake and run and besides her family get-together doesn't start for another hour. She snaps a few pictures of the cake and decides to sit down on a stool at the kitchen island. As she's scrolling through her phone, Alec walks into the kitchen.

He pauses when he sees her. "Oh, I thought you left."

Her eyebrows lift in surprise. "You thought I'd leave without saying goodbye?"

He lifts a shoulder. "I don't know."

After an uncomfortable silence, Morgan asks, "So, what's it like to work with your dad?"

He shakes his head. "Nope, no, I know what you're doing. You're spying for her, aren't you? Did she ask you to get information out of me?"

"No, well yes, but I was asking because I genuinely care. It'll stay between us." She holds out her pinky. "I pinky promise."

Twin dimples show as he takes her pinky in his. Then his hand falls away along with his smile. He takes the stool next to hers and confesses, "It sucks."

"Really? What are you doing there?"

"My dad works in construction, well, kind of. He works

higher up for the construction company. He's just a sleazy salesman who lies his ass off all day to get people to do what he wants. I've been shadowing this guy named Rob this week. He's leaving the company because he's afraid the shit's going to fall on him, which is exactly what my father told me he's going to do. Rob is going to be the fall guy, which is bullshit."

"Alec, you have to quit!"

"I can't quit. It's shitty, but it's still the best job I've ever had. I get paid a lot to do things I actually like. I just wish I didn't work for such a shady asshole and I wish that asshole wasn't my dad."

"Is there another place you could go and do the same thing?"

"Not if I can't list this place on my resume. I've got to stick it out a little longer."

"Sounds like your mom is right about your dad."

Alec rests his elbows on the island. "The best thing that man ever did for me and my mom was to stay away."

Morgan takes a breath, wishing she could carry his pain. Not sure what to say, she taps his leg with her foot: two taps, a pause, tap.

Alec wonders how she does it, how she can turn such a small gesture into a beautiful gift. She breathes her strength into him without even realizing it, and all he can do is give her a half smile. He aches to lavish her with perfect adoration. He wants to bundle her in his arms and carry her off to his room where he can unwrap the flawless package that is Morgan.

He knows he's breaking some unspoken rule, but needing to feel her; he drops a hand to her leg where he taps his finger against her knee.

Her little intake of breath doesn't go unnoticed. He lets his hand linger on her knee, wanting to break all the rules. Slowly, she lays her hand on top of his, gently repeating the simple tapping pattern. His heart jumps, and he turns his body towards her, watching her as she stares at their hands, wondering if she feels it too. Hoping she does, he flips his hand so their palms meet and their fingers interlace. He knows she feels it when her eyes close and tears slip out from beneath her eyelids.

She whispers, "I can't do this, Alec."

He wipes her cheek with his free hand, but his touch only makes her tears come faster. Fuck, he's hurt her so much more than he knew. Why didn't he see it before? She slips her hand out of his and pulls away. He wants to comfort her, but instead, he extricates himself, offering, "How about I box up the cake for you?"

She nods and wipes at her wet cheeks while he goes off to box it up. She stands from the stool and grabs her coat. Slipping into it, she puts an extra barrier between Alec and her heart. She fears it doesn't matter because he wormed his way in there a long time ago. Great, now she has heart-worms! She doesn't know how to get rid of the pesky bastards, and she definitely doesn't know how to repair the damage.

Alec walks back into the kitchen holding the boxed-up cake. "I'll help you out with it. I think it's still raining."

Morgan nods and sets cash on the counter for Cindy. "Will you tell your mom thank you for me? She did an amazing job."

"Of course. She loves you, ya know? You're her favorite out of all my friends. You always have been."

"She's my favorite, too." Morgan smiles, opening the front door. "There were days I came by just to see her."

The rain has slowed to a drizzle, and Morgan thinks about telling Alec to go back inside, but she doesn't know when she will see him again, and she's not ready for another goodbye.

After loading the cake in her car, Alec says, "I hope you still come by, Morgan."

Her smile slips as she looks up at him. "Not sure that's a great idea right now, Alec."

He can't let her go like this. They have something—something real, and he can't let her walk away. Not caring if it makes him sound desperate, he asks, "Why didn't you ever say anything before?"

She shrugs. "What was I supposed to say?"

"I don't know, but you should've said something."

"It doesn't matter anymore, Alec."

She doesn't mean to rip his heart out with her words, but there he is, chest wide open, bleeding on the pavement. His pain turns to anger, and he accuses, "Why, because you have perfect Preston now?"

"No," she says without hesitation, "because you don't get to make me feel worthless and then turn around and expect me to pick up the pieces Sadie left behind. I didn't choose Preston over you. I chose myself over you. Preston is my boyfriend, but he is not your replacement, Alec, because you never had that place."

She moves to get into her car. She doesn't cry this time because as much as it hurts to walk away from him, she knows it's the right move.

BEN AND EMILY arrive at Ben's apartment. It's the first time they have been completely alone, and they are eager to make up for lost time. Emily peels off her coat, dumping it on the floor before forcing him out of his shirt. Their mouths fuse together, tongues and hands becoming desperate. She unbuttons his jeans and pushes them down where they pool at his ankles. She pulls him closer, feeling his excitement while he strips her of her shirt. They're moving toward the bed as Ben unclasps her skinny jeans and she pulls them down where they get stuck around her calves. They try to keep moving, but in their haste, they completely immobilize themselves. Emily squeals as they almost tumble over. Ben catches them before they fall, and he begins to laugh which makes Emily giggle.

"Thwarted by our own jeans," Emily says, clinging to him.

"Give me a second." He bends down and slips off his shoes and socks. He steps out of his jeans and in only his boxers, he picks her up and carries her to the bed. Laying her down, he peels her jeans down her calves, freeing her.

"My hero," she whispers, the laughter from a moment ago all but forgotten. She's looking up at him with lust and anticipation. He puts a knee to the bed and crawls up her body, placing a kiss at her hip, her belly, right over her heart and then along her jawline.

Her hands dive into his hair and slide down his neck.

"Careful Emily, Adelaide doesn't like this," Valla speaks into her mind.

Emily has been exposed to a lot in the last several months, but she wishes she didn't have to share this moment with anyone except Ben. Losing her virginity is a big deal, and it should be her choice to make, not Valla's and certainly not Adelaide's. She continues, ignoring the warning. She pushes Ben to his back and rolls over him, straddling him.

She loves him so much and can't imagine her life without him. She unclasps her bra and lets it fall from her shoulders.

He stares at her in awe as his hands glide up her sides. "You are perfect."

She leans down to kiss him, and he rolls them back over. He hovers over her, positioned right between her legs. Her hips rock up to meet him, touching their most sensitive parts together with only a thin sheath of fabric separating them.

Ben pulls back, hooking his fingers in her panties, and slides them down. Slipping them off, he stands to remove his boxers. He takes a moment to appreciate the most beautiful thing he's ever seen. "Look at you," he says in a reverent tone. He can't believe this is finally happening.

"Ben," she whispers, "come here."

He does as she says, kneeling back on the bed and positioning himself above her. "I need to get a condom."

She pulls him down, too impatient to wait another second, but images begin flickering through her mind. She tries to stay focused on Ben. "Kiss me," she says, and he does, but the images become harder to block out. She pulls away from him, squeezing her eyes shut.

"What's wrong?" he asks.

"Shit!" Emily curses and Ben lets her free.

"Emily, what's happening?"

"Adelaide," she whimpers, still fighting to free herself. "She's showing me images of all her past lovers."

"What can I do? Should I call Patrick?"

"No!" She shakes her head and continues, "Just give me a minute and I'll get it under control."

"I fought her off as long as I could," Valla says. *"I told you she didn't like it."*

Ben covers her with a blanket, snuggling next to her while he waits helplessly for her to recover.

She has botched this so many times. Slowly the images flicker out, fading away along with the anger she felt from within.

She opens her eyes and turns into Ben's arms. He holds her against him, kissing the top of her head. They stay like this for several moments before Ben asks, "You okay?"

"No, I'm mad that Adelaide is in my head. I'm mad that I can't have sex with my boyfriend. I'm mad that I rely so much on Patrick. And I hate that I let you down. Again."

"Emily, look at me."

When she looks up at him, he says, "You are not letting me down. I love you."

"See," she says, "It's even harder when you say things like that. Why can't you just be a jerk? Tell me I'm too high mainte-nance and I'm ruining your life because when you're sweet, it makes me want to pick up where we left off."

"Is that an option?" Ben wonders.

She shakes her head, lowering her face into his chest. "I don't think so. Not until Adelaide is gone. She put up quite a fight. She's not happy about us."

"Do you know why she's fighting so hard?"

"Let's just say she has a type and they don't look like you." After a pause, she says, "But maybe we can try other things without her getting in the way." Her hand glides down his chest to dip beneath the blanket.

THE TELEVISION IS BLARING in Patrick's apartment—his attempt at drowning out his thoughts—but no matter how high the volume, his thoughts remain several decibels louder. It is eleven thirty and Emily hasn't made it home from her date with Ben. She told Patrick she would come back to the apartment tonight.

Patrick tries not to create a picture in his mind of what might be keeping her out so late. He is neither an anxious parent, nor a jealous boyfriend, but still, he waits up for her, an uneasy possessiveness growing in him.

Patrick senses the moment Emily arrives in the parking lot. He lowers the volume and pretends to be entranced in the movie he's watching, only to realize the credits are rolling.

"Hey, Patrick," she says, as she enters the apartment.

He turns to her and his heart aches. Her hair is messy and cheeks slightly flushed. She's not trying to hurt him. She didn't come back to parade her 'just been fucked' look in his face. The only reason she came back at all is because she doesn't trust herself to stay overnight with Ben.

Emily needs Patrick, but for how long? And will he still see her once she doesn't need him anymore?

"So," she pauses, "something weird happened tonight."

Patrick schools his features, trying not to cringe at the intimate details she is about to give him. Calmly, he says, "Oh, yeah?"

She sits on the couch, pivoting her body to face him. "So, I don't know how to say this, so I'm just gonna go for it. Adelaide has a type. Blond hair, blue eyes, basically, every Olvasho male.

She doesn't like Ben and me together. Tonight, when things started heating up, she forced all these images inside my head, and I felt this unbelievable anger. She's a constant presence in my mind, but it's harder to block her out when I'm with Ben, especially when we're—"

"I get it," Patrick cuts in. "It sounds like she doesn't approve and she's trying to force her feelings upon you. Could you fight through her influence?"

"Well, I didn't kill Ben, so she didn't get her way completely, but neither did I. She wouldn't let Ben and I be . . . intimate. I mean we could do some things, but—"

"She won't let you have sex?" Patrick guesses.

"No."

Patrick wants to lecture her, but again, he reminds himself of his place in all this. "Eventually, Adelaide will be gone," he says. "Until then, be careful."

She nods and in a small voice, says, "Thanks, Patrick. I'm sorry to bring this up with you; it's just, there is no one else who understands the way you do." She leans forward to place a kiss on his cheek before walking toward her room.

Before she gets to her door, Patrick calls, "Emily?"

She turns to face him. "Yeah?"

I love you. "You can always come to me, no matter what." His eyes burn with sincerity. "I'll always be here for you."

Feeling her body warm from his gaze, she gives him a tender smile before escaping into her bedroom. She closes the door and leans against it. She thought her time with Ben tonight would erase her attraction to Patrick, but perhaps her feelings are too convoluted to undo with one night.

CHAPTER FORTY-THREE ~

"HE'S GETTING AROUND BETTER," Samantha says, pushing open the door. "His physical therapist said he's never seen anything like it." Finished with their meal, Samantha and Emily walk out into the crisp, mild evening, unseasonably warm for December in Ohio.

As they climb into Samantha's car, Emily comments, "We both know Dad is no ordinary man, he's superhuman."

"He must have the superman gene because he's blowing past all kinds of records in the last two weeks. At this rate, he'll be able to walk me down the aisle instead of using the wheelchair."

"They said the exercises you did with him really helped."

Samantha smiles, proud she did something right. "How are you feeling? Any headaches today?"

Emily can't exactly explain being possessed by an evil Olvasho and the side effects that come with it. So, whenever she has trouble controlling the power within her, Emily says she has a headache from the same head trauma that caused her to forget who she was for four months. She is having *headaches* less and less, but she still has to call Patrick for help occasionally. She's too nervous to stay with her sister for long, fearing she might have another episode.

"The headaches seem to be getting better. I haven't had one today."

"That's great!" Samantha says. "I feel like things are finally becoming normal again. How are you and Ben doing?"

"We're good. He works most of the time, but we've seen each other almost every day. I'm going to the coffee shop on Fifth to see him play tonight. I guess a girl from the coffee shop has joined him on stage a few times. She sings while he plays. He says she's really talented. Do you want to come with me?"

"That could be fun," Samantha says. "Do you mind if we stop by one more store? I want to get dad this levitating phone charger I saw on TV."

"I don't mind. Did you pick up Dad's tux today?"

Samantha shakes her head as she stops at a light. "Dan picked it up when he got off work."

Emily loves the support and adoration Dan shows Samantha. He stuck with her through her most difficult times and Emily feels good about the man who stole her sister's heart. "Samantha, I'm really happy you have Dan."

A secret smile lifts her lips, and she says, "He's my soulmate, my prince charming." She looks at Emily with that same gushy smile. "I hope Ben is that for you and if he's not, I hope you find your soul mate."

"I don't believe in soulmates," Emily counters. "I think some people are better matches than others, but if there is really only one person for everyone then how would anyone ever meet their other half? This world is too big for soulmates."

"Maybe everybody has a couple of people their soul connects with. That way you're more likely to find a match," Samantha theorizes.

"But what happens if someone finds more than one?"

Samantha is quiet for a minute, thinking before she finally jokes, "Maybe that's why some people have more than one spouse."

Emily smiles, but inside, her heart is being split in two. Ben is her home, her best friend, but Patrick is her solace, her rock. She hates that these thoughts keep repeating. She feels like she's cheating on Ben when he's the only one she wanted—wants. He's the only one she wants.

CHRIS DID a great job keeping things running while Mark was away; however, Mark is still playing catchup. "Chris, do you know where the files for Waldo are?" Mark asks from his desk.

Chris is sitting on the leather loveseat in Mark's office. He looks up from his laptop, saying, "You mean, where's Waldo?" Chris laughs at his own joke before answering, "I haven't seen a file labeled *Waldo*."

Mark isn't smiling. "Maybe it's on the server downstairs."

"Do you want me to get it for you?"

"No, I'll get it," Mark says, backing up his wheelchair. He runs into the side of the desk and curses, "This damn wheelchair. My walking is getting steadier, but I don't think I can do two flights of stairs, yet."

Chris stands. "Let me get it. I'm not having you fall down the stairs ten days before your daughter's wedding." He makes his way to the bookshelf.

"Chris, it contains some sensitive information. Please don't open the file."

Chris throws his arms out. "Have I given you any reason to doubt me?"

"No, but I've given you plenty of reasons to doubt me."

"Never. I will never doubt you. You saved my life too many times, man. I trust you."

Chris goes down to the hidden basement apartment to retrieve Waldo. It takes him twenty-five minutes, but he finds it. Mark hid it well, and he hid it on purpose. Chris puts the USB into the computer to download the file but accidentally hits the wrong prompt, opening the file instead of downloading it. "Oh shit!"

He goes to close the window but hesitates as one of the images catches his eye. His curiosity grows when he finds a picture of the man with the face tattoos. He scans the thumbnails hoping to find answers but only becomes more intrigued. Ultimately, it is the picture of his parent's house fire that has him questioning what Mark is hiding.

After printing out pages from the file, Chris climbs the stairs and marches into Mark's office. He slams the pictures down in front of Mark, demanding, "What is this?"

Mark's shoulders become stiff as he stares at the pages, before glancing up at Chris, saying, "I told you not to open it."

Chris places his palms on the desk, leaning forward. "Did you have your arsonist set the fire that killed my father?"

Mark takes a deep breath through his nose. "Christopher."

"Do not Christopher me. You aren't my father or my brother. My sister overdosed twenty-two years ago, so don't pretend we're still family."

Mark uses the desk to pull himself up so he can stand eye to eye with his first wife's little brother. "I consider you my brother whether you want the title or not. Have I ever done anything to hurt you?"

Chris loses the harshness from his voice. "Sit down, old man, you're not sturdy."

"How many times did I bail you out of trouble when you were younger? How many times did I pick you up after your father drank too much? How many times did I track you down to make sure you weren't making the same mistakes your sister made?"

"I never touched drugs!" Chris shouts.

"I'm proud of the man you've grown into, but Chris, I did not kill your father. I had my arson specialist look into it to make sure there was no foul play, and he found the same thing everyone else found. Your father passed out drunk with the cigarette in his hand. He never had a chance at making it out of there alive."

Chris closes his eyes, stepping back from the desk.

Mark continues, "The man was a bastard, but he was your father. I wanted you out of his house, but I would never stoop to that level."

Chris points at the file, accusing, "Why did you try to hide this from me if everything is legit?"

"There is a lot of incriminating evidence in these files. Not with your parent's house, but some of these other cases weren't accidental."

Chris asks, "Why would you burn down a bunch of abandon mansions and warehouses?"

"It's better you don't know. And before you ask, no one got hurt in those fires."

"What kind of shady things are you into?" Chris asks. "First, someone abducts you. Then Emily and Patrick can do things no one should be able to do. You're beaten into a coma and no one is talking about it. You aren't pressing charges or pointing a finger at anyone." Chris shakes his head. "The people who abducted you are dead, aren't they?"

Mark looks confused. "What happened to never doubting me?"

"I never thought I would, but you have a lot of secrets and it's getting harder to ignore."

Feeling unstable on his feet, Mark sits back in his chair, contemplating what to disclose. "There are others out there like Patrick and Emily. Only, instead of using their abilities for good, they are destructive, dangerous individuals. They go unnoticed by authorities because they can mold and manipulate minds. It's a scary thought many people would be more comfortable not knowing."

"What about Samantha? How does she fit into this?"

"Sam doesn't know about it, and she's safer not knowing. She has been through enough. I'm sorry I've had to burden you with it."

"You know I love both of your girls. I think of them both as my nieces, and I'll do what I can to help." Chris pauses. "Mark, I appreciate everything you've done for me. The truth is, if it weren't for you, I probably would've ended up just like Cara. I owe everything to you. I'm sorry I accused you of killing my dad. I know you better than that."

Mark nods, "I hope you do."

Chris looks down, saying, "I'm gonna go close everything down. It shouldn't take long, and then I'll drop you at Sam's."

"Good plan. I'm just finishing up here," Mark says, waiting for Chris to leave the room before looking down at the remains of Chris and Cara's childhood home. He hadn't lied. Chris's father set the fire, but Mark had his suspicions that his second wife, Selma, manipulated him into lighting that cigarette.

Selma loved fiercely and she protected what she loved. She was also a killer. She wouldn't hesitate to murder the man who repeatedly beat his son and raped the daughter who eventually turned to drugs to escape the pain. Selma wasn't around to save Cara, but she loved Samantha like her own and she grew to love Chris, too. Selma protected those she loved, by any means necessary. Mark may not agree with her actions, but he will never tell another soul of his suspicions.

THE COFFEE SHOP is busy when Emily and Samantha arrive. The staff and half the patrons are wearing full Christmas garb. Santa hats pepper the crowd of ugly sweater-wearing customers, and a giant sign on the far wall announces an ugly sweater contest.

Even Ben is sitting on stage in a dinosaur Christmas sweater and an elf hat while he plays a special rendition of Jingle Bells. The woman singing next to him looks to be in her early twenties. She is petite next to Ben, and her husky voice doesn't seem possible for such a small body. Emily feels a spark of jealousy but dismisses it immediately. She knows Ben. The whopping engagement ring on the woman's finger also makes her feel better. The woman throws her hands out to the crowd, encouraging them to sing along, and they happily oblige.

"Oh my God, this is so much fun!" Samantha says, leaning into Emily.

"Come on, let's order something before we find a seat." Emily loops her arm with her sister as they move to the counter to order.

Even the drinks are holiday themed. While Emily orders a Candy Cane Mocha, Samantha orders Santa's Treat, which has blended cookies mixed into it. While they wait for their drinks, Emily takes in the rest of the crowd.

She finds her group of friends. Instead of sitting at a table, they are lined up in chairs against a wall. Alec is closest to them, talking distractedly to Ashley, who is sitting on Jeremy's lap. She leans back and her hair falls across Patrick's shoulder as she whispers something in his ear. Patrick shakes his head and leans into Morgan, who is sitting next to her boyfriend, their hands interlaced. Emily notices Morgan is as far from Alec as she can get and is pretending not to notice the looks Alec keeps sneaking. Emily has been spending so much time with her dad and sister that she hasn't seen how much her friends have changed.

Patrick's eyes land on Emily first, giving her a look begging for help. She smiles while Ashley turns to see where Patrick is looking. Seeing Emily, she squeals and hops up, rushing towards her. *Okay, maybe not all of them have changed.*

"Emily!" she shouts, picking her up in a hug and spinning her around. "I'm so happy you're here!"

As Emily's feet hit the floor, she says, "It's great to see you, Ashley."

"And you brought Sam!" Ashley wraps Samantha in a hug.

They grab their drinks from the counter and join the group. Pulling over a few stray chairs, Emily and Samantha sit next to

Alec. Except when Samantha's eyes fall on Patrick, she walks over to him and wraps her arms around his shoulders. He's surprised by the hug at first but seems to warm to it when Samantha doesn't let go.

His face turns gentle as he whispers soft encouragements. Emily watches the interaction as long as her heart can take it, and then she looks toward the stage to watch Ben. He has matured in the last few months. He is a real adult now, entirely on his own and thriving. He's broken out of his shell, playing his guitar for a crowd who clearly loves him, when only a few months ago she could barely talk him into playing just for her. She's proud of him. No matter how much she feels like she needs Ben, he's proven that he doesn't need her. He wants her. And she wants him. So why is she confused?

It doesn't help that instead of staying with her boyfriend, she's going home to Patrick every night. At first, it was for everyone's safety, but she's doing better now. She's stable enough to try staying overnight with Ben, even if they can't do all the things she wants to do. She will take it slow, and someday Adelaide won't be there to hold her back.

Alec squeezes her shoulder. "Burk, you're looking much better."

Turning to Alec, she says, "Yeah, I'm sorry about showing up at your door like that."

Alec shrugs. "Don't worry about it. I'm glad you're okay. I mean, you did scare the shit out of me, but . . ."

"I'm sure I did. I scared myself, too. I appreciate you, though, and I'm glad you called Morgan instead of Ben. I'm glad he didn't see me like that." She doesn't know why she's telling him this. Being back here, being around her friends, keeps bringing up emotions she can't quite get a handle on.

Alec leans into her. "I'm pretty sure it wouldn't have changed his mind about you."

Alec still thinks something is going on between Patrick and Emily, but he doesn't comment on it. Emily looks at Patrick to find Samantha crouched on the floor in front of him, wiping tears. Sam credits Patrick for Emily's safe return, and she's thanking him in a very heartfelt, very public way. Eventually, Morgan grabs Samantha's attention to introduce her to her boyfriend. Emily decides it's about time she meets the guy, too.

First, she asks, "Alec, what's your take on Morgan's new boyfriend?"

Alec takes the opportunity to glance at Morgan. "He's a good fit for her, except for the giant rod he has shoved up his ass."

Emily grins, wondering if his assessment of Preston is correct. She stands, groaning, "Well, I guess I should go try to pull it out."

Alec laughs, showing off his dimples and sparkling hazel eyes. Emily wonders why two smart people can't figure it out and then she remembers her own drama with Ben. Perhaps intelligence has nothing to do with it because insecurities and tricky emotions can blind anyone.

After a quick meet and greet with Preston, Emily returns to Alec's side, saying, "I hate to break it to you, but I think he was born with the rod shoved up there. I think it will need surgical removal at this point."

Alec's good humor returns, his cheeks punctuated by matching dimples. "See, it's not just me."

More seriously, Emily admits, "But he seems to make Morgan happy, rod and all."

His dimples deflate and he nods. "I know."

Emily reaches over to squeeze his hand.

In a mock whisper, Alec says, "Emily, stop it, Ben will see."

She nudges him and he wraps his arm around her shoulder for the next two songs, before Ben calls him up to the stage.

Alec leans into Emily. "See, he's so jealous."

Emily laughs while Alec goes up on stage with Ben to play the djembe for the last few songs.

Morgan thinks about leaving early, but she isn't going to let Alec ruin her night. Preston leans in, saying, "Will you come to my parent's dinner on Christmas Eve?"

Morgan looks stunned. "I thought you said they had some fancy overdone dinner party on Christmas Eve?"

"They do, so you'd need to dress up, but I'd like them to meet you."

Her eyebrows lift in surprise. "You want me to meet your parents?"

"If it doesn't make you uncomfortable. I'm not going to lie; I'm pretty sure they think I'm making you up."

"You told them about me?"

"Of course. Your parents know about me, don't they?"

"Yeah, but your parents sound intimidating."

"You don't have anything to worry about," he says. "They'll love you."

"Okay, but you're coming with me to Ashley's this time to find a dress. I don't want to wear the wrong thing."

"How about you let me take you shopping? I'll pay since it's my idea."

Morgan smiles at him. "Are you for real?"

He leans in for a kiss, pausing a second to request, "Stay with me tonight."

Morgan nods as his lips find hers.

Emily notices the change in Alec on stage the moment Morgan and Preston begin kissing. Of all people, Alec drags his eyes to Ashley, who shrugs with a look of sympathy.

Emily wonders when those two became close. Patrick distracts her from her thoughts when he sits down in Alec's vacant seat and asks, "How are you feeling?"

"I'm confused. I was only gone a few months and all my friends are different."

"You're different, too."

"Yeah," she sighs. "I guess change is inevitable." She pauses, waiting a moment before breaking the news. "I'm going to stay at Ben's tonight."

She expects him to argue, so she's thrown when he says, "Do you need anything from the apartment?"

"No, I have everything I need."

He nods. "I'm really glad you're feeling better."

If he is faking, she can't tell. Changing the subject, she asks, "Have you heard an answer from Lathe?"

"Not yet," he says. "I'm giving him until January first. After that, we move on."

"I can't believe he threatened me."

"Neither can I. That's not typically Lathe's style, but then again we did just remind him of his unfaithful dead girlfriend."

Ashley leans over from the seat next to Patrick. "Did I hear you mention Lathe's dead girlfriend?"

"Eh, yes," Patrick stumbles, wondering how she heard him.

She flips her hair saying, "Is he coming tonight?"

Patrick shakes his head, saying, "No, he lives a few hours away."

"Oh," Ashley says, "Where?"

"Fort Wayne," Patrick answers, exchanging a concerned look with Emily.

Ashley nods, trying to play it off. "Okay, good to know."

Ashley would have missed it, but Lathe is on her mind a lot these days. The fog over her memories is lifting, and she remembers more and more of the story Lathe told her in the bar. *"You paid for your hair. I paid for my face,"* he'd said. Ashley remembers leaning toward him to touch his face and he shrank away from her, demanding, *"Don't touch me!"*

She wants to ask more questions about him, but she doesn't. Her attraction to him, which she doesn't understand, isn't healthy and she doesn't need to complicate her life with the likes of someone who doesn't even want to be touched. Maybe his obvious aversion to touch has something to do with the dead girlfriend he didn't mention.

PATRICK FISHES his phone from his pocket as he leaves the coffee shop. Lathe has been blowing up his phone all evening. Patrick puts him out of his misery by finally answering, "Hello, Lathe."

"We don't see eye to eye on a lot of things, Patrick, but we both want Emily to take on the leadership of the Olvasho, right?"

"Correct," Patrick agrees.

"I will take on Leona as long as Emily takes on leadership," Lathe offers.

Patrick sighs. "Then we just need to find a way to persuade her to take the role," Patrick says, running his fingers through his hair, knowing it is easier said than done. "I don't imagine we will have to worry about a vote. Seeing everyone's reaction to her at the meeting tells me she's already got the role."

Lathe says, "If she wants it."

"Let's make sure she does," Patrick responds before hanging up.

Patrick decides to wait to tell Emily. She is happy for the first time in a long time and he doesn't want to remind her of the evil living inside of her.

EPILOGUE ~

"Only twenty-four hours until you walk down the aisle," Ben says as he exits his Corvette. He walks around to open the passenger door for Emily, but she's already getting out of the car.

"That makes it sound like I'm the one getting married," Emily complains. "Samantha is the one walking down the aisle. I'm just there for moral support."

Ben grabs his guitar from the trunk, saying, "I can't wait to see you in your bridesmaid dress."

"You mean my slutty bridesmaid dress?"

Ben closes his trunk and takes Emily's hand. "I mean your sexy dress. Samantha wouldn't let you guys look slutty."

"We're wearing plunging backless halter dresses. We're barely keeping it PG-13. But I'm not complaining. It's what Sam wants, and after the hell I've put her through, I'd wear a string bikini if she asked me to."

Ben groans. "Mmm, it's not too late. I could suggest it to her."

Emily elbows him. "Not if you want to live."

"I wouldn't do that to myself. I'd be too distracted to play."

"Thanks again for doing this. I had no idea Sam would ask you to play."

He drops her hand to grab the door. "I'm happy to do it."

As she enters, he looks back over his shoulder, feeling as if someone is watching them. He scans the parking lot of the event center. Finding nothing out of the ordinary, he follows Emily into the building.

The first person they see when they walk through the giant glass doors is Dan's sister, Leah. She looks nervous as she approaches. "Emily, can I talk to you for a minute?"

Emily shrugs. "Sure."

Ben kisses Emily on the cheek. "I'll go set up," he says, before walking away.

Emily watches him for a moment before facing Leah. In high school, Leah was such a bitch to her, making her life miserable. As Emily surveys her now, she can't bring herself to hate someone who looks so pathetic.

Ever since Patrick persuaded Leah into confessing all of her cruel behavior, she has been different. Even as the effects of his persuasion are wearing off, honesty continues to leak out of her.

Leah fidgets. "I'm sorry I've been so mean to you. I started counseling, and I realize I have some anger issues. I'm working on them."

Emily is genuinely shocked by her candor. "It's in the past, Leah. Let's just forget about it."

Leah fights back her tears, so Emily changes the subject. "Are you coming to the salon in the morning?"

Leah nods. "Yeah, I'm getting everything done there."

"Me, too." Emily wiggles her fingers. "We all know what happened the last time I painted my own nails." She pokes fun of herself.

Leah laughs, before throwing a hand over her mouth.

"It's okay to laugh." Emily smiles. "You were right about my botched paint job."

Mark walks in and pauses. "Oh, hi, Leah."

"Hi, Mr. Burk."

Emily places a hand on her dad's arm to prevent the angry

words he wants to speak to his daughter's high school bully. "Dad, shouldn't you be using your cane?"

"I'm not an invalid. I'm doing fine without it."

"Let me walk you in," she insists. "Leah, I'll see you in there."

Mark and Emily enter the ballroom where the wedding ceremony and reception will be taking place.

Mark murmurs, "How did that go?"

"She apologized."

Mark stumbles, and Emily holds tight to his arm, waiting for him to correct himself. He's been healing incredibly fast, but he isn't one-hundred percent. "Let me sit down here for a minute." They sit down in a row of chairs, and he admits, "I think I did too much, but I wanted to get the rest of my things out of Sam's house today. You're welcome to come stay with me."

"In the bunker? No thanks."

"The bunker?" Mark laughs. "I like that. I always called it an apartment, but the bunker sounds way cooler."

Emily shakes her head, thinking of the hidden apartment in the basement of her dad's office building. "I don't have fond memories of that place."

He wraps an arm around her shoulder. "I know you don't."

She turns to him, asking, "Why didn't you tell me about Chris, before?"

"What's to tell?"

"Oh, come on, Dad. I wondered why he was so loyal to you. Patrick and I didn't exactly make things easy for him. He pushed a few times to get the truth, but mostly he just had this blind faith in you. I had to know why."

"He's a good man."

"He is, and you've been good to him. He respects you. You basically saved his life."

"He was only a kid when his sister died, and his parents weren't around much. I kept an eye on him over the years. I couldn't let him die like Sam's mom."

"He knows he's Sam's uncle."

It's not a question, but Mark nods. "He also knows you aren't my biological daughter."

Emily scoffs, "You know he thinks I'm an alien, right?"

Mark chuckles, "No, he doesn't."

"I swear he does!"

Before Mark can say more, someone from the front of the room announces wedding rehearsal will be starting soon.

Samantha walks into the room arm in arm with her fiancé, breaking away when she spots Emily and Mark. Sitting down next to them, she asks, "How are you feeling, Daddy?"

While Mark answers, Lathe's mother appears in the doorway, distracting Emily. The mysterious woman is wearing a formal blue gown with red tennis shoes, and her wild hair is less crazy than normal. Emily stands from her seat, excusing herself to meet the dangerously confused woman.

"Emily," Evelyn coos, looking overjoyed to see her again.

Emily reaches out for her, grasping nothing but air. The woman is merely a projection of herself. "Can the others see you?" Emily asks.

"No."

"Why are you here?"

"To warn you." A tear glistens down Evelyn's cheek. She reaches out, letting the back of her ghost-like hand caress Emily's face, whispering, "She rises only to fall. She will die to pr —" She stops abruptly, her eyes becoming unfocused. She looks at Emily with a blank stare before saying. "Don't look so sad, dear."

Lathe's mother vanishes without a sound, leaving Emily to stand in the doorway alone, questioning her fate.

ACKNOWLEDGMENTS ~

Thank you for hanging on with me through this journey. I am so grateful to be surrounded by such an amazing group of supportive individuals. I couldn't have done this without your continued interests and feedback. I am so thankful for each and every one of you who continue to follow Emily's story.

I would not have been able to complete this book without Mary Catherine Kline. Editing can be a painful process, but we laugh our way through it. I absolutely adore our time together. Thank you for always understanding what I meant to think.

To my mom, my number one fan, I love you. I love that you talk about my characters like they are real people, and I am so grateful to have someone who believes in me so much. Thank you for all of your encouragement.

To my wonderful sisters, Sarah, Heather, Marissa, and Jenna. You have all unknowingly given me material to use for my stories. Thank you for carving out the time to help me. I am lucky to be blessed with such amazing women.

Melissa DiRienzo, my book buddy, I am forever grateful for your encouragement and friendship. I don't know how you do it, but you somehow manage to look at my rough draft and tell me exactly what it's missing. That's part of what makes you such an exclamation point in my life!

Thank you to Sara Wilson who swooped in at the end to save me when I knew something was wrong but couldn't put my finger on it. You made an enormous impact on this book, and you continue to challenge me to become a better writer.

To my Dad and Father-in-law. I am so blessed to have two dads who love me so much. Thank you for reading my books and encouraging me to continue writing.

Justin, my husband and my miracle, I love living life with you by my side. Thank you for supporting me through this even though sometimes I act like a crazy person, and other days (or weeks) we barely see each other because I'm locked away in my writing room. You are my favorite person, and I don't know what I'd do without you.

With *Guardian of Latovia*, the third book in the Valla Series.

Guardian of Latovia

PROLOGUE

EVERYONE BORN WILL EVENTUALLY DIE. It's a fact so basic, so logical, so inevitable, yet it's something most of us are never ready to face. Is it fear of leaving those we love or fear of the unknown? No one can be sure when death will strike, but every day is priceless to those who acknowledge the Grim Reaper lurking just over their shoulder.

If we knew when we were going to die, would we live our lives differently? Would it change our decisions?

The casket at the front of the room stands like a declaration of failure. He watches from the balcony, separating himself from the people pouring into the room below. It makes him angry to see how many gifted individuals show up today. He wants to berate them for being here. They don't belong here, but then again, neither does he. After all, he let this happen.

GUARDIAN OF LATOVIA

CHAPTER ONE

THREE MONTHS earlier -

LATHE PACES THE HALL, crumpling the sheet of paper in his hands. With powers of healing, mental manipulation, and mind-reading, it is vital to have someone police the gifted Olvasho group. The Olvasho Council was created to do just that. It was originally set up to run like a democracy. Their primary job was to prevent the Olvasho from causing harm while keeping them safe from discovery, but during Sky's long reign, it became corrupt, running like a criminal organization.

The night Sky died, the council lost four members to abandonment and death, leaving only eight members in their council seats. Now, nearly five months later, the Olvasho are about to vote for a new leader and council members.

Lathe knows the next head of the Olvasho needs to inspire change in order to fix the corruption. Unfortunately, the list of candidates is anything but hopeful.

Lathe pulls out his phone to call Patrick.

Answering with a sigh, Patrick says, "You're losing your edge, Lathen. Your predictability is getting old."

Lathe growls, "You know why I'm calling."

"To wish me a Happy New Year?"

Lathe rolls his eyes and says, "They announced the final four candidates."

"Don't spoil it! I missed last night's episode."

Lathe grinds his teeth. "You think this is a joke? This is the future of the Olvasho."

"You have no sense of humor, Lathe." Patrick sighs. "Do I know any of them?"

"Three are sitting council members and the fourth is just for show. I've never heard the name, and no one will vote for him."

Patrick scoffs. "Of course, they rigged the election. They need to make it look like someone outside the council has a chance at winning. Is Keith on the list?"

Lathe groans, rubbing at his facial scars. "He's favored to win."

Keith had once been eager to become Sky's second in command. He would carry out all kinds of nefarious deeds, trying to capture Sky's attention. It was never Patrick's desire to be Sky's *protege*. He would've handed it to Keith in a heartbeat if Sky had let him.

After Sky's death, Keith did a one-eighty, preaching anti-Sky to the masses to gain their support. It made Patrick hate him even more.

Lathe continues, "The Olvasho respond to power above all else. Emily has power. The people love her. She has the blood of a leader, and the backing of the prophecy." He has no doubt his half-sister would win, but she still refuses to run.

Patrick sighs. "I can't make her do it, Lathe. And she is sick of hearing about the prophecy. She said she's not going to let a poem decide her fate."

Lathe's mother had premonitions of the future and years ago

374

gave a prophecy they believe to be about Emily, though they didn't know until recently.

Bred to be orphaned, pursued but not found,
The weak build the strong to find light underground.
Rising from nothing to fight for a cause
A victim, a killer, an innocent one.
Finding freedom for souls, we believe to be lost,
By crossing lines that cannot be crossed.
Fear breeds allegiance that is easily broken,
While love builds loyalties that remain unspoken.
Rising from evil, from death, from ash
To encompass abilities no other can have.
Garnering gifts from mother and father alike,
Her blood will awaken three sisters to fight.
Saving us all, for it is fated,
Unless she befalls, incinerated.

LATHE OFFERS, "Did you tell her I would take on Leona if she takes leadership?"

"I did, and your ultimatum didn't go over very well with her." Patrick sighs. "She's too involved with getting her life together. She's not about to throw it away to lead a group she doesn't like or trust."

Lathe huffs, "This is our window! It's our chance to change everything, and you're coddling our most powerful asset!"

Patrick remains unruffled. "I'd love for her to run, but I can't make her. You have power, Lathe. Your mother might be the most powerful Olvasho alive. If you're so keen to change things, why don't you run? Why don't you give up your life to serve the Olvasho? You can't expect your sister to give anything to the people who have persecuted her. To her, they are all like Keith."

"That isn't a fair assessment, Patrick. Most of the Olvasho are innocent. They have every right to be frightened. Their leaders have misled them, but we can put an end to it!"

"Sounds like your campaign speech is practically writing itself. The people will love your conviction."

"I can't run!" Lathe barks.

"Why? Being the head of the Olvasho will still allow you to look after mommy dearest."

A growl comes through the phone. "Don't pretend to understand my life!"

"Stop being so touchy."

"You're not taking this seriously!"

"Lathe, I don't have time for this. I have to get myself and Maggie ready for a wedding."

"I'm trying to save the future of the Olvasho, and you're going to a wedding?"

"Yes."

Lathe lets out a long sigh, trying to calm himself. He grumbles, "Who gets married on New Year's Eve?"

"Samantha. You know, your half-sister's sister."

"Fine, but while you're there, try persuading her to take leadership."

The line goes dead, and Patrick looks to Maggie and shrugs. "Some people take life too seriously. Come on girl, we have a wedding to prepare for."

Patrick jumps up and Maggie follows. The scarred Doberman Pinscher has basically become Patrick's dog since Emily has been staying with Ben. Not to mention, the dog can sense the entities living inside of Emily and they make her uneasy.

Adelaide is evil and must be destroyed, but to get rid of Adelaide, they must awaken the three creators of the Olvasho. Emily already possesses Valla, the first of her bloodline. And a few weeks ago, Patrick took on the spirit of Isa, the first of his bloodline. Except for making him more powerful, Isa is an amiable presence in his body. The only entity missing is Leona.

Patrick knows they need Lathe to take on the spirit of Leona, but he doubts Emily will ever give into Lathe's demands. Either way, he doesn't have time to think about it now. They have to get ready for a wedding.

"IT'S GOING to drop down into the twenties tonight," Ashley says, as she pushes Emily down into the chair in the fancy bathroom that adjoins to the ballroom. "Let me fix your makeup."

"Ash, my makeup is fine, and you know I don't want to look all made up."

"That's too bad because this day isn't about you. It's about Samantha and Dan, and they told me to make you look smoking hot."

"No, they didn't!"

Ignoring Emily, Ashley pulls out a giant bag of makeup and sets it on the counter. "Now, close your eyes."

Ashley's face is already done up with smoky eyes and bold lipstick. Her ultra-blond hair is spun into an outrageous updo. Put together with her willowy frame, Ashley looks like the love child of a supermodel and a rock star.

As Ashley works, Rochelle, the only bridesmaid Emily likes, hurries into the bathroom, complaining, "Alison and Eva might be the most depraved human beings I have ever met. They are out there rationing rice cakes. Rice cakes!" She throws herself into the lounge chair next to Emily. "And here we are hiding out in the bathroom while they get the bridal suite."

Ashley uses the makeup brush to point to the crystals sparkling in the chandelier above her head. "At least it's a nice bathroom."

"That's true," Rochelle admits. "Would you have time to do my makeup, too?"

EMILY WALKS to the bridal suite to help her sister into her dress. As she enters, her sister pulls her into the adjoining dressing room, pleading, "Emily, they are driving me crazy! They told me I wasn't allowed to eat anything because I didn't want to look fat on my wedding day. I am starving, and they won't shut up."

"Who? Eva and Alison?"

"Yes!"

"I'll take care of it, Sam. Stay here. I'll be right back with some food."

Emily walks past the girls in the bridal suite and goes out into the hall.

For a while, Sam thought she would have to postpone the wedding because her dad was in a coma and Emily was missing, but a few weeks earlier Patrick brought Emily back to town and that same week their dad, Mark, woke from his coma.

To explain her four-month disappearance, Emily told Samantha she suffered from amnesia. In truth, she suffered the spirits of her ancestors, Valla and Adelaide, who share possession of her body. Where Valla is benign, her mother Adelaide is cancer. For four months Adelaide had control over Emily's psyche, living through her body until Patrick found a way to suppress her temporarily. Now Emily is doing everything she can to make it up to her sister.

Emily walks down the hall to the room where Patrick is keeping Maggie. Entering the room, she pauses. Patrick's dazzling sapphire eyes settle on her, and she melts a little. His usual unruly blond hair is exquisitely groomed, and his contoured cheeks sport a natural glow despite it being winter in Ohio. A perfectly tailored black suit showcases his tall, lean body. "Wow, look at you! You look . . .." She doesn't know what's safe to say and she doesn't like her reaction to him, so she says, "You're going to break some hearts tonight."

She's wearing one of the silk floral robes Sam bought for all her bridesmaids. As she stands there stumbling over her words, Patrick feels the charge between them intensify. He's having enough trouble holding out against her increasingly tempting looks, so he's relieved she's been staying with Ben for the last two weeks. She and Ben have been friends for a long time, but ever since they started dating, nothing has gone smoothly.

"Beautiful doesn't even begin to do you justice, love."

Maggie nudges against Emily's leg, drawing her attention away from Patrick. "Maggie," she coos, bending to pet her dog. Years ago, Emily found the emaciated Doberman Pinscher curled up on her front doorstep. The dog's ears were clipped, her tail docked, and the scars down her sides were evidence of abuse. Emily adopted the pup and named her loyal companion, *Maggie*. "You are just the girl I was looking for." Glancing at Patrick, she says, "I need to borrow her. Would you do me a favor and grab some food from down the hall and bring it to the bridal suite? Lunch was catered, but Samantha didn't get anything to eat."

"Sure," he says, walking out behind her. While Emily and Maggie enter the bridal suite, Patrick continues down the hall to find the food.

"What is that dog doing in here?" Alison says, backing to a wall.

"This is Maggie. She's the ring bearer."

"What! I was expecting like a poodle or something."

"Nope, this is Maggie. I have to get her ready. I think this might go better if you're not here. You're making her nervous." Right on cue, Maggie starts growling. "See?"

Alison and Eva back to the door and slip out. Leah, the groom's sister and Emily's former bully, stays in the lounge chair, pulling her legs up as if that will protect her from Maggie.

"Relax, Maggie won't hurt you," Emily says, glad she and Leah worked things out. Maggie circles around to find a good spot on the floor while Emily calls, "Sam, it's safe to come out."

Samantha comes out of the dressing room and looks relieved to have both girls gone. "Where's Rochelle?"

"Ashley is doing her makeup. They should be done soon."

"It's almost time to change, and I'm still starving!"

"Don't worry. Patrick's bringing food."

After a small knock at the door, Rochelle enters carrying a platter piled with food. "Patrick asked me to bring this in."

"God love that man!" Samantha says grabbing a few finger sandwiches before Rochelle can set down the tray.

AN HOUR LATER, the girls in the wedding party are back together in the bridal suite.

"The guests are arriving," Leah says, peeking out the window.

Couple by couple they arrive dressed to the nines and carrying gifts. The black-tie event has women wearing evening gowns and men sporting tuxedos. Guests pile their offerings on the gift tables, check their coats, and allow the ushers to escort them to their seats.

Eva and Alison push Leah out of the way and peer through the window, searching for eligible bachelors. "I still call dibs on the dog handler," Eva says.

From the side, Leah sniggers, "Good luck with that."

"Ooh, what about him?" Alison says, pointing toward Alec. "Isn't that the girl who was doing your makeup, Rochelle? What's their story? Are they together, together?"

After Ashley finished Rochelle's makeup, she left to pick up Alec, who doesn't look happy to be here. Of course, Ashley talked him into coming in hopes that he and Morgan could work things out, but Morgan is bringing her boyfriend, Preston, tonight.

"He's spoken for," Emily cuts in. "As is the dog handler." She is fine with Patrick finding someone tonight, but it isn't going to be Eva or Alison.

A light knock has Emily turning away from the window to open the door for her dad. Mark takes in the room filled with beautiful women, but his eyes stop on the girl in white. "Samantha," he says softly, as he walks forward, "you look stunning."

"Thanks, Daddy," she says, tearing up. She wasn't sure he would be healthy enough to attend her wedding, and now here he is to walk her down the aisle. She couldn't be more pleased.

Samantha steps forward, and Mark whispers, "Don't cry, sweetheart."

"I'm just so happy you're here. You and Emily," she says, stepping into his arms.

Judy, the mother of the groom, bustles into the room, announcing, "It's time."

Before she knows it, Emily is walking down the aisle. She holds her flowers with both hands, attempting to match her pace to the lovely music Ben is playing at the front of the room.

Ben is the epitome of tall, dark, and yummy. His hair is as dark as night, and his eyes are warm chocolate to make one melt with hunger. Surrounding those delicious eyes are lashes long enough to make any girl envious. Teaching Taekwondo has enhanced his already broad shoulders and kept his muscles toned. Emily is distracted by his body until their eyes find each other. Love fills her heart, and she gives him her warmest smile.

Following Emily down the aisle is Dan's five-year-old cousin. She's wearing a miniature princess dress with pink bows adorning her cascading curls. She does her job perfectly, dropping flower petals as she goes. Her dad is one of the groomsmen, and when she sees him, she runs up to him, gaining her an "Ahh" from the guests.

Maggie walks in, and Patrick closes the double doors behind her. She has flowers draped over her shoulders and is holding a small white basket in her mouth. She saunters down the aisle coming to sit right in front of Emily.

Then the music changes and the double doors reopen. All the guests stand, turning to get a look at Samantha on her dad's arm. They glide forward, Samantha's gown and veil flowing elegantly behind her.

Both Dan and Samantha tear up during the ceremony. When prompted, Maggie steps forward with the basket of rings, and the service continues. The couple is pronounced husband and wife and the crowd cheers as they kiss.

After an hour whirlwind of posing for photos, they announce the bridal party to the reception. A live band is playing, bringing the party to life. Food is passed around, the open bar is handing out drinks, and Samantha and Dan have their first dance before Emily can break away.

She finds Ben at a table with Morgan and Preston, Ashley and Alec, and Morgan's sister and her boyfriend. Emily sits in the empty chair next to Ben and gives him a kiss. "I can't believe I'm just now saying hello to you. This day has been one thing after the other. I am never having a big wedding."

Ben pulls her close and whispers, "I need you to come with me for a minute." Not waiting for an answer, he grabs her hand and drags her from the room. Ben seems to be searching for somewhere to go, so Emily takes charge, pulling him into the bridal suite down the hall. Once they're inside, Ben attacks, groping and kissing and doing everything aside from stripping her naked and having his way with her.

"Ben," Emily pants, pulling away. "Ben, we can't miss the whole evening."

Ben rests his forehead against hers, trying to rein in his desires. "This dress is going to kill me, Emily."

She smirks. "Sounds like a good way to go."

Ben pulls away. "I'm serious. You look so sexy in that dress. I hate that anyone else gets to see you in it."

She caresses his cheek. "But you're the only one who gets to peel me out of it later."

Something between a groan and a growl emanates from him, and he's ravishing her mouth again. She rarely gets to witness this side of him. He's always so controlled, and she loves the possessive glint in his eye that promises so much pleasure.

They eventually make it back to the reception and Ben

leads her directly to the dance floor where a love song is play-ing. He doesn't want to miss the opportunity to hold her. He notices Mark and makes a mental note not to grope her . . . too much.

They enjoy a few slow songs before a groomsman taps Ben on the shoulder. "Hey man, sorry, the band is asking if you'll move your guitar."

Ben nods and says to Emily, "Let me just run it out to my car. I'll be right back."

"Should I go with you?" she offers with a hint of teasing.

"If you go with me, I won't bring you back," he says, leaning in to kiss her before moving away.

"Emily," Sam says, rushing up from behind. "They said they're going to lock the bridal room. Will you help me get a few things out of there?"

"Sure," she says, following her sister. They pack up Saman-tha's things, and Emily helps her load it into the limo parked out front. It takes longer than expected, and Emily searches the parking lot, spotting Ben's Corvette but not Ben. He's probably inside looking for her.

Once back in the reception hall, Emily goes to sit at Ben's table. He isn't there, but Ashley and Alec are, and currently, they are having a contest to see who can hold a spoon on their nose the longest.

After watching Alec lose, Emily asks, "Have you guys seen Ben?"

Ashley puts a hand on her hip. "What? Are you embarrassed to be seen with us?"

"Of course, she is. You guys are children," Patrick says from over her shoulder.

Emily spins in her seat. "Hey, where have you been?"

"I had to run Maggie to my uncles. I didn't realize it would take so long. Traffic is a nightmare. There are DUI stops everywhere."

"Thanks for taking care of her, Patrick."

"I couldn't deprive Samantha of a family member. Come dance with me, love." He offers his hand.

"I'm waiting for Ben."

"He can come steal you away from me. Come on, just for a moment."

"Okay," she says, as he leads her to the dance floor.

CHAPTER TWO ~

A LEC IS STANDING with his back against the bar sipping his drink while watching Morgan on the dance floor. Alec heard she already met her boyfriend's parents at a fancy-schmancy Christmas party. They loved Morgan. Alec isn't surprised. Morgan is pretty hard not to love. The look on her face as she dances with Preston makes Alec grind his teeth.

Ashley nudges him, saying, "You've got a real stalker vibe going. Come on, tiger, let's go get some air."

"It's freezing outside," he says incredulously.

"It'll be good for you to cool off. I'm not taking no for an answer."

He downs the remainder of his drink and sets his glass on the bar. They grab their coats before exiting.

"Brrr, it's freaking freezing out here," Ashley complains, leaning against the side of the building. "You better cool down fast."

Alec's phone vibrates, and he pulls it out to find another message from Sadie, his ex. He broke up with her earlier this month when he found out she had faked a pregnancy as a way to trap him. She's been trying to win him back ever since, but he is relieved to be done with her and the nude photos she sends him don't tempt him the way they once did.

Ashley peeks over. "Is that Sadie, again?"

He nods and ignores the text, putting his phone away. Alec is trying to get his life together. He continues to work for the father who walked out on his mother when she was pregnant with him. Alec hates the man, but he needs the money and the experience, even if it means spending time with the devil.

"Are you still looking for your own place?" Ashley asks as she blows on her hands to warm them.

"I don't think I can afford it, but I'm trying."

"You have, like the best mom in the world. No one could blame you for staying there forever."

"I need my own place, Ashley. As much as I love my mom, it's time to prove to myself and Morgan that I can make it on my own."

Ashley exhales loudly and watches her breath in the freezing air. "This night isn't as much fun as I thought it'd be. I feel like everything has been weird since Emily came back. Like, have you noticed people acting different lately?"

"Weird shit's been going on longer than that, darlin."

Ashley sighs. "I keep throwing myself at Patrick and nothing! He's like, always with Emily, like lurking over her shoulder or something. He's even more of a stalker than you. Don't get me wrong. I like Patrick. He can follow me around like that anytime, but Emily doesn't seem interested in him. I don't know, their relationship is . . . Shit, I'm gossiping! I don't mean to be gossiping about this."

"Patrick and Emily slept in the same bed together. I mean, he . . . I don't get it. I don't know how Ben puts up with it. I've known Em for a long time, and she seems . . ."

The screech of tires steals their attention, and they watch a black car speed through the parking lot. Just beyond the first row of cars, the vehicle slows. The back door opens just long enough for something to tumble out. Then, the car speeds off. Alec steps away from the building to get a view of the license plate as it pulls away.

"What was that?" Ashley asks.

Alec heads into the parking lot. "I'm gonna go check."

"Be careful!"

Peering around vehicles to get a better look at whatever fell out of the car, Alec sees a shadow on the ground and shouts, "Ashley, get over here!"

He rushes to the shadow, not just a shadow, a body. Ben is lying on his side, clutching his chest.

"Fuck!" Alec shouts. "Ashley, call 911!"

Rushing over to join him, she pulls out her phone.

Alec gets down on the ground and curses, pushing Ben to his back. "Ben, what the . . ." He reaches out but doesn't know where to touch his barely recognizable friend. Underneath a torn suit jacket, blood soaks through his white dress shirt. His face looks like someone smashed it in with a baseball bat. Alec swallows hard to hold back his emotion. "What happened to you, man?" Alec stumbles over his words, as he scoots closer to his friend.

Ben's lips are moving, but no sound escapes.

"It's okay, man, you don't need to talk," Alec soothes.

"Oh, my God!" Ashley gasps and hits *send* on her phone.

Alec continues reassuring Ben, "An ambulance will be here soon. Hang on, bro. Hang on."

Blood is dripping from Ben's moving lips as he keeps mouthing the same thing over and over. Alec leans closer, asking, "What's that?"

"Em," Ben breathes. He coughs, and blood sputters out of his mouth.

Ashley paces in the background, talking rapidly into her phone.

"Ashley, give them the address, tell them to hurry!" Alec urges.

She stops pacing to look for the number on the building.

Ben is choking, and Alec turns him on his side, but that only seems to make matters worse, so he rolls him back.

"Ben . . . Shit! Just . . . Shit! Hold on!"

Ben's body convulses, fighting to survive while he drowns in his own blood. Alec doesn't know how to fix this. Tears pool in his eyes and he yells, "There's gotta be a doctor in there!"

Ashley hangs up, wiping at her eyes, smearing black eyeliner across her cheeks. "Stay with him. I'll go get help."

Alec runs his hands through his hair, disheveling his chestnut waves. He leans back down to Ben, who is turning blue. Ben's body stills and his head lolls to the side.

"No, no, no, Ben, no, come on man! No, come on!" Alec puts his ear against Ben's chest but doesn't hear anything. He checks for a pulse, but his own heart is pounding so hard, he can't feel anything but his own thunderous heartbeat.

"Fuck!" he yells, as he starts chest compressions. "Ben, come on man!"

PATRICK AND EMILY sway together on the dance floor. "You're terribly clumsy, aren't you?" Patrick says in a deep silky voice. "Those were my first words to you. You've certainly proved me wrong."

In a mock baritone, Emily says, "It's rather endearing to find such a beautiful woman whose movements completely contradict the elegance a body like yours suggests." Switching to her normal voice, she says, "You were such an ass."

Patrick smiles. "I must have made an exceptional first impression since you still remember my exact words."

"Do you remember my first words to you?"

"You were yelling at me for laughing at you and calling you clumsy."

"That sounds right," she says, as they continue to sway.

"Patrick, none of this would've been possible if you had given up on me."

"I'd do anything for you, love."

"Do you think—" Her words end abruptly and her face drains of color. She looks toward the doors leading to the parking lot. "Patrick, do you feel that?"

"Wha—"

"Something's wrong," she gasps, taking off at a frantic pace, pushing and weaving her way through the crowd of dancers. Patrick follows close behind. As soon as they reach the foyer, Emily spins around. "Patrick, something has happened to Ben. He's . . . It's . . . something's happened."

"Emily, it's all right," he soothes, moving forward to console her.

She backs out of his reach, shaking her head. "No, Patrick, it's not all right!"

He catches a glimpse of a panic-stricken Ashley as she bursts through the glass doors from outside. Her black eyeliner is running, ruined by the tears streaming down her face. Her lips quiver as she looks at Emily and shouts, "We need a doctor! Now!"

Patrick steps forward. "Ashley, what—"

Emily shoves past both of them, darting out into the cold night.

CONTINUE READING in *Guardian of Latovia*.

ABOUT THE AUTHOR

Anna Rezes has been passionate about writing since she was a child. When she's not busy honing her superpowers or traveling to other worlds full of fictional characters, she is spending time with family and friends. She lives in Central Ohio with her husband, their two dogs, and the cat they love and hate. Anna is the author of *Unraveling Emily, Descendant of Valla, Guardian of Latovia, Broken Alliance*, and *Pink f*cking Moscato*.

For more from Anna Rezes visit:
www.annarezes.com
www.instagram.com/anna_rezes
www.facebook.com/annarezesauthor
www.twitter.com/annarezes